THE ORPHANS OF RACE POINT

ALSO BY PATRY FRANCIS

The Liar's Diary

THE
ORPHANS

OF
RACE
POINT

A NOVEL

PATRY FRANCIS

HARPER ● PERENNIAL

NEW YORK ● LONDON ● TORONTO ● SYDNEY ● NEW DELHI ● AUCKLAND

HARPER ● PERENNIAL

HarperCollins books may be purchased for educational, business,
or sales promotional use. For information, please e-mail the Special
Markets Department at SPsales@harpercollins.com.

FIRST EDITION

Designed by William Ruoto

Library of Congress Cataloging-in-Publication Data has been applied for.

ISBN 978-0-06-228130-2

14 15 16 17 18   OV/RRD   10 9 8 7 6 5 4 3 2 1

To Ted

*Love is not blind; that is the last thing it
is. Love is bound; and the more it is bound,
the less it is blind.*

— G . K . CHESTERTON

THE ORPHANS OF RACE POINT

PROLOGUE

From the journals of Gustavo Silva, Jr.: Last Entry

JANUARY 9, 2011

In prison, you learn that no one is innocent. It doesn't matter whether you were wrongly convicted, if your crime was justified, or if life constricted your path so brutally that even the most heinous act came to feel inevitable. The cell accepts no excuses. There, no matter who you are, the truth will come looking for you in all its darkness and mercy. Either you look back unflinchingly or you die.

Of all the people I have known, there have only been a handful whose eyes reflected that kind of death. Pray for them—yes—and then stay away. There's nothing else you can do.

PART ONE

THE WIDOW'S WALK

{ 1978–1979 }

Sometimes I feel the need for religion
so I go outside to paint the stars.

—VINCENT VAN GOGH

CHAPTER 1

It was late October, the first cold night of the year, when nine-year-old Hallie Costa followed the bobbing arc of her flashlight to the roof, where she was irresistibly drawn to the black sky, the brackish taste of the wind that shuddered off the bay, and the companionship of the gull who slept near the chimney. She knew him from the slight bend in his right wing, and his unbalanced flight—her father had diagnosed an accommodation to an old injury. *Asa Quebrada*, he called him. Broken Wing.

Hallie had been on the roof before, but that night was different. She would never be sure whether her sleep had been disturbed by the shift in temperature or by a sound that entered her room as stealthily as moonlight. *Was it singing?* By the time she opened her eyes and sat up in bed, it was gone. For some reason, she thought of how the old people wept when they played fado music at the annual Portuguese Festival. *Saudade*, her great-aunt Del called it: homesick music. But according to her father, the emotion was about more than place. It was a profound longing for everything that was lost and would never be regained.

When she heard the sound, Hallie had turned on the light and taken in the objects in her room. Everything was in place. The glowing face of the clock read 3:07. Her dutiful side, inherited from the Costas, reminded her that it was a school night. But at that hour, the unruly spirit of her mother always prevailed. She switched off her lamp and reached for the flashlight under the bed and a jacket that hung on a hook shaped like a clamshell.

Usually, she was careful not to wake her father when she crept through the dark. But that night she tiptoed down the hallway toward his room. The door was ajar, and she considered crawling into his bed. She could almost feel his warmth, the arm inserted beneath her neck; she could hear his sleepy murmur. *Nightmare, Pie?*

A nightmare: Was that what it had been? She buttoned her jacket against the chill that had infiltrated the house and looked down at her pale feet, wishing she had put on her red Keds. Her father groaned and shifted in bed as if sensing her presence. If she stood there another second, he would surely open his eyes.

The sign outside his office advertised Nicolao Costa as a GENERAL PRACTITIONER, but his patients also knew him as a psychiatrist specializing in common sense, an unorthodox marriage counselor, and a friend they could call when they were too drunk to make it home from the Pilgrims Club down the street. When the latter happened, Nick would ask his friend, Stuart, who lived in a renovated fish house next door, to come and watch Hallie. Stuart groused about being disturbed so late at night; but even before he hung up, the light in his dormer window flicked on and he could be seen pulling on his pants.

On the rare nights when Stuart wasn't available, Nick would rouse Hallie from sleep and take her along. He made his house calls at the bar in faded pajamas, hair spiked with sleep. Syl Amaral, who owned the place, would have a shot of bourbon waiting for him after he'd returned from getting the offender home safely. Hallie would watch as Nick downed it quickly, cursing the *bacalhau* who'd dragged him out, and vowing never to do it again. To his consternation, everyone in the bar would laugh.

But even she knew that Nick was too haunted by the drunk-driving accident that had claimed her mother to ignore any late-night call. If one person, one family, could be spared what he had seen, or the loneliness he had endured following the collision on the infamous stretch of road known as Suicide Alley, he would be there.

Hallie was surprised that her father, with his famously keen sense of observation, hadn't yet discovered her secret excursions to the roof. The only one who knew was her best friend, Felicia.

"I think you just miss your mom," Felicia had said, twisting her wheat-colored braids and studying Hallie like a therapist, after she confided to her on the playground. "You go up there because you're *looking* for her."

"Liz Cooper's got nothing to do with it," Hallie insisted, wishing she hadn't brought it up. "Besides, it's *scientifically* impossible to miss someone you can't remember."

She would never admit that she didn't go onto the roof to find her mother; she did it to escape her. In many ways, Thorne House still belonged to Liz Cooper, whose fledgling renovations and dreams of a family large enough to fill the place had ended abruptly on the highway. Though the first floor had been gradually taken over by Nick's rambling practice, it was cluttered with her memory.

Hallie and her father confined themselves to the kitchen and the large room that most people would have referred to as a living room. Nick preferred to call it his study. One wall was covered with maps that told the story of ancient societies, and newer ones that defined the world as it was now. There were charts that explored the intricacies of the human body right down to the cellular level, and others that mapped the heavens.

"Either one will give you a view of infinity," Nick liked to say.

Another wall chronicled a different kind of history. Nick's mother's family had arrived with the first wave of Portuguese immigrants nearly a hundred years earlier, but on his father's side he was only second generation, and the ties with people "at home" were still strong. Photographs of family in the Azores mixed with shots of Nick's friends from Provincetown and Harvard. There were pictures of him and Liz Cooper on the leafy, brick streets of Cambridge, where they'd fallen in love, at their small private wedding, and then holding their newborn daughter. But most of the wall was taken up by images of Hallie at every stage in her young life. At the bottom of a baby picture, her mother had inscribed her proper name in a dramatic left-handed slant. *Hallett*. Since the accident, however, she had become, irrevocably, Hallie. Nick's shining happiness. The only thing that had stopped him from walking into the sea after he lost his wife.

The real proof of Liz Cooper's continuing dominion over the house could be found on the second floor, where the desolation of her absence settled like a thick dust. The doors to three spare bedrooms were kept closed, as if the children the couple would never have were sleeping behind them. The ghost rooms, Hallie called them.

Only the widow's walk was hers alone. Most of the spoke railing had rotted away, and what was left tilted precariously toward the sidewalk, but the platform remained as solid as it was when a whaler named Isaiah Thorne built the house. According to town lore, his wife, Mary, would sit up there for hours, often at night, watching for her husband's ship to return. The first time Hallie heard the story, her curiosity was aroused. *Just once*, she had promised herself, knowing how her father would react if he found out. But as soon as she felt the proximity of the stars, she was spellbound. She extended her arms and took in the night air, pretending she was wearing a long white dress with a peplum and high-button shoes instead of mismatched pj's and bare feet, and that she was waiting for a handsome sea captain to return. An exhilarating sense of release, and something else—*possibility*—assailed her whenever she pushed open the heavy door. Despite her vow, she was drawn to the roof regularly, sometimes as often as once a week.

The sole obstacle between her and the place where she could be anyone she wanted to be was the painter who rented the attic for his studio. People called him Wolf for his preternatural leanness and the almost predatory way he took in the landscape. Nick, who treated his asthma and admired his work, was the closest thing he had to a friend.

Three years earlier, Wolf had convinced Nick to rent him the space to use as a studio, but it soon became apparent that he wanted far more. He extended the hours he spent in the attic until it was time for dinner, knowing that he only had to pause outside the kitchen for Nick to set another place at the table. Still, Hallie had been startled the first time she stumbled upon Wolf sleeping on a futon in the corner during one of her late climbs to the roof. Fortunately, the energy that fired his work also exhausted him. Once he succumbed to sleep, he almost never stirred.

Hallie trained her light downward and thus navigated the detritus in the attic. Careful not to disturb Wolf, she pushed open the trapdoor to the sky. The stars were sharp and cold, closer than they'd ever been. There was no wind, but she sensed the kind of pressure system that preceded a nor'easter. It was so strong that when she put her hand to her chest, the ladder, nailed to the wall for more than a century, seemed to dodder.

Her first instinct was to pull the door shut, and scurry back to her room. But remembering the fearsome quiet that had driven her out, she clambered onto the roof and focused on the steadying green eye of Long Point Light. The dinghies, iridescent in moonlight, floated nearly motionless on the water. *Asa Quebrada* opened one eye, ruffled his black-tipped wings, and went back to sleep.

Hallie took her usual perch next to him. When her feet grew numb with cold, she drew her knees to her chest and covered them with her pajamas. Finally, she stood up and wandered to the edge of the roof and cast the little beam of her light over the town, searching for something she couldn't name.

As far as she could see, every house in Provincetown was dark; the crooked roads, nearly impassable in the bright days of summer, were empty. All but a few restaurants and bars had been shuttered for the season, returning the town at the tip of Cape Cod to the people who lived there year round.

The gray-shingled houses that huddled tightly together in the village usually made her feel secure. But at three a.m., the spit of sand surrounded by dark, unpredictable waters seemed particularly vulnerable. Hallie was startled by her fear, and by the fat tears that suddenly spilled down her face. As unpredictable and powerful as the east wind, a deep sorrow entered her bones and left her shaking. Her heart hammered in her chest. The sound of an engine revving, and a lone car starting down the road made her jump. *Asa Quebrada* spread his wings and emitted a long, disgruntled *cawww*. Hallie normally loved his trilling squawks, but as he swooped over the bay, he sounded more like a crow. She cried out for her father with the name she rarely used. *Papai!*

She was still yelling as she sprang toward the door and down the ladder. The trap flapped open again behind her, admitting the brittle stars, the incipient chill of winter, but she didn't go back. Near the window, Wolf churned in his blankets, jerking awake. His face, caught in her careening light, revealed the demons he worked hard to hide during the day. "Jesus Christ, Hallie. What the—"

Hallie heard him cursing some more as he emphatically latched the door behind her. *Goddamn kid.*

She raced down the stairs and through the hallway, her flashlight casting erratic splotches of brightness on the walls and the floor as she went. The sound of her own voice scared her as much as the way she'd felt on the edge of the roof, or at the sight of Wolf's unguarded expression.

"Papai! *Nick*—" she yelled as she pushed into his room. But when her flashlight found the empty bed, she stopped short. The phone handset on the nightstand emitted a harsh bleep. Hallie crossed the room and returned it to its place. From the window, she could see Stuart's bedroom light. She wondered how she had missed it from the roof, and why he hadn't turned it off the way he usually did.

Hallie went to the top of the stairs, and listened for the soft sound of the stereo Stuart kept on while he napped on the couch. Instead, she heard him crossing the study for what felt like a prescribed number of steps, before he paused and returned.

She was about to go down and ask what was wrong when

the pacing was replaced by Ella Fitzgerald singing about airplanes and champagne. One of Nick's favorite songs. Stuart kicked off his shoes. *One, two.* Closing her eyes, she imagined him lining them up beside the couch the way he did before he pulled the quilt over himself. The world, momentarily askew, clicked back into place.

Hallie had never liked Ella much. (*Too goopy,* she complained, suspecting that the romantic lyric and the aching voice reminded her father of Liz Cooper.) But now as she slipped into bed, she clung to the scrap of melody like an amulet. She didn't sing the words, but they spun in her mind like a record playing on the turntable Nick had used since college. She heard them in his voice . . . *But I get a kick out of youuuu.*

If he had been there, she would have admitted the truth about her secret forays onto the roof in the deep of night, and told him about the bewildering emotions that had sent her reeling. But as it turned out, she would never tell anyone what she'd experienced that night. Not her father or Felicia. Not even the boy who huddled in the back of a closet across town as Hallie finally gave in to sleep. The boy with whom her spirit had become entangled in a way she would never, not in all her life, be able to explain.

CHAPTER 2

The house was dead quiet the next morning, and the clock was wrong. Eight forty-three? *Impossible.* Nick, who was up and moving around the house at five, always woke Hallie promptly at seven. She was so focused on the clock's deceitful face that it took her a full minute to notice that someone was sitting in Liz Cooper's ancient rocker. As far as she knew, no one had used that dusty wicker chair since her mother had rocked her to sleep when she was a baby.

At seventy-three, Aunt Del was a perpetual cyclone of activity and chatter, but that morning she was so still and pale that Hallie didn't recognize her. Blurry with sleep, she blinked at the apparition until she came into focus and then turned back to the clock. *Eight forty-five.* So it was working.

"I missed the bus!" she cried, leaping out of bed. "Why didn't Nick—" Before she voiced it, she answered her own question. "My dad went out on a call. He still isn't back?"

The gulls outside reminded her of the mournful singing she'd heard the night before. Hallie went to the window that her father, a great proponent of fresh air, kept open at night, no matter the season, and closed it.

She wanted to ask more questions, but she could no longer ignore her great-aunt's appearance. She was dressed for work right down to her pantyhose and pumps, but black rivulets of mascara defined the creases in her face. Hallie had never before seen the older woman's lips when they weren't slicked a vibrant fuchsia, and she was shocked at their pallor.

"What's wrong, Aunt Del?" Hallie said, hating the way her voice had grown small.

"Is Nick—"

"Your father's fine," Aunt Del answered quickly. She grabbed a tissue and wiped her face. "I didn't mean for you to see me like this, honey."

"*Uncle Buddy?*" Hallie asked, referring to Del's troubled son.

Aunt Del shook her head and blew her nose into the soggy Kleenex before she continued. "It's Mrs. Silva. Something happened to her last night. Something bad, Hallie."

Mrs. Silva. Hallie pulled her curly yellow hair into a knot at the base of her neck and tilted her head to one side as she processed what Del had said. There were lots of *Mrs. Silvas* in town, but the one people talked about most lived on Point of Pines Road. Even Nick turned to watch when she walked by. "You mean the Captain's wife?"

Codfish, the adults called him for his prowess at sea; and at school, their son was proud to answer to Little Cod. Young Gus was easily the most popular and athletic boy at Veterans Memorial Elementary, which didn't much impress Hallie. But when the boys chose teams for a game in the playground, he often picked the weakest players first. The kindness that radiated from his eyes when he called their names had won her over.

"Whatever it is, you might as well tell me," she said to Aunt Del. "I'm going to find out when I go to school anyway. Nick says it's always better to hear bad things from an adult."

Del fidgeted in her chair. "Yes, and he should be the one—"

"Never mind. I'll just ask Felicia. Her mom listens to the

police radio half the night. Luanne knows who's going to jail before the cops even leave the station."

"You know, Nick insists you're going to be a doctor," Aunt Del said when Hallie started for the door. "But I see you as a lawyer, or maybe a detective who specializes in getting people to talk."

Hallie returned to her spot on the bed. Miguel, the white kitten Nick had recently accepted from a patient in lieu of payment, leaped onto her lap. They both regarded Aunt Del expectantly.

"Your father got the call around three-thirty or four. Apparently, their neighbor, Deb Perry, had heard some screaming. When she got up, she noticed the door was wide open and the Captain's truck was gone."

Hallie remembered the face of the clock when she'd awakened, and the hour it had displayed. "Three oh-seven a.m.," she said out loud.

Fortunately, Aunt Del didn't seem to hear her. "Codfish would have gone ballistic if she'd called the cops, so Deb put on her housecoat and went over to check on Maria herself."

Hallie gazed out the window at the calm bay as she struggled to keep her expression neutral, but inside she again felt the rising pressure she'd experienced in her chest the night before.

"Deb stood on the stoop and called Maria's name, but there was no answer. Finally, she took a couple of steps into the kitchen and yelled louder. That's when she got spooked." Aunt Del paused and picked invisible lint from her dress.

"You can't stop now. What did she see?" Hallie spoke so vehemently that Miguel startled and leaped from her lap.

"Nothing. She ran back home, locked her door, and called nine-one-one. It was Officer Perreira who found the body."

"The body?"

"Oh, Hallie, I knew we should have waited for your father."

"But where was Gus?" Hallie persisted. "Was he sleeping?"

"Nick will—"

"Please, Aunt Del. He's in my class. I need to know."

"Gus's room was empty. At first, they thought his father had taken him or he'd run off. But a couple of hours ago, Nick went back to the house, and found him. The poor kid was folded up like a beach chair in the back of his mother's closet."

"You mean—" Hallie whispered.

"Oh, no, he's alive, thank God—but he was in such a state of shock that he was rigid. Catatonic."

Though Hallie didn't know what the word *catatonic* meant, silent tears, like the ones that had ambushed her on the roof the night before, streaked down her cheeks as she thought of Gus alone in the closet.

"Is there school?" she finally asked, unsure what the protocol was for an event like this. Someone's mom, who had stood at the bus stop just the day before, her black hair pulled up in a scrunchie, had become a *body*. Would the town shut down?

"There is, but your father wants you to stay home. The streets are already buzzing with rumors."

Hallie spent most of the day watching Wolf paint, stealing sips from his cold coffee, and sucking on the toffees he kept on his worktable. The attic was probably one of the last places in town news of the murder hadn't penetrated. Focusing on the vibrant canvas, Hallie could almost pretend it had never happened.

However when Nick finally came home in the late afternoon, there was no avoiding it. The darkness he'd tried
to shield her from was there on his face. Nestled in his lap,
Hallie had many questions, but it was clear her father was in
no mood to talk.

She settled for one: What had he said to Gus when he
pulled him from the closet?

It took a minute for Nick to recall his instinctive response.
"'*Oh, sweetheart*'—that's what I said. Then he removed his
glasses and wiped tears from his eyes. "Oh, my poor sweetheart."

CHAPTER 3

Do *you think he means it?"* Hallie asked one night over a mix of boxed macaroni and cheese, chopped tomatoes, and chorizo that Nick called "the Costa special."

Nick glanced up at his daughter. "What exactly are we talking about here?"

"The *Captain*," she said impatiently. Two months had passed since the murder, but it remained the dominant topic of conversation in town. "He said he never wants to see Gus again."

Wolf looked in the doctor's direction, as if he needed to hear the answer, too.

Nick continued to focus on his pasta.

"Where did you hear that?" he finally said.

"Neil Gallagher told me. When the Captain spoke in court, that's what he said. He didn't want his son coming to that prison. Not ever."

Even Wolf had heard the story when he stopped into Birdy's for some art supplies. "Then he told the judge that he'd already given himself the stiffest penalty possible; he expected no mercy from the court," he added.

"But he can't just quit being Gus's dad!" Hallie blurted out, banging the heel of her fork on the table. "Even if he killed Maria. Even if he's in jail forever. He's still Gus's dad. Well, isn't he?"

Wolf laughed bitterly, shattering the silence that followed. "Maybe some men aren't meant for fatherhood. Did you ever think of that? The way I see it, he did the kid a favor."

When Nick glowered at him, the painter rose from the table and scraped the remains of his dinner into the sink. The aging garbage disposal grumbled into action. "That meal was an abomination. Why do you people feel the need to add your greasy sausage to everything?" Wolf said. He didn't so much walk toward the stairs as lunge at them.

"You're welcome, Wolf. Please—feel free to join *us people* again," Nick yelled after him. Then he pushed back his chair. "Come here, Pie."

"Wolf's right about fathers, isn't he? Some of them just quit," Hallie said, frowning as she remembered how Felicia and her brother Hugo had wept when their dad loaded up his truck and moved out.

"You didn't need Wolf to tell you that," Nick answered quietly.

"But this was different. Gus was always with his father on the wharf, almost like you and me."

Nick nodded. "Little Cod. Far back as I can remember."

Hallie slid onto his lap and leaned against his chest. "Do you think he'll change his mind?"

"Codfish has always been pretty stubborn."

"It's because Gus has gone crazy, isn't it?" Hallie said, thinking of the rumors she'd heard on the bus. "Even his own dad doesn't want to see him anymore."

"Crazy? Is that what the kids are saying?" Nick sat up straight, his eyes flashing.

Like everyone else in town, Hallie knew better than to repeat the stories she'd heard to Nick. But almost no one had seen Gus since his mother died, and the longer he stayed away from school, the more outlandish the tales became. Recently, people had begun whispering about a new hypnotic power

in his eyes. They'd given him a new nickname, too: *Voodoo.*
Hallie first heard it from Felicia.

"My mom's friend, Cilla, says that if you look him in the
eyes he'll put a *feitiço* on you," Felicia had warned. "You'll go
to bed fine as ever, but when you wake up the next morning,
you'll be as crazy as he is."

"I don't believe in *feitiço*," Hallie said. "Besides, what
would you know about it? Your family came over on the
Mayflower. And so did Cilla Jackson's."

"So what? I'm still part Portuguese," Felicia answered.

"What part is that?" Hallie challenged.

"The part that lives in Provincetown."

Hallie might have laughed if she weren't so disturbed by
the subject of Gus's voodoo. Since the murder, Gus had been
staying on the edge of town with his aunt and uncle, Fatima
and Manny Barretto. She wondered what would happen if
she ran into him in the A&P with one of them. Would she
dare to stare directly at him? She decided she *would*—just to
prove Felicia and the others wrong.

But now, ashamed that she'd disappointed her father by
listening to superstitious talk, Hallie felt her skin grow hot.
"But he doesn't talk or go to school and he won't come out
to play—even though Neil goes to his house every single
day."

"Give the boy time, Pie. He'll do all those things again—
when he's ready," he said. "Now let's clean up our *abominable*
supper and check on your homework."

*B*y *spring, when the boy still* hadn't spoken a single word,
Nick and Gus's stalwart friend, Neil Gallagher, were the only
ones who believed he ever would. Hallie thought so, too,

but her faith was based on the conviction that her father was never wrong.

At least once a week, she overheard someone ask Nick why he didn't *do something.*

"What do you think I am—a shaman?" he'd say when Deb Perry confronted him near the cash register at Lucy's Market.

"You mean you're *not?*" Steamer Cabral asked from behind the counter. "Hell, I wouldn't have waited three weeks for an appointment if I knew you were just a regular doctor."

Everyone laughed but Deb. "Little Cod and Maria were so close, Doc. I'm afraid he might never come back from this."

Nick sighed as he pulled a few crumpled bills out of his wallet to pay for his purchases. "Fatima's taking him to Children's, Deb. To one of the best child psychiatrists in the country. Sure, I'd like to stick my head in and check on him, but the family wants to be left alone right now. I've gotta respect that—and so do you."

But several weeks later, when he heard the Barrettos were considering a "placement" for Gus, Nick changed his mind.

Hallie was rereading a biography of Amelia Earhart in the study when she heard her father on the phone. She put down her book and crept to the kitchen door.

"You've gone with the fancy experts in Boston, Fatima," Nick said. "Might as well give the local doctor a shot. I'll be there Saturday around one."

He hung up before she had time to object.

A small crowd had gathered outside the Barrettos' cottage even before Hallie rode her bike to Loop Street. It was located out past the two main streets, not far from Felicia's house. She immediately spotted Neil, hiding behind the leggy rhododendrons and neglected forsythia bushes in front of the house. Hallie tossed her bike at the edge of the lawn and hunkered down beside him, urging him to move further back. "And put your hat on," she added, handing him the baseball cap that was sitting in the dirt. "You can see that hair from Route 6."

"Who are you to come in my friend's yard and tell me what to do?" Neil said. Then, obviously used to playing the role of sidekick, he reached for his cap and scrunched it on his head. "Satisfied?"

Hallie tucked a recalcitrant red curl under Neil's cap and nodded. "Much better."

She turned her attention to the crowd. From her vantage point, she could see Gus's uncle, Alvaro, and his muscled sixteen-year-old son, Varo, Jr., who lived across the highway, leaning against their truck, sipping beer, and feigning boredom. The dark half-moons beneath young Alvaro's eyes told a different story. Since the murder, people had been saying that a curse hung over the family. Three years earlier, the Barrettos' only son, Junior, a high school football star, had drowned after a night of drinking. And now *this*.

The rest of the crowd was composed mostly of elderly relatives, who were already clacking their rosary beads, and a few of Fatima's friends. It was exactly the atmosphere Nick had hoped to avoid.

"Jesus *Christ*," he bellowed, hopping out of his truck. "What the hell is this? And you can put those damn beads away. The sea isn't going to part no matter how many Hail Marys you say—not in Provincetown, and not this afternoon." When he got no response, he shook his head and released a string of Portuguese curses as he made his way through the silenced group.

He turned around and faced them at the door. "Listen, if you want to waste a perfectly good Saturday afternoon standing out here like a pack of fools, I don't suppose there's anything I can do to stop you."

The onlookers, momentarily cowed by Nick's anger, lowered their heads, discreetly tucking prayer beads into pockets, and beers out of sight, but didn't budge.

"Okay, then," Nick said. "If you're going to stay, at least have the decency to keep quiet."

A hush fell over the group. Almost unconsciously, Neil Gallagher squeezed Hallie's hand between his. She'd never held hands with a boy before. Neil's grip was so ferocious that she felt as if her bones might break, but she didn't let go. "Do you think we should pray?" he asked.

"Me and Nick are atheists. We don't pray," Hallie said, repeating the word her father often used. Then, in spite of her disavowal, she closed her eyes and imagined being on the roof with the darkness all around her, recalling the rush of emotion that had invaded her on the night Gus Silva lost his mother. Silently, she whispered to the invisible stars: *Pleeease!*

Nick *was known for taking his* time with his patients, so no one was surprised when an hour passed and he still hadn't emerged. However, when Manny pressed an ear against the door and pronounced the parlor mysteriously quiet, the determined gathering was baffled. *What was he doing in there?* One of Alvaro's friends speculated that he was ashamed to admit he'd been stumped by a silent nine-year-old and had escaped out the back door.

"Keep your opinions to yourself," Manny told him sharply.

The first long hour passed into two and then three. Fatima's Aunt Elesandra announced she was going home for a nap, while the other women, who'd completed the fifteen mysteries of the rosary twice, complained about their arthritic fingers. At the edge of the property, Alvaro asked if the good doctor was giving Gus a brain transplant in there. Hallie and Neil played a tense game of marbles in the bushes. "You're good," Neil complained when Hallie swiped his last one. "Uncle Buddy taught me," she said, enjoying the feel of the marbles rattling in her pocket. Then she returned them. "I've got a whole jar at home."

By the time they reached the four-hour mark, Alvaro's six-pack was empty. He looked stripped and forlorn on the hood of his car. Fatima's friends had left, claiming they needed to get supper ready for their families, but they were soon replaced by Aunt Elesandra, who returned with some curious neighbors. By then everyone was starving, so Manny went into town to pick up pizzas. The scent of the food drew the crowd around Manny's car—among them Neil and Hallie, who were so hungry that they decided a slice was worth whatever punishment they got for defying Nick's orders.

"I should've known *you'd* show up!" Fatima said when she spotted the boy she shooed away from her door on a daily basis.

But Manny was focused on Hallie. "Nick's been in there for half the day, and we haven't heard a sound out of either of them. What the hell is he doing?"

Hallie felt the eyes of the crowd on her; and in the background she thought she heard someone whisper the word she hated most: *genius.* Since she knew no more about what was going on than anyone else, she looked toward the house, and put her finger to her lips, reminding them of Nick's request for quiet. The reminder couldn't have come at a better time, because a minute later the long, almost otherworldly, silence was broken by a voice.

"It's Voodoo! He's talking!" Fatima's friend Sherry cried out as the old women crossed themselves in unison. Alvaro leaped from the hood of the car and pumped a fist in the air. But the loudest whoop of all came from Neil Gallagher. Hallie looked to the window, wondering if Gus could hear him, and if he had any idea how many hours they had spent outside the door, refusing to give up.

A few moments later, Nick came out smiling. He lifted his arms like the Pope and announced that the boy was going to be all right. *Fine.*

"What did you do?" Fatima looked up at him, weeping openly.

"Did I ever tell you I was Veteran Memorial's all-time champion of the staring contest?" Nick said. "Well, let's just say I successfully defended my title."

"You and Gustavo had a *staring* contest?" Fatima glanced at her watch. "For five hours?"

"Something like that. I looked into Gus's sorrows, and he looked into mine, till eventually he broke."

"What did he say?" Fatima asked, clearly expecting something profound.

"He said what anyone says at the end of a staring contest: *I give.*"

CHAPTER 4

A week later, Hallie appeared at the Barrettos' door. She hesitated for a full minute before she dared to knock. When Gus's aunt opened it halfway, Hallie took a step backward and picked up the gifts she'd brought. In one hand she carried a thick book, holding it against her chest like a Bible salesman; in the other, a swollen plastic bag secured with a wire tie. Two minnows swam inside it. Fatima Barretto let out a long exhalation. She looked past the girl suspiciously. "So where's your little boyfriend—hiding in the bushes again?"

"Neil's not here—and he *isn't* my boyfriend," Hallie said, though she wasn't quite sure she was right on either count. Neil still spent most of his free time skulking around the house on Loop Street, waiting for the Gus he once knew to come out and play. And since he had started sitting with Hallie on the bus almost every day, she'd heard the word *boyfriend* whispered more than once.

At first, Neil just wanted to talk about Gus, but one afternoon right before they reached her stop, he asked if she'd ever kissed a boy. When she squinched up her nose and replied, "Of course not," Neil smiled. "Me neither. Never kissed a girl, I mean. But when I do, it's gonna be you." Hallie hadn't contradicted him. She wondered if that made him her boyfriend.

Mrs. Barretto continued to bar the doorway, but Hallie sensed an opening.

"Nick sent me," she said, though she hadn't exactly told Nick where she was going. She held the book and the fish in the air. "Follow-up treatment."

Mrs. Barretto tilted her head to read the title of the book. "*David Copperfield*? How's that supposed to help my nephew?" she asked, but she opened the screen door and let Hallie pass.

"It's about an orphan," Hallie said, speaking with more certainty than she felt.

"Well, that should cheer him up." Mrs. Barretto took in the scraggly fish. "And what are those—minnows? I know you mean well, Hallie—*everyone* means well. But those fish belong in the tide pools, and the last thing Gustavo needs is a story about an orphan."

"Not just any orphan," Hallie replied. "An orphan who becomes the hero of his own story."

Mrs. Barretto sighed. "We were so happy when Gustavo spoke to Nick on Saturday. But that was it. He hasn't said a word since."

Hallie bristled at the hint of criticism toward her father. "That was just part one of the treatment."

"I see. And you're part two?" Fatima folded her arms across her chest, as if she wished she'd never opened the door. "You and your orphan book?"

"Yup." Hallie took in Fatima's collection of statues. Dolorous replicas of the Virgin Mary were everywhere, their blue ceramic cloaks grayed by dust, their eyes glazed. Though he wasn't home, Hallie could smell Manny's scent—a mixture of drugstore cologne, the sea, and pure meanness. For the first time, she wondered if Mrs. Barretto was right; maybe she shouldn't have come. But she banished the thought by sitting up extra straight on the couch and smiling like a prim visitor, the book resting on her lap like a lady's purse.

Mrs. Barretto emitted a long sigh, then relented. "Gustavo!" she hollered as if the house were a many-winged mansion instead of a winterized five-room cottage. The name reverberated, as did the silence that followed.

Fatima Barretto knocked on his bedroom door. "Dr. Nick's daughter is here to see you. It looks like she brought you a—a *present*." Again, she shook her head disdainfully at the common minnows. Then she returned to the living room.

"Maybe he's sleeping," Hallie said, when Gus still hadn't come out after several, long uncomfortable moments. "I'll come back some other time."

But before she could get away, Gus appeared in the hallway, looking as if he'd just woken up from a nap. His eyes were dark and glistening, but they clearly weren't crazy. Hallie quickly decided that Gus Silva was just sad—more sad than anyone she'd ever seen. He was so sad he couldn't utter a single word. Her heart clenched.

Mrs. Barretto cleared her throat. "Hallie's come to, um, *read to you*, Gustavo." She spoke loudly, as if Gus wasn't only mute but deaf, too. From the way she emphasized the words, Hallie sensed that reading—especially the passive act of being read to, had never been Gus's favorite activity.

Mrs. Barretto picked up the book, and skimmed a few pages. "I was in high school before I even heard of Dickens. Don't you have something more appropriate?"

Hallie grimaced, as she always did when anyone referred to her precociousness. "This is one of his books for children," she said as Gus took a seat opposite her.

Mrs. Barretto tested its heft and squinted at the small print inside. "Doesn't look like a kids' book to me."

Gus, however, was focused on the fish.

"Nick took me to Herring Cove this morning," Hallie explained. "This big one here—I named him after Johnny Kollel because he's a bully. And the little one is Silver because—well, just because I thought it was pretty. Now that she's yours, I guess that makes her Silver Silva."

Gus blinked at her with his sorrowful eyes.

"How about I get you a snack, then I'll leave you and your pet fish alone," Mrs. Barretto offered. "That okay with you, Gustavo?"

Hallie was glad his aunt didn't call him Voodoo like people in town did. And yet even as she denied the power of his spell, she felt it.

Mrs. Barretto set down a platter of *trutas* and two glasses of milk in mismatched tumblers. She'd also retrieved an old fishbowl for Johnny and Silver. It was milky and stained with a ring of algae.

Though Hallie had never liked the sweet potato pastries, she took a polite nibble. In spite of the sugar and spices, it still tasted like a vegetable to her, and it had to be at least a week old. (Even her father, who adored *trutas*, said they were only good the first day.) "Mmm . . . thank you," she said, in the spirit of Nick's *cortesia*. The word meant "courtesy," but when Nick pronounced it in Portuguese, he was giving a name to his personal religion: a profound respect for the unknowable spirit in everyone he met.

When Gus's aunt left the room, Hallie discreetly spit her cookie into a napkin. Then she poured the two fish into the cloudy bowl, pulled a small canister of fish food from her pocket, and set it beside Gus. "They're yours now. If you don't take care of them, they'll die."

Gus watched everything she did intently, but made no

response. Hallie decided there was something comforting in being with a mute. She could say whatever she wanted—or she could just relax and say nothing at all. As for Gus, he seemed to be at ease with his own silence. He didn't squirm when spoken to, nor did he look away. If he could speak, he might say that he didn't want to spend a sun-dappled afternoon listening to a girl he didn't know very well read a nineteenth-century novel.

But he neither complained nor teased Hallie when she opened the heavy book crammed with tiny print and filled the living room with David Copperfield's story. Hallie stood when she read, as if it were a performance; her voice rose in the dramatic parts, and changed for each character.

When she peeked obliquely at Gus, he was holding the plate of stale *trutas* on his lap, clearly absorbed in the tale. Hallie smiled and went on reading. For at least a little while, it looked as if he'd forgotten to be sad. She read for over an hour before she suddenly stopped in the middle of a critical scene and slammed the book shut.

Gus blinked like he'd just awoken from a dream, almost dropping the plate of pastries on the rug.

"I'll have the bus drop me here on Monday so we can read some more," Hallie said. Knowing there would be no response, she didn't bother with goodbye. "Thanks again for the *trutas*, Mrs. Barretto," she sang out as the screen door slammed, its elbow hinge long broken.

As she stepped into the garden, Neil Gallagher jumped up from under the same scrawny bush where the two had hidden the week before.

"What are *you* doing here?" Hallie said in a harsh whisper. She looked back at the house to make sure Gus's aunt

wasn't watching them. "If Mrs. Barretto thinks you're following me, she'll never let me back in the house again."

"Old *witch*," Neil muttered. "She got mad just because I
hooked her ripped screen with my fishing pole. Then when I
broke a window in Manny's stupid shed with a ball, she really
freaked." After retrieving the sporting equipment he had been
using to try to lure Gus outside—this time a catcher's mitt, a ball
and two bats, he hobbled after Hallie. "Wait up! I got a charley
horse waiting under that bush so long. Did Gus talk to you?"

Hallie didn't stop or answer his question, but she slowed
down and let him catch up. "You should sit down and mas-
sage that leg if you want the cramp to go away."

"Oh, so you're a doctor now?" Though he was still limping, Neil refused to slow down.

"Not yet, but I'm Nick's number-one assistant."

"Well, *la-di-da*."

Hallie laughed out loud. It sounded like something Aunt
Del would say—not a boy with a charley horse, wearing a
baseball cap backwards.

"So what did you do in there?" he repeated, oblivious to
her laughter. "And why did you bring that huge *book*?"

Hallie ignored his questions. After a peaceful hour with
the mute Gus, she had already become used to speaking only
when she felt like it. Neil skipped ahead of her with his sore
leg and forced her to look at him. "Well?" His face was so
expectant that she giggled again.

"What's so funny? Did Gus say when he's coming back
to school?"

"He didn't say anything," Hallie admitted. They had
reached the road where she turned off, so she stopped briefly.
"Not *yet*."

Hallie resumed walking, clearly done with their conversation.

"But he will, right, Hal?" he yelled, standing on the corner of his street, a wide smile stretching his freckled cheeks. "He's gonna talk just like he used to!"

Hallie continued in silence a few more yards. Then she turned back, wearing a smile that matched Neil's. "Yes, he will," she said into the bright wind that came off the bay. She didn't know how she could be so sure, but she was.

That night, Hallie was relieved when Linda Soares, the town librarian who'd spent years trying to impress Nick with her low-cut shirts and book recommendations, joined them for dinner. Hallie had rehearsed how she would tell Nick what she'd done, and she hoped the presence of a guest might soften his reaction.

She finally blurted it out in the middle of dessert.

Nick pushed back his plate. "Let me get this straight. You *lied* to me about going to Felicia's," he said sternly, seeming to forget that anyone else was there. "Then you rode your bike all the way to Loop Street, and showed up at the house of a grieving family with a book and two fish?"

"*You* went there."

"I'm a doctor. It's my job to help people."

"From what I heard, you had a five-hour staring contest with the kid," Wolf snorted. "If that's what you call medical treatment, I prefer Hallie's idea."

Nick ignored him. "I don't believe in all that nonsense about *feitiço* and voodoo, but Gus Silva is deeply troubled, Hallie."

"When I got to the door, I wanted to turn around and go back so bad, but the water from the plastic bag was starting to leak, and I knew the fish would never survive the trip back. And—"

"And when you decide to do something, you don't let anything stop you—just like your mother. There are going to be consequences for this one, though, Hallie."

"I'm sorry, Nick, but—"

"But nothing. You lied to me and you went somewhere you had no right to be. I can't believe Fatima Barretto even let you in, or that Gus was willing to see you."

"I thought my fish were going to die before he came out, but he finally did." Though she knew she was in trouble, Hallie couldn't keep the excitement from her voice.

"And he sat there listening to you reading Dickens?" Linda asked. "That's pretty heavy going for a nine-year-old—in the best of circumstances."

"Didn't take his eyes off me for a whole hour."

Though Nick was listening intently, he said nothing. When he got up to clear the table, the tension was palpable. Wolf grumbled something and slipped upstairs; and Linda, who suddenly remembered she had something to do, offered to pick up her pie pan the next day.

Hallie and Nick dried and put away the dishes in strained silence.

"I suppose you promised you'd go back?" Nick finally said.

"Well, I hoped . . . I mean, if it's okay with you. Please?"

Nick pulled out a chair at the table, scraping the floor, and then sat down. "I'll consider it—with certain conditions, of course," he said.

Sensing her victory, Hallie threw her arms around his neck, but her father held her at arms's length.

"I said I'd *consider* it," he repeated. "But first there's the matter of your punishment. That sleepover you planned with Felicia for the weekend? Consider it canceled."

The following Monday, Hallie went to the Barrettos', where she would return every day for the next three weeks including Saturdays and Sundays. Neil Gallagher was always somewhere nearby, either caught in an inhospitable nest of cat briars and Japanese honeysuckle, spying from his perch high in the crabapple tree, or sitting among the old traps and fishing lures in Manny's disheveled shed. Sometimes, when he got tired of hiding from Fatima, he came out and tossed a ball in the air outside the window, singing the theme songs to Gus's favorite TV shows.

Then, one afternoon, just after they'd entered their fourth week, she noticed Gus taking an interest in the world around him. She slipped into the kitchen for a glass of water, and when she returned, he was standing in the window, shadowed by the dusty gold drapes. Outside, Neil threw a ball higher and higher, as if aiming at the sun while Gus followed its bright trajectory. When Neil caught it, Gus smiled for the first time.

But when Hallie picked up the book, his attention returned to the narrative Hallie was slowly unspooling in the living room. An hour later she reached the scene where David Copperfield waved goodbye to his mother for what would be the last time and Gus looked stricken. Hallie wondered if his aunt had been right. Maybe she'd chosen the wrong story. "Do you want me to stop?" she asked. Gus shook his head vigorously, and Hallie sensed that he didn't just want to hear more; he *needed* to hear it.

She read extra long that day, not stopping until her father showed up to ask if she ever planned to come home.

That night Stuart brought over his famous potato leek soup and Nick made omelettes. They were in the middle of dinner when Hallie announced that her visits to Loop Street were almost over.

"Did you finish the book?" Nick asked.

"Don't need to," Hallie replied, thinking of the way Gus had smiled as he watched Neil tossing the ball. "Gus will be wanting to go out and play soon."

"So, Dr. Hallie's treatment is almost done?" Stuart said.

"Yup." Hallie was surprised by the hint of regret in her voice. She would miss the hours she spent in the Barrettos' living room, just her, Gus, and David Copperfield.

The next day she reached the point where David hears of his mother's death. She closed the book gently, and set it on the table. Gus looked up, startled.

"You'll have to finish the rest yourself," she said. Then she reached out to shake his hand like her father always did when he was finished with a patient. Gus stared at her extended palm, refusing to accept what it meant.

After she left, he followed her into a street that was exploding with pink clover, grape hyacinths, and rugosa roses. Hallie inhaled the scents, and wondered how she had failed to notice them before. Had they just appeared that day? Her heart thumped wildly at the sound of his footsteps behind her, but she didn't look back. If he had something to say, he would have to speak. *Now was the time.*

"Wait!" he finally called. "You know I can't read that book."

Hallie turned back and met him eye-to-eye. "You *can*."

"No, I—"

"You *have to*," she said, stopping him with the firmness in her voice. "Because if you don't, you'll never know the end of the story."

Abruptly, she turned the corner, leaving Gus behind. She tried to stay cool, as if it was the most normal thing in the world for him to speak to her, but everything inside her—blood, heart, and spirit—was humming one word. *Yes!*

She walked another half-mile. Then she looped back to the house, where she found Neil in the crabapple tree, watching Gus through the window.

"Will that branch hold both of us?" she asked in a low voice, mindful of the open window.

Neil reached out his hand to pull her up. The tree offered the cover of foliage, while still providing a clear view into the bedroom and access to the sounds coming through the open window. Gus was straining over the small print, the oversized words. He appeared to give up and hurled the book across the room. But a minute later he leaped up and went to his cousin's bookcase. The shelves were lined with the model boats Junior had once made with his father, but there was a tattered copy of *Webster's Dictionary* on the bottom shelf. Gus pulled it out, retrieved the novel from the floor, and tried again.

It clearly wasn't easy for him. The first words he used when he returned to David Copperfield's interrupted story were in Portuguese. Though Hallie didn't know their meaning, she recognized the curses Nick had forbidden Uncle Buddy to use in her presence.

Hearing him, Neil laughed so hard that he almost fell out of the tree; and Aunt Fatima marched into Gus's room and threatened to spank his *cu* if she ever heard such language from his lips again. Then she confounded the message as she hugged him and began to weep. "That Costa girl did it! She's going to be just like Nick someday."

Hallie smiled, though she didn't believe it. She had only been the messenger. Charles Dickens owned the magic. Impulsively, she pressed her lips on Neil's mouth, hard the way her father kissed her cheek when he was excited about something.

"That was it," she said, as surprised as he was. "Your first kiss." Then she jumped from her perch on the tree and ran home.

CHAPTER 5

In the fall, Hallie often saw Gus and Neil together on the bus and in the playground. Neil smiled and lifted his hand in a triumphant wave whenever he caught her eye. *Hallleee!* He'd holler, letting the wind take the elongated syllables. Most often, he was looking over his shoulder at her from a bike, or running across the playground. Every now and then he'd skid up close enough to ask if she was still his girlfriend.

"I never said I was," Hallie replied when he hung around long enough to listen.

"But you *kissed* me. That means—"

"I kissed you because I was happy! If you weren't there, I would have kissed the tree."

"The *tree*? Thanks a lot." Neil would pretend to be heartbroken, but a week or two later, he would ask again.

As for Gus, he *had* come back, just as they'd all prayed he would. Still, Hallie noticed a new ferocity in his play, an *edge*.

"Of course, he's different," Nick said when she told him about it. "Underneath all the sorrow, he's plain angry. He's got to be."

Hallie caught a glimpse of that anger when Johnny Kollel taunted Gus with the rhyme he'd made up after the murder:

> Little Cod, Little Cod,
> the orphan of Race Point.
> Mommy's in the graveyard,
> Daddy's in the joint.

Johnny was older and stronger, but he was no match against Gus's rage. The gym teacher intervened, but two days later, when Johnny joked with his friends about how Little Cod had "gone mental over a silly poem," skinny Neil had put his head down and charged him like a bull. The older boy had Neil on the ground and was pummeling him when Hallie spotted them from the window of the art room. As soon as she saw blood spurting from her friend's nose, she dropped the brush she was using to decorate a pumpkin for Nick, marking the floor with what looked like an exclamation point in black paint. "Sorry—emergency!" she yelled to the startled art teacher as she streaked outside.

Hallie had never been in a fight in her life, but she dove onto Johnny's back and pounded him with her small fists. The crowd whooped, finally alerting the playground monitor, who had sneaked around the building for a cigarette. She rushed toward them, her words indecipherable to Hallie in the heat and exhilaration of the fight. Johnny tossed her off just as Gus, careening out of the school building, a flash of jet black hair and speed, arrived.

Though blood was still spraying from Neil's nose, he scrabbled to his feet. "I guess I showed him!" he said. Then he pulled Hallie into their defiant circle. "I mean *we* did. Right, Hal? She fights pretty good for a girl; doesn't she, Gus?"

Gus touched a scrape on her cheek, then ducked out from under Neil's arm. "You could have gotten hurt," he said. There was gratitude in his tone, but also a sternness that made Hallie think of her father.

Neil ended up with several stitches, a scar on his upper lip, and a discolored tooth that would mark the day for life.

They were all suspended for a week. Nick grounded Hallie for the duration, exiling her from the sweetest week of Indian summer, and gave her a serious lecture about the dangers and futility of fighting.

"I understand why you did it, Pie," he conceded a few days later. "You were defending a friend. But if you ever try something that irresponsible—and just plain *stupid*—again, you'll be grounded till you're fourteen. Got it?"

Hallie assented gravely, but all she heard was *I understand*.

Throughout the fall and winter, Hallie kept her promise, but one Thursday in May, Neil convinced her to get off the bus at the wrong stop and go to Beech Forest. He and Gus had planned a blood brother ritual. *Blood brothers, and a sister if you come*, he added, snapping his jackknife open. Gus and Neil were drawn to the older boys who swore and played rough games on the playground, and Hallie couldn't believe they wanted to hang out with her. Initially she said no, but at the last minute, she jumped from her seat and followed them as they got off the bus.

When they reached the spot they had chosen, Gus frowned at Hallie. "This is dumb, Gallagher. We should head back to town before she gets in trouble." Though he was speaking to Neil, he continued to look at Hallie.

But Neil had already cut himself. "You can't back out now, Gus," he said, triumphantly squeezing a drop of blood from his index finger. "We're going to be brothers, remember? Your blood in me and mine in you."

Turning back to his friend, Gus quickly repeated the ritual, pressing his finger against Neil's. But when Hallie reached for the knife, he gripped the handle tightly. "Not you. This is for blood brothers only."

Determined not to be shut out, she pushed the tip of her finger against the blade just as he jerked away. Blood flared.

"Jeez, Hal. You were only supposed to get a drop." Neil went so white that even his freckles looked blanched, while Gus tore a piece of cloth from the sleeve of his shirt and handed it to her. "My cousin's house is down the road," he said. "I'm gonna call Nick."

"You don't have to do that," Hallie said firmly, imitating the calmness her father always displayed on house calls. While the boys watched, she tore the cloth into strips and wove it expertly around her finger to stanch the bleeding. Then she started toward the path. "And don't either of you try to follow me, either."

She started off slowly, but once she was out of sight, she broke into a run. She didn't notice anyone was behind her until Gus sprinted to her side on Route 6.

"Man, you're fast," he said when he caught his breath. "And you bandaged that finger just like Dr. Nick."

"See, it's okay." She held up her injured hand. The blood had turned the yellow strip of fabric orange, but it wasn't leaking through.

"That's not why I ran after you." Gus looked down and crossed his arms the way he had when he challenged Johnny Kollel to a fight. "There's something I need to tell you."

"Now?" Hallie said, feeling confused. She glanced toward the road that led into town as if expecting to see her father's truck on the hill.

"It won't take long, and if I don't do it now . . . Look, I just want to say I don't need anyone coming over to read me stories, or cutting herself up to be my blood sister. And I sure don't need a girl getting in fights for me. Us Silvas, we take care of ourselves. Got that?"

"I told you I was okay."

But Gus shook his head, clearly determined to finish. "And you can have your book back, too. I can't read it, and even if I could, I wouldn't want to."

Those last words struck their target. "Are you saying you don't want to be my friend?" Hallie wasn't sure if she was more offended for David Copperfield or for herself.

Gus stared at the ground.

In that instant, Hallie's hurt turned to anger. "Well, fine. But if you don't want the book, take it down to the pier and throw it in the harbor. 'Cause us Costas? When we give something, we don't take it back. You got *that*?"

Gus glanced up at her. It only lasted a second, but the compassion she saw made her chest ache. *So that was what this was all about.* He wasn't excluding her or trying to hurt her; he was protecting her. She darted into the road so quickly that a man on a bike had to weave perilously close to an oncoming car to avoid her. She turned and recognized Stuart's boyfriend, Paul, who had nearly succumbed to a serious bout with pneumonia that winter. Hallie was as surprised to see him as he was her.

"Hey, Hallie, watch where you're going," he yelled. He stopped on the side of the road, straddling his bike. "What are you doing over here, anyway? Does Nick know where you are?"

"I'm sorry, and no . . . and *I've got to go*," she called back from the other side of the street. She was unsure if she was apologizing to Nick for disobeying him yet again, to Paul, or to Gus Silva. When she reached the bottom of the hill, she stopped and looked back, half-expecting to see Gus behind her. The street was empty. She stood there for a full minute, tears stinging her eyes, before she spun away and ran the final half-mile back to her father.

PART TWO

RACE POINT BEACH

{ 1985 - 1987 }

Hallie loaded her backpack carefully: a pound of Jamaican coffee, a woolen hat for the winter that would soon be upon them, some Truro honey, and two books, one a heavy ocean-ography tome she'd borrowed from her father and the other a volume of poems by Kabir. Before she hiked out to the dunes, she planned to stop at Cap's and pick up some oyster stew.

It had been six weeks since she or her father had seen Wolf. Just after her sixteenth birthday, a letter from the Park Service had arrived informing him that he'd been granted a lease on one of the storied shacks in the dunes. Hallie hadn't expected to miss him as much as she did. Since she'd entered high school, she was home less, and often preoccupied, but the house felt empty without him. She begged Nick to go out to the shack and convince him to come home, but her father was as adamant as Wolf had been. "You know, I kind of miss the old crank myself—and I'm worried about his health, too, but this is important to him."

The shack was buried so deep among the dunes that Hal-lie thought she'd never find it, and the heavy pack cut into her shoulder blades. Then, just when she was about to give up, it came into view. Poised between two crests of sand, it offered a stark view of ocean. Hallie never failed to inhale sharply when she hiked across a high dune and saw the mus-cular swells of Race Point Beach. The shades in the shack were down, and a hand-painted KEEP OUT sign was staked in the sand out front. She marched to the door and knocked.

When it winged open, she took a step backward, startled by the man who confronted her.

A patchy beard obscured Wolf's bony face, and there was something wild and untamed in his eyes. *Had he really been so feral-looking when he lived with them?* she wondered. Her father's words rose to mind: *Don't romanticize him. He's nobody's uncle, Pie.* But as soon as Wolf spoke, she relaxed.

"Jesus Christ, girl! Now you're going to torment me out here, too?" The hint of a smile crossed his face.

"I hiked for an hour carrying this heavy pack, and that's all you have to say?" she joked back, wondering how long it had been since he'd seen another person.

"Oyster stew," he said, catching a whiff from the take-out container she'd brought. "From *Cap's.*"

"So are you going to invite me in or not?" Peering over his shoulder, Hallie saw that the shack was laid out remarkably like the attic had been, with the futon in the corner, a small table and solitary chair where he took his meals near the window, and his easel in the center of the room.

Wolf was looking past her, too, and abruptly his mood changed.

"*No one* comes in here," he growled, like an animal defending his den. "That's the point."

When Hallie didn't budge, he grew agitated. "Don't you get it? I want to be left alone." He took the container of stew from her hands, muttering the most ungrateful *thanks* Hallie had ever heard as he slammed the door.

Hallie raised her fist to knock again, but it lingered in the air. Nick was clearly right. Wolf, the eccentric uncle, or the wayward older brother, was as much a figment of her imagination as the romantic sea captains she used to conjure when she sat on the roof. She kicked the door, wondering what had gone wrong.

"Well, thank you, too!" she yelled. "The hospitality was amazing." In her mind, she heard her father's robust laugh. She had always loved its sound, but like many of her father's formerly endearing traits, it had recently begun to annoy her. Did he always have to be so right? *You visit a hermit and you expect to be invited in for tea?* he'd say later.

She turned to escape the unstable porch when she was startled by the sight of Neil Gallagher sitting cross-legged on top of a nearby dune. He was wearing a pair of jeans with a hole in one knee and a sweatshirt with the words PROVINCE-TOWN THEATER emblazoned across the front.

"Gallagher, what the hell—" she said, realizing why Wolf had turned her away. "You *followed* me out here?"

"I didn't mean to interrupt anything," Neil said, holding up his hands in surrender. "Honest. I didn't even know where you were headed when I—"

"When you what? Tracked me like a bloodhound and ruined my visit? Do you know how long it's been since I've seen Wolf?"

But Neil looked so open-faced and apologetic that her anger quickly fell away. When she reached the top of the dune, Hallie offered him a hand up.

He stood, brushed the sand off, and took Hallie's backpack from her. "The least I can do," he said. "What's in this thing anyway—rocks?"

"Presents for Wolf," she replied, listing the contents.

"I see nothing has changed," Neil laughed. And when Hallie answered with a curious glance, he said, "You still think a book can cure anything."

"And you still don't know how to dress for the weather. It's November, Gallagher. Don't you own a jacket?" Hallie studied the moody clouds that were easing toward them. "We probably should get going."

Neil looked up as if noticing the weather for the first time. "Jeez, it does look like rain. But now that you dragged all this stuff out here, don't you think you should leave it for him? It's a long walk to the road. And since I stopped pretending I was a jock, I'm out of shape."

"Nope. He already got my oyster stew. If he wanted the rest of it, he should have invited me in," Hallie said before she visibly softened. She stopped and looked back at the shack. "Stubborn fool. I bet he's dying for a good cup of coffee."

Quietly, she carried the bag back to Wolf's porch, where she carefully stacked her gifts.

Neil was smiling when she climbed toward him.

"What?" she said.

"*You*, that's what. I knew you couldn't deny him his presents." Neil took up the lightened pack again as they started toward the road.

"Shouldn't you be home practicing for your play or something?" Hallie said, feeling embarrassed by the admiration in his eyes.

In freshman year, when he failed to make the basketball team, Neil had been crushed. But after an English teacher suggested he try out for a school play, he'd discovered his passion. He'd starred in every production since; and recently, he'd landed a part in a famed local theater.

"I'm practicing or thinking about it wherever I go," he said. "In fact, when I was hiking out here, I put on a one-man show for the gulls."

"How did they like it?"

"The reviews were unanimous: I'm gonna be the next big thing."

Hallie laughed. "How about trying your lines out on a real critic?"

Neil didn't need a second invitation. As they trudged through the sand, his voice resonated through the dunes, captivating Hallie.

They'd walked halfway to the truck when Neil wandered off the path and sat down. "Break time," he announced. "Anything to drink in this thing?" he said, opening the pack.

Hallie passed him a bottle of orange-mango juice as she took a seat beside him. "The seagulls were right, by the way. You were awesome."

Neil grinned widely. "You really think so?"

"I wouldn't lie. Now it's your turn to be honest. I want to know what you're doing out here. And please don't tell me you wanted to meditate in the dunes."

"I wouldn't insult your famous intelligence." Neil picked up a stick and concentrated on drawing in the sand. Interlocking squares and circles, looping ovals and blunt triangles. The sand was so thick and dry that the shapes vanished as quickly as he drew them.

"Last spring you asked me why Gus acts so strange around you, why he never flirts with you like he does with every other girl on the lower Cape," he finally said. "Do you remember that?"

Hallie took a deep breath. "You want me to believe you walked all the way out here to talk to me about some stupid conversation we had last spring? Come on, Neil. This is *me*."

But Neil, who had always talked to her so easily about any

subject suddenly seemed edgy and evasive. "Do you remember or not?"

"Okay, I might have mentioned that it's kind of weird the way he avoids me, but I never said anything about *flirting*."

"Well, did you ever think it's because he's had a huge crush on you for years? Ever since you first showed up at his house with that book. In fact, *crush* isn't a big enough word to describe it."

Hallie shifted uncomfortably in the sand, hoping Neil didn't notice. "That was a long time ago. I hardly know Gus anymore."

After he had ended their friendship on that desolate strip of highway, Gus had remained polite but distant. Hallie had been secretly relieved when she heard that he was transferring to the regional school twenty miles away for freshman year. Still she couldn't help hearing about him. By the time he was a sophomore, he was playing quarterback for the varsity team, and half the town was making the trek to Eastham to watch him play.

He even made the pejorative name he was called after his mother's murder his own, choosing it over the one he'd inherited from his father. He was Voodoo now, Voodoo who could charm a spiraling football or a girl with equal ease. Voodoo who lived with his aunt and uncle in the run-down house on Loop Street but was rarely home. He seemed equally untouched by its dismal atmosphere, and those who tried to chain him to the past.

Neil closed his eyes as if he was determined to get through his prepared speech. "Listen, some of us are going to hang out at the beach on Saturday night if you want to come. We're gonna build a bonfire and drink a few of my special rum and Cokes."

"You mean a *party*?"

"More like a few couples. I'm going with Christina," he said, referring to the girl he'd been seeing for several months. "And Voodoo really wants to hang out with you."

Hallie's color deepened. "What is this—a summons? The great Voodoo Silva has chosen me as the girl of the week? I thought he was going out with one of Daisy's cousins from Truro, anyway."

"Over," Neil said with a dismissive swoop of his hand. "Come on. What do you say? He would have called you and asked you all nice and proper. It's just—well, like I said, he gets nervous around you."

"Are you trying to tell me Voodoo is shy? Please. He's got to be the most *arrogant* boy I've ever met," she said.

She got up and resumed walking, but Neil didn't immediately follow. He was out of breath when he finally caught up to her.

"Listen, if you don't want to go out with him, fine. But don't talk about him like that. Not to me."

Hallie turned around and hugged him. "I know you love him, Neil . . . but sometimes I wonder if he deserves your loyalty."

Neil, who was usually easy and affectionate, pushed her away gently. "Don't go there, okay?"

Hallie was confused. Was he talking about the hug or her doubts about Gus? She started down the path, grateful for the sand that pushed back against her feet, giving her something physical to resist. Soon she heard Neil behind her. She waited for him to sing out the lines he'd been practicing earlier, or to break out in a song from Metallica or Cole Porter as he often did, but he stayed silent.

It wasn't until the rain came down in great splashing buckets that he caught up to her. "First you call my best friend an arrogant asshole, and now we're caught in the middle of a typhoon. Thanks for ruining my day."

"I ruined *your* day—excuse me? If it weren't for you, I'd be sitting in a cozy shack drinking a nice cup of Jamaican coffee and checking out Wolf's newest paintings. And I never said Gus was an *asshole*. Well, not exactly."

"So you've changed your mind about Saturday? How does nine o'clock sound?" Neil said as he raced toward the road.

"You never give up, do you?"

"You should know that by now."

Hallie wondered why it mattered so much to him that she go out with Gus, but she was too wet and cold to pursue the discussion. She had just reached the truck when Neil darted into the middle of Route 6, opened his arms, and lifted his face to the unexpected downpour. "You've got to feel this, Hal. This just might be the best moment of our lives."

"You know something? You really are insane," Hallie yelled, but she followed him into the road, laughing as she swallowed the needles of water.

CHAPTER 7

The following Monday, Aunt Del discovered a sheet of paper folded like an origami bird wedged inside the mailbox when she went out for the mail. "Apparently this is for you," she said, lifting her penciled eyebrows when Hallie came home from school.

"For me?"

Aunt Del indicated the name that was scrawled across the wing: Hallie Costa. "Looks like you've got a secret admirer."

"It's probably from Felicia," Hallie said. "She's always making cool things." Then she grabbed a jacket and took it onto the porch to open alone. Inside the folds was a smudged note in recklessly male handwriting: *It's you or nobody. Always has been, always will be.*

Hallie turned the creased paper over, looking for a signature. Finding none, she spun around to see if someone was watching for her reaction. The street was empty. She thought of the way Neil had described Gus's feelings for her: *Crush isn't even the word for it.* There had been something almost mocking in his tone, but now she wondered.

Hallie scrunched the note into a ball and jammed it in the pocket of her jeans. A light snow began to fall as she spotted Felicia coming around the corner.

"I can't believe you didn't tell me Gus Silva asked you out," Felicia said, sounding offended.

"Actually, he didn't. Someone else asked for him. How did you hear about it?" Hallie opened the door and started for the stairs, a finger to her lips when they passed the door to the office.

"How do you think? Neil told me. He acted like he was hurt on Gus's behalf," Felicia said.

"They've always been like that. Cut one and the other bleeds." Unconsciously, Hallie touched the scar on her finger as her mind was drawn back to the ceremony in Beech Forest when they were nine.

She closed the door of her room, and popped an R.E.M. tape in the cassette player. Their favorite band had become a necessary backdrop to every important conversation that year. Felicia flopped across Hallie's bed on her stomach.

"So you really said no?" Felicia asked when Hallie joined her on the bed. Miguel, the fat white cat, took his position between them.

"Is that so shocking?"

Despite the coolness of her words, Hallie's skin felt hot as she produced the note from her pocket and watched as her friend absorbed it.

"Holy *shit*," Felicia said when she looked up. "Who would have thought Gus was so romantic?"

"You really think he wrote it?" Hallie asked. "I mean, it's not signed, and I didn't see—"

"*Of course*, he wrote it. Be logical, Hallie."

"Logic is my middle name, but the last time Gus and I really talked, we were kids."

"And you think *lo-o-ve* is about meaningful conversations, especially for guys? *Please*." Felicia jumped up impulsively, and went to Hallie's desk, where she foraged for paper and the nearest writing implement, which happened to be a purple crayon. She drew a crooked heart.

"What are you doing?"

"You've got to write back, don't you?"

"I couldn't answer even if I wanted to—which I don't," Hallie said. "I'm still not convinced—"

"Come on, Hallie. Gus Silva crooked his baby finger in your direction the other day and you said no. He must have been crushed. I mean, rejection is something that happens to other kids—not the great Voodoo."

"I guess his spell didn't work on me, huh?" Hallie said. But her smug tone masked a confusing disappointment. Was that all the note signified—a popular boy's injured pride?

"Exactly. So he had to pull something else from his book of charms." Felicia waved the crinkled paper they'd been staring at all afternoon. "*Voilà!* The love note spell."

"Well, from what I know about *feitiço*, a spell won't work if you don't deliver it personally," Hallie said, still annoyed that Gus had asked Neil to speak for him. She took the note and tore it in two. Then she tossed it into the trash.

Felicia watched the waste basket suspiciously, as if it might catch fire. "I hope you don't think that's the end of it. 'Cause anyone who sends a message like that? They're obviously not about to give up."

Though Hallie pretended to be impervious, her heart felt as delicate and fragile as that origami bird in her chest. Secretly, she wondered if her silence would force Gus to ask her out—all nice and proper—as Neil had sarcastically drawled. But when nothing happened after a few weeks, she willed herself to forget. She walked away when Gus's name came up among her friends; and if her mind drifted to the precisely folded note, she mentally tore it up all over again.

In early June, when Neil's play opened, Hallie sat in the first row between Felicia and their friend Daisy, nervously clutching Felicia's hand. The little theater in Wellfleet was sold out, and Neil was the only amateur on the bill. Felicia squeezed her hand back.

However, as soon as Neil took the stage, playing the role of a young heroin addict, Hallie forgot her anxiety. He inhabited his character so completely that even his eyes seemed to change color. But what really overwhelmed her was the torrent of emotion that hid behind his self-deprecating slouch and lazy smile. After the first act, she headed for the exit to catch her breath; and in her rush to get outside, she nearly collided with someone. It took her eyes a moment to adjust to the darkness before she realized who had caught her shoulders. Gus Silva left his hands in place for a second too long before he released her.

"Hallie!" he said, letting her go. It was the first time he'd called her by name in years, and he seemed as astonished by the sound of it as she was.

"I'm sorry," he said, somehow managing to imbue ordinary words with a rare sincerity. Was this what they called his *voodoo*?

Gus nodded before he lowered his head, and disappeared inside, leaving her with a whiff of his cologne. Hallie felt as if she'd drunk half a liter of Aunt Del's *vinho*.

In the slash of light created when she opened the door to the theater, her eyes found him. Like his hands on her shoulders, the brightness only lasted an instant, but it was long enough for her to see that he was watching for her, too.

Then, just as the door swung closed behind her, she saw the girl nestled beside him.

The words of the note taunted her as she made her way to her seat. *You or nobody*. Had she believed that, even for an instant? She knew she had no right to her anger. After all, she hadn't even bothered to respond. But there it was—one accidental touch in the doorway, the smell of his cologne, and she was curiously lifted up, shaken—and now *jealous*? How dare he, she thought, though she couldn't name his offense.

She remained aware of Gus's presence throughout the rest of the play—and that, too, incensed her. When the cast came out to take their final bow, Gus's voice, hooting for his friend, rose above the clamorous standing ovation. Neil lifted his head and smiled in Gus's direction, his eyes full.

When she started for the exit, Hallie was relieved to see that the seat Gus had occupied was empty. In the foyer, Neil was surrounded by friends who were eager to congratulate him. Hallie could feel him beaming at her from across the room. When he caught her eye, he blew her a triumphant kiss, and she returned the gesture.

It was chilly for early June, but their friends were already planning an impromptu celebration on the beach.

Sean Mello approached the girls. "Voodoo went to see if his cousin can get us some beer. You guys coming?"

"Not me," Hallie said quickly. "I promised to get Nick's truck home by ten. But maybe you can give Felicia and Daisy a ride. They probably want to go."

"You sure?" Felicia said, obviously feeling torn.

Hallie reached into her bag for her keys. "Have a good time. And give Gallagher a hug for me, will you? He's such a superstar I can't even get close to him."

That night around three, Hallie awakened the way she used to when she was a little girl. Almost like a sleepwalker she climbed down from her high bed, and turned on the mermaid night light Nick had plugged into an outlet when she was small. Or maybe it had been there even longer. It had been years since Hallie used it, but whenever she tried to throw it away, her father always found it, and managed to slip it back into place. As if such talismans could still keep her safe from the world. Safe from her own dreams.

She slipped out of the tank top and pajama bottoms she wore to bed, and revealed her sixteen-year-old body to her mother's antique mirror. In the dim light, she traced her cheekbone, the lines of her jaw, her lips, and then lifted her chin and discovered her long neck. *This* was what Gus had seen.

When she rested her hands lightly on her shoulders, she felt the imprint of Gus's palms on her body. Almost hypnotized, she tested the weight of her breasts and touched the arc of her hip. It occurred to her that Gus had probably traced a similar cartography on another body that very night. Again, she was assailed with unreasonable anger. At him—yes, but mostly at her own foolishness. What had he done to make her feel she might be different from his other conquests? Say he was sorry for nearly bumping into her? Stop the collision with his hands on her shoulders? God, she was as bad as the lovestruck girls who had undoubtedly believed—if only for a day or two—that it was *them or nobody*.

Hallie unplugged the mermaid light, pulled on her pajamas in the dark, and carried the dinged sea siren into the bathroom. She wrapped it in tissues so Nick wouldn't see it and threw it away for good.

CHAPTER 8

That summer, Hallie helped out in her father's office, as she did every year. Trapped in the claustrophobic waiting room, she couldn't avoid the latest chapter in the Silva saga. After seven years of steadfastly refusing to see his son, Codfish had apparently changed his mind. He was not only willing to see Gus; he *demanded* it. Fatima's friends said she wept when she came home with the news. But her joy had been transformed into fury when her *ungrateful* nephew flat out refused to visit.

The ensuing standoff had been so bitter that Gus spent two weeks sleeping on the couch in his football coach's house in Brewster before his uncle's truck roared into the driveway, kicking stones everywhere, and Manny insisted he come home.

Hallie tried her best to tune out the exaggerated updates, but she couldn't help reacting. She left the room when people said that the football player known for his politeness and his brilliant smile had lost his temper "just like Codfish." Others insisted that it was Fatima who'd turned violent and driven the boy out. But the heart of the gossip was Gus's refusal to see his father, and everyone who passed through the office was compelled to express an opinion about it.

"People who don't forgive go to hell. It's as simple as that," Izzy Brodeur said to a full waiting room one Monday morning in July. As the Sunday cantor at St. Peter's, she didn't merely say the words, she *pronounced* them. "That boy needs to get himself to Millette State Prison before it's too late."

"And what happens to people who judge, Izzy?" Nick

asked, bursting out of the examining room, a tongue depressor still in hand. "From what I recall, there's something about that in your holy book, too."

Everyone in the office laughed—especially Nick—when Izzy huffed out of the office, saying that from now on, she would seek treatment from a doctor who wasn't known as a *quack* all over the Cape.

In the corner, the usually taciturn Bobby Cleve, who'd been a crew member on Codfish's boat, the *Good Fortune*, spoke up. "Not that it's anyone's business, but the kid *did* go to see his father. Manny told me he was planning to take him up last week."

For a moment, the waiting room fell silent as all eyes turned to Bobby. "Planning doesn't mean much," Aunt Del said. "How do you know they actually went?"

However, when pressed for details, he returned to a tattered copy of *Field and Stream* that had been in the office for years and muttered, "No one's goddamn business but the family's."

But two weeks later, everyone seemed to have forgotten Nick's outburst and Bobby's enigmatic statement. All they remembered from the incident was Izzy's prophetic words: *before it's too late.*

In the office of Nicolao Costa, M.D., the morning when the news came, the doctor had taken a rare half-day off due to a toothache. Hallie busied herself by organizing the files. A natural lover of order, she lost herself in the task, sorting the active from the inactive charts, and restoring their alphabetical sequence. She kept the shades down to mute the heat; and for once, she filled the office with *her* music. As she sang along with an old Joni Mitchell song, she felt suffused with a calm happiness.

She was even glad that Aunt Del was late for work. However, when her great-aunt still hadn't shown up at ten, Hallie began to worry. She had the phone in her hand when she was stopped by the ferocious rat-a-tat of Del's stacked-heel sandals on the walk.

Sensing trouble, Hallie got up and opened the door. But Aunt Del sailed past her as if she didn't even see her. "Close that," she ordered. "Maybe they'll think no one's here."

"They?" Hallie said, looking under the window shade to see if someone had followed her aunt. It took her a moment to realize that *they* referred to the town itself.

"I thought for sure someone would have called by now," Aunt Del said, sinking into her tired swivel chair. "Not that Nick could do anything about it, but there are people who dial this number as a reflex. Hurricane comin'? Call Dr. Nick."

"What kind of hurricane are you talking about this time?"

Aunt Del let out a strangled sob. "Poor Codfish finally finished the job."

"What are you saying? You mean he—"

In response, Delores made the sign of the cross. "They found him hanging in his cell. People should have known something was up when he asked to see Gus."

Hallie wasn't sure what brought on the wave of nausea she felt—the thought of Codfish's act, Aunt Del's obvious sympathy for him, or the mention of the son who hadn't visited.

While Aunt Del searched for the number of Nick's dentist—as if she, too, believed he had the answer to every disaster, Hallie wandered into the examining room. She shut the door, hoping to quell the hammering of her heart, which had reacted to the news with one word: *good*. She knew it was wrong, but she couldn't forget the desolation, the sheer *ruin* in Gus's eyes that day she came to read to him, or Nick's description of how he'd found Gus near catatonic in his mother's closet. *Filho da puta!* she shouted at the dead man. At the same time, tears sprang into her eyes.

On the wall a framed quote from Mother Teresa that Nick had received as a gift from a patient, seemed to taunt her.

IF YOU JUDGE PEOPLE, YOU DON'T HAVE TIME TO LOVE THEM

It had hung in the room for years, an unspoken, imperfect contract between Nick and every patient who entered—even wife beaters and murderers. If there had been a bowl or a vase handy, Hallie would have hurled it at the pious words. But since there was nothing, she turned the framed quote to the wall.

"You all right in there?" Aunt Del said, knocking on the door. "I shouldn't have blurted the news out like that. It's just that I was so upset—"

"Upset—over a *killer*? I don't understand this town. In fact, sometimes I don't even understand my own family." Hallie walked past her aunt and retrieved her bike from the alley.

As she navigated Front Street, she suddenly confronted the same impulse that had directed her course when she was nine. She had to see Gus Silva.

The center of town smelled like fried seafood and popcorn. It was clotted with cars, and with vacationers on foot who'd come to point at the drag queens on the street, to be titillated or entertained by the artists who were happy to take their money. (When Hallie had complained to Nick that tourists only saw their own stereotype of Provincetown, never the complexity of what it really was, he only laughed. "We don't see *them*, either. We just see a google-eyed horde reeking of suntan lotion, cameras dangling from wrists. Don't you think they're more than that—every one of them?") Recalling the words, Hallie felt even more impatient and annoyed—not only with the *google-eyed horde* that stood between her and her destination, but with Nick, too. Did he always have to wax philosophical over everything—even the annual invasion of outsiders? Couldn't he just complain along with everyone else?

As she took the turn, the question inside her suddenly caused her bike to skid to a stop. *What was she doing?* She hardly knew Gus. Why would he want to see her now? The emphatically penciled note rose up in answer: *It's you or nobody. Always has been. Always will be.* Even the wind seemed to agree. It propelled her forward as she pedaled toward the outskirts of town.

From the corner of the street, she could see the cluster of cars that had been parked askew in front of the Barrettos' house. She recognized Fatima's Buick, a new pickup that belonged to the Captain's brother, Alvaro, and Alvaro Jr.'s muscle car. But there was no sign of Neil's familiar Jeep. Hallie wondered if he'd already come and taken Gus out.

The Barrettos' house looked even more forbidding than Hallie remembered. Fatima's statue of the Virgin had tumbled onto the ground, probably during a high wind. Over the years, the long grass had grown up around it. The shutters, which had been red the last time she was there, were chipped and faded to a wan coral.

Hallie paused, her eyes unaccountably stinging—not for

Codfish Silva, but for Gus. For the five constricted rooms where he returned every day from school, or from his job at the A&P. A pot of yellow mums with a card and a bow on the porch only emphasized the gloom that surrounded it. If she came back in a week, Hallie was sure she'd find the neglected flowers in the same spot; and five years from now, a pot full of dirt.

She left her bike and crossed the street, wondering what she would say to Gus.

His cousin Alvaro opened the door. Not long ago, their seven-year age difference had been the vast gulf between childhood and adolescence. But recently she'd caught him staring at her on the wharf. *Is that little Hallie Costa?* he'd said. *My, my.* Several of the men from his boat picked up the sinuous tone in his voice and turned to look. One of them laughingly pulled him away. "You leave Dr. Nick's daughter alone now, Varo."

Now he pulled the door open wide and eyed her warily. "What're you doing here?"

Hallie looked past him to Fatima, lying on the couch in a blue T-shirt and sweat pants, her eyes red from weeping. From the kitchen, Hallie could hear the low rumble of male voices. "Is Gus home?" she said, ignoring the question she couldn't answer.

Manny wandered into the doorway that led to the kitchen and, leaning against the frame, downed a glass of whiskey. "Hallie Costa," he said. "Now that's one girl I haven't seen around here before. Are you and Gus *friends*?"

Hallie hated the way he pronounced the word, as if describing his own sordid pickups at the Pilgrims Club. Alvaro drifted into the kitchen.

He's not like you, Hallie wanted to shout at Manny. But instead she spoke with as much dignity as she could manage. *Yes, we're friends.* And in that instant, she knew it was true.

Whether Gus acknowledged it or not, they had been friends ever since the day she presented him with the minnows, Johnny, and Silver, and he accepted them.

"Well, sorry to disappoint you after you've come all the way out here, but Voodoo's not home," Manny said.

"Do you know where he went?"

Manny snorted. "The kid never tells us anything."

"What scared me was the way he acted when I told him. He didn't say a word," Fatima said. "Just kind of nodded his head, and the next thing I knew——"

"He took off," Manny said, finishing her sentence. "The kid eats my food and lives under my roof, but otherwise, he ain't got the time of day."

"Have you called Neil?" Hallie asked.

"His mother said he went down to Hyannis to buy concert tickets with Chad Mendoza early this morning."

"How'd you get here, anyway—walk? *In this heat?*" Manny said.

"I rode my bike. So you have no idea——"

Apparently bored with the talk about Gus, Manny tried out a roguish smile. "No clue, honey. Can we get you a drink or something? Fatima, don't we have any soda or anything for Nick's daughter?"

The hospitality felt jarring. "No thank you, Mrs. Barretto," Hallie said quietly, her hand already on the door. "I just remembered there's somewhere I have to be."

Even in the height of summer, there were places at Race Point where you could be absolutely alone. On the twisting miles of coastline, the tumultuous rhythm of the waves silenced everything else and created a pocket of solitude.

The sky was a deep, cloudless cobalt, the ocean Race Point blue, a glittering shade somewhere between royal and midnight. Despite the heat, the cars in the parking lot were sparse. Feeling the high wind, Hallie suspected that undertow warnings had been announced, keeping all but the most foolish swimmers and surfers away from the National Seashore.

As she walked down the beach, she encountered two men walking a dog, and a naked sunbather, camping close to the dunes, but there was no sign of Gus. The farther Hallie walked, the more she doubted herself. Not just about coming to the beach, but about the instinct that had driven her to look for him. *Always has been, always will be.* The tumbling surf echoed it back to her, making a mockery of her foolish belief that she could ever own such a sentiment. It belonged to the waves and wind, not to humans with their brief lives and flickering loyalties.

She turned around and headed back toward the parking lot where she'd left her bike, forced to admit that she had no idea where Gus would go when he got the kind of news he'd received that morning. She hoped that Aunt Del had gone home so she could have an hour of quiet in the office. She would play some old Beatles songs—the simple ones, from their early years—as she returned to her filing. And she would *not* think about Gus Silva's latest tragedy.

The wind was against her as she started back, so she lowered her head and took her favorite shortcut home. When she passed the parking lot of the church, she noticed a bike that had been jettisoned near the edge of the lot. The salt-abraded red Columbia was Junior Barretto's old bike, the same one Hallie often saw parked outside the A&P.

She pulled into the parking lot, leaned her own bike against the fence, and wandered past the garden dedicated to Our Lady of Fatima. In the center, a larger version of the statue displayed in so many homes in town seemed to open her arms to her just as it did to the plaster children who knelt before it. It was as welcoming as the old pastor who occupied the rectory was not.

Father D'Souza was known as a prickly old man, small as a gnome, who railed against the drama club's choice of Othello and frequently chewed out local waitresses when they got his finicky orders wrong. What kind of consolation could Gus get from a man like that? Hallie wondered. She'd started back to her bike when she noticed that the side door to the church was slightly ajar. Curious, she walked to the main entrance and tried it; to her surprise, it gave way.

The church was hushed, dark, and cool. A lingering fragrance of incense and candle wax pulled Hallie deeper inside, where she felt overcome with an ineffable sense of pooling peace. Of course, it wasn't the first time she'd been inside St. Peter the Apostle's. She and Nick had attended countless weddings and funerals, even a couple of baptisms there.

She'd stood for what felt like a long time, savoring the deep quiet, when she spotted Gus sitting alone near the front of the church. He was slouched so low in the pew that if it weren't for the glow of his cigarette, Hallie might have missed him in the dim light. He didn't react when she walked down the center aisle. She slid into the pew beside him.

"Cigarette?" he offered, breaking the silence as he pulled a pack from his pocket.

Hallie shook her head. "Aren't you afraid God will strike you dead if you smoke in here?"

Gus's eyes were inscrutable. "Not the God I know," he said, retracting his Camels.

He continued to stare straight ahead, enjoying his smoke. Hallie took in the sense of spaciousness created by the vaulted ceilings and the sculpted shafts of light that poured through the stained-glass windows. "Do you come here a lot?" she asked.

Gus didn't exactly smile, but a trace of the flirtatious boy everyone knew crossed his face. "Either that's a really bad pickup line, or Father D'Souza sent you to find out why I haven't been at mass lately."

"Or maybe I just want to know."

Gus was quiet for so long that Hallie thought he hadn't heard her. Then he said, "Uncle Manny and Aunt Fatima don't go to church much anymore, but when I was little, we never missed mass. Best clothes. Ten-fifteen sharp. This pew. Tell you the truth, I kind of miss it. There's a moment when the priest lifts the Communion host in the air and we pray: *Just say the word and my soul shall be healed.* Sometimes it really felt true."

Hallie nodded, though she always felt uncomfortable when people like Aunt Del talked about their faith. "I can't believe they leave this place open. Aren't they afraid it'll be robbed?"

"Has been—more than once. Don't you read the *Banner*? That's why Father D'Souza gave me this." Gus pulled a key from his pocket. "When I was a kid, I used to come here sometimes—usually at crazy hours. One night when I was ten, I crawled out my window in the middle of a huge storm, and rode my bike here. By the time Father D'Souza heard me knocking on the door, I was drenched."

"Didn't your aunt come looking for you?"

Gus stared at the altar. "Aunt Fatima checked out after she lost Junior. Woman never even knew I was gone. The next day the priest came to the house—kind of like your dad making a house call. He told me if I ever did that again, he'd give me a beating I'd never forget. When Uncle Manny asked what was going on, he just said, 'Parish outreach.' Gotta love that guy."

He gave Hallie a long look. "So now that you know all my crazy secrets, what are *you* doing here? From what I heard, Nick's an atheist and he brought you up the same way."

"I saw your bike out back."

Gus continued to watch her, waiting for the full explanation.

"And I heard about your dad." Her voice had sunk to a whisper.

Gus looked toward a stained-glass window depicting a storm at sea. "I suppose everyone's heard by now. This whole nosy town." He turned back to Hallie. "So you're here to offer your condolences? Avoid the rush, maybe? Well, thanks but no thanks."

Feeling as if she'd been slapped—and worse, that she deserved it, she rose to go. "I'm sorry. I had no right to come in here."

He grabbed her arm. "No, please—*I'm* sorry. *Again.* And don't go. I know I'm an asshole, but I could use the company."

"Not what I'd call a very appealing offer." Hallie was still on her feet. "And like you said, I'm not used to hanging out in churches."

Gus grinned, and in spite of the setting and the circumstances, she felt her skin flush.

"I can't do much about my mood, but we could at least go somewhere else," he said. He mashed his cigarette on the church floor. Then, apparently having second thoughts, he retrieved the butt and put it into his pocket. Hallie noticed a small bottle of Jack Daniels protruding from its fold. When he thought she wasn't looking, he bowed his head and crossed himself.

"We better get out of here before Father D'Souza shows up and gives you that beating he threatened you with when you were a kid," she said, starting down the aisle.

Once they were outside, Hallie was startled by the bright day. In the unforgiving light, it was obvious that Gus Silva was drunk. She wondered how she had missed that in the church.

"Where were you thinking of going?" she asked, realizing how little she knew him. This grown-up Gus whose gleaming black hair and bright teeth reminded her of his father's. "I really should be getting—"

"I only know where I *don't* want to go," Gus said before she could finish. "Not to my house. Or yours. Not into town, or to the beach or the wharf. Nowhere we might run into anyone we know."

"That pretty much rules out our entire world."

"I know a place," Gus said, impulsively taking her hand. Hallie felt a current go through her as he tugged her toward the cemetery.

The grave was located out near the highway. Gus sat down on the broad, flat stone inscribed with his mother's maiden name: MARIA BOTELHO. There were no dates, no BELOVED WIFE or MOTHER, not even a carved angel to soften it.

"Her family only agreed to bury her here because of me. I promised my grandmother I'd visit the grave every day."

"Do you?"

Gus looked straight ahead. "Only came once. The night of that storm I told you about. I kept thinking of her, out in the rain alone. I don't know what I thought I could do about it, but I had to come. Pretty dumb, huh?"

"No. Not dumb at all," Hallie said softly, imagining the night, the storm, the boy he had been when she showed up at his door. And she thought of her own predawn wanderings. Though she never went further than her own roof, she understood the impulse.

"When I finally realized she wasn't here, it was a huge relief—and the worst moment of my life. It meant nothing could ever hurt her again—not the weather or my father or anything else," he said. "But it also meant that I couldn't climb out my window and find her. I couldn't protect her, and there was nothing she could do to help me, either."

The temperature was in the eighties, but Hallie wrapped her arms around herself like she'd caught a chill. "You walked straight to the spot as if you came here every day. Just like you promised your grandmother."

"It's not something you forget," Gus said, as he lit another cigarette. He edged over to make room for Hallie. "Have a seat."

She hesitated, feeling superstitious about sitting on a gravestone—and a little bit wary of being that close to Gus. "I should probably get back. I left a ton of work at the office."

"You can't leave now. Maria will be offended if you don't sit for a few minutes." Gus patted the stone like it was a couch in his living room. "'What can I get you to drink?' she'd say. She was like that. Traditional mom, you know?"

He pulled the pint of Jack Daniels from his pocket. "Sorry I don't have a glass. Mom would have made sure you had some ice, too."

"I kind of doubt she would have served me *that* either," Hallie said. She waved away the bottle, as she sat beside him on the stone. Even half-drunk and sitting on his mother's grave, Gus Silva was so handsome, she felt dizzy.

"Always the doctor's good little girl, right?" he said and shrugged. "I guess that means there's more for me." He took a long pull from the bottle.

Hallie cringed at the image she'd been trying to live down all her life. *The girl genius. Dr. Nick's perfect daughter.*

"Not as good as you think," she said, taking the cigarette from his hand. She dragged the smoke into her lungs. Nick would have been more shocked and angered by the smoking than if he'd caught her drinking whiskey with Codfish Silva's son. On his mother's grave, no less.

The cigarette tasted of nicotine, but also of something else. It took a minute before Hallie realized it was Gus himself. It reminded her of the scent that had followed her into the foyer, and trailed her home on the night of Neil's play. She inhaled deeply, and began to cough.

Gus laughed, extending the bottle in her direction. "Now you have no choice. You have to accept my hospitality."

"I think one new vice is enough for today."

"Come on. Please?"

Hallie laughed. "Why do you care? Like you said, if I don't have any, there's more for you."

But Gus remained serious. "If we both drink, it will be easier to tell the truth, and I want us to tell each other everything. Even the stuff we never told anyone else."

Holding his eyes, she accepted the bottle of whiskey. Then she threw back her head like he had when he drank. Her throat burned, and her eyes watered.

"*Jesucristo!*" she yelled. "That's worse than smoking! Are you trying to kill me?" But even as she jumped up and shouted, she was reaching for the cigarette from Gus's mouth.

"I'd slit my wrists before I ever hurt you," he said. "I hope you know that." Then he undermined his seriousness with a loud hiccup.

"I didn't mean . . . I never thought—" she stammered, wondering how she could have been so insensitive. She sat back down on the stone, so close she could see the amber flecks in Gus's dark eyes. She'd only had one gulp of alcohol but she felt intoxicated.

"I know," Gus said, putting a finger to her lips. "But I *do* mean it. All my life, my biggest fear was that I would grow up to be like him. And I wasn't the only one. Whenever I went to New Bedford, I could see it in her family's eyes. They loved me; I was all they had left of my mother. But they couldn't look at me without seeing the man who killed her. Eventually, I gave us all a break and stopped going."

"I don't see much of my mom's family, either," Hallie said, passing the cigarette back to him. "Not since my grandmother told Nick he should put me in boarding school where I would be *properly* cared for. They never thought he was good enough, you know? Even with a Harvard education and his medical degree, he was too Provincetown, too eccentric—and probably too *Portagee*, too. They couldn't believe their debutante daughter had married a fisherman's son."

"Their loss, right?" Gus said. They fell into a strangely

comfortable silence as they looked out on the landscape of carved stones.

"Do you still miss her?" Hallie finally asked.

"Not like I did when I was a kid, but yeah, I miss her. You know what scares me? There's so much I already forgot. And if I don't remember her, who will?"

Hallie reached for the whiskey bottle. She pushed back the wavy gold hair that slanted across her face, determined to hide nothing. "Do you want to know the worst thing about me?" she asked. "The thing I've never told anyone?"

Gus waited.

"I've always been glad my mother wasn't around. I *like* having Nick to myself."

"Maybe that makes it hurt less," Gus said, absolving her like she imagined Father D'Souza did in the confessional. Or like Nick did in his own way. "Besides, it's not like you wished her dead. You just adapted to the way things were."

"Don't let me off so easy. I was jealous of her," Hallie admitted. "Nick *adored* Liz Cooper."

"Adored. That was the same word my father used," Gus said. He laughed bitterly. "What *bullshit*. You know what pisses me off more than anything?"

A cigarette dangling from his mouth, Gus reminded her of James Dean or Marlon Brando in the campy old movies that played at the theater in town. "Today's her birthday. Of all the days on the calendar, he chose this one."

Hallie took the cigarette from his lips and drew the smoke into her lungs.

So *are you ready to hear* the worst thing about me?" Gus asked.

Hallie nodded, though she wasn't sure she was. In the last hour, she'd already learned that he loved the mass like an old woman clutching her beads, that as a boy he'd wandered around in the rain searching for his dead mother, and that he came to the church to drink and smoke.

"It was my fault," Gus said abruptly.

Hallie stayed quiet, willing him to keep talking, but at the same time afraid that he would.

"The night she died I stayed in my room. I closed my eyes and covered my ears. I counted backward from a hundred and let the Portuguese song she taught me run in my head like a tape. I *sang*."

Despite the heat, Hallie shivered as she thought of the voice that had awakened her that night. The sound she had never described to anyone.

"And you know what else I did?"

It had been many years since she'd thought about what Johnny Kollel used to say: that Gus Silva was crazy; that he was the one who'd really killed his mother. Codfish had only gone to jail to protect him. But now the memories, the rumors from that dark time crowded in on her.

"*Nothing*," Gus said. "I was right there in the next room and I didn't even try to save her."

"You were *nine years old*!" Hallie was ashamed of her thoughts—and of the relief that flooded her. "You didn't know what was going to happen. And even if you did, what could you have done?"

"Did your dad ever tell you about the time my mother went to him with a dislocated shoulder, her whole arm covered by bruises?"

Though she knew Nick harbored regrets about the in-

cident, Hallie hesitated. Her father had taught her that anything she overheard about a patient in the office was strictly
confidential. But this day, this encounter seemed to be happening outside all the rules she'd ever known. She nodded
almost imperceptibly. *Yes, she knew.*

"Every fight they ever had, it was the same story. Codfish
would be drinking and someone would say something about
my mother—maybe that they saw her when she was host-
essing, and man, she was lookin' good. You know how men
talk, but my father went crazy over that shit. It was like he
blamed her for it. So he'd have a couple more shots to make
himself *feel better.* By the time he got home, he had convinced
himself she was sleeping with every guy in town.

"Anyway, when I heard her scream, I got out of bed and ran
into the room. I was small, but that night my rage was as big as
his—no, bigger. I threw myself against him with everything I
had, pounding his stomach and his chest with my fists. I don't
know what I was yelling—or even if it was words."

"So he stopped?"

"*Stopped?* Are you kidding me? Codfish never stopped.
He accused my mother of turning his only son against him.
He said I was a mama's boy, a spoiled little Provincetown
cabrao. He wasn't sure if I was even his son. And when I said
I hoped I wasn't, he threw me against the wall so hard I
couldn't breathe.

"The next thing I knew I was on the floor, and both my
parents were crying. At that point, my father was himself
again, the guy who taught me how to dig for clams and read
a navigational map, the dad I was so proud to walk through
town with. Almost as if the shock of seeing me hurt had so-
bered him up on the spot.

"He was like a kid that way, you know? He thought he could throw the biggest tantrum he wanted, that he could hit my mother—once he even pushed her down the basement stairs—and no one would really get hurt. He was always shocked when he saw the marks on her—as if someone else had done it.

"I didn't know I'd been knocked out until we were in the car heading for Hyannis, and I didn't care either. All that mattered was that the fighting had stopped. Even when I found out I had a concussion and had to spend the night in the hospital, I felt like I'd won."

"But if you were at the hospital, why didn't they treat your mother's shoulder? Why did she wait till the next day and go to Nick?"

"The people in the emergency room were already suspicious—even though my parents stuck to the story that I'd fallen off my bike earlier in the day. If the doctors had seen my mother's arm, that would have blown the whole thing. It was the kind of hot spring day we never get on the Cape and she'd just gotten the beating of her life, but she was wearing long sleeves, and holding my father's hand like they were the happiest couple this side of the bridge."

"And you didn't say anything?"

"Gallagher might be a great actor, but he couldn't touch me that night. I said I'd been speeding on my bike when I hit a patch of sand, and I didn't tell my mother I'd been knocked out because I had a farm league game that day. By the time we left, the doctor was clapping my father on the back, and telling him he had three sons of his own. *Boys will be boys, right?* And Codfish was flashing that smile of his. 'One's enough for me. This kid's already taken ten years off my life.' He sounded like he believed it himself.

"The next day my mother was late bringing me home from the hospital. She'd already seen Nick, but she hid her sling in the car until after we left. 'Your father wanted to come, but he's out on the boat. Won't be back for three days,' she said, talking to me in code in front of the nurses. But when we looked at each other, this calm I can't explain passed through us. You'd have to live like we did to understand. *For a few days, things would be normal.* I didn't realize how much pain she was in until we got into the car. I had a black eye and this huge egg on my forehead, but we were so happy we sang all the way home.

"We didn't talk about anything till after dinner when she pulled me into the living room and cried. Cried and called me her little hero. Then she took me by the chin and looked at me more seriously than she ever had before. 'I need you to take a vow, Gustavo. Do you know what that is?' I didn't answer. 'It's a promise you can never break, no matter what,' she said. 'Because if you do, you will grow up to be a man without honor.' It sounded like something a Jedi knight would do. I stood up straighter and said I was ready. I wouldn't break my vow no matter what."

At that point in his story, Hallie noticed the sheen in Gus's eyes. "She asked you to promise that you would never get in the middle of a fight again."

"I vowed that when my parents argued, I would never come out of my room again. I would cover my eyes and block my ears, count from one hundred backwards, and sing the song she taught me.

> *Atirei o pau au gato tu, tu*
> *Mas o gato tu, tu*

Nao morreu, reu, reu
Dona Chica, ca, ca . . .

"In all these years, I never knew what it meant. Do you?"

Hallie had immediately recognized the rhyming song her great-aunt used to sing to her. Though most people in town knew only a handful of phrases in Portuguese—usually prayers or curses—a few, like Maria, whose family had immigrated to New Bedford when she was five, or Aunt Del, still retained their native tongue. Though not fluent, Hallie had been taught by her father, who had taken the opportunity to study the language in college.

"It's about a woman trying to chase a stubborn cat away," she said. "All the kids learn it in Portugal, according to Aunt Del. Kind of like 'Twinkle, Twinkle' for us."

Gus looked sadly over the horizon. "So that's what I was singing while it happened. A nursery rhyme about a cat."

"You were a little boy doing what your mother asked you to do . . ." Hallie said, though she already knew that no words, no spell could take away his guilt.

"But instead of becoming a Jedi knight, I lost my mother—and my father, too. I counted and sang through all the yelling and scuffling and doors slamming. When I finally stopped, the house was quiet, and my father's truck was gone. Usually, when he left, I went and crawled in bed with my mother. But this time she wasn't there. At first, I thought she'd gone out, too, even though she never left me alone. I was scared, but I refused to cry. If my father came back and caught me crying, it would start all over again. So I curled up in the bed. On her pillow, I could still smell the Ponds cold cream she always put on before bed. By then,

I was so tired from trying to keep my vow, I almost fell asleep."

He paused, as if trying to stop time before he added five grim words. "And then I saw her."

Hallie closed her eyes and tried not to imagine the terrible hours between that moment on the bed and the time when Nick found a nearly catatonic Gus hiding in the closet. Her first instinct was to hold him the way Nick had that day after he removed the door and lifted him from the small space.

But Gus was no child anymore. He stared straight ahead for a long time, an unlit cigarette hanging from his lips, his face a mask.

Abruptly, he leaped to his feet and extended his hand to her. "Let's get out of here," he said abruptly. "There's nothing in this place but old bones and stories no one wants to remember."

Hallie wasn't sure if it was the cigarette and the alcohol or the shimmering heat—or just everything she'd heard and tasted and felt that afternoon—but she was wobbly.

"You know something?" Gus said. "I've never talked about that day to anyone, and here I am, spilling my guts like I've known you all my life."

Hallie wanted to tell him that they *had* known each other all their lives. Had he really forgotten? And what's more, she *wanted* to hear it. But instead she blamed the Jack Daniels.

Gus stopped in the middle of the sidewalk. "That's not the reason," he said. "It's just that there's never been anyone close enough to tell. Not till today."

CHAPTER 9

That night when she went to bed Hallie felt like the dimensions of her room had changed; it was far smaller than she'd imagined it. On the other hand, the moon outside her window was huge, and so bright it seemed to pulsate. Even the air she breathed felt like it had been charged with a secret intoxicant.

By morning, the ordinary road she had walked every day of her life was new, too. It was the last place she'd seen *him*. If she looked hard enough, she could almost see him disappearing down the road, his spine arrow straight in spite of the Jack Daniels, and what had happened that day. If she listened hard enough, she would hear the gravelly music of his voice. *I'll see you, okay?* Now as she looked out the window toward the spot where he had vanished, she had only one question: *When?*

All day, the street remained a desert, even as it hummed with activity. Gus didn't come. Hallie wondered if she had imagined what had passed between them? Had he only told her his secrets because he was vulnerable? Or had it been the Jack Daniels after all?

Though she once abhorred the gossip in the office, she now listened obsessively to the speculation about Codfish. Would there be a funeral? How was the family holding up? Would he be buried in Provincetown? All of that ended when word of the suicide note got out.

"It was more like the list of orders he used to leave for the guys," Diane Cleve announced in the waiting room. Fatima had invited the crew from the *Good Fortune*, including Diane's husband, Bobby, to hear the note read. The office fell silent as she recited Codfish's final requests.

1. Cremate the body.
2. No ashes are to be preserved.
3. No mass or memorial.

She paused before she recited number 4, the only personal piece of the note: *I loved her.*

The note was signed and dated the way he once formalized his business correspondence:

Captain Gustavo Silva
The Good Fortune
Provincetown, Massachusetts

"Nothing addressed to his son?" someone asked when Diane finished.

"Nothing," she said with finality.

After learning about the note, Hallie was so addled that when she answered the office phone, she drew a blank. She was jerked back to the present when the caller spoke to someone in the background. "I've been dialing the same number for ten years now. It's *got* to be Dr. Nick's."

"Yes, *it's Nick's*," Hallie managed to get out before the woman hung up. "We've just been, um, having some trouble with the line this morning." When Aunt Del looked up sharply, Hallie disappeared into the bathroom, where she pulled out the Camels she'd impulsively picked up at

Lucy's Market that morning. She locked the door and lit one up.

With the first inhalation, her afternoon with Gus returned. The heat, the rough lettering of Maria Botelho's name, the dry salty wind in her nostrils. But most of all the *saudade* in his eyes. *No, she hadn't imagined it.* She hadn't imagined any of it. With the phone ringing in the background, Nick's nurse, Leah, pummeled the door. "What the hell are you doing in there, Hallie? It's a zoo out here."

"Be right out," Hallie said. She took one more puff from the cigarette before she flushed it and sprayed the narrow space with a scent that smelled like baby powder. Just to be safe, she opened the window.

G*us didn't call or show up* that day or the day after that, but a week later, when Hallie had almost given up watching for him, he walked into the office.

"I guess there's no chance you can get off," he said, as if they were already in the middle of a conversation.

Hallie glanced around the room where every seat was filled. "You're kidding, right?"

Old Tony Poillucci tapped his cane on the floor impatiently. "This was a place of business the last I checked—not a high school social. Make your dates on your own time, Silva."

But Gus didn't seem to hear him. "I know you're busy, and that it's the worst possible time, but—" Then, as if he'd reached the top of a mountain, he took a long, deep breath.

"But?" Hallie repeated.

"But I stayed away as long as I possibly could—to the minute."

Ignoring the jangling phone, the charts piled high on the desk, and Old Tony, who was waiting to make an appointment, Hallie stood up and led Gus by the hand onto the porch.

"Your family needed you; and I figured you wanted some time alone, too," Hallie said. She couldn't begin to imagine how difficult his days had been since they'd talked in the cemetery.

"That's not the reason," Gus said. He looked downward for a long minute before he met her eyes. "You know when I told you I could never do anything for my mother again?"

Hallie nodded.

"Well, I was wrong. There was one thing I could do for her. One last thing she really wanted from me."

Hallie waited for him to continue.

"I could refuse to let him hurt me ever again, especially with his bullshit list. So while the house filled up with his old buddies, all blubbering about what a great guy he was, I rode my bike further and further every day. Most days I went to Eastham, and hung out with my friends."

"That's forty miles, round trip."

Gus shrugged. "Football practice starts in a couple of weeks, and I've been smoking a pack a day all summer. If I showed up in that condition, Coach would bench me. By the time I got home from Eastham, I was too tired to listen to the shit that was flying around the house. Too tired to think or feel. But I couldn't get something out of my head."

Hallie tilted her head curiously.

"I couldn't stop thinking of how close you were the other day in St. Peter's. Or how you looked. Sometimes when I closed my eyes, I almost expected you to be there."

Hallie thought of how she'd watched the street with the same sense of his presence, and she smiled to herself. "Why didn't you come sooner?"

"Are you gonna make me say it?" Gus said. "Okay, then. I was scared. More freaking scared than I've ever been in my whole life."

"Voodoo Silva—scared of a girl? Do you really expect me to believe that?"

Gus put his hands on his narrow hips, and gazed into the street.

"This is something different, Hallie. I mean, *isn't it*? This is something I never—" He shook his head, and left the sentence unfinished.

Unconsciously, Hallie nodded. Standing a couple of feet from him, she felt as drunk and exhilarated as she had in the cemetery; and this time, there wasn't a drop of Jack Daniels to blame.

But before she could speak, the screen door snapped open, and Nick stood in the doorway. "*Jesucristo!* There's an office full of people in there, Hallie. What do you think you're doing?"

"It's my fault, Doc," Gus said quickly. "I knew Hallie was working and I—"

"To tell you the truth, Gus, I don't care whose *fault* it is. The phone is ringing off the hook, and if Tony Poillucci doesn't get some attention in about thirty seconds, he's gonna have a coronary right there in my office." Nick slammed the door and went back inside.

"I better go," Hallie murmured..

"I hope I didn't get you in trouble," Gus said. "But even if I did, I'm glad I came. If I didn't smell your hair or hear your voice, I was seriously going to lose my mind."

He started down the street where he had disappeared the other day.

Her hair had a scent—and Gus *remembered* it? She seized a clump of pale hair and pressed it to her face, inhaling the fragrance of her everyday shampoo.

When she looked up, she saw that he had come back. He smiled at her outside the gate. "Hey, one more thing. Since our first date was at the cemetery, maybe next time we should do something more traditional. You know, go to a movie or something."

"That was a *date?*"

Gus grinned. "Pretty pathetic, I admit, but I'll make up for it. I promise."

"As long as it doesn't involve whiskey. The morning after our first *date*, I felt like I was going to die."

"No JD. No church candles, and no ghosts," Gus said, grinning. "Just us. Tomorrow night?"

"I have to go to my grandmother's summer house in Maine for the weekend," Hallie said, rolling her eyes. "Once a year, Nick makes me go up there and pretend they're family."

"They *are* family," Gus said. "Maybe you should give them a chance. Anyway, another time."

"You could at least be disappointed," Hallie blurted out.

"I stopped believing in disappointment a long time ago," he said, as he walked away. He turned abruptly. "And besides—you and me? We've got *time*."

"*We do?*" She wasn't sure if her voice was audible, or if she'd just thought the question until Gus responded.

"Yup. All the time in the world."

CHAPTER 10

All the time in the world. For a while, that's how it felt. The way Gus's face changed when she came into view made her almost certain it was the same for him. And yet he never talked about needing to see her right now, *this second* the way he had in the office, nor did he tell her his secrets like he had in the cemetery. And after three weeks, he still hadn't kissed her.

"So are you two *seeing* each other?" her friends asked.

The simple answer was yes—almost every day, if only for a few minutes on the wharf when he got out of work. But *seeing each other*, the way people said in school? Hallie didn't know herself.

A week before Labor Day, they sat on the pier at dusk. You could already feel the end of summer in the air, the subtle diminishing of the crowds. Gus had started preseason practice, and was trying to quit smoking, but that night he sneaked a couple of puffs with Hallie. They passed the cigarette back and forth, kicking their bare feet over the edge in a coordinated rhythm. "So are you ever going to kiss me?" Hallie asked.

Gus fixed his eyes on Long Point's unwavering green light. "Maybe."

Maybe? Was he teasing her? Hallie mashed out the cigarette they'd shared, and looked over at him.

Before she could read him, he was on his feet. "I probably should get going. Coach wants us to start getting to bed earlier." His face was a mask, but clearly, he was lying. The coach's rules would never keep him from spending time with a girl—if he was interested.

Later, lying in bed, she felt restless. She was tormented by the memory of Gus's scent and the closeness of his mouth, but also by the fear that his feelings for her resembled hers for Neil. Friendship. An almost familial bond. Love, even. Just not *that kind*. Up on the widow's walk at one in the morning, she promised herself she would ask him directly the next day. She practiced what she would say as she walked up and down the treacherous slates.

Do you remember last night on the pier when I . . . (Did she really want to bring up the most embarrassing moment of her life?) *Gus, there's something we need to talk about . . .* (Wrong again: she sounded like her father when he wanted to discuss an issue.) *Listen, if you want to keep our friendship the way it is, I'm cool with that.* (But she couldn't even say the words on the roof without her voice giving her away.) No, she wouldn't allow anyone, not even Gus Silva, to turn her into a liar.

When she tripped over a loose shingle and came dangerously close to the edge, she felt the same exhilaration she'd experienced when she asked him to kiss her.

"Hallie! What are you doing up on that roof at this time of night? And who exactly are you talking to?" The voice seemed to come out of the night itself. But when Hallie looked down, she spied Stuart sitting on his balcony with someone else. Their faces were in shadow.

"Stuart! You should have told me you were there," she mumbled, embarrassed to be caught talking to herself, and stunned to find Stuart with a date. It was the first time she'd seen him with another man since his partner Paul died four years earler. "I was, um, practicing for a play."

Stuart laughed. "I know that play well, honey. In fact, I've played the lead more than once myself."

"Do you have any idea how lovely you look up there in your pajamas, talking to the night? Your hair is pure gold," his friend said. "Whoever he is, he isn't worth it."

"Michael hasn't seen him, has he, Hallie?" Stuart added. He paused to sip his wine.

"Oh, he's worth it, all right," Hallie said, a mixture of hopelessness and pride flooding her.

"So come right out and tell him, then. None of this 'maybe we should be friends' stuff," the man named Michael advised. "You're already out there on the rooftop. Make the leap."

"A poorly chosen metaphor, Michael," Stuart said, nearly dropping his wineglass. "And, Hallie, much as I sympathize with the reckless impulses of the lovelorn, as one of your father's closest friends, it's my duty to tell you that you really must get off that roof. *Now*."

Still embarrassed that her meandering soliloquy had been overheard, Hallie blew Stuart a kiss. "You won't tell him, will you?"

"As long as you promise you'll stay off that widow's walk—at least not until Nick hires a contractor and gets some work done."

"Don't worry. I've been coming out here since I was eight"—Hallie smiled—"and I haven't fallen yet." She opened her arms as if to tempt the wind.

"*Please*, girl! The heart isn't what it used to be, and the only doctor in town is getting some much-needed rest. Now get inside. And, Hallie?"

She turned to look.

"I wouldn't worry about the boy. I've seen him with you. Uncomplicated friendship is *not* what he has in mind."

"Here's to complicated friendship," Michael said, clinking his glass against Stuart's. "The best life has to offer."

The next morning Hallie rode her bike to the West End and climbed onto the Barrettos' dilapidated porch. The inner door had been left open, but the house was utterly still. Hallie thought briefly of turning back. Then she remembered how she felt on the wharf when Gus almost kissed her. Or almost *didn't.*

She called his name, pressing the screen door open an inch.

She heard the sound of feet hitting the floor and then the word *shit.*

"Did I wake you up?" Hallie asked, taking a step backward when Fatima Barretto appeared at the door.

"Hallie? Jesus . . ." Fatima said, blinking at the light. "What time is it?"

"Almost eight," Hallie said, though it was closer to seven. "I shouldn't have come so early, but—" And then she stopped. Did she really expect Fatima to understand what it felt like to stay up half the night, talking to the stars about her doubts, her hopes, her wild overwhelming need to kiss Gus?

Before she had time to finish her sentence, Gus appeared behind his aunt. He was wearing only a pair of drawstring pajama bottoms.

"How did I forget? Hallie and I were supposed to ride our bikes to Truro this morning," he said to his aunt. "Looks like I overslept."

His aunt shuffled back to her room, muttering to herself.

"I'd offer you coffee, but we're out of milk," Gus said.

"I didn't come for coffee."

Taking her hand, Gus led her back to the stoop.

"You lied," Hallie said.

Gus laughed. "Yeah, I lied, but it's practically the middle of the night around here. I had to tell her *something*. Now I guess we have to ride to Truro—given how you feel about honesty and everything. Just give me a couple of minutes to throw on some shorts, okay?" He gestured toward a rusted green lawn chair on the porch before he started back inside.

But Hallie stepped into his path. His chest was smooth and taut. It took everything she had not to reach out and touch his skin.

"Aren't you going to ask why I came?"

"You think I don't already know?" he said. Then he walked past her and disappeared into his bedroom.

Hallie knew she should stay outside and wait as Gus clearly wanted her to do. Or better yet, she should leave. But instead, she followed him and pushed open the door of his room.

Though the small bedroom was perfectly organized, there was almost nothing of Gus in it. His cousin's old posters of the Grateful Dead and Frank Zappa remained on the wall where they'd been tacked up a decade earlier. Junior's football trophies lined the bureau, their false bronze veneers peeling away. An ancient crucifix, probably brought from Portugal generations earlier, was affixed to the wall. Hallie switched on the light in the shaded room, wondering where Gus kept *his* trophies. Her eyes drifted to the corner of the room where his sports equipment was stored in a duffel bag—as if he still considered himself a visitor. The only personal object rested on top of the bureau: her old copy of *David Copperfield*.

"You didn't think I'd really throw that in the harbor, did you?" Gus said, following her eyes. And suddenly Hallie felt ashamed of her impatience.

He stood in the center of the room, holding a pair of shorts and a T-shirt.

"It's way too early, and I wasn't invited here," she said. "I'm gonna go."

Gus stepped forward and kissed her forehead like a protective older brother. "I thought we were going for a bike ride."

Hallie turned her back while he changed, wondering if that chaste kiss had been her answer. She closed her eyes and touched the spot where he had kissed her head.

"This place is basically an eat-and-sleep deal for me," he said, reading her thoughts about the room. He pulled on his T-shirt. "Once I graduate, I'm gone."

Where? she wanted to ask. Gus Silva, who transformed the air in a room just by speaking her name, or resting his hands on his hips the way he had when he suggested a bike ride, was still a mystery to her.

"I'm sorry," she said, shaking off the question.

"Don't be. I'm *glad* you came. Remember what I told you in the cemetery that day? I want you to know everything about me. And this, as it happens, is where I live."

"I love it," Hallie said. How could she not love the room where he slept every night, the window that framed his first morning view? "I'm gonna take a rain check on the ride to Truro, though."

All she could think of was the words he'd said on the porch. *He knew why she'd come.* She was suddenly grateful that the dim light hid the color on her cheeks.

Gus walked her to the door.

Outside, she picked up the bike, but he reached out and touched her arm. "You can come back and get that later. I'll walk you home."

She was about to say he didn't need to do that, but his eyes, usually so full of energy, were calm and thoughtful.

She leaned the bike against the house and started for the street while Gus fell in beside her silently, not quite close enough to touch. Still she felt his presence acutely, both as he was now in his familiar shorts and T-shirt, and as he'd been when she followed him into his dim bedroom—shirtless in his drawstring pajama bottoms.

Halfway to her house, Gus stopped abruptly. "So you want to know why I didn't kiss you last night?"

"I haven't really thought about it," she said. The bay had just come into view.

Gus laughed. "Now I know why you hate lying so much. You're a total failure at it."

"Or maybe I just think honesty is really important."

"Admit it, then. The reason you showed up at the house of the living dead this morning is because you wanted to know how any kid in his right mind could turn you down."

"Don't make me sound so pathetic! Or conceited! For one thing, I didn't *ask you to kiss me*. Well, not exactly." Hallie frowned. "Okay, maybe I did—but I won't again. In fact, I wouldn't kiss you now if you begged me—" She picked up her pace, taking the lead again.

Gus grabbed her arm, and tugged her back to him—perhaps closer than he intended. They were eye-to-eye, and for the first time since the cemetery, there was nothing between them. "I hope you know that once I start kissing you,

I'm never going to stop. All these great conversations we've been having? Forget it. And we better tell our friends not to call for about a year cause we're gonna be too busy. Hell, I might even have to give up football, not to mention my great career at the A&P."

He took her by the shoulders and kissed her right there in the middle of the street. It was the shortest, gentlest kiss imaginable, but it pricked her, infected her, forever altered the colors of the landscape where she'd spent her whole life. And, yes, it answered the question that had driven her out of the house that morning.

"God, Stuart was right," Hallie said, putting her hand unconsciously to her mouth.

Gus laughed. "Who's Stuart? And what does he know about how bad I needed to kiss you?"

"Stuart's my next door neighbor, and he's very intuitive, especially when it comes to things like this. Last night when I was up on the widow's walk thinking about you, he heard me."

"He heard you *thinking*? Wow, I guess the guy *is* intuitive."

"Okay, I was talking to myself, all right? Talking to myself and pretending I was talking to you. Are you happy?"

"Yeah, to tell you the truth, I *am*. This last month, I've been happier than I've ever been in my whole messed-up life."

"Me, too," Hallie said softly, but she didn't dare to speak the words too loud. She knew about that kind of happiness and she mistrusted it almost as much as Gus did. It was in every photograph of her parents together. It beamed from Liz Cooper's eyes as she smiled at the man behind the camera. Briefly, it had made her and Nick invincible, and then it stripped them naked. Happiness, Hallie thought, had ruined her father's life. But now she understood Nick's secret: it had been worth it. For him, it was *still* worth it.

"One favor?" she said.

Gus lifted his chin.

"Promise me you won't fight this anymore. Promise me you'll let us have it."

Gus didn't say anything. He just stood there with his hands resting on his hips. The answer was a blaze in his eyes, a subtle upturning of his lips.

"I'll be over to get my bike later, okay?" she said, signaling she didn't want him to come any farther. Then, while Gus stood on the corner where he had grazed her lips with his mouth, she wove through the colorful street. She started off walking, but by the time she reached her house, she was running. And breathless.

*L*ater, *Hallie went to the phone* and dialed his number. It was after midnight, but she was sure Gus would be awake. He answered on the first ring.

"Do you want to see my roof?" she said.

"*Now?* Nick would probably nail me with Captain Thorne's whaling harpoon if he caught me."

"There's a wrought-iron fire escape out back. No one's used it in years, and it's pretty rusted, so be careful. I'll bring a flashlight."

"You're sure?"

"I went to your church," she said. "Now it's time for you to visit mine."

When she heard the dial tone, Hallie thought they must have been disconnected. But within ten minutes, she saw Gus smiling up at her from the bay side of the house. She shone her light on him as he climbed the precarious fire escape to the roof. Then he sat beside her on the quilt. The stars were particularly bright against the black night. Her cathedral had never been more glorious.

When Hallie tried to speak, Gus put his finger over her lips. "Don't you know you're not supposed to talk in church?"

"My church isn't like that," she started to say. But he shushed her with his mouth. The kiss began as gently as the one on the street, but this time nothing could keep back the hunger behind it. When a loose board crackled beneath them, Hallie pulled away. "Maybe we should go inside."

Gus lifted the hatchway door that led to the attic. "You're sure your father's asleep?"

"He gets up at five," Hallie said, as if that were an answer.

The attic was dark and littered with the detritus of the past. Stuart's lights were still on next door, and not wanting to attract his attention, Hallie resisted the impulse to illuminate the space. In the weak moonlight, they could see the outline of old boxes filled with Liz Cooper's possessions, things Nick found too valuable to throw away, though no one would ever use them again.

Gus kissed her in the center of the room. He lifted her up and spun her in a slow circle, still kissing her until they moved dizzily across the room, then pressed her against the wall. All the riotous emotions they had been storing up in the past month, maybe for all their lives, were in that kiss—wonder and love, hunger and thirst, and, yes, the wild happiness that had terrified them both. But didn't anymore.

It ended when they tripped over one of her mother's boxes, producing a clatter. "Ouch," Gus cried out, clutching his shin and laughing, but still not letting her go. A moment later, the light flashed on in the hallway, followed by Nick's voice. "Who's up there?"

"It's me, Nick. I was just, um, looking for something I need for a project," Hallie said, watching Gus, who was already straightening his clothes, studying his escape route.

"At one in the morning?" Nick said. By then, he was just outside the door that led to the attic stairs. "What could you possibly need up there?"

Hallie turned on the light before Nick came any farther and saw she was in darkness. "Just some of Wolf's old art stuff—and I found it. I'll be right down."

Nick hesitated, but didn't immediately retreat. "Next time, work on your projects in the daytime, okay? I was in the middle of a good dream."

"So was I," Gus whispered, already standing near the ladder.

Hallie took a step closer, but he stopped her. "If you don't go down now, your father will be up here," he said. "And, besides—"

Hallie was confused only for a moment before her face erupted in a slow smile. "Yeah, I know. We've got time."

Gus grinned before he disappeared up the ladder and through the hatchway onto the roof.

"Now you're catching on."

CHAPTER 11

After the night on the roof, time did funny things. It slowed
torturously during the hours Gus was at the A&P, or when
Hallie sat behind the desk in her father's office, but then it
raced ahead. They sped through the waning days of summer.
And when they returned to school, Hallie would watch the
clock obsessively, waiting for four, when Gus's football practice ended.

Gus would pick her up at the monument in the latest junk
car Alvaro had provided, and they'd drive to Loop Street.
They banged the door behind them every day, rarely making
it to the bedroom in the empty house before they were kissing, tearing at each other's clothes.

Once, lying on Gus's bed, she asked him if he thought
anyone else had ever experienced what they had.

"No one in the world," he said, pulling her closer. "This
right here? This belongs only to me and you."

Sometimes Hallie wanted to tell him about the October
night when *Asa Quebrada* had flown away for good, about
the strange song she had heard in her sleep, or the way she
had stood at the edge of the roof and cried for something she
didn't understand. But after the day in the cemetery, Gus
never spoke of the past again so she kept her secret to herself.

Hallie had never liked football before, but that year she attended every game Nauset played. The night games were the
best. Everything she loved about Gus was there beneath the
lights, the sheen of his black hair, the grace of his movements

and the ferocity that reminded her of the way he pulled her toward him in his room.

Neil dated Melissa Perreira for most of the year, but he always went to the football games with Hallie. "She talks too much during the games," he explained. "I want to *watch*."

Neil liked to sit apart from their boisterous friends, and sip rum and Coke from a Thermos, waiting for the inevitable moment when Voodoo took control of the field. Sometimes Neil was so tense and focused—almost reverent—during the games that Hallie wished she had stayed below with Daisy and Felicia. But usually she was happy to be at the top of the bleachers, where nothing impeded her view.

At the beginning of the season, she hoped Gus might look for her between plays, but he never did. Only at the end of the game would he lift his face in her direction and zip her a smile, a triumphant fist in the air. In that moment, it felt like her victory—even when the team had lost. She and Neil would leap to their feet and respond in kind.

"Do you have any idea how much I would give to do what he did tonight?" Neil said, after a game in which Gus had run for three touchdowns, one in the final minute. "The kid is a god out there."

"What are you talking about? You're the one who's going to be famous someday."

For a moment, though, it seemed as if Neil hadn't heard her. He was focused on the celebration under the lights. "Don't you get it? It's not the game. It's who he is. I could win six Academy Awards and I'd never have that."

Eager to join Gus, Hallie reached for her jacket. "You're not making any sense, Gallagher. Gus doesn't even care about awards or stuff like that."

But Neil was fired up, the way he was when he was on-stage or narrating a story to their friends. "Come on, Hal. You can't tell me you don't see it. It's what made you fall in love with him. What turns people like me into loyal lapdogs for life, willing to do almost anything for him. Whether it's voodoo or that thing my director calls *presence,* it's fucking magic. And you're right. It means nothing to him."

Hallie picked up his Thermos and shook it. "Aha. I was wondering what got into you tonight. You drank this whole thing and didn't even offer me any? Come on, take my arm before you break your neck."

At first, Neil protested, but then he laughed and allowed her to help him down the bleachers. "Maybe I did have a little too much, huh?"

On Saturday nights, she and Gus drove around with Melissa and Neil in Neil's Jeep, looking for a party. At some point, they always ended up at the beach. Freshman year, Gus had begun the habit of taking a short swim every day, no matter what the season; and when the temperature rose over sixty, he convinced his friends to join him.

"You want to freeze your asses off, fine, but swim in the goddamn daylight," Uncle Manny said angrily one evening when he'd caught them sneaking towels out of the closet. They all knew he was remembering what had happened to Junior.

"Don't worry, Mr. Barretto," Neil finally said, slinging his arm over his friend's shoulder. "We only go in the water when there's a bright moon, and Gus here is never out of my sight."

Manny walked away, mumbling that it would kill Fatima to go through that again. "Do you hear me? *It would kill her.*"

Gus didn't say anything, but he was strangely quiet for the rest of the night.

Later, on West End Beach, after their swim, Neil tried to dispel the mood. "You know why people like your aunt and uncle get old? It's fear." The two couples had dressed quickly after their dip and were sitting on an overturned scull at the water's edge.

"Cell death might have something to do with it, too," Hallie said, shaking as she nestled closer to Gus.

Neil jumped up and climbed on top of another small boat. "And what do you think makes cells die? Honestly, think about it. Ever see those worry lines parents get in their foreheads? That's the start of it . . . *Don't drive too fast. Watch out for riptides. Ooh . . . I hear there's sharks off the coast of the Vineyard. How old is that shrimp, anyway? Might get food poisoning . . .*" His voice rose with every warning. "Well, I'm not buying it. I think that if you never give in to fear, you just might live forever."

"Or at least till the shark off the coast has you for lunch," Hallie said. But feeling Gus's arm around her, a salty breeze on her face, she almost believed Neil was right.

All her life, she'd been afraid of growing up and leaving her father, but as the spring of senior year approached, Hallie rarely thought of Nick at all. She kissed him carelessly on the cheek or on the top of his head as she rushed in and out of the house—always on the way to somewhere else. His love, which frequently took the form of a question, was almost an irritant. *Where are you going? When will you be in? Who's driving?* And the most dreaded of all: *When are you going to make a decision about college?*

Sometime in March, just after Neil sent his confirmation to NYU's theater department, Gus and Hallie brought their college acceptance letters to the beach and read them out loud by the light of a bonfire. Then they folded them all back into the envelopes and talked about what they really wanted.

It was crazy! Plain stupid! was what Felicia and Daisy said when Hallie told them about their plan. Daisy had been accepted to Cornell, and Felicia was going to Salem State if her father could come up with the money. *No one throws away college and their future for a guy. Not in 1986! And if Gus's family cared enough to notice, they wouldn't allow it, either.* Everyone knew he was a lackadaisical student, but he'd been offered several football scholarships. *Does he think these opportunities will come again?*

"If I wanted to hear this lecture, I could have stayed home," Hallie told them. "College is all Nick talks about."

On a quiet Tuesday, Neil spotted Hallie reading in the window seat, and stopped in. Though he tried to act nonchalant, they both knew he'd been looking for her.

"Have you reconsidered?" he asked, picking up the pile of acceptance letters that lay beside her on the cushion. He held on to them as he sat in the window opposite her.

"Not a chance." Hallie slammed her book shut.

Neil flipped through the letters, summing them up with a whistling sound. "Personally, I vote for Columbia. Think about it, Hal. We'd both be in the city, and if you and Gus are still together, he could come down on weekends."

"*If* Gus and I are still together?" Hallie seized the letters and slapped Neil's hand with them. "Get out of my house, traitor," she teased.

"Just testing," Neil said, putting up his hands in surrender. "Everyone knows you two are going to be married for seventy-seven years and make a bunch of Portagee babies."

"Only seventy-seven?"

Hallie and Gus had decided to give themselves a year in Montana, a place as unlike Provincetown as they could imagine. *Just one year,* Hallie finally told her father one Friday night over dinner. One year away from everything that had protected and constrained her and Gus from birth, one year far from the wild Atlantic that had defined their families' fates for generations. Hallie pulled out bank passbooks, maps, and listings for apartments in Missoula to prove that this was no impulsive lark. They had even sent for some local newspapers and circled several possible jobs—one in a medical office for her, a couple of restaurant and deli positions for Gus. "I was also thinking of asking for a deferred acceptance to Columbia."

When Nick remained implacable, Hallie quickly reminded him that she was turning eighteen. No one could force her to go to college.

"I don't care if you're a hundred and eighteen. I'm still your father," Nick said, sounding more like an old world *papai* than her own famously open-minded father. "Once you get to Montana, you could change your mind. I won't have you throwing your life away on—"

"*Don't* say it," Hallie said before she slammed out of the house.

Nick followed her onto the porch in bare feet. "Or what?"

"Don't say it, or I swear, I'll never forgive you, Nick. Never." Then, heart hammering, she hopped on her bike and pedaled furiously toward the Point.

She returned in the dark. Still not ready to confront her father, she leaned her bike against the side of the house and walked through the narrow alleyway to the back garden. She planned to climb the fire escape in the back of the house, but when she passed an open window, she heard the low murmur of Nick's voice coming from the study. Peering through the window into his study, she saw a familiar sight: her father sharing a drink with Stuart.

"I love the kid myself," Nick was saying. "Have since he was a small boy."

"Your sweetheart," Stuart said quietly.

"Christ, is there anyone in this town who doesn't know what I said that day?"

"Not one. This *is* Provincetown." Stuart refilled their glasses.

"It's just that sometimes I look at him and all I see is goddamn Codfish. I know it's not fair, and you're probably the only person on earth I'd admit it to, but I do."

"You're right. It's *not* fair, and it's absolutely beneath you. And, unfortunately, most of us entertain similarly despicable thoughts all the time."

"*Despicable?* Did you just call me despicable in my own house?"

"Apparently, I did. Impertinent little bastard, aren't I?" Stuart laughed softly and Hallie heard the ice cubes clinking in their glasses as they paused.

"But seriously, Nick, you're fighting a battle that you can't possibly win. When it comes to deciding between a parent and the kind of love Hallie has for Gus, the choice is heartbreakingly easy. If you don't believe me, go see my father." He lowered his voice before he delivered his final punch. "Or maybe you could save yourself a trip and call Liz Cooper's mother."

"Her name was *Costa*. Elizabeth Costa. And it's not just about Gus, Stuart. Hallie's been accepted at Columbia and

Dartmouth, not to mention my own alma mater. Is it a crime if I want my daughter to get an education?"

"Your only crime is underestimating her. Hallie's going to go to school, Nick—if not this year, then next. She even said she'd request a deferred acceptance. Everything you've given her in the past eighteen years, not to mention her own inborn drive—it's all still there. Isn't Missoula a college town? Perhaps you could compromise and suggest she take a couple of courses in the fall."

Nick merely grunted.

After Stuart said goodnight and walked through the light on the front porch, Hallie crept out of the alley and hugged him.

"Dear God, girl, you startled me. What are *you* doing out here?" And then, taking her two hands, he answered his own question. "Eavesdropping on a private conversation? I'm shocked."

"Thanks for what you said in there," Hallie whispered, glancing toward the window where her father was alone in the study. Not reading. Not listening to music. Just sitting.

She had never seen him look so lonely. "Do you think he listened?"

"Nick always listens. That's what makes him a great diagnostician, and an even finer human being."

"So you really think he'll—"

"Whoa, there. I said he listened. I didn't say he agreed with me. The man has his own mind as you well know."

"He's so obsessed with this *college* thing; he'll never give in."

Stuart took her face in his two hands and kissed her on the forehead. "As I told your father in there, have a little faith, dear. This isn't an easy time for him, either, you know. Wherever you go, he's losing his little girl."

After Stuart had gone inside, Hallie wandered to the back of the house, where she sat on a fractured cement seawall, hugging her knees as she looked out on the bay.

A few days later, Nick slapped a course catalogue from the University of Montana on the table. "One year," he said. "And you have to promise to take at least two courses a semester."

"I've got the same catalogue in my room," Hallie said. "If you check it out, you'll see that I've circled organic chemistry and freshman English."

When Nick released her from the bone-crushing Costa *abraço*, they both had tears in their eyes. Hallie quickly turned away.

That night, she told Nick she was sleeping at Felicia's, but she and Gus took a sleeping bag and braved the wind off the point. The moon was obscured by clouds, and they could see nothing as they started to kiss. Despite the unseasonable chill, Gus impulsively stripped off his sweatshirt and thermal in one deft move. In the dark, he found the buttons of her jacket and undid them expertly.

"Gus, we can't . . . not out here," she protested. "It's too cold, and besides, someone might see us."

"It's not, and they won't. Not tonight. *I promise.*" He tossed her jacket in the sand, lifted her sweater over her head, and unhooked her bra, letting it fall. When he pulled her against his skin and looked intently into her face, both her shivering and her doubts dissipated. All she felt was his heat. "See? It's magic. Now do you believe me?" he whispered.

Hallie unhooked his jeans and then took off her own. "I never believed in anything more."

In the absolute darkness, the powerful presence of the surf was magnified. The sand, lifted by a strong gust of wind, stung their skin, but Gus's promise held: on this night, nothing and no one could reach them. She was astonished by the suppleness of his body as it fitted itself against hers, by its smoothness and strength, by the tenderness that turned ravenous as they wrapped themselves in the sleeping bag and moved against each other.

"Do you have any idea how beautiful you are?" he said when they were finished. "So . . . incredibly . . . beautiful."

"You, too," Hallie said, nestling into his shoulder. "So . . . incredibly . . . beautiful."

Around three, when Gus was in a deep sleep, Hallie slipped out of the sleeping bag and found her clothes. The clouds had lifted and the sky was overcome with stars.

"Gus, look!" she said, shaking him. "It's brighter than my church."

"I still like your church better," Gus said, as he roused himself, dressed, and joined her. "That was the first place we kissed."

"Wrong. The first place we kissed was on Commercial Street."

"I mean *really* kissed." Gus grinned at her.

"The other kiss was real, too." As if to prove it, Hallie leaned over and grazed her lips with his.

Gus closed his eyes. "Mmm . . . Honeysuckle."

"What?"

"That's what the street smelled like that day; it was everywhere," he said. "Did you really think I forgot?"

Hallie laughed. "Honeysuckle and beach roses. The most amazing fragrance on earth."

They'd stayed awake the rest of the night, savoring the surf, the sharp stars, the powerful sense of connection that had begun on the night his mother died. She didn't understand it then— she *still* didn't—but leaning against him, she already knew that nothing in her life would ever be more real.

"This just might be the best night of our lives," she said. Then she remembered that Neil had said something similar the day they were caught in a rainstorm just after he'd told her about Gus's "crush."

"What about the first time we see Glacier National Park?" Gus said, pulling her back to the present as he held her tighter. "Or when our kids are born—little Hallett and the boy we'll name anything but Gus."

They'd tacitly believed all those things would happen, but neither of them had ever spoken about them before. Hallie felt thrilled—and just a little terrified. But before she could respond, Gus turned back into the eighteen-year-old boy he was. "Hell, what about your big prom next week?" he teased. "You really think that a sky full of stars and a sleeping bag are better than that?"

Hallie kissed him, feeling wistful. "I can't believe it's all happening so fast."

CHAPTER 12

Since Gus could only afford one prom, they had chosen hers in Provincetown. He and Neil had been joking about it for weeks. *All that money for what—to march around the gym in a monkey suit?*

"Maybe we should hold the un-prom out on the beach," Neil had suggested. "The three of us and Reggie." He and Melissa had broken up three weeks earlier, after he'd vigorously denied cheating on her with Reggie Aluto. When he asked Reggie to the prom, it seemed like a slap at Melissa, and Hallie told him so.

"We were together for almost a whole year and she takes some stupid rumor over my word? If you ask me, that deserves a slap or two," Neil blurted out, his color deepening.

Hallie had been almost physically taken aback by his vindictive tone. She suspected that there was more to it than the breakup. Though he had every reason to be excited about his future, Neil had been increasingly moody as the school year wound down. She was having trouble saying goodbye to friends, too, but it was different for Gus and Neil. Inseparable since they were five, they finished each other's sentences, played straight man for each other's jokes, and had rescued and defended each other more times than they could count. Though Gus was the orphan, Neil had always seemed to need him more.

Once when Neil was alone with Hallie at a party, he looked at Gus across the room. "Honestly, I don't know who I'll be without him. Pretty sad, isn't it?"

Hallie rested her hand on his knee. "You're going to be a student in one of the most exciting cities in the world. *That's* who you're going to be. Hell, by October, you'll probably totally forget us."

"Hallie *who*?" Neil joked, but there was no hiding the misery in his eyes. She wished they could have talked about it longer, but they were interrupted by Sean and Daisy, who had some news to share: Sean had decided to join the Air Force.

And now, before she could react to Neil's harsh comment about Melissa, he quickly turned to Gus and changed the subject. "Once we get through the ape parade, it should be a cool night, though. Chad's brother already picked up enough rum to light up the Point. Think you guys can get the Coke?"

When the night came, Neil and Reggie picked Hallie and Gus up at her house. Hallie was secretly relieved that her father had been called out on an emergency. Like all the other parents, he wanted to snap some pictures of them in their formal clothes and, undoubtedly, repeat his last-minute warnings about drinking and driving as well, but Hallie was grateful to avoid the sadness, and something else—*doubt* perhaps, that appeared in his eyes whenever he saw her with Gus these days. Hallie gave Gus a silk scarf she'd found in a vintage clothing store in town. Like her dress, it was almost the same color Wolf had named Race Point blue: midnight with a hint of cerulean. When Gus draped it around his neck, the effect was electric.

"That scarf is so cool!" Reggie gushed when she saw Gus. "You look like one of those guys in the old movies my grandmother used to watch—you know, Gary Cooper? And it makes your eyes look so—so brown."

"Gus has nothing in common with Gary Cooper," Neil said. "Except they both always play the good guy."

Hallie felt sorry for Reggie, who seemed out of place with the established trio, but she also couldn't help being protective of Neil. The tuxedo hung on his narrow frame; and no matter what he tried, he'd never managed to tame his wayward hair.

She pulled him into the bathroom and added a dab of gel to it. "Much better," she said, standing back. "And next time I'll find a scarf for you, too. A mix of green and brown like your eyes."

"There are no next times after tonight, remember? This is it for our class," Neil said. "Incredible dress, by the way. The color doesn't do a thing for Gary Cooper out there, but it's a knockout on you."

When they rejoined Reggie and Gus in the kitchen, Neil filled a two-liter bottle with his trademark drink and cracked a joke. Hallie studied him covertly. Getting laughs and ratcheting up the energy in a room were what he did, but he seemed to be trying too hard.

They passed the bottle around in the car when they reached the school, and Hallie felt a surge of warmth pass through her.

"Okay, let's get through the dancing and pictures so we can get to the real party on the beach," Neil said. He stashed the bottle, and threw open the door. A slash of light cut across the backseat.

"Let's have one before we go in," Gus pulled a Camel from his pack. He and Hallie crossed the street to the monument where they met for a smoke every morning before Gus left for Eastham. Gus made a cup of his hands, lit the cigarette, and took the first drag. When he passed it to Hallie, it tasted like vanilla and salt. They could hear the music emanating from the gymnasium. It was Whitney Houston. *I wanna dance with somebody . . .*

S*he and Gus didn't spend much* time with Neil and Reggie, but during the slow songs, Hallie couldn't help noticing how Neil's lanky form was welded to Reggie's curves. Melissa, who hadn't found another date, was conspicuously absent.

"You know, this prom thing isn't so bad," Gus said, sensing Hallie's wistful mood. "Holding you? Watching every guy in the place wish they were wearing my lucky blue scarf? I can deal with it." He kissed her again.

A couple of hours later Neil clapped a hand on Gus's shoulder. "I hate to interrupt this tender moment, bro, but we need to get the bonfire started. Provincetown's finest will be out in full force as soon as this gig is over." His eyes looked bleary, but bright at the same time.

"I can drive if you want," Hallie offered, though she knew Neil never let anyone behind the wheel of his Jeep.

"We're going to Race Point," he said, leading them out to the parking lot. "I could get us there drunk, high, and blindfolded. And, lucky for you, I left my blindfold at home."

Hallie thought briefly of her father, whose face clouded with dread when he cautioned her against getting in the car with anyone who had been drinking. She was acutely aware that she was his only child—*all he had*. She stopped short a few feet from the Jeep.

Sensing her hesitation, Gus took off his jacket and slung it over her shoulders protectively. "I think I left my tie behind, anyway. We'll catch a ride with Sean and Daisy."

Hallie reached into the pocket of Gus's jacket and felt the bow tie he'd removed after the photos. Then she squeezed Gus's hand.

"Whatever you say, Voodoo," Neil said. After slamming the door of the Jeep, he roared toward the highway.

The party started off like so many others. The joking and flirting around the crackling fire, the taste of rum and vanilla. Hallie only remembered having two of Neil's drinks, but both were stronger than usual, particularly the second one. Hallie remembered Gus saying, "Dude, did you forget the Coke? Then he laughed as he brought the cup to his lips and passed it to her. She couldn't count how many times a joint had come her way—or recall when Reggie had produced a bottle of tequila. Had she really drunk that, too? Again, she heard her father's unwelcome voice: *There's something about Cape kids. Maybe it's the constant drumbeat of the ocean, like a clock reminding them how short the time is, or maybe it's just the loneliness of the long winters . . . but they party more than anyone else.*

Hallie and Gus had always been an exception to that rule. They enjoyed the parties on the beach, the illicit gatherings in the homes of absent parents, but the only time they'd ever been close to drunk together had been that afternoon in the cemetery. Hallie had too much respect for her father, and Gus had his own reasons to fear drink. "Alcohol was what brought Codfish down," he told her one night after his friends had teased him for passing on a bottle of vodka. "It killed my mother as surely as his hands did."

Hallie nodded. "Mine, too," she had said.

Eventually couples began to drift into the dunes, including Neil and Reggie. They were holding hands as they walked away. But when they returned, the easy rapport Hallie had noticed in the auditorium was gone. Neil disappeared down the beach for a walk, uncharacteristically alone. Hallie and Gus were about to go looking for him when they spotted him, ambling along the shoreline, with his pants rolled up to the knees.

"The water is awesome!" he yelled. "Who's coming in?"

"You're drunk. The tide is wicked strong, and I left my lifeguard certification card at home tonight," Chad Mendoza called back to him. "How about you do something productive and make us some more drinks?"

Everyone laughed, including Neil, as the undertow unbalanced him, proving Chad's point. He started up the beach. "Okay, okay. If you guys want booze, what can I say?"

While he mixed the last of the rum and Coke, Reggie gradually drifted to the periphery of the group. Her eyeliner had blurred; the hair that had been piled on top of her head in studied spirals collapsed; she leaned her knees together and stared out at the ocean, looking lonelier than ever.

Hallie guessed that it was around four, the hour when the water turned as gray as a black-and-white photograph of itself. After they finished their drinks, Gus, Neil, and some of the other boys worked to resuscitate the bonfire that had flamed out, refusing to surrender the night, or the years that had led them to it. Sean Mello's mother had promised pancakes, eggs, and *linguiça* at seven, but the only thing Hallie hungered for was sleep. She sighed when someone produced a football. Gus kissed her before he went off to join the game.

Hallie was wobbly on her feet as she made her way toward Reggie. "Stupid heels," she said, which made Daisy and Christina laugh. Then, realizing she was barefoot, Hallie giggled, too. She crossed the sand with as much dignity as she could muster and managed to lower herself onto the spot beside Reggie without toppling. Reggie stared into the fire, ignoring her.

"Any more of that tequila?" Hallie finally asked.

Reggie reached into the pocket of Neil's tux jacket and produced the empty bottle. "Gallagher chugged it," she said. She threw it into the bonfire, where it shattered.

"Is everything okay between you guys?" Hallie said. "You seemed to be getting along great back at the school."

"Yeah, we're already planning the wedding. Maybe you and Gus can live next door, and once a year we'll play the swappy game. That's one way to keep Gallagher around."

"*Excuse me?*" Stunned by the comment, Hallie attempted to scrabble to her feet, but she was too dizzy to stand. "Neil is like my brother. Has been since we were kids."

"You really believe that, don't you?" Reggie laughed so caustically that Daisy turned to look. "And you're supposed to be the town genius."

"I don't know what your problem is, but I'm not listening to this," Hallie said, again trying to rise. But this time Reggie tugged on her dress, easily pulling her back onto the sand.

"Wait. I didn't mean to pick on you," Reggie slurred, reaching for a Coke bottle that was wedged in the sand. "You've always been nice to me. Just jealous, I guess."

"Well, don't be. I'm not any kind of genius. It's just that my dad was teaching me science and math when normal kids were watching cartoons."

"I'm not jealous of your *mind*. You think I want to sit around doing calculus all day? Or go to freaking *Har*vard?"

"I'm not going to—" Hallie said.

"It's Gus I want," Reggie blurted out. "Just like my date has always wanted you. Pretty ironic, huh?"

"I remember you guys sharing snacks back in first grade," Hallie said, attempting to bring the conversation back to neutral territory. "Everyone thought he had a crush on you."

"My mother could never get it together to pack me a snack, so he would slip his into my cubby. Usually an orange, with the peel already slit, and a napkin in the bag. His mom thought of everything. It must have been his favorite fruit, but when I tried to give it back, he always claimed he didn't like them."

He *still* loved oranges, Hallie thought, remembering his smile as he split one in half and offered it to her in her kitchen just the day before.

"Anyway, I was the one with the crush, and it was never mutual. I mean, I believed it was. I didn't think anyone could be as nice as Gus unless they wanted something in return. But turns out that's just him. He's even like that with Mavis Black at the A&P. Carrying her bags to the car. Giving a biscuit to that ugly little dog of hers."

"Mavis still doesn't trust him. Says he reminds her too much of Codfish." Hallie glanced at Gus, wishing she'd never left the fire. "God, I hate people like that."

Reggie nodded before she turned her attention back to the water. "You think Neil's going to take us home soon?"

"I'm going to go get my cigarettes out of the car, and then I'll talk to him," Hallie said, then successfully launched herself onto her feet. "You okay?"

"Yeah, just a little tired. And, Hallie? Sorry for being such a bitch before."

The strangely serious conversation had almost made Hallie feel sober, but when she started to walk, she again felt dizzy. Seeing the way she swayed as she navigated the sand, Gus called after her.

"Just going to the car," she yelled back. Then she pulled his jacket more closely around her, inhaling his clean scent and headed for the parking lot. She'd almost reached the car when she heard footsteps behind her.

She turned around, expecting Gus. But in the dawn light, another figure emerged.

She slowed down and waited. "Gallagher! Jeez, you scared me."

"What are you trying to do—steal my car, and leave me and Gus behind?" Neil joked, panting as he caught up. It was bright enough that Hallie could have traced the map of his freckles.

"Don't forget Reggie," Hallie said.

"Reggie will find a way back, don't worry. She'll just flash those tits of hers like she always does. I'm sure somebody will be happy to take her home and tuck her in."

"Don't talk about her like that."

"Why not? She your new best friend or something? I saw the two of you bonding over there in the sand."

"Maybe she is."

"What can I say? The girl can't hold her liquor. Did you see her? She's a mess, babbling on about Saint Gus from Miss Iverson's first-grade class again. You were right. I only asked her to the prom to frost Melissa. Guess karma got me back, huh?"

"She told you that story about first grade, too?" Slowly registering the reference to *Saint* Gus, Hallie cracked open the back door of the car and retrieved her cigarettes. She was suddenly eager to get back to the fire.

"Oh, she told me all right. Pretty pathetic all around, if you ask me." Neil took the pack of cigarettes from her hands, removed two, and lit them. He passed one to Hallie.

"Are you calling Gus pathetic?"

"Bad choice of words." He only smoked on rare occasions, and after he inhaled, he gave in to a brief coughing fit. Then he returned to the subject of Gus. "Fucked up is more like it. Fucked up for life."

The moment was so surreal it left Hallie speechless. It reminded her of the night when he had played a desperate addict onstage so convincingly that she no longer recognized him. But this time he wasn't acting.

"Come on, Hallie," Neil continued, his voice growing louder. "Open your eyes. I know him better than anyone, and I love him, but—"

"You *don't!*" Hallie yelled. "You wouldn't say that if you did." She tossed the cigarette on the ground and began to walk away. She hadn't made it more than a couple of feet when Neil sprang after her. He spun her around and kissed her hard on the mouth.

"*This* is what I know," he said as she struggled to get away. "It was supposed to be me. It was supposed to be us; and if you weren't so blinded by Gus's fucking voodoo, you'd see it, too."

"*Never,*" Hallie said harshly. "Even if there was no Gus, it would never have been you." In an instant, her words accomplished what all her strength could not. Neil let her go.

Gus's jacket fell to the ground as she reeled backwards. But before she could regain her footing, she felt his long freckled fingers, digging into her arms. "Bitch," he said in a slurry voice. "Nick's spoiled little bitch."

When she again tried to jerk herself free, Neil tore at the strap of her Race Point blue dress, exposing the whiteness of her breast. Enraged, Hallie pushed back with enough force to land him in the asphalt. "If you ever come near me again, I'll—" she began, backing away as she tried to cover herself.

Before she could finish her threat, she heard Neil crying. Crying and saying that he loved her. *Don't you understand? I love you.* And then he was reciting the words of the note that had brought her and Gus together. The note she had never talked about with anyone but Felicia. How did Neil know what it said? *It's you or nobody. Always has been. Always will be.*

Hallie was struggling to absorb it when she heard the gunfire rhythm of approaching footsteps. Though they'd been alerted by the sound, Gus still seemed to come out of nowhere—the way he did on the football field in the most thrilling moments of the game. But this time there were no lights, no chanting crowd, no victory. He threw himself at Neil like he hurtled himself toward the end zone, the hands that had glided gently over every inch of her skin, transformed into a pair of remarkably efficient fists. She was stunned by the audible *thwack* of knuckles against flesh. The primal, metallic odor of blood left her instantly nauseous. Spurting from Neil's nose and spraying across his face in the pale light, it was more black than red. But above all, she was shocked by the appearance of a Gus she'd never seen before, the one he and her father had tried to warn her against: *Codfish Silva's son.*

Though he was hitting Neil, it was Hallie's name he was

saying. "Shit, Hallie. With my best friend?" And Neil was talking to her, too, even as he swiped his nose with his sleeve, and attempted to evade another punch. "Do you see this, Hal? Do you get it now? What did I tell you?"

Gus took his friend by the shoulders and heaved him against the hood of the car. *Again.* And again. At first, Neil attempted to resist, but then his body went pliant and limp. Still Gus continued.

"Stop, Gus! *Stop before you kill him!*" Hallie heard herself yelling just before she threw herself between them. The words seemed to be coming from someone else. The inky blood pouring from Neil's face, his unfocused eyes, were the last things she saw before the morning was erased and blackness swallowed her.

CHAPTER 13

Hallie saw her father even before he realized she was awake. He was sitting on the edge of her purple quilt, where he had taken to drinking his coffee before work, and his forehead was creased with worry. He'd lost so much weight that even his bones looked diminished.

According to the calendar on her wall, Hallie had been home for eleven days. During the weeks she'd spent in a coma, most of the summer had disappeared, and with it, everything she had planned. What she once confidently called *her future.* Nick had been at her side when she woke up, too. She remembered his tears, and the way he had covered her face with kisses, telling her he loved her over and over in Portuguese and promising her that she would make a full recovery. He was sure of it.

Recovery? Hallie had thought, taking in the squares of white mineral board on the ceiling, the hospital machinery, the sound of the staff's brisk footsteps in the hallway. She'd attempted to form a word, but it was hours—or even days— before it came. Time had become irrelevant. *Gus. Where's Gus?*

By then, Aunt Del and Stuart had arrived. And they, too, were crying and kissing her hand, hugging Nick and promising her and each other that she was going to be fine. But even when she spoke louder, no one would answer her question.

"Rest, my darling," Nick had said. "You need to rest."

And though she wanted to argue back, Hallie gave in to exhaustion.

Still she'd called for him repeatedly. She knew something had happened between her and Gus. Something bad. But the images floating to the surface of her mind made no sense. Had they been in an accident? Was Gus hurt? *Dead?* No, she couldn't bear to think of it; and yet she couldn't imagine anything else that would keep him away.

Not now, her father said, echoing her thoughts. *You have to focus on healing.* And on the days when she grew agitated: *Gus is all right. I promise you, Pie. Now no more questions. Please, you have to trust me.*

If he's all right, then why isn't he *here*? she wanted to say. But again, she was too weak to form the words. Too tired to make sense of the answers.

Even Aunt Del left the room when the subject came up, repeating Nick's stock lines as she went: "There will be plenty of time to think about that, but first you have to take care of yourself. You've done so well, sweetie."

Now, back at home, her father was clearly trying to steer her thoughts toward the future. However, when he brought up college, Hallie turned toward her window.

"If you keep working hard on your therapy, you could take a couple of courses at the community college in the spring. Linda said she'll sell me her old Corolla," he persisted, the determined optimism in his voice never waning. "Thing's got some miles on it, but it would get you to Barnstable and back for a few months."

"You know the reason I work so hard at therapy?" Hallie asked—more sharply than she intended. "It's not so I can get a car. Or go to college. Or hang out with my friends. I'm doing it for one reason and one reason only."

She shook off Nick's hand. "I'm starting to remember

what happened that night on the Point, and I know why Gus has stayed away. He probably thinks it's all his fault."

"I'm glad you're starting to remember, Pie, but the situation is more complicated than what happened that night. You don't understand—"

"No, *you* don't understand, because if you did you'd know I'll never give him up." Hallie shouted, startling her father with the newfound power in her voice.

Nick set his coffee cup on her bedside table next to a copy of *Jane Eyre* he'd brought upstairs. The novel she could never resist, even though she'd probably read it a dozen times, remained untouched. He gave a perfunctory glance at his watch, signaling that he was through with the discussion. "I've got to get to the office—"

"If Gus won't come to me, then I need to get strong enough to go to him. That's what I'm working for . . . what I'm *breathing* for."

A flash of anger darted across Nick's face. "Gus Silva is thinking about his own future, Hallie. You need to do the same."

"How do *you* know what he's thinking about? Have you seen him? You've got to tell me the truth." Against her will, Hallie began to tremble.

She expected her father to come back and sit on the bed again. To comfort her like he always did. Instead, he stood firmly in his spot. "I'm sorry, Hallie. Truly, I am. But if you started to plan a little bit, some of this might become easier."

"*Some of this?* You mean knowing that Gus is torturing himself for something he didn't do? That only the blackest despair could keep him away from me? Or maybe feeling like I'm going to lose my mind if I have to go through another day—another hour—without seeing him?

"All I can say is that it will get easier. I can't tell you when, but it will," her father said with the same compassionate but professional stolidity he used when he told a patient he or she had a terminal illness.

"I don't want it to get *easier*," Hallie snapped. "I want to see my boyfriend!" By then, the tears were running into her mouth, and onto her chin.

Nick stood in the doorway, the shadows on his face emphasized the light that poured through the door. "You want to know Maria Silva's worst mistake?" he asked finally. "She thought she could save Codfish. Even when her own life was threatened, she kept believing she could save him. I'm sorry, Hallie, but I won't allow that to happen to you."

Hallie blinked back fiery tears, as the objections formed in her throat. *Gus was not like the Captain. He was nothing like him.* But when she looked again, the doorway was empty; her father was gone. All that remained were the dust motes spinning in the light and the echo of his words.

*H*allie *had been home for three* weeks, growing stronger and more lucid every day. She had been eager to see her friends, but when Felicia and Daisy pivoted quickly away from the subject of Gus, she stopped taking their calls.

Then one day Hallie heard the coltish click of Felicia's heels on the stairs, her friend's impatient hammering on the door. "I'm not taking no for an answer, Hallie. Open up," Felicia demanded. When that didn't work, she wheedled: "*Please?* I've got music, and a ton of gossip—even a couple of your precious books."

"That's not what I want and you know it," Hallie called back.

Felicia released an audible sigh. "I swear, Hallie—I haven't seen him. No one has. And even if I knew where he was . . ."

In spite of her weakness, Hallie climbed out of bed and made her way to the door. *"Even if you knew—what? Finish the sentence."*

Felicia seemed stunned by her friend's pallor, the hand that shook as it held the door.

"You need to get back in bed, Hal," she said, gently taking her elbow.

But Hallie just shook her off as she glared defiantly. "Finish the sentence, Felicia."

"Listen, you almost freakin' died out there on the Point whether you know it or not. Your dad's worried about you, okay? Nick only let me come because I promised on my life that I won't talk about . . . *him."* Felicia's voice sunk to a whisper as she pronounced that last word.

Hallie looked her directly in the eye before she firmly closed the door. Though she believed Felicia, she couldn't pretend to carry on a normal conversation until her questions were answered.

Images of Gus tormented her. Gus in his blue scarf on prom night, or regarding her with a mixture of skepticism and vulnerability that day she found him smoking in the church. The mute child, his hair askew from lying on his bed all day, looking at her with eyes that had swallowed the whole world and all its sorrow. Gus climbing the rickety ladder to the roof, the brightness of a starry night eclipsed by the yearning on his face.

No one would ever know him as well as she did. Nor would anyone else understand what the accident on the Point would do to him or where it would take him. *Fucked-up for life . . .* Neil had called him. Hallie shut out the words, her memory of Neil's thick, sour breath.

Nick was surprised when she asked if she might have a phone installed in her room. Though he was glad that she was well enough to want something—*anything*—he balked. "You know I'd love to hear you talking to your friends the way you used to, but you also need to spend less time in your room. If you want to call from the kitchen, I promise not to listen in . . ."

But when Hallie continued to beg, he relented. "One caveat," he said, when he entered the room with a slender phone. "Don't try to contact the Silva boy. And no calls from his buddy, either."

"I have nothing to say to Neil—not ever. But do you really think that anyone can keep me away from Gus? If you don't want me to talk to him in your house, I'll find another way."

Nick, who was sitting at the table checking his schedule for the day, closed his appointment book and returned her gaze. "Don't you understand? Gus will be in serious trouble if he speaks to you."

"What happened that night was an accident, Nick. I've told you that—"

"Was it an accident what he did to Neil Gallagher's face? Not that the *cuzo* didn't deserve it. But Gus could have killed you, Hallie—whether he intended to or not," Nick said softly. "The kid's lucky he's not in prison. *Damn* lucky."

"So you're saying he's *not* in jail? Then where is he? Why won't anyone tell me?"

Nick rose from the chair to go to the office as he did every day, but that morning he looked particularly tired. "If you try to call him, he won't talk to you. Gus has . . . something else in his life now, *someone* else. He doesn't want to see you."

Someone else—Gus? It was impossible. "That's a lie!"

"I'm sorry, Hallie. I didn't mean to blurt it out like that, but sooner or later, you had to find out."

Hallie refused the Valium he offered, and she pushed away the steaming cup that Aunt Del brought later.

"I don't want tea, Aunt Del. I want answers. Gus *couldn't*—" Hallie began before something she saw on Del's face stopped her in mid-sentence. She realized she was shaking violently. This time, when she was offered the small blue pill, she accepted it.

The next day, though, she steeled herself and picked up the small white phone. In spite of what she'd promised her father, what she vowed to *herself*, the first number Hallie dialed was Neil's. She still had no desire to talk to him, but if anyone would tell her what she needed to know, he would.

Neil seemed as shaken by her voice as she was by his. "Please, Hallie. Don't hang up. I know I can never explain, but—"

"No, you can't," Hallie said, closing her eyes against the images that rose against her wishes. "You can never explain; and right now, it would probably kill me if you tried."

The line went quiet.

Finally, Neil said, "Then why—" Then he stopped himself. "Of course. You're calling to ask about Gus, and here I am thinking about myself again."

Hallie's head hurt. Was he being sincere or sarcastic? Somehow her brain couldn't tell the difference anymore. Nick was right: it had been a mistake to call him.

Before she could put down the receiver, he spoke again, "I mean it, Hal. You've been through hell; you probably have no idea where Gus is; and the first thing I do is dump my guilt on you."

"So you've talked to him, then? After everything that's happened, you two—"

Neil hesitated. "It's not the same, and it probably never will be if that's what you want to know, but yeah, I had to see him."

Not wanting to think about that reuinion, Hallie repeated what her father had said verbatim . . . *Gus has . . . someone else. He doesn't want to see you.* It had been so difficult to speak the words that she felt herself growing breathless, as if she'd run across the dunes. "It's not true, is it, Gallagher?" she finally asked. "It can't be true."

At first, she thought Neil had put the phone down, or they'd lost their connection. But then she realized that the silence on the other end of the line was his answer.

She hung up, and waited for it to ring again, but the phone remained eerily silent. More than anything, Hallie needed to get out of bed and scale the ladder to her roof, where she could think. But when she opened the door to the third floor, she saw shadows of herself and Gus in every corner. It was as if she had stepped directly into that night of beginning, and experienced it again. Even her private church would be contaminated with Gus's presence now. Exhausted, she stumbled back to her room and locked the door as if she'd been chased away by her own ghost.

Two days later, Neil finally called back. He didn't bother with social niceties. "Gus wants to see you. Not now. And definitely not at your house. But when you're strong enough to come out to the Point, he wants to talk to you one more time."

"*One more time?* What are you saying, Gallagher?"

There was a long pause.

"He's going away, Hal," Neil finally said. "I'd say more, but I don't really understand it myself. Anyway, he wants to be the one to tell you."

Hallie felt a thickening in her throat. "God, Neil, *tell me*! Is he going to jail?" she asked, wondering if her father had lied to protect her.

"No, nothing like that. There wasn't even a trial."

"So they realized it was an accident?" Hallie was flooded with a mix of relief and confusion. If Gus wasn't being physically kept from her, then why wasn't he here?

"Not exactly, but he had a great lawyer; a couple of pillars of the community came forward to speak for him; and I certainly wasn't going to testify against him. It could have gone a lot worse."

"But he didn't do anything wrong—" Hallie began, and then she thought of Neil, his lanky body unresisting, being smashed repeatedly onto the hood of the Jeep.

"Listen, I gotta go, but I'll be in touch, okay?" Neil said.

Throughout August, Hallie redoubled her efforts to regain her strength. During the weeks she'd been in the hospital, her muscles had atrophied; but above all, her brain was tired. Tired of trying to arrange the thoughts in her head, of organizing her words so people would understand what she meant, of trying to get out of bed when there seemed so little reason to do so. Everyone told her how lucky she'd been, how little cognitive or physical damage she displayed on various charts and scales. Her prognosis was excellent. But she, who had always felt like the luckiest of girls, now inhabited a treacherous universe. Was there a scale to measure that, she wondered.

Only when she heard that Gus was going away did her urgent sense of purpose return. Finally, she had a goal: she had to get strong enough to see him; *she had to change his mind.* For the last two weeks, she'd worked hard, performing her physical therapy twice a day like the high achiever she was. She began taking walks around the yard, and then to the corner, and finally into town, where people poked their heads out of shop doors and apartment windows to greet her.

Everyone seemed to be rooting for her. Even Wolf was now making regular visits to the house for the first time in two years. He had come because he was missing a saw and thought he might have left it behind. Or because he forgot the color of the sky in one of the paintings he'd abandoned in the empty bedrooms and he needed to know. He'd come because after years of drinking Nick's abominable coffee, nothing else was quite strong enough to jolt him awake. Usually, he just stayed long enough to bolt a cup of the dark brew and to peek in on Hallie. If she was awake, he grumbled an angry, unpracticed *Hello!* and quickly escaped, his footsteps clattering down the stairs as if he were being pursued. But if he thought she was asleep, he would pace around the room, watching her and muttering cholerically, the way he had once done in the attic. Much of his grumbling was incoherent, but sometimes Hallie heard him cursing *the stupid boy,* or *the stupid girl,* or his own stupidity for caring. In her bed, she cried silently for all of them.

CHAPTER 14

Finally, three days before Labor Day, Neil called to say the meeting was set. He even offered to drive her out to the Point. It had been easy for her to absolve Gus for nearly killing her, but she didn't think she could ever forgive Neil. Whenever she thought of him, the memories came back in hard, violent shards. The drunken kiss. Her exposed breast. Him calling her a bitch. *Nick's pampered little bitch.* Was it possible that her friend had really thought that of her all along? And then there were the things he'd said about Gus.

But most of all, she couldn't forgive him for loving her. For *still* loving her. She could hear it in his voice.

"Thanks, but I'll get out there on my own," she said before she hung up.

The day of the planned meeting Felicia drove her to the beach. "Did Neil tell you where he'd be?" she said when they reached the parking lot.

"He didn't have to tell me. I know." It was where they always went—beyond the area where tourists set up their patchwork of towels, the same place where they had built a bonfire on prom night.

Exhausted from the walk, she sat and waited until she spotted Gus in the distance. As usual, he was running. Even far off, everything about him was familiar—from the dark-blue track shorts he wore to the black of his hair against the sky and the disciplined, fluid motion of his body. She had thought of him so much that the sight felt like a kind of miracle. *He really existed; she hadn't imagined him after all.*

He stopped a good yard away from her, still breathing hard from his run, but he was looking at her the same way—as if he could hardly believe she was really there.

"You look good," he said at last. His eyes were wet.

"You, too—beautiful." Hallie wondered if he remembered the last time they had said those words to each other. They were only yards from the spot where they had camped that night in a single sleeping bag.

She waited for him to come closer, to pull her up and embrace her, but he remained frozen where he was. That didn't matter, though, Hallie told herself. He was *there*. He was *right there*, and he obviously still loved her. How had she ever doubted it? She got up and took a loping step toward him, until she was close enough to inhale his familiar smell—tobacco, the fresh sweat from his run, and the most intoxicating scent of all—*just Gus*.

But instead of reaching for her, Gus looked out over the water, hands resting on his hips. "I don't deserve to see you, Hallie," he said, as if beginning a prepared and difficult speech. "But I appreciate you coming out here."

Appreciate you coming out here? He sounded like one of Nick's patients after a house call.

"So, you're okay?" he asked, turning back to her. "You're *really* okay? Everyone told me you were doing better than anyone expected, but I had to see for myself. Just once, I had to see."

"Physically, the doctors and therapists say I've made remarkable progress. But okay? *Without you?*" Hallie was unable to quell the tremor in her voice. "Can't you at least give me a hug? I'm dying here." It was exactly what she *didn't* want to say, but standing this close to him, there was no way to keep back the truth, or the tears that rolled down her cheeks.

But Gus remained where he was. Hallie followed his gaze out over the sea.

"I promised I wouldn't see you again, Hallie," he said. "And I intend to keep my word. But before I do, there's something I need to tell you."

"Who would ask you to make a promise like that?" But even as Hallie spoke the question out loud, she already knew the answer. *Nick.* Aside from Gus, the person she loved most in the world. She wondered what her father had given Gus in return. Had he paid for the high-priced attorney that Neil told her about? Maybe even shown up in court in his ancient suit, the frayed red tie he pulled out for funerals and weddings? Had he testified on Gus's behalf—not merely as a "pillar of the community" but as the father of the victim?

"He had no right," Hallie said. "This is my life we're talking about here. Our lives." A new rage sluiced through Hallie's blood. At Nick, who had betrayed her in the name of protecting her. At an anonymous court system that knew neither her nor Gus, but thought it had a right to decide her fate. At everyone who had withheld the truth from her. But especially at Gus. She would have served fifty years in prison before she agreed to give him up. Had he been willing to sacrifice their future—to sacrifice *her*—for a favorable outcome in court?

As if reading her mind, Gus said, "I didn't do it for them, Hallie. The only promise that ever mattered to me was the one I made to you."

"What are you talking about?"

Gus took a long, deep breath. "Don't you remember that day in the cemetery?"

"Do I remember? *Everything* began that day for me," Hallie whispered, once again fighting tears.

"No, it didn't," Gus said. "You had an incredible life before me, and you'll have it after I'm gone. It's in your eyes right now; I can see it. You are so strong, Hallie—more strong—"

She interrupted before he could finish. "We said we'd always tell each other the truth. Even when we couldn't tell anyone else. *That's* the promise I remember from the cemetery."

"There was another one, though. Maybe you didn't hear it; maybe you took it for granted. But I didn't. I couldn't. I was sitting on my mother's grave when I promised I'd never hurt you."

"It was an accident, Gus. You didn't—"

But something steely and distant in Gus stopped her. "I asked you to come out here because there's something I have to say," he said, meeting her eyes with a disconcerting directness. "I didn't want you to hear it from anyone else."

An image of Reggie Aluto came into her mind. All the girls and women who were drawn to Gus. Was it possible Nick was right—that there was someone else?

"I'm going away," Gus said, intruding on her thoughts with the words that had haunted her since Neil first spoke them. "I'm—"

"No, *we*—we're going away. To Montana. Remember, Gus? We're going to live someplace so open that nothing can limit us. We're going to a town where no one remembers what happened to your mother, or looks at me and sees Nick's daughter. I know my accident slowed us down, but we can still—"

She hated the way her words rushed out in a panicky torrent and the note of pleading she heard in them.

"That was a great dream, Hallie. And if I was someone else—"

"I never wanted you to be anyone else; you know that."

She was sure that he was about to hug her like he always did when she cried. Draw her close and say that *of course*, he knew that. And of course they'd go to Montana, just like they'd planned.

But instead he looked at her, his eyes full of the blinding compassion that had drawn people to him since he was a small boy. "I'm entering the seminary as a postulant in three days, Hallie. I know it must sound crazy to you. How could it not? But it's the right decision for me."

He reached out to take her hand, but Hallie jerked away. "The *seminary*?" The words made no sense. Though she knew he found solace in the quiet of an empty church, he never even attended mass.

"Is this a joke? You—a *priest*? No one does that anymore, Gus," she blurted out. "I didn't even know you really believed all that stuff."

"Well, I do. I believe it, Hallie. Don't you remember when you found me that day in St. Pete's? You must have known—"

"You were *drunk*—drunk and grief-stricken and smoking cigarettes on Old Man D'Souza's hallowed ground. Now you're trying to tell me that you were having a religious experience?"

"You're right, I *was* drunk. Drunk and screwed-up—just like Neil said I was. Probably more so. But I went to the church for a reason. It's where I've always gone when—"

Hallie took a dazed step backwards, stumbling in the sand. "Don't try to make this about God, okay? Because it's not. This is some crazy guilt trip you put on yourself because of what happened to me."

"Not what happened to you—what *I did to you*. Do you think I can just forget that?"

"It was a drunken accident, Gus," Hallie pleaded. "And it's never, ever going to happen again."

"You might believe that, Hallie—and you know why? Because you don't have it in you to hurt anyone. But me? Well, obviously I do. I beat Neil badly, and I almost killed you."

"It's not true. And even if it was, do you really think that becoming a priest is the answer? If the Church wasn't so desperate, they wouldn't even consider you."

"Maybe they are desperate, but so was I. So *am* I—and you know what? It's okay. In fact, some people would say desperation is the first step toward redemption."

"What people—*Father D'Souza?*" Hallie snapped. "Don't you think a religious vocation should be about more than running away?"

Gus sat down in the sand and folded his arms loosely around his knees. "I suppose I *was* running away at first, and the church was the perfect hiding place. None of my friends would think to look for me there, and since half the police force belongs to the parish, they wouldn't say much."

"So that's where you've been all summer?" Hallie asked, sitting beside him.

"The first couple of nights, I slept on the pews; then I'd hide in the confessional when a few parishioners straggled in for the morning mass. I guess I thought I was getting away with something till Father D'Souza pulled open the curtain one morning. 'If you're going to stay here,' he said, 'you better come over to the rectory for breakfast. I can't have anyone starving in my church. What have you been eating?' I pulled out an empty bag of Doritos I'd taken from Fatima's house before I left. Believe me, my first impulse was to take off right then and there, but I was so hungry I would've sold my soul for breakfast."

"It sounds like you did."

Gus laughed wryly, but Hallie refused to return his smile. "Father D'Souza is an old crank who's mad at the world, and you know it. Probably because no one cares about his church anymore."

"I admit the guy's a little old-fashioned. And, yeah, he might push the fire-and-brimstone bit too far. But he took me in when the whole town was ready to lock me up in my father's cell. He took me in and didn't judge me."

I didn't judge you, either. I never judged you, Hallie thought, recalling the summer she'd spent defending him. She had never stopped believing in him.

"I couldn't stay at my aunt's house anymore," Gus continued. "Between Fatima crying and Manny screaming about what a typical piece of Silva shit I was, I couldn't take it. Besides, Sean and Daisy, and everyone else from town, they were all showing up constantly. I didn't want to see anyone. I couldn't."

It was the first thing he'd said that Hallie truly understood. "I didn't want to see anyone either," she said, then lowered her voice to the intimate whisper that had always pulled him to her in the past. "Just you."

Gus gazed in the direction of the Race Point Light as if he hadn't heard her. "That day over breakfast, Father D'Souza gave me the lecture of my life. Then he offered me a spare room in the rectory. Nothing but a bed and a dresser and a little cross on the wall."

"The old coot probably realized you were vulnerable."

"It wasn't like that; he left me on my own. The cook even served me supper in my room."

"What did you do all day?" Hallie thought of the weeks she'd spent in a hospital bed, but even there, she'd had her father's daily presence, the staff who had become friends during her stay, and the rhythms of the ICU and then the floor where she was transferred to anchor her.

"At first, I thought I was going to lose my mind. Then I remembered that Sean's father found a stash of booze when he went to fix the sink at the rectory—gifts from parishioners who didn't know Father D'Souza was a teetotaler. Mostly it was sweet *vinho*, the kind my grandmother used to drink, but I didn't care. As soon as he went out to say the seven-o'clock mass the next morning, I snuck down and got a bottle. I know it didn't make any sense. I mean, alcohol had ruined my life twice, but I didn't know where else to turn. I stayed drunk for two weeks straight."

"I was waiting for you," Hallie whispered. "Even when I could hardly speak, I called for you."

"You asked for me? They never told me when I checked with the hospital—"

"Just like no one ever told me you called."

"I didn't leave my name. I was considered a threat to you."

Hallie closed her eyes. If they could have spoken—even once—when she was in the hospital, would they be sitting here now? Would she be listening to his desperate plan? In her mind, she cursed everyone who had kept him away: the nurses who had pretended to be her friends, the police, *her father.* "So you crashed at the rectory and stayed drunk for two weeks? Then what? You realized you had to stop?"

"More like I ran out. One day, I went to look for a bottle under the kitchen sink and there was nothing left. When I looked up, a strange little man was standing over me in a T-shirt and his polka-dotted boxers. I'd never seen Father D'Souza without his collar before."

"Has anyone? I thought he was born in it."

"So there he was—no longer the powerful priest, bellowing from the lectern, but a feeble old man. 'It's gone,' the old man said. 'And it doesn't look like it worked very well, does it? Maybe it's time to try something stronger.'"

"Let me guess. He was talking about *prayer.*" Hallie struggled to keep the skepticism out of her voice. Though she hadn't been brought up in a church, she found the words to many of the prayers she read beautiful, especially the St. Francis Peace Prayer. And occasionally, when she was in trouble, she secretly found herself importuning some unseen force for help. But now all she could feel was resentment at a Church that had tricked him into a vocation.

"Probably. But at that moment, I couldn't even think," Gus said, impervious to her anger. "I had become someone I promised myself I would never be. I was my father—a violent, jealous drunk who would do anything to get what he wanted. That night I called my cousin, Sunny, in New Bedford."

"Sunny? You mean the—"

"That's the one. The crack addict. Or maybe it's heroin now. Whatever she can get her hands on. She hadn't heard from me in years, but an addict is always happy to bring someone into the fold. I told her I was coming down. Could she hook me up? I was hoping I'd OD before the cops ever caught up with me."

"But you never went," Hallie said, almost disappointed. It seemed that anything—even drug addiction—would have been easier to fight than what now possessed Gus.

"I made it onto Route 6, and the first car stopped for me. It was sputtering along at about thirty miles an hour."

"D'Souza." Hallie recalled the jokes she'd heard about the priest's driving. "The old buzzard followed you."

"Honestly, I wasn't gonna get in the car, but you know him—he plays hardball. He threatened to send me back to my aunt's house. And I couldn't do that—no matter what. My room was so full of you, I could taste you as soon as I went in there. When I woke up in the middle of the night, I felt your hair spilling across my chest. If I even walked through the door, I knew I'd break."

It was the first time he'd acknowledged their afternoons in the house on Loop Street, or that *he loved her*. But as he spoke, he looked out on the ocean, as if he were seeing something far away, not something real and vital the way it felt to Hallie.

"We'll be together like that again, Gus. Not in Junior's room, but in our own place. In Montana." This time, though, her voice no longer sounded convincing—even to herself.

When he looked at her, she saw the anguish on his face. But also an unmistakable resolve.

She steered the conversation back to the highway, where his story had the potential to turn out differently. She imagined Gus standing before the priest's hearselike black Buick, making one of the most critical decisions of his life while the old crank stared him down. "So you went back," she said.

"I went back and hid in the spare bedroom at the rectory, but there was no escaping myself. I felt the insane rage I experienced when I saw you and Neil together. I didn't just remember it, Hallie. I *felt* it—heart hammering, fists ready to pound someone, the whole thing. You want to know the worst of it?"

Hallie wanted to say no; she didn't want to know, but she couldn't summon the word.

"The worst was how *good* it felt when I was hitting Neil. Like being on the field under the lights, the whole town cheering for me. A minute on the clock, I had the ball, and no one, no matter how fast they ran, was ever gonna stop me. Except this time someone did."

"*Me*," she whispered.

"One thing you need to know: no matter how crazy I was that night, I never meant to hurt you. I was going for Neil—and out of nowhere, you were there. I don't care if the judge believed that or this whole stupid town believed it, but it's important to me that you do."

"Do you think I ever questioned that?" Hallie asked.

"The next thing I knew you were on the ground. You weren't moving, and there was blood in your hair. I didn't live it once, Hallie; I lived it a thousand times a day. I'll probably never stop living it."

"I've got something I wanted to say to you since that night, too. One thing *you* need to know: I never kissed Neil and I never wanted to. There was never anything—"

"You think I don't know that?" Gus reached out to touch her face, but then retracted his hand. "The problem wasn't you; it wasn't even Neil. It was *me*. The way I reacted when I saw your dress—it was like a bomb went off inside me. Something that had been dormant for a long time. If it hadn't exploded that night, it would have happened another time."

"It was five in the morning, and you'd been drinking all night. It isn't who you are, Gus. And even if it was, do you think your God can change that?"

"He already has," Gus said quietly. "Once the booze was gone; once I stopped cursing myself and my blood, there was nothing left but me and that quiet room. By the time I was ready to go downstairs and sit at the table with Father D, I wasn't the same person."

When he finished speaking, a calm had replaced the grief in his eyes. Finally, Hallie understood that all her protests were useless. Her father was right: Gus belonged to someone else now; and even if his new love seemed like an illusion to Hallie, it was utterly real to him.

She felt a surge of fury to think that a few weeks in the rectory could have stolen both their future and their past. *How could he just forget that he loved her?*

"So you brought me out here to tell me you were going away before I heard the gossip in Nick's waiting room? That's really thoughtful of you, Gus. I appreciate it."

"It's not like that—"

"I didn't understand what my father was hinting at, but he knew," Hallie said. "I guess everyone who visited me knew. Felicia and Daisy—people I ran into at Ina's. Everyone. Hell, even Wolf probably knew."

"Felicia and Daisy knew I wanted to tell you myself, that I had to see you before I let you go." This time when Gus looked at her, it was as if he really did see her.

But Hallie was thinking about the weeks she had spent in the hospital, and cosseted in her room, fighting to get well enough to be with him, weeks Gus had used to leave her behind, and find a new vocation.

"So now I'm supposed to say goodbye like an old friend and pretend I understand, right?" she said. "Pretend you're doing it for *me*? Is that what I'm supposed to do? Well, you want to know the truth? What you're doing right now is far worse than anything I went through in the hospital, and a thousand times more painful than what happened on the Point. So fuck you, Gus Silva. *Fuck you*."

Tears blinding her, Hallie turned and started up the beach. Gus called her name just once. The sound of the gulls cut through her like a late-October wind. She kicked off her sandals and walked faster. At first she felt dizzy and weak, but then she forgot what her body was or wasn't ready to do and just ran. She felt the sand kicking up behind her, and Gus's eyes as he watched her disappear. And she also felt the truth growing stronger with every step: Gus wouldn't come after her. Not this time. Not ever again.

That fall, when most of her friends left for college, Hallie stayed home and walked. Every morning she walked from the East End, where she lived, to Loop Street in the West End. She stood across the street from Manny and Fatima's forlorn cottage with its dangling shutter and the fallen Madonna out front, wondering what drove her there. Did she expect to see Gus, bounding out the front door the way he once did every morning, hungry to see her? Or maybe the shadow of the girl who had waited for him on the porch? The foolish girl who had laughed as easily as she breathed.

From Loop Street, she'd go back home for her bike and ride out to Route 6. It was a long trek through the dunes to Wolf's shack, but every day she brought him a Thermos of coffee. He always greeted her the same way: "What the fuck, Hallie? Don't you know I'm trying to work out here?"

But as she had when she was a child, she found solace watching Wolf paint.

In the afternoon, she'd wander into her father's office for lunch and end up hanging around. She'd help Aunt Del with the paperwork, smiling as Nick joked with his patients or castigated an elderly woman in Portuguese for refusing to follow orders. Gradually, Hallie began to take on more responsibilities. She learned to take blood pressure readings to help Leah out on busy days and researched nutritional information for patients on special diets. And when her father brought home the files for a particularly challenging case, she studied them, too.

Occasionally, in the evenings, she'd drive around with Felicia and Reggie, who had ended up staying in town, and the three of them would share a six-pack or a bottle of fruity wine on the beach. They'd talk about movies, and the beauty school Felicia was attending in Hyannis, and how *boring* Provincetown was in the winter. They'd bemoan the fact that all the best-looking men in town were gay, and then swear they didn't care about guys anyway. The only subject that was off limits was the past.

But wherever she went, she felt his shadow. He walked out of the sea; he called her name from the top of the monument; he sat on a bench in the center of town near the memorial where members of both their families were listed among the war dead. Once, in a dream that left her particularly shaken, he walked into the office wearing the black T-shirt from Lou's, and smiled at her the way he had on the day of his father's funeral.

*N*eil had his own way of coming back, too. Hallie turned her head when she caught sight of a red Jeep, or spotted a rangy boy in a white dishwasher's outfit like the one he wore for his summer job. Even the sight of the school bus where they had first become friends filled her with a private ache. Time made the "accident" on Race Point increasingly unreal, but her friendship with Neil was something tangible.

She wasn't sure she was ready to forgive him, but as the weeks passed, she knew she had to see him again. Thanksgiving break gave her the opportunity she was waiting for when she heard that Neil was home alone. Although his family had gone to Boston for the weekend, he had insisted on remaining behind.

The Friday after the holiday, Hallie borrowed Nick's truck and drove to the West End. Steeling herself, she knocked on the door—at first tentatively and then more insistently but there was no response. She was in the driveway heading toward the truck when Neil appeared on the porch. Despite an unseasonable cold snap, he was wearing only ripped jeans and a New York Knicks shirt and his feet were bare. He didn't speak.

"Wanna go out for coffee?" she finally asked.

Neil shook his head. "Not a chance."

Hallie was about to leave when he continued. "If we walked into Ina's together, half the town would know every word we said before we made it home. But you can come in here—that is, if you're not afraid of me."

Hallie could see the bones of his shoulders protruding through his T-shirt. She followed him through the house and into the kitchen Neil's mother had decorated in a seashell motif.

"Sorry, but I don't know how to make coffee," he said, studying her as he leaned against a counter. He indicated the table with its severely angled chairs. "You want to sit?"

She noticed that he'd gotten an ear pierced, and that his hair had grown shaggier. Her eyes were drawn to a scar on his cheek that was shaped like a crescent moon, an obvious souvenir of the night on the Point.

"I don't know what I want, Neil," she said. "I just know I had to come. Ever since you and Gus went away, I've been trying to understand how it happened. How any of it happened . . ."

Neil took a step forward to hug her like he had done a thousand times before, but then retreated. He slouched into a kitchen chair and put his face in his hands.

"*How it happened*. It's my undeclared major. I'm practically flunking out of school, Hal, because all I can think of is that night. The horrible stuff I said. What I fucking *did*. Last summer, when I called you, I wanted to apologize. Imagine that? As if any apology in the world could cover it."

"I'd like to say I'm sorry that you're in pain, but I'm not. I can't be, Neil."

"You think I want you to be *sorry for me*? That's the last thing I want," Neil said.

"Why didn't you ever tell me you were the one who wrote the note?" Her voice was so low that she wasn't sure it was audible.

Neil reddened. "Shit, Hallie. I'd been telling you how I felt all my life. I thought you'd know it was me—"

"And when I didn't?"

"You mean, when you immediately assumed it was Gus? Well, it was clear who you wanted it to be, no matter what you said in the dunes. I thought you and Gus would eventually talk about it, and I'd have to admit the truth, but you never did."

"When he didn't bring it up, I thought he was embarrassed by it. Or maybe that I'd been wrong."

"But still, you never connected the dots."

"Like you said, I wanted to believe it was Gus."

Neil nodded. At that moment he reminded her more of his child self than ever. His nose was running, and his eyes were leaking, and the scar on his cheek had turned a flame color that nearly matched his hair. Hallie handed him a tissue.

"I guess we were all wounded that night, weren't we?" she whispered. She wasn't even aware that she was crying herself until Neil pushed the tissue box in her direction.

He was still sitting at the kitchen table with his head in his hands when Hallie let herself out.

A few days later she called Sean Mello and got Neil's number at school. She dialed immediately before she could change her mind.

"I just wanted to tell you I've been thinking about what you said, Gallagher. I'm not a judge, but I want you to know one thing: what you did that night was horrible, maybe even unforgivable, but you didn't ruin anyone's life. Gus is out there doing what he wants to do, no matter how much it kills me; and someday you're going to be a famous actor. And me? Don't count me out yet, either." Then, before he had a chance to respond, she hung up.

She didn't know what the revelation did for Neil, because he didn't call her back. But it released something in her. She stopped passing by the house on Loop Street in the morning. Though she still dreamed of Gus, the dreams were less frequent; and shaking them off in the morning, less painful. When she took her daily walks, the past still accosted her like the Black Flash, a legendary ghost that all of the older people swore they'd seen at least once during the lonely winters in Provincetown. But increasingly she was too preoccupied to stop for it. The future, *her* future, was a fire that burned more brightly inside her every day.

*O*ne *pristine winter evening when she* and Nick were walking home from Cap's, sated and entranced by the stars, her father stopped dead. "You always used to sing around the house. Ever since you first learned 'Twinkle, Twinkle,'" he said. "I miss it."

She shrugged and kept walking. "I guess I lost that in the accident," she said over her shoulder.

"Lost what—your singing voice?"

"No. Just the desire to sing." She wasn't ready to admit that she was afraid of what her voice might contain.

Nick hitched the backpack he substituted for the traditional black bag up on his shoulder and resumed walking. "It will come back," he said.

"Yes, it will," Hallie said, feeling a surge of the optimism that had been slowly building since Thanksgiving. "It will be different, maybe, but it will come back."

Nick studied her obliquely. "In the meantime, what are you going to do with your life?" he asked. It was the first time in months that he had suggested she might want to do more than visit Wolf, putter in the office, and read with him in the study in the evenings.

"Do I have to *do* something? Can't I just stay here and be Hallie, like I always was?"

"Just *be*? Might be fine for a Zen monk or an old hippie, but not for my Pie."

"In case you haven't noticed, I'm not your Pie anymore. I'm all grown-up, and I get to decide my own future." Hallie speeded up slightly when she noticed nosy Mavis Black scurrying to catch up with them. Mavis was waving wildly, the eyebrows she'd painted orange to match her hair lifted in interest at the raised voices.

"You're also someone who has a lot to give. And if you don't find a way to give it, you might be the proud master of your own fate, but you'll never be happy," Nick said, turning back to confront her.

Then, spotting the woman he called his favorite hypochondriac, he cupped his hand and whispered, "Look at poor Victoria. Mavis has got that poor dog dressed up like something out of *Dr. Zhivago*."

Hallie giggled.

Though she couldn't have heard their voices, Mavis got the idea that the doctor was avoiding her. She harrumphed so loudly that even Nick laughed; and when Hallie finally turned around, Mavis and her fur-clad dog were trotting at a huffy clip in the opposite direction.

They walked the next half-mile in easy silence, Nick's question still between them: What was she going to do with the rest of her life? The answer had been growing inside her throughout the long fall as she helped out in the office, as she and her father discussed a particularly tricky diagnosis in the study at night. She wondered if he'd seen the new batch of catalogues that had arrived in the mail from Duke and Tufts.

"Okay, I'm going to apply to a couple of schools for next year, but I'm especially interested in Berkeley."

"I hear they have an excellent premed program." Though he tried to sound cool, Nick couldn't quite pull it off.

"Nick! You already *knew*!"

"I've known since you were a little girl. And so have you. I was just waiting for you to remember."

Waiting for me to forget, is more like it, Hallie thought, following her father as he turned the corner. It was the exact spot where Gus had left her that afternoon when she found him in the church. But now she felt a different kind of possibility opening up inside her, and this time she passed the corner without allowing herself to sink back into that moment with Gus.

The truth was no longer something to be argued with, or even mourned. It was just the truth: Gus wasn't coming back. Her old strength and energy coursed through her veins. It hadn't come from Gus, and he couldn't take it away. Her father was right. She had something to give, something to *do*; and give and do she would.

"It's pretty far away," she said, a little offended that her father hadn't balked at the distance that would be between them.

"Far away is hard, but sometimes it's good—necessary even." Nick stopped where he was. "There are too many shadows around here. If you stay in Massachusetts, you might never escape them."

Like you? Hallie thought, but didn't say it out loud. Instead, she turned and hugged him the way she used to when she was a little girl. He returned it with a bone-crushing Costa *abraço*, lifting her off her feet.

By then, they were standing outside their front gate. When Stuart pulled his Saab into the driveway next door, Nick waved wildly.

"Hey, Stuart!" Nick yelled before their neighbor had a chance to climb out of his car. "Have you heard? Hallie's gonna be a doctor!"

Embarrassed, Hallie rolled her eyes. "Don't listen to him, Stuart." And then to her father: "I'm applying to an undergrad program, Nick. Don't get the lab coats monogrammed yet, okay?"

But, as ever, when Nick was excited about something, whether it was an outburst from Coleman Hawkins' saxophone or the discovery of a new star, there was no keeping him quiet. Hallie threw up her hands helplessly in Stuart's direction. Then they both laughed as Nick raced into the middle of the street, and turned toward the center of town, making his hands a megaphone. "You hear that, Provincetown? My daughter's gonna be a doctor! A *doctor*!"

PART THREE

ST. BEN'S

{ 1999 }

G*us had been at St. Benedict's* for six years, assisting in
the parish and serving as chaplain in the hospital, when the
woman showed up. Normally, he would have been downstairs watching the Red Sox game with his pastor, Jack, and
their housekeeper's daughter. Julia, who turned fifteen that
year, claimed she didn't like sports, but she seemed to enjoy
the blare and hum from the TV and the grumbling banter
between the two priests as she studied. But on this particular Monday, Gus announced he was going to bed early and
headed for his room.

"*You*—miss a game against the Yankees? What's the matter? You pick up a bug at the hospital or something?" Jack
said, following him to the bottom of the stairs. Gus's dogs
were confused, too. When she realized he wasn't coming
down again, Jane, a Lab mix with dolorous eyes and an over-
protective streak, crept up the stairs loyally, while Stella, the
rat terrier, tucked in her tail and clattered off toward the
familiar drone of the game. Both dogs had been inherited from terminal patients Gus met during his rounds at the
hospital.

"You might say that. But don't worry; it's nothing a good
night's sleep won't cure," Gus said, stroking Jane's ears as he
avoided Jack's eyes.

In his room, Gus lay down, arms folded behind his head,
and studied the ceiling. His old friend Neil Gallagher had
called earlier to say he was in Wellfleet, playing in summer
stock again, and he was planning a reunion of their old high

school crowd. Would Gus be there? After all this time, it shouldn't have bothered him, but somehow the call derailed his day.

For eight years after Neil left for New York and Gus entered the seminary, they had kept their distance. But when Neil's brother, Liam, took a job in Emergency Services at Cape Cod Hospital, he began to pass news between the two former friends. *Neil's in a play Off Broadway . . . an amazing performance . . . He's waiting to hear about a part he really wants. Something big . . . He worked with this prestigious director (whom Gus had never heard of) . . . that well-known actor (ditto.) He was nominated for a Tony in a supporting role.* There were a dizzying series of girlfriends, a tall redhead, a gorgeous Colombian, a dancer who promised to leave her husband but didn't.

Sometimes he wondered what Liam said about him. That he ran on the beach and swam all year? He said mass? He comforted the sick and the dying? He watched sports with Jack and played touch football on the lawn outside the rectory with Julia? And then, the next day, he did the same thing again? There were no awards. No triumphs. No stunning announcements or crushing disappointments. Yet his life had never been fuller. How could he explain that to Neil?

Gus picked up *The Rule of St. Benedict*, which Jack had given him for a recent birthday. He was usually too exhausted in the evenings to read, but now he opened it to the prologue. His eyes settled on the words *Run while you have the light of life lest the darkness of death overtake you.* They described the urgency that had driven him since he was a child, and the reason he felt so used up at the end of the day.

He'd only got through a few paragraphs when he heard a knock at the front door, first so light that Gus thought he might have imagined it, and then more resolute. The sound of someone who wouldn't disappear until they were heard.

He listened for Jack's predictable grumbling as he headed for the door. "They just won't leave me alone, will they? Even when the bases are loaded. Julia, let me know if they score."

Gus waited for Jack to invite whoever it might be into the living room to watch the game. There in the middle of his usual sports talk, they would manage to get to the heart of whatever the visitor had come to share.

He could almost see Julia frowning in annoyance that her family time had been interrupted. Then she would gather her books and scurry back up to the apartment she shared with her mother above the garage.

"Night, Dad," she teased before she retreated up the back stairway.

Detecting the susurrus of a female murmuring, Gus got up and pushed open his door.

"I'm sorry, but Father Gus wasn't feeling well tonight. He's already gone to bed," Jack explained.

Gus stepped into the hallway. "I'm still awake, Monsignor," he said, formally.

"You have a visitor," Jack said, when he saw him. "*A young lady.*" An arch of his unruly white eyebrows conveyed all he needed to say about the matter. "Says she has an *appointment*, too."

Jack stepped back so that Gus could see the woman standing by the door.

His first impression of the stranger was that she was indeed *young*—perhaps still in her teens, and ethereally pale. No make-up, with a scarf wound around her head and neck, she was wearing a sweater although it had been a hot day and the air was still close. His first thought was that she must be Muslim.

As he walked down the stairs, Gus quickly realized that all he'd gotten right was her pallor and the incongruity of her sweater. The long ponytail that protruded from beneath her scarf indicated that it wasn't a *hijab*.

"I'm Father Gus," he said, extending his hands. "Have we met?"

"Don't you remember? I spoke to you after the noon mass on Sunday," she said, in heavily accented English. "I asked if you might have time to talk with me about a—about a personal issue."

"It's Miss Cilento, right?" Jack said, slyly watching both of them.

"*Mrs.*," the woman corrected, addressing Gus. "But, please—call me Ava."

"I'm sorry, but I'm afraid I *don't* remember." Though he was certain they'd never spoken, there was something familiar about her. Up close, it was also clear that she was older than he'd first guessed—probably around his own age: thirty-one. "In any case, Monsignor does most of the pastoral counseling here. Usually in the afternoon."

"If it's important, we can talk now—as long as you don't mind a little baseball in the background," Jack offered.

But Ava continued to speak to Gus as she pressed her lie. "I told you I could only come in the evenings—when my husband is out. You suggested tonight."

If they had met, Gus knew it couldn't have been on Sunday. He'd been in New Bedford for the funeral of a former parishioner the previous weekend. Politely, he shook his head. "I'm sorry."

"Obviously, I've knocked on the wrong door. Please forgive me for the . . ." She searched for the right word, then pronounced it with emphasis. *"Intrusion."*

"If you'd like to schedule an appointment, I have my calendar in the other room," Jack said.

Still looking at Gus, Ava replied curtly. "No, thank you. Obviously, I made a mistake coming here." She turned to Jack and gave him a taciturn nod. "Goodnight, Father."

Later, Gus thought how easily that might have been the end of it. But as she turned to go, she bit down on her lip so fiercely that blood pearled at its edge. Instinctively, Gus pulled out the handkerchief he carried with him everywhere.

When he'd first arrived and asked for advice on his hospital ministry, Jack had told him simply, "Always carry a handkerchief, and make sure it's clean." Gus had nodded politely, but he laughed inwardly. *A handkerchief? Did they even sell them anymore?* Over the years, however, it had proven remarkably useful.

Appearing embarrassed, Ava accepted the white cloth and blotted her lip. "I'm sorry . . ." she muttered, looking down at the smear of blood, her disdain transformed into palpable despair. "I didn't know I—"

"How could I have forgotten?" Gus said. "Last week after the noon mass, you stopped me. You said you could only come in the evening when your husband was out."

As Gus repeated her lie almost verbatim, Ava Cilento closed her eyes, expressing a mixture of gratitude and anguish. "I knew you would remember."

"We can talk in the kitchen," Gus said, directing Ava to the right.

As he made a move to follow her, he felt Jack grasp his arm. "Mind if we have a word?"

"Make yourself comfortable," Gus said to Ava. "I'll be right there."

"We both know where you were last weekend," Jack began when they were alone. "Exactly what—"

"Weren't you the one who told me to regard anyone who came through that door as Christ?" Gus interrupted.

"Don't use my pious quotes against me. You know what I meant."

"So you're saying those are nice words in theory, but in practice—"

"I meant those words literally, and you know it, Gus. But when Christ comes in the form of a good-looking broad, you've got to be careful."

"A good-looking broad? What I see is a woman on the edge. Did you catch what happened out there? She's so distraught she didn't even know she'd bitten her lip."

"Now you're really starting to make me nervous."

"Why?" Gus peered in the direction of the kitchen. Whatever had driven the visitor here, it had taken her an extraordinary amount of courage to come; and he knew she might bolt at any moment.

"Because whenever you get that sympathetic look in your eye, someone or something else moves into the house." Jack gestured at the dogs. "Exhibit A. And we won't even talk about the girl who just called me 'Dad.' What's next?"

"Tell me Sandra's not the best housekeeper we've ever had," he said, speaking of the woman he had first met when she was in the hospital, trying to outrun her addictions, a lifetime of bad relationships, and the health issues that had resulted from both. Since then, she had licked two out of three.

"You know I love Sandra and Julia; hell, even the mutts

have grown on me, but that's not the point. In case you haven't noticed, this isn't the MSPCA, or the shelter in Hyannis. This is a parish rectory, Gus."

"Okay, I promise not to offer the woman your room. Feel better now?"

"Let me leave you with one word," Jack said sternly.

Gus cocked his chin in the old priest's direction.

"Detachment. *Detachment with love*. It's an old AA slogan."

"That's three words," Gus said as he started toward the kitchen. "Do I get to choose the one I want?"

"Nobody likes a wiseass, Gus. You hear me. Nobody likes a wiseass."

Ava Cilento was seated at the table, her hands folded, when Gus entered. He began the ritual of making coffee, attempting to make her comfortable with small talk.

"Nothing to drink—please," she said, nervously glancing at the door. She got up and began to pace. "This is not a . . . social visit."

"If you want reconciliation, we can close that."

"Reconciliation? You mean *confession*?"

"Whatever you prefer to call it—"

To Gus's surprise, tears appeared in Ava's eyes. "With all my heart, I wish I still believed a man had that power. A long time ago, when I was a little girl in my First Communion dress, I felt that kind of trust, but no more, Father."

Gus sat down at the table. "Then why don't you start by telling me why you're here. How can the Church help you?"

"Not the Church, Father. *You*."

"But we're strangers," Gus said though he was increasingly convinced he had seen her somewhere before. "Why did you lie about having an appointment with me tonight?"

"You lied, too. Does that mean we both need to do penance now?" There was a new hint of defiance in her voice—and something else, perhaps the determination he'd sensed in the foyer.

"I need penance every day, but this isn't about me. You obviously needed to talk to someone pretty bad. Why you chose me, I don't know—"

"*Talk*," Ava said with obvious scorn. "You Americans think that talk—*words*—can fix everything. Sometimes you are so naïve."

Gus raked a hand through his black hair in frustration. "Let's make a deal, okay? You don't stereotype me or tell me what I believe and I'll extend you the same courtesy. Now, if you want to—"

Instead of responding, Ava lowered her eyes in shame, and pulled the scarf from her head and neck, revealing a necklace of purple thumbprints around her throat. "This, Father," she said, still unable to meet his eyes. "This is why I came to you."

It felt as if the oxygen had been sucked from the room. Gus could almost hear the Portuguese rhyming song his mother had taught him as it mixed with the sound of his father's rising voice. Even on the nights when Codfish didn't touch her, the violence of his movements, his steps, his intonations had made mother and son quake. Until this moment, Gus had almost forgotten how it felt.

He got up and closed the door, sealing himself and Ava in the kitchen that Sandra had already set for breakfast. The cracked coffee cups and mismatched spoons mocked him with their promise of semi-predictable days as he took in her bruised neck.

"Your husband?" he asked, attempting to mask his own reaction as he rejoined her at the table.

Ava barely nodded.

"Bastard—" Gus snapped before he could stop himself. "Do you need a place to stay?"

Despite his promise to Jack, Gus was already thinking of Sandra's crowded apartment above the garage. Ava could even sleep on the couch in the living room—at least until morning, when he would find a shelter for her.

"Don't you understand?" she said, her voice both tremulous and vehement. "There is no *safe place* for me. Not here. Not anywhere on this earth. I've made my peace with that."

"The man tried to kill you. You don't make *peace* with something like that."

"You are the hospital chaplain, Father. Surely, you see terminal cases. Diseases that have no cure. Patients who wait too long . . ."

"But you don't have a *disease*."

"Disease isn't the only terminal condition, Father. But I didn't come here to talk about myself." She rifled through her purse, her hands trembling more violently as she pulled out a small photograph. She shoved it in his direction. "She's the only one who matters now."

Gus stared into the bright face of a girl who looked to be about six or seven. The resemblance to Ava was unmistakable. The same green eyes. The same thick chestnut hair, though the child's was divided into two ponytails. He turned the photo over and read the name written in pencil on the back: Mila. "*Milla?*" Gus pronounced.

Ava smiled with a sorrowful, maternal pride. "*Mee-la,*" she corrected, elongating the syllables into something beautiful. "Named after my sister, Milena. She would have loved her so."

"*Would have?* Did your sister pass away?"

"I haven't seen my family in many years, Father—and it's not likely I will. But I don't complain. As far as my family is concerned, Robert has been very generous. He bought my mother a home, and my niece and nephews go to the finest school in Bratislava. That is why . . ." Her voice trailed off.

"Why you married him," Gus murmured, finishing her sentence.

"Don't misunderstand. I wasn't just—what is that ugly word? A *golddigger*." She looked toward the window reflectively. "I was a waitress in Robert's restaurant when we first met, here on a temporary visa. I was flattered by his attention, of course, but also a little bit intimidated. And yet he was so good to me, so very attentive. Though I wasn't in love, I believed I could make him happy. In his own way, he needed me as much as I needed him. He still does, perhaps even more so . . . It's just that the cost is so high."

"But your family—surely, they call. You have contact."

"On occasion, with Robert listening to every word, and hating them for their claim on me. I have been so alone in this country. You can never imagine. So alone in my husband's house. But I didn't come to talk about that. After Mila was born, it seemed I hadn't lost my family after all. I saw them in the lines of her face, the way she moved. Once again, I had a reason—" She paused for a long moment before she looked up at him directly. "I'm begging, Father. Will you help her?"

"Yes, of course I will, but you must know I can't help the child without helping her mother as well."

Ava glanced nervously at her watch. Obviously, she had stopped listening. "We've wasted too much time on things that don't matter. I have already chosen a guardian for Mila," she said hurriedly. Then she pulled a file from her purse and handed it to Gus. "Instructions for my attorney—everything—it's all here. Please. Read it."

"I don't want that," Gus said, with mounting anger. "Let me ask you one more time: *Why did you come to me?*"

"I need a witness, Father," Ava sputtered. "Someone who has respect in the community. Someone who will make sure the court never leaves my Mila with—with him."

Gus attempted to respond, but she was determined to finish. "There are two things you must know about my husband. Robert has a lot of money and many important friends. No matter what he does, he will never go to prison."

"The man's brainwashed you with his own delusions. All murderers think they're above the law. Invulnerable. And you know what? All of them are wrong."

Ava shook the papers at him. "You're not listening. I need someone to help Mila when I'm not here. The last time I was in the hospital, a nurse slipped me a piece of paper with your name on it."

"So let me get this straight. You come here and show me those marks on your neck; then you expect me to stand aside and do nothing while you wait for him to finish the job?" Gus said.

Ava picked up the photograph of her daughter and tried to hand it to him, but Gus refused to accept it. "Maybe *you* should look at your daughter. That kid has already seen too much. And if something happens to you, her life will never be the same. Never."

Ava turned her face away.

"Listen, I understand your fear. More than you know, I understand," Gus said more gently. "But I have friends on the police force, good men who will help you."

"No," Ava spat out. "No police. I already told you—my husband has contacts there, too. I'm asking you to save my daughter—"

"If you won't let me report this, or at least help you and your daughter find a place to stay, there's nothing I can do for you," Gus said in frustration. He got up, pushed open the door and confronted Jack, gaping at him from the couch.

Apparently, Gus's voice had risen enough to be heard through the door.

"So you're asking me to leave?" Ava's tone was oddly flat.

Gus passed her the scarf she had used to cover her injuries. "No, that's not what I'm asking. I'm asking you to let me help you. And you're refusing."

Without a word, Ava deftly restored the scarf to its former position and started for the door. "I'm sorry for interrupting your game," she said to Jack as she passed him in the living room.

Gus stood in the doorway of the kitchen, silently watching her go. His dark eyes burned with frustration.

"What happened in there?" Jack asked. He walked to the window and lifted the curtain.

"Weren't you the one who told me that some people can't be helped? Cases you have to turn over to God? Well, that woman proved your point."

"And you said you could be detached. Look at you; you're *enraged*."

From outside, there was the sound of a car door slamming.

Taking Jack's place in the window, Gus studied the dark-colored vehicle. He imagined Ava collecting herself before she drove back to whatever waited for her at home.

"*Merda!*" Gus muttered. "I blew it; didn't I?"

Before Jack could respond, Gus was across the room and out the door. He barely felt the stones under his bare feet as he ran toward the slowly moving car.

"Wait, please—*Ava!*" he called to her.

She accelerated, backing rapidly down the driveway and into the parking lot before turning toward the road.

Gus sprinted after her and hurled himself in front of her car.

The brakes whined as she stopped within inches of him. Flushed with anger, Ava jumped out of the car. "Are you insane? I could have killed you!"

"Now you know how it feels when someone tries to implicate you in their death wish," Gus said, feeling oddly exhilarated.

Ava's chest heaved. "You are a madman!" she shouted.

"The nurse who gave you my name should have warned you," Gus said, grinning. "Let me have another chance, will you, Ava? Not just for your sake, but for mine. I can't explain now, but if I let this happen again, it will kill me."

"Again? What do you mean?" Ava said, before she was distracted once more by her watch. "I have to go. Robert will be home any time now."

"When can you come back?"

She climbed into the car and opened the window. "So you will help my daughter?"

"I already told you I would," Gus said. "Have you got

anything to write with in there? I want to give you my cell number."

"No. No paper for Robert to find. I'll keep your number here." Ava tapped her temple.

"You'll never remember it."

"I have an excellent memory for what matters, Father. When I get home, I'll call and prove it to you."

Gus recited the number, expecting her to repeat it back to him.

Instead, she again glanced anxiously at her watch. "My God, it's so late. I have to go." And then, without another word, she closed the window.

He watched as her car roared out of the parking lot and disappeared.

Jack was standing in the doorway when Gus came back inside.

"I tried," Gus said. Then he ducked into the kitchen to clean out the coffee machine before he heard about it from Sandra in the morning.

After he finished, he was stopped in his place by the photograph Ava had left behind on the table. He picked it up and studied the child's face. The wisps of hair slipping from her ponytails, the way her head tilted sweetly to one side, made his chest ache. After slipping it into his pocket, he went out to join Jack for the end of the game. But as he stared at the screen, all he saw was the girl's eyes. He checked his cell phone to be sure it was charged.

The call didn't come till after midnight. Jarred from sleep, Gus reached for his phone.

"It's me," Ava said, her voice low. "I'm sorry I called so

late, but Robert . . . he came home early and found me gone. It—wasn't good, Father; every time it gets worse. But I have memorized your number. And your promise to Mila—I know that by heart, too."

Then, before Gus could remind her that it was a promise to her as well, she disconnected.

After the nine-a.m. mass, and before Gus left for the hospital, he stopped for breakfast in the rectory. Jack read the sports page out loud, leaping to his feet when he recounted how the Sox had bungled a game. Often, he used this time to work in a question about Gus's ministries, and this morning it was again about "that woman who stopped by the house late at night."

"It was only nine, and no, I haven't heard from her," Gus said, frowning as he wondered if he ever would. Now that three weeks had passed, the question had become less frequent. He shook his head tersely, adding, "Don't think I'm likely to, either."

Gus and Jack hadn't always been so close. Before he came to St. Ben's, Gus's priesthood had been considered a "problem vocation." His heritage had made him a natural for placement in the Portuguese parishes in New Bedford, but a succession of pastors had been troubled by the number of young women who sought counsel from a curate who was both dangerously handsome and excessively sympathetic.

Finally, the diocese decided that St. Ben's, with its older parishioners and a pastor who'd been an ex-boxer and was known to "brook no nonsense," was the solution. Jack Rooney, who had run the parish alone since hip surgery ended his vigorous city mission, had hardly been thrilled with the placement. The first day Gus arrived, he looked him up and down before he shook his head and pronounced his verdict: "Why me?"

When Gus thanked him for the welcome, the old priest, who tried to mask his limp with an even more pronounced swagger, pointed toward the stairs. "Your room's directly at the top. While you're up there, maybe you can shave your head or something."

Gus had heard about Jack Rooney's famous sense of humor, but he could see he was dead serious.

Nor did Gus glimpse much of his jovial nature during the next few months when the pastor found fault with nearly everything he did. If Gus turned down a beer, Jack snapped, "Watching your weight?" When he was particularly kind to an elderly parishioner, the pastor suspected it was because he'd heard about the beautiful granddaughter who visited every summer. Gus bore the needling patiently, mostly because of his growing admiration for the man.

Though Jack never bragged about it and would have been furious if anyone brought it up, his work with the poor in his former parish was legendary. When he first came to Quissett, he'd shocked his well-heeled parishioners by selling the luxurious furnishings in the rectory and replacing them with castoffs from a thrift shop. A *Protestant* thrift shop, no less, a member of the parish council had huffed.

Soon, however, Jack's passionate homilies and his willingness to live the demands he asked of others had inspired his flock to give more, and do more. They boasted that St. Benedict's fed more of the hungry, and sheltered more homeless, than any other parish. "No one with a genuine need gets turned away at our church," they said. "No matter where they come from or what religion they are."

But when Jack found fault with Gus's daily runs, the younger priest finally rebelled.

"Can't you find something better to do with your time?" the pastor heckled one morning when he saw Gus lacing up his sneakers.

Gus looked at him evenly. "To tell you the truth, Monsignor, I can't." He opened the door and started outside.

"I'm not surprised," he shot back. "Vanity first, right?"

Gus slammed the door and faced him. "You want to know the reason I run? It's my way of letting go of all the bullshit in my life. And since I've been here, I probably put more miles on these sneakers than I did in the last five years."

Jack's berry-blue eyes opened wide, and he never questioned the morning runs again. But it wasn't until the now-retired Father D'Souza dropped in for lunch that things actually changed between them.

Gus had been livid when he'd walked in and seen the two old priests sitting at the kitchen table. Father D'Souza had grown so small that he looked like a white-haired child in the seat. Gus and Jack made eye contact, but the increasingly deaf D'Souza didn't see or hear his former parishioner.

For the next two days, neither Gus nor Jack spoke about the visit, but at odd moments, Gus would feel the pastor's eyes on him. Jack would turn away or offer a ready complaint every time the younger priest caught him. "Six paper towels to clean up one small spill? Ever hear of good stewardship?" Or "I happened to be in the sacristy during your nine-a.m. mass. Not a very challenging homily."

On the evening of the second day, Jack unexpectedly asked if he'd like to watch the Patriots game with him. "Thanks, but that little radio in my room is still working," Gus said.

Gus was startled to feel the old priest's hand on his shoulder. "Listen, Gus. I think we got off on the wrong foot here—and it was my fault. But if we're gonna live in this house together, we should—"

Before he could finish, Gus sunk into a chair opposite him and stopped him mid-sentence with the look in his eyes. "You think I don't know what this is about, Monsignor?"

"It's Jack. And if you think you've got my number, you can think again. Better men than you have tried to figure out this brain of mine—including me," he said, tapping his fuzzy white skull.

"So this has got nothing to do with D'Souza's visit and the sad story he undoubtedly told you?"

"*Father* D'Souza to you. I believe the man was your pastor when you were a boy. And sob stories are a dime a dozen. If I let them get to me, I would have floated away on a river of tears years ago."

Gus studied him. "Okay, if you didn't invite me to sit on your musty couch and watch your crappy black-and-white TV out of pity for my tragic childhood, then why?"

Jack circled the room the way he'd once danced around an opponent in the ring. "Listen, Gus, I'm gonna say this once and once only. What you went through as a boy or as a teenager—all of that means nothing to me. Hell, I've heard worse stories. *Much* worse. What struck me is how you reacted to them. And the boy D'Souza described? The man you grew up to be? Well, he sounds like someone who deserves more respect than I've given him. Even sounds like someone I might want as a friend."

Gus eyed him for a long moment before he said, "Don't you think you should call him *Father* D'Souza? After all, he's probably the only priest in the diocese who's older than you."

Then he got up and turned on the TV.

But for the past three mornings, neither of them had even opened the paper. Nor did Jack ask any probing questions. They moved around the kitchen uneasily. "You know where she keeps the sugar? The bowl needs to be refilled," Jack said, staring into the cupboard.

"Nope. And we're out of butter, too."

Neither wanted to admit what really worried them. Sandra had been hospitalized for the third time in six months; and each time she returned to them, she was a little thinner and a little paler, though still as feisty as ever. During the four years she'd been with them, she had done so well on her drug regimen that it had been easy to pretend she wasn't sick.

"I thought people weren't supposed to die of HIV anymore," Jack grumbled as they sat down at the table and stared at the phone. Gus was about to call Liam Gallagher, to ask his medical advice. "You need to ask him why she keeps getting sick."

"Whoa, Jack. You sound like it's Liam's fault," Gus said, defending the friend who had conferred with Sandra's doctors as a personal favor.

His eyes nervously glued on Jack's, Gus picked up the phone. He was close enough to see the broken capillaries in the pastor's passionate blue eyes as he spoke.

"It's liver disease that's killing AIDS patients these days," Liam explained when Gus relayed Jack's question. "And unfortunately, Sandra hasn't responded to treatment."

"You helped that guy from home get a liver transplant," he said. "What was his name?"

"Ray Lima," Liam supplied. "I referred him to a surgeon in Boston."

"So why can't you refer Sandra?" Gus asked impatiently.

"Use your influence and get her name up the list. Something. The woman's got a daughter to raise, Liam. A *fine* daughter, I might add."

"Ray Lima didn't have HIV, Gus. Unfortunately, Sandra's not a candidate for a transplant. We're hoping that will change, but right now . . ."

"*Unfortunately.* That's his favorite word," Jack said after Gus hung up. Both priests peered through the French doors at Julia, who was on the couch, studying, an eclectic mix of music blaring in the background, Stella nestled comfortably in her lap.

Though she had always been an excellent student, in recent months Julia spent more time studying than usual, losing herself in complex math formulas and the predictability of the periodic table.

"She's too serious," Jack said, his brow furrowing.

"And shy," Gus added. "The other night she turned sixteen shades of red when we ran into a boy from school at the store. Then she went out and hid in the car."

"She doesn't exactly fit in with the kids around here; her mother's dying and she lives in the apartment over a church rectory. How's she supposed to make friends?"

They kept their voices low, but Julia got up from the couch and sauntered toward the doorway. "You two whispering about me in there?"

They both did their best to deny it, but finally Jack said, "How did you know?"

"You've got the same worried look on your faces that Mami gets," she said.

Sandra had forbidden the priests to discuss her illness in front of Julia, and with equal determination, the girl seemed to resist knowing. Even when she visited her mother in the hospital, she carried her books with her, holding them against her chest, as if they could protect her.

One *morning over coffee, Jack scowled* as he put down the sports page. "I stopped at the hospital to see Sandra last night when I was out."

Gus looked up. "Why didn't you tell me?"

"Because she looked like hell, that's why. I didn't feel like talking about it."

"Worse than ever," Gus acknowledged. "I caught her doctor in the hallway the other day and—"

But when Julia appeared with her backpack to say she was off to school, the conversation abruptly ended.

"Not without breakfast you don't, young lady. How do you expect to ace that history exam without proper nourishment?" Jack roared.

Immediately, Gus was up, pouring the last of the orange juice, digging up an overripe banana, and a package of instant oatmeal.

After one bite of the banana, Julia tossed it into the trash. "That was mush. And don't even bother with the oatmeal; the milk's almost sour. This, I'll drink," she said, quaffing the orange juice. "Just to keep my two *dads* happy."

Jack cringed. "As if the church didn't have enough problems."

The men trailed her to the door, followed closely by the dogs. As she walked down the drive, Gus called, "Do you have your lunch money?"

"Will you be home after school?" Jack added, maneuvering himself into the doorway. "You can invite a friend over if you want."

"Yes, and maybe. I'll call," Julia said impatiently, but her sly smile showed that she enjoyed their awkward ministrations.

When they returned to the kitchen, the gloom returned. "What's going to happen to Julia when her mother's not around?" Jack said, finally broaching the question they'd avoided. "Sandra's the only family she's got."

"She'll stay here, of course. Julia's had too much instability in her life already. And besides, you heard her. She thinks of us as her two dads."

"That will go over great with the bishop. Are you out of your mind, Gus?"

Gus sniffed at the milk they had used in their coffee. "She's right," he said, pouring it into the sink. "This is on the verge. I can't believe we didn't notice it."

"Incredible," Jack said. "And I'm not talking about the milk. You actually think we could keep her here, don't you? If it came to a fight, you'd probably give up your vocation rather than send the kid to a foster home."

"You're right. I wouldn't send Julia to a foster home—no matter what. And neither would you. But don't worry. She's only got two more years of school, and her mother has vowed to see her graduate. No matter how bad she looks, Sandra's got some major willpower going for her." He cleared his coffee cup, and a half-eaten piece of toast. "If you pick up something for dinner, I'll cook. How's that for a deal?"

"Lousy. You know I can't find anything in that damn grocery store. And I've experienced your cooking . . ."

Gus was leaving the kitchen when Jack stopped him with his rusty voice.

"I almost forgot. Yesterday when you were at the hospital,

you had a call." By his tone, Gus immediately realized who it was. Her name, as well as the dark moons beneath her eyes and the bruises on her neck hadn't left Gus's mind for a moment, but it was the thought of her child that affected him most. From the night he first found it, he'd carried her picture in his pocket wherever he went.

"Ava Cilento. Did she leave a number?" he asked.

"She just about hung up on me when I asked for one."

"She'll probably call back," Gus said, wondering why she hadn't tried to reach him on his cell. Then he remembered the silent message that had been left on his phone the night before.

As if he expected the ailing Sandra to appear at any moment, Jack surveyed the cluttered kitchen and glanced down the hall before he sat down with his coffee. "I just hope it's not in the next couple of days. I'm going out to Notre Dame to receive that damn award, and I don't think you should meet with her alone."

The *award* Jack referred to was the Laeture Medal, one of the highest honors the Church bestowed. This distinction, like all the ones he had received before, would be accepted with grousing embarrassment, then tucked away into a drawer or an attic. "Why the hell did they pick me?" he would say. "There's so many others who do more." If his humility were not so utterly genuine, it might have been cloying.

"You saying you don't trust me, Jack?" Gus asked.

Jack cleared the table. "It's her I'm worried about," he said. "She's not a member of the parish. Why did she come to you? Hell, how does she even know you exist?" Then he looked around for his shoes."Speaking of intractable problems, I'm off to meet with the St. Vincent de Paul Society. It seems Barbara Malloy's been showing up at meetings half in the wrapper again . . ."

Catching sight of the kitchen clock that Sandra had picked up at a yard sale, Gus realized he was late for the hospital himself.

Jane and Stella took their spots at their respective windows as Gus started the car. He played back his most recent cell-phone messages. There were two from Sandra, one sounding woeful, the second simply determined:

Listen, Gus, you got to get over here. Things ain't lookin' good. I need the Last Rites—or whatever it is you call it these days. And then, when you're done praying over me, you can get me the hell out of here.

Then, an hour later: *Hey, Gus, forget that damsel-in-distress call I made a little while ago. These people been poking at me and bothering me so much, I'm too pissed off to die. And I won't be need-ing a ride, either. I got my own plans.*

The elevator at the hospital was so slow in coming that finally Gus took the stairs two at a time. He burst through the third-floor door with his usual greeting to the nurses and aides. Cocking his head in the direction of Sandra's room, he asked, "How's she doing?"

"She called a cab about ten minutes ago," a nurse named Robin said. "I'm surprised you didn't run into her. Barely able to stand, but she wobbled out of here on those spike heels of hers, holding the cabbie's arm like they were heading for a dance."

"AMA?" Gus said, using the hospital shorthand for *against medical advice*. It wasn't the first time that Sandra had gotten impatient with her illness and left without a discharge.

"You got it," Robin said while two aides nodded their head in semi-amused agreement.

"Thanks, Rob. I'll give Jack a buzz and let him know." Gus set out on his rounds in a distracted state, but as always his work made him forget everything else. In the pediatric ward, Gus retold the old fishing legends his father had recounted when he was a boy, fantastic stories about fishermen in the Azores who had hauled in mythical creatures and monsters instead of fish, who disappeared for years into kingdoms beneath the sea only to be returned to their families full of mystical knowing and secret powers.

In the adult wards, he prayed with and anointed those who wanted it, and listened to those who had grown bitter at the Church, but who accepted his obvious kindness. The old, and those who had forgotten any identity but pain, clung to him with particular fervor. "Everything's going to be all right," he said gently, but with conviction. "I promise." The healing words he'd learned from Nick when he was a boy never failed to soothe.

In the car, he checked his cell. A few new messages had accumulated during the hours he'd spent at the hospital, including two from a blocked number that were silent.

He was thinking of Ava and her daughter when Neil's voice burst through the phone, reminding him again about the reunion at the Last Knot.

Gus couldn't help smiling. Though he enjoyed Liam's stories about Neil, he never expected to rekindle the relationship with his childhood friend. Then one night when he and Liam had stopped off at a local bar for a beer after a game of pickup basketball, the subject came up.

"You were more of a brother to him than I ever was, Gus," Liam said. "I tried. We all did. But when it came to the family, Neil seemed to be born with a chip on his shoulder."

Gus stared into his brew. "Your parents didn't even show up when he was nominated for a Tony. Isn't that what you told me?"

"Guess it all comes down to that old conundrum about the chicken and the egg."

"Yeah, and in this case, I know what came first," Gus said. He finished his beer and rose from his stool.

"See what I mean? You always stood up for him—no matter what. You're *still* doing it."

"It was the other way around. I was the kid from the bad family, remember?"

"Okay, it worked both ways, then. Do you have any idea how rare that is?" Liam said. "Sure, Neil's got a ton of friends in the city, but he's never really gotten close to anyone since he left Ptown."

"I think about him and pray for him every day—even though I know he'd hate that. Last summer, I even went to see him when they did *The Importance of Being Earnest*. He was terrific."

"He saw you in the audience, but then you disappeared. I think he's afraid you've never forgiven him for—"

"Of course I have," Gus said uncomfortably. "Neil was so drunk that night he probably doesn't even recall what he did. Unfortunately, I remember my actions."

"So why don't you call him?"

"Maybe I will," Gus said.

Before he had a chance to follow through, Neil called him. "I hear you've been hanging out with my tightass brother," he said, as if ten years hadn't passed. As if they'd just spent a night driving around, or hanging out at the beach. "Is what he said true? Do you really forgive me?"

Gus could almost see Neil before him. "On two conditions. First, you forgive *me*."

There was a pause on the other end of the line. "Three lives were never the same after that night, including mine—because of what *I* did."

"Don't give yourself so much credit. You never hit me once. I was the one who—"

"Listen, I may have been half out of it, but I knew what you were feeling, and I kept pushing. In my own way, I was hitting every bit as hard as you were."

"So you won't say you forgive me?"

Neil sighed into the phone. "The kind of friends we were, Gus? We shouldn't even be having this conversation. But sure, I forgive you. Now what's your second condition?"

"Two tickets to your show when you come back to Wellfleet? I want to take our housekeeper's daughter."

"They'll be waiting for you at the window. Opening night. Fifth row, center."

Gus hadn't realized how much he missed his friend and everything he stood for—childhood and home and the fierce loyalties that belonged to both—until he heard his voice. Still, he was surprised when Neil seemed to choke up as they said goodbye.

They'd seen each other once or twice every summer since then, and though it would never be the same, things had been remarkably easy between them. They went fishing a couple of times like they had when they were boys; they took a few bike rides, laughing after they raced each other up a hill; and every summer, Gus attended Neil's play.

Still, he was surprised when Neil showed up for one of his masses. Gus was reading the Gospel when he spotted his friend in a pew near the back of the church, watching him so intensely that when their eyes met, Gus shuddered and looked away. The next time he glanced toward the rear of the church, Neil was gone.

Later, Gus thought of bringing it up, but then he decided against it. Who knew what had drawn Neil to the church that day? A desire to see Gus in his element? A vague nostalgia for the religion he'd been taught as a child, and then rejected in adolescence? Perhaps even embarrassment at being seen? Whatever it was, Gus didn't want to know.

Though he doubted his old friend would ever understand his life, he had begun to look forward to their occasional get-togethers. Still, the idea of a larger reunion scared him. He barely even visited his own family.

O*n the beach road, Gus rang* Neil's number. "The Knot? Can you find a bigger dive?" he asked when Neil picked up.

"I prefer to think of it as a place with atmosphere," Neil laughed, his old infectious enthusiasm brimming in his voice. "You mean you're coming?"

"I didn't say that. I've got to see what's going on at the house, Neil. My housekeeper—"

"Hallie isn't going to be there, if that makes a difference."

Gus drew a sharp breath at the mention of her name. Though they had cautiously talked about home, she remained a forbidden topic. "That's not it," he said quickly, eager to change the subject. "But as you pointed out, the Church is in enough trouble without a priest skulking around the Knot."

"You don't have to *skulk*; you can sit at the bar and drink

Shirley Temples if you want to. Come on, Gus. There's supposed to be a good band. And how long's it been since we've
gotten together?"

"Okay, I'll come—but I can't stay long," Gus said. He was
approaching the place where he began and ended every day,
no matter what the season. "Listen, my phone's flickering in
and out," he said. "I'll call you later. Or, better yet, I'll just
see you there."

Before he said goodbye, Gus was peeling off his jacket and
then his shirt, climbing out of the car to drop the jeans that
covered his bathing suit, shedding his day. The wind spit a
sharp flurry of sand against his legs. Forgetting everything,
Gus tossed the phone through the car's open window, and
followed the dogs, who were already racing toward the surf.

G*us was the first one to* arrive at the Knot. Dressed in jeans,
a hooded sweatshirt, and a Patriots cap, he reveled in the
chance to represent nothing more exalted or controversial
than the local fish-and-chips place whose name was emblazoned across his sweatshirt. He ordered a draft and slipped
the bartender a generous tip.

Though Neil had told him Hallie wouldn't be there, he
found himself scanning the crowd for her. Liam was the one
who had broken the news to Gus when she got married. "I
know you don't like to talk about her, but I thought you should
know. As you can imagine, everyone was pretty stunned."

What shocked Gus wasn't so much *who* she had married.
The choice made sense to him in a strange sort of way. It was
that he knew so little about her life. "If you see her, tell her I
said . . ." Then he shook his head. "No, on second thought,
don't. She already knows what I wish for her."

While he was lost in thought, two women sat down at the bar. Gus glanced over at them discreetly, wondering if he might have known them in what felt like another lifetime.

"Mmm. Bailey's. Best clam rolls on the Cape," the one who was seated at the next stool said. "Do you work there or something?"

Gus laughed as he looked down at the logo. "Sometimes I wish I did. Actually, I'm a priest."

The woman's face froze for a minute, and then erupted in laughter. "Good one. I'm Jill," she said. "And you're Father— Father Bailey maybe?"

Her friend giggled. "If you're a priest, the least you can do is buy us a couple of drinks. The Catholic Church messed me up for years. The way I see it, you guys owe me."

Gus lowered his head and laughed briefly. Though he hadn't been in a place like the Knot in years, he felt oddly at home. It reminded him of some of the bars in Provincetown, places where his father occasionally bought him a ginger ale when he came home from a successful fishing trip. He signaled for the bartender.

After ordering drinks for the women, he nodded and picked up his beer. He'd started toward the jukebox when he caught sight of Melissa, Neil's ex-girlfriend from high school. She'd apparently been watching him for several moments from a booth in the corner.

"Gus Silva," she said, shaking her head. "All that prayer, all those hours on the altar still haven't managed to destroy it."

He slid into the vinyl seat opposite her. "What are you talking about?"

"Your voodoo, of course." Melissa glanced in the direction of the women at the bar.

"Those two were just trying to con someone into buying them a drink." Gus felt himself grinning ridiculously at the sight of his old friend from home. And when Daisy appeared in the doorway with Sean Mello, he wondered why he had stayed away so long. They exchanged enthusiastic greetings before Gus excused himself to go to the men's room. When he returned, Neil had arrived with Chad Mendoza and his wife, Erin.

"Too bad Hallie and Sam didn't come," Melissa was saying. "Since they're on the Cape."

"I guess she thought it would be awkward," Daisy put in.

"She's been married for what—five years now?" Neil said. "And he's a priest, for Christ sake."

Daisy sighed. "Though he sure as hell doesn't look like one. What a waste."

"So tell me, Daze. What's a priest supposed to look like?" Gus said, as he stepped into the circle and gave her a hug.

"Not like you, bud. And they're not supposed to feel this good either. *Damn.* It's probably a good thing Hallie didn't come."

"Anyone see the beer I left at the booth with Melissa?" Gus asked, changing the subject as he took a seat between Chad and Erin.

"Forget the beer. It was piss warm, and tonight we're having something better," Neil said, producing a bottle of vanilla extract from his pocket. He was smiling, but his mood had clearly changed. "I already ordered a round."

On cue, the waitress appeared with her tray, and set it directly on the table. "Captain and Cokes for everyone, right? The taste of old times."

While the others reached for their drinks, Gus quietly

told the waitress that he'd take another beer. No one but Neil seemed to notice when he discreetly pushed his mixed drink to the side.

"You okay, bro?" he asked from across the table. "You're looking a little pale over there."

Gus smiled. "I'm great—even if I feel like I'm in a time warp. I've been here five minutes and Daisy's already giving me crap, and everyone's getting buzzed on rum and Coke. The next thing you know someone's going to ask me to build a bonfire."

"Not a bad idea. How far is it to the beach?" Daisy asked.

When everyone else got up to dance, Gus turned to Neil. "I heard you talking about Hallie. Have you seen her?"

Neil took a long drink from his glass and then claimed the one Gus had abandoned. "She and her husband came to the theater last night."

"I didn't even know you two were in touch."

"Not often, but yeah, we talk. I apologized to Hallie a long time ago, Gus, and somehow she accepted it. I would've mentioned it, but, I don't know, it's still weird for us, isn't it?"

"If it is, it shouldn't be," Gus said. "You like him, then—the husband?"

"You know, I used to think no one would ever deserve Hallie. But Sam comes pretty close."

Gus nodded slowly. "I'm glad for her."

"I know you are, but it's gotta hurt a little—"

If he'd gotten a chance, Gus would have said that he was happy in his life, too. However, before he could speak, his cell phone rang. "I'll take this in my office," he said, heading for the only quiet spot in the bar—the men's room. However, by the time he got there, the caller had hung up.

He was listening for a message when he caught sight of his own face in the cloudy mirror over the sink, and saw what Neil did when he asked him if he was okay. Suddenly, he knew he couldn't sit at the table littered with glasses that reeked of vanilla and the past. He didn't want to listen as his friends talked about Hallie. Or conspicuously avoided the subject. Neil was right about that, too. It *did* hurt. Imagining her in Provincetown. At Neil's play. With the husband who had given her the life he never could. He slipped the phone into his pocket, and headed back to the table, where Neil seemed to be in a deep conversation with Melissa.

"Sorry to interrupt, but that was the hospital. Someone needs the Sacrament of the Sick."

At first, it didn't seem to register amidst all the noise. But when it did, Neil's eyes flashed. "Jesus Christ, Gus. Can't you give the holy-roller bullshit a rest for a few hours? This is *us*."

Gus tossed a ten-dollar bill on the table, tension rippling through him. He nodded in Melissa's direction. "Tell everyone I said goodbye."

He heard Neil calling his name as he walked away, but he made no answer. And then he was distracted by someone in the back corner of the bar. He was shocked to recognize Ava Cilento, her straight hair pulled back severely. Of all the people he might expect to see in this rowdy bar, she was the last. Gus pivoted toward the small table where she sat, alone, with a drink that looked untouched.

But as he approached, Ava rose, pulling on the same thin, wheat-colored cardigan she'd worn the night they met, and started for the door. Despite her unadorned appearance, heads turned. Jack had been right, of course. She was a stunning woman. Somehow that only made Gus pity her more. Even her beauty had become someone else's possession. He suspected it had brought her little but grief.

"Ava!" he called through the thick crowd that now filled the bar.

She turned, briefly acknowledging that she'd heard him, then moved more purposefully toward the exit.

Gus struggled to follow her, but he was stopped when Melissa seized his arm.

"He can be a real prick sometimes, can't he?" she said.

Gus glanced back at the table where Neil sat alone. "It's the booze. Never brought out the best in any of us."

"The hostility back there? The cracks about your vocation? There's a lot more than rum behind that," Melissa said. "Wake up, Gus. *It's Hallie.* He still blames you for stealing the love of his life."

"That's ridiculous. There was never anything between Neil and Hallie. Nothing real anyway. Why would he—"

"Maybe not in your mind. Or Hallie's. But to Neil, nothing on earth was more real. Obsession doesn't even begin to describe it. I was his girlfriend. I knew. The only thing that surprises me is that it's still there."

Gus kissed her on the cheek. "Well, whatever it was, it's over. For all of us. Listen, it was great to see you, but I really do have to go."

"The hospital, right?"

"Actually, the holy roller lied. It's something else, but right now it feels just as urgent."

Gus scanned the room for Ava, but she was gone. By the time he reached the sidewalk, it was as if she had never been there. He was rounding the corner to the next street when he spotted her unlocking her BMW. She had parked directly behind his Corolla.

Catching sight of him, she looked panicked—as if *he* was the one who presented a danger to her. He sprinted after her, but she slammed the door before he reached her. Seeing the set of her jaw—so fixed on escape—Gus experienced a sudden instinct to let her go. Perhaps it was Jack's voice warning him. Or maybe it was the priest who had coached him and his fellow seminarians in the skill of walking away, of knowing when it was time to leave a problem to God. But in spite of those voices and Ava's clear rebuff, Gus pressed the palm of his hand against the car roof.

"Can't you see I want to be left alone?" she said, lowering the window.

"If that's what you want, what are you doing here? Why did you follow me?"

"You flatter yourself, Father."

"I probably do—but not in this case. You came here looking for me tonight, which makes me pretty uncomfortable," Gus said. "If you wanted to see me, I gave you my number."

She turned away, exposing the long neck where he'd first seen the bruising. It had faded, but the yellowing shadows still rattled him. "All right, I *confess*. I called the rectory, and the girl who picked up told me you would be here tonight."

Gus remembered how intrigued Julia had been when he told her that he was meeting his old friends.

"She seemed to believe I knew you from high school," Ava explained. "Anyway, I didn't think you would notice me—or try to talk to me."

"I already know all about your aversion to talking. Is that why you've been leaving those silent messages on my cell?"

"How are you so sure it's me?"

Gus sighed. "Intuition. The question is why you do it. If you don't have anything to say to me, why dial my number? If you don't want to see me, why would you follow me?"

When her eyes filled unexpectedly, Gus offered her the handkerchief he'd pulled out the first time they met.

"You know, sometimes you remind me of my grandfather in Bratislava," she said. "With your old-man handkerchief. Your old-man church."

"I heard enough of that crap in there—from my friends," Gus said, looking back toward the bar. "Now are you going to tell me why you've been calling me or not?"

"I meant no insult. My grandfather was a kind man, Father." Ava said, as she folded the handkerchief into increasingly small squares and triangles, a complex geometry of anxiety. "I mentioned him to honor you."

Gus took the handkerchief from her hand. "You barely know me, Ava."

"So you want to know why I call? For the same reason I came here tonight. The same reason I go to your beach in the morning when you run. To hear your voice . . . to watch."

Yes, that was where he'd seen her, Gus thought, recalling the times when he'd spotted a lonely-looking figure sitting on the jetty at dawn, her hair fluttering in the wind. Once he'd even stopped to warn her that the tide was coming in; she needed to get back to the shore. Then, after she'd waved and started to walk down the broad flat stones toward the beach, he'd resumed his prayer. Forgotten her. Or so he thought.

"You come to the beach at dawn to watch me? Do you know how crazy that sounds? If I did that to you, I'd be arrested for stalking. And those calls, those wordless messages. If you don't want my help, then why?"

Ava's eyes glittered. "Do you really want to know? Because in you I see something I lost a long time ago. And sometimes I need to see that again. There are days when I would risk my life to believe in that goodness for one hour. And when I can't get out of the house, yes, I dial your number. I listen to your voice."

Gus shook his head. Then he laughed softly. "I just walked out of that bar because I felt like popping a guy in the mouth. A close friend. That's your good man for you. Like you said before, we all have something to confess."

"But you don't *pop the guy*. You walked away. That's the difference."

Gus leaned against the car and smiled. "Most people walk away from their worst instincts—out of sheer self-interest if nothing else. I've got three masses tomorrow, and I'm expected at the hospital. I don't have time to spend a night in the can."

Then he turned serious. "You took a fair amount of trouble to track me down tonight. Why don't you follow me back to the rectory so we can talk about your options? Maybe work out a plan?"

"I told you before, Father, I already know what I have to do. When the time is right, I'll say more." She inserted her key in the ignition, eyes straight ahead. "But not now. Again, you have kept me too long." Then she yanked the door closed and pulled away.

Gus watched as she rapidly accelerated and disappeared. He was still staring down the dark road that had swallowed her car when he spotted someone cloaked in shadow across the street. His oldest friend leaned against a building, smoking a cigarette.

"*Gallagher!*" Gus called, wondering exactly how long he had been standing there, what he'd seen and how he interpreted it.

Neil looked embarrassed, as if he'd witnessed something Gus meant to keep secret. He tossed the small flame of his cigarette into the black road and went back inside without answering.

Gus thought of following him back into the bar and attempting to explain, but quickly decided against it. If Neil misinterpreted the scene, nothing he could say was likely to change his mind. Besides, there was some place he needed to be. Though it wasn't the hospital, it felt equally urgent.

The night was starless, and the beach so dark Gus couldn't even see the water, but it didn't matter. The tides always quieted him. Without uttering a word, he was at prayer.

Thirteen years had passed since that day on the beach when he told her he was entering the seminary; and, faithful to his vows, Gus had not spoken to her again. But in dreams, Hallie returned as vividly as ever. Hair shot through with sunlight, skin smelling like salt, the baby oil she used for tanning, and her citrusy fragrance—she came back to him as she had been in his small, neat room on Loop Street.

However, he hadn't dreamed of the bungalow on Point of Pines Road until a few days after he met his friends at the Knot. He was a child again, sitting at the table in the old kitchen. Before him was an empty plate and a glass of milk. Amália Rodrigues, the fado singer Maria loved, on the tape, singing "Gaivota," the song about a seagull, and the narrow room full of the scent of her spicy meat pies, the flowers she picked from her garden, and, even more strongly, her presence.

He knew the things people said. The words Hallie used when she tried to assuage his guilt. That he was nine years old. That he was just doing what he promised his mother. What she surely *wanted* him to do. That he might have been killed himself if he tried to stop Codfish. But he also knew that if he'd broken his promise, if he'd left his room, if he hadn't been *afraid*, the night might have ended differently. Nothing could change that—even the private resolution he'd made when he emerged from the months of silence that followed her murder: he would never act out of fear again. No matter how scared he was or how truly imperiled he might be, he would always choose courage.

The morning after the dream, he woke up with the smell of her cooking in his nostrils, the memory of the empty blue plate before him and an insatiable hunger for home. He'd planned to take the dogs for a hike, then meet up with Liam and another young doctor to shoot hoops. The day usually ended in a bar on Route 28 where he stopped for a hamburger and a beer.

Instead, he showered and dressed quickly; and when the dogs followed him expectantly to the door, he stooped down to pet them. "Sorry, girls," he said. "But where I'm going, I gotta go alone."

"And where might that be?" Sandra said, leaning against the door that led to the kitchen. Though it was only six a.m., she was in full makeup and heels. (*Excuse me? If I'm going to be a maid, I'm at least gonna be a sexy one*, she said when Jack asked her how she could work in those shoes.)

It was the first time she'd been out of bed since she'd discharged herself from the hospital a week earlier. The pants that had once emphasized her curves now hung from her, and no amount of makeup or determination could mask the grayness of her skin. Gus reached out his hand to her with the intention of helping her back upstairs.

"Sandra, honey—"

But the housekeeper stopped him with a pointed finger, tipped defiantly in red polish.

"Don't look at me with those sorry eyes of yours, Papa Gus. You hear me, *don't*. I may be dying, but I'm not doing it today. Not with this place in such a damn mess. Pardon my French, but *Jesus Christ*. Either you or Father Jack ever hear of a broom?"

"Better not use that kind of French around Jack; he doesn't mind swearing, but *that* he takes sorta personal," Gus said, scanning the room. "And I think the place looks pretty good. Maybe not up to your standards, but, really, Sandra, I don't want you—"

"Don't change the subject. You were about to tell me where you were off to so early."

"Home," Gus said, as if it were a common occurrence. "To Provincetown."

"The past ain't nobody's home, Papa Gus," Sandra said. "But I guess that's something you gotta find out for yourself."

Gus leaned over and kissed her cheek. "You're a wise woman, Ms. Perez. In fact, sometimes I think you should be made bishop."

"I woulda cleaned house on those child abusers, I can tell you that," she said, sashaying toward the kitchen. "Call if you're gonna be late for dinner, okay?"

"You promise to get back in that bed as soon as you feel tired and I promise to be home in time for dinner. Deal?"

Still possessed by his dream, Gus drove too fast down Route 6—as if he had to get home before it vanished. But by the time he reached Point of Pines Road, the narrow streets of Provincetown forced him to a crawl.

He parked the car on the corner of his old block, got out and walked. The closer he got to home, the more powerfully he felt his parents' presence, the turbulent brew of love and rage, exuberance and fear that was Codfish and Maria Silva's life. How could a family that felt so real simply be *gone*? He could almost hear his mother's voice calling his name. *Gustavo! Time for supper.*

The house looked pathetic—especially contrasted to the other well-tended bungalows on the street, and to his memory. After the murder, he had gone to great lengths to avoid the lane. The shutters his father had painted a bright cornflower blue and the window boxes had disappeared; the shingles were abraded by salt and time. But most devastating of all, his mother's once resplendent blue garden had become a field of weeds.

When he entered the seminary, Gus had officially transferred ownership of the house to his Aunt Fatima. A succession of renters had passed through, each leaving the mark of their makeshift aesthetics, their fervid or apathetic cleaning. But no one was committed enough to restore the garden or replace the warped shingles. Finally Gus's cousin, Alvaro, had taken over the place. Still single, he worked hard at pulling a living from the sea and was rarely home. Perhaps that made him the perfect occupant for the wood-framed house that leaned slightly into the wind from the bay.

Gus was not surprised when he turned the door handle and found it open. "Varo?" he called, entering cautiously. "Anyone home? It's me—your cousin, Gus." *Voodoo. Little Cod. Stavo.* He thought of the nicknames his cousins had called him. Probably still used when they spoke of him. If they did at all. A family like his would forgive anything but desertion. And though he hadn't intended it, he supposed that was how they saw his long absence.

The house was clearly empty. In the kitchen, Gus found a storm of beer bottles, overflowing ashtrays, takeout containers from Cap's. From the pots on the stove and the plate on the table, he surmised that the last meal to have been cooked in the house was *linguiça* and eggs for one. The caked-on food suggested Alvaro had been away for several days, perhaps even weeks.

The house had known more than its share of sorrow and loss, but upon entering it Gus remembered the nights when his mother set two blue plates on the table and they ate alone; he recalled Codfish and his friends laughing so hard it caused the walls to vibrate; he thought of the holidays when the relatives had filled these rooms to bursting with fado, homemade baked goods, tureens of kale soup, and stories. Eager to escape his lost family, Gus had forfeited the brightest memories of his childhood as well.

He walked through the house, allowing the pungent odors of Alvaro's life (fish, sweat, the sweetish scent of stale beer, sausage grease) to mix with his memories. In the bedroom, he nearly tripped over a pair of Alvaro's boots. There were piles of dirty clothes, more ash, and empty bottles.

Gus opened the shades and surveyed the messy bed where Alvaro would collapse when he returned. He was immediately drawn to the glass that hung over the bureau—his mother's mirror. Gus almost expected to see her leaning into the mirror, inspecting her reflection for signs of age—the hint of crow's-feet, a stray silver hair. But she always shook her head defiantly, tossing her magnificent hair as if she already knew that age would never have its way with her. However, the mirror revealed only his own face. In the muted light, he looked older than he did in his bright bathroom at the rectory.

Gus was so lost in the past that he didn't hear the footsteps on the walkway, or the sound of someone entering the house until the door closed.

"Hello?" he said, scrambling to come up with an explanation for his presence. But when he turned, expecting to confront his cousin, he found himself looking into a pair of dark eyes he'd thought he would never see again—least of all there.

The figure in the doorway was silent for a beat too long as she took him in.

"Hi, Gus," Hallie finally said, letting the impact of those two common words settle in the room. *Hi, Gus.* As if it had been hours, not years, since they'd seen each other.

"*Hallie?* I don't understand—What on earth are you doing here?"

She turned toward the kitchen where she began nervously switching on lights, lifting shades, anything to banish the shadows. "I was about to ask you the same thing. From what I hear, you never come home to Provincetown—much less *here.*"

Gus pulled up a chair, and absorbed the sight of her. In jeans, a sweater, and a pair of red Doc Martens, she was as lithe and beautiful as ever. "You first," he said.

"That's obvious, isn't it?" she whispered. "I came looking for you."

Hallie removed an unread stack of *The Banner* from a chair and sat opposite him. She reached out her hand, but then quickly retracted it.

"Just like you did in the church that day. You saved me that day, Hallie. I probably never told you that, but you did."

"We saved each other," Hallie said. "That's how it works, isn't it?"

Gus continued to stare at her. If Maria's ghost had walked in the door, he couldn't have been more startled. "You still haven't told me how you knew I was here."

"Gallagher called this morning. He had just spoken to your housekeeper."

"I told Sandra I was going to Provincetown, but I didn't mention this house," Gus began. "I didn't even know I was coming here myself."

"That part I figured out on my own."

Gus shook his head. "Hallie Costa. Apart from God, no one knows me better than you do. Even after all this time. So you figured I was heading home to square off with my old demons. I suppose Neil told you what he saw outside the Knot last night, too. It wasn't what it looked like."

Hallie paused, then she pushed back the hair that had fallen across her face. "You know the promises kids make in high school? Promises to always be there for each other and all that corny stuff? Well, I meant those things, Gus. Every silly adolescent word of them."

Gus smiled, momentarily forgetting where he was and what had driven him there. "I never doubted that. And, for the record, I meant them, too. But there's nothing exactly urgent going on here."

"Come on, Gus. If it wasn't urgent, you wouldn't be here," Hallie said. "In high school, you used to walk blocks out of your way to avoid this street."

"You noticed that?"

"You were my first love. I noticed everything about you. The way you held a cigarette. The incredible shine of your hair. Your crazy enthusiasm for the perfect french fry, the perfect tide, the perfect guitar solo . . . everything."

She looked out the window for a minute, and then continued. "You can still talk to me, you know. Whatever's going on . . . What I'm trying to say is, I'm on your side."

"It's my day off. I came down to see my cousin. That's as dramatic as it gets. And as far as this house goes, it's about time I came home, don't you think?" Gus cocked his chin at her. "Now it's your turn. What are you doing in Province-town in the middle of the week?"

Hallie shuddered almost imperceptibly.

Scanning the disordered kitchen, now illuminated by a merciless flood of light, Gus saw it through Hallie's eyes. Suddenly he felt ashamed for Alvaro, for himself, for the entire Silva clan.

"We should go someplace else," he said. "There's got to be more bacteria per square inch here than anywhere you've been in years."

"My life isn't as sanitized as you think, Gus," Hallie said, getting up to check the fridge.

As Gus suspected, it contained nothing but a twelve-pack of beer. She pulled out two cans of Bud Light.

He watched as she cracked one open and took a long pull. "Now I *know* something's wrong. Hallie Costa drinking beer at—uh—" He stopped and consulted his watch as if it could explain more than the time. "Ten thirty-eight on a Friday morning? Aren't you supposed to be in Boston, looking down some kid's throat or something?"

"I've been on a leave of absence for three weeks. Didn't Neil or Daisy tell you?" she said, suddenly on the verge of tears. "Nick's got pancreatic cancer."

"Shit, *no*," he murmured. "Oh, God, Hallie, I'm so sorry. Are they treating it? I've heard there are some new—"

Hallie shook her head. "Not for Nick. They're giving him two months, Gus. Felicia and Linda Soares have been helping out as much as they can. And Sam—my husband—he comes down every weekend."

"Is Nick at home?"

"He's staying out by the Point. After Wolf died, he picked up the lease on the dune shack. His summer home, he calls it, though he never got away from the office long enough to get much use out of it. Not till now, anyway."

Gus had heard about Wolf's death when he went home for his aunt's funeral four years earlier. An asthma attack, people said, adding that he'd been dead for nearly a month before anyone knew it. Nick had been the one who finally hiked through the biting winds in the dead of winter and discovered the body.

He got up, pulled her from her seat and hugged her. The move was instinctive, but when her hair brushed his cheek, and he inhaled her scent, he was overwhelmed by the same longings that had infiltrated his dreams.

"I'm sorry," he repeated, pulling away. This time he wasn't sure he was expressing sadness for Nick's illness, for everything that had come between them, or for the way he felt when he held her.

She, too, appeared shaken. "Remember that day on the Point when you told me you were going into the seminary?"

Gus watched her, knowing the question needed no reply.

"I wanted you to touch me like that so badly. It tormented me for longer than I care to admit."

"And now?"

"Now I understand why you didn't."

He walked to the window and looked out on the street. Several moments passed before he spoke, but the silence between him and Hallie felt as natural as it always had. "I always thought Nick was immortal," he finally said. "The man seemed to know everything; and though he was exposed to every virus in town, he never got sick."

"Everyone thought that. Especially me." Hallie smiled sadly.

"When you first came in, you made it sound like I was the one with the problem. And here you are dealing with something like this."

"That's what I've been trying to tell you. You *do* have a problem," Hallie interrupted. "One significant enough to take me away from my father. Neil told me—"

"Listen, Hallie—I don't know what Gallagher thought he saw the other night, but he was wrong. *Totally* wrong. That woman in the car—she came to me for counseling."

He instantly realized how foolish he must sound. Spiritual counseling? In a *bar*? Or worse, in a car parked outside it?

"Whatever you were doing, it's your business," Hallie said. "And much as I enjoy sharing a morning beer with you, you shouldn't be here. If they find you in this house, it will look incriminating." She rose and set her beer can on the counter. "Provincetown is the last place you should have come, Gus."

Gus laughed. "You're losing me, Hallie. Find me? *Incriminating?*"

Hallie drew a long breath, looking surprised that he didn't know. "That friend of yours—Ava something? Liam treated her in the ER. Apparently, someone assaulted her last night or early this morning—pretty badly from what I hear. Her daughter found her sometime around six and called nine-one-one."

Gus jumped to his feet, raking his hand through his hair as the questions rushed out in a torrent. "What? *Is she going to be all right?* And what about the little girl?"

"I don't know what happened to the child, but the mother's doing well enough to speak to the police. She's even named her assailant."

If Gus were not so relieved, he would have picked up on the edge in Hallie's voice.

"Dammit, Gus, don't you get what I'm trying to tell you?" she said. "She told them it was *you*."

At first, Gus didn't absorb the words. Then, like a man catching a hint of thunder in the background, he felt Hallie's anxiety spreading into his brain: *What did you say?*

"That's why Neil called me. Apparently, the police talked to Liam at the hospital this morning. She told them about the affair, and how she tried to end it last night. She says that you followed her from the bar and completely lost it—"

"Affair? She didn't say that. She *couldn't have*, Hallie. Maybe her *husband* . . ." Without waiting for an answer, Gus started for the door. "She's at the hospital now?"

Hallie grabbed his arm. "Are you out of your mind? There's no way you can go there."

Gus turned back, his hand holding the screen door open, and surveyed the house that held his best and his worst memories. "Yeah, I probably am, but I'm telling you, there's something wrong with this story."

Hallie opened her mouth to speak, but Gus held up his hand.

"I *have* to go, Hallie. If anyone knows that, it's you. I may not be able to do anything to save this woman. But if I don't try, I'll never live with myself."

"Go within a mile of that hospital, and it will look like you're trying to silence her. Or worse."

"The man's her next of kin, Hallie. He has complete access. While the police are busy looking for me, he could get in there and—"

"*He?*" Hallie said. "Then it wasn't—" She stopped herself, but not in time.

"Wait. You really thought I did it?"

"No—*no, I didn't*," she stammered. "I mean, I don't know what I thought. This whole situation makes no sense."

Gus nodded silently, remembering why he'd left home and never come back. In this house, even with Hallie, he could never entirely escape the past.

"I'm sorry," she said. "I wanted to help, not to add to your problems."

"Don't apologize. You were probably right. Given the right circumstances. If I really had been in love with her the way . . ." His voice trailed off. "In this case, though, I didn't hurt her."

Hallie turned away and put her face in her hands. When she looked up at him, he saw the confused girl he'd left on Race Point twelve years earlier. It had taken all his strength not to turn around that time. It was no easier now.

"Please, Hallie, don't say any more. For both our sakes, don't say any more," Gus said. Then he walked away; and this time she didn't try to stop him.

CHAPTER 17

A broken rib, some internal bleeding. *One side of her face is badly swollen. She looks pretty bad, Gus.*"

So came Robin's report on Gus's cell phone. After calling various wards and asking for nurses he knew personally, he'd finally located Ava on South 3, the same ward where Sandra had landed for her most recent hospital stay.

"She's gonna be okay, though, right?"

"Dr. Gallagher was in earlier, and he said she was stabilized." Robin lowered her voice to a whisper. "I probably shouldn't be talking to you about all this, Father Gus, but I just wanted to say—well, I know you couldn't hurt anyone like that."

Gus took a deep breath. Though he knew she was attempting to be kind, his first instinct was to tell her that he didn't need anyone defending him.

"I'll be there in five minutes," he said, more curtly than he intended. "What room is she in?"

"There's an officer posted outside her room. If you step off that elevator, they'll arrest you on sight."

"Let them, then. I have nothing to hide," Gus said before he hung up.

Soaring down the highway, he refused to think of Robin's warning—or Hallie's. All he knew was that he had to see Ava and convince her to tell the truth. Not for his sake— even if he was arrested, he was sure he would be quickly exonerated—but for her own, for her daughter's.

Gus slipped into the hospital through the laundry and

greeted the three Brazilian workers in Portuguese. Though he hadn't learned his mother's first language growing up, it had come easily when he was first assigned to a Portuguese parish in New Bedford, and he was now a fluent speaker.

"I thought it was your day off, Father," a woman named Eliana said. Apparently, the gossip that was swirling on the upper floors had not yet reached them.

"It is. This is a personal visit." Just then, the service elevator announced its arrival with a loud clank. He got in and rode it to the third floor.

Robin had obviously been watching for him.

"Sorry if I was rude on the phone," he said, touching her arm as he passed the desk. Before she could say a word, he headed down the corridor. An older nurse named Evelyn called after him, "Father Gus, you can't—"

"Morning, Evelyn," he fired back.

Gus knew most of the men on the Barnstable police force, but the officer who sat in the hallway, sucking on a cup of Dunky's, must have been new. A beefy blond guy around Gus's age, his name tag identified him as Officer Ryan Whiting.

"Hello, Officer," Gus said, extending his hand. "I'm here to see Mrs. Cilento. I won't be long."

Rattled out of the tedium of his job, Whiting looked for a place to set his coffee. Finally, he put it on the floor and stared at the proffered hand. "Immediate family only," he said.

"Unfortunately, the immediate family consists of a child and the man who did this to her," Gus said, speaking loudly enough to hopefully penetrate whatever drugged slumber might have swallowed Ava Cilento. Moving quickly, he opened the door, and called to her directly. "Ava, it's me— Father Gus. Can you hear me?"

Whiting charged into the room. After calling for backup, he ordered Gus to turn around and face the wall slowly. Gus cooperated, even putting his hands behind him so that Whiting could put on the cuffs.

"I'm the hospital chaplain, officer. I don't want any trouble."

"If you didn't want any trouble, you shouldn't have assaulted the woman, Padre," Whiting said. "And stopping by for a little visit probably wasn't the best idea, either."

In the bed, Ava appeared to be asleep. Gus called her name again, this time more loudly, but she didn't stir. Was she unconscious? Or perhaps just unwilling to face the man she'd falsely accused?

"What did you guys expect me to do—leave town? I haven't done anything wrong," Gus said to Whiting, the fury rising again. "If I'm going to be arrested, I might as well do it right here."

Whiting made no answer; and in a moment, two more officers arrived. Gus recognized one of them as Willard Duarte, who regularly attended the Portuguese mass he said on Saturdays in Hyannis. "Sorry, Father Gus," he muttered as he led him out.

Gus said nothing, but inside his head he was screaming. Eyed suspiciously in the hospital where he spent so many of his days? Arrested by a parishioner? *How could this be happening?*

*I*nside the police car, he could smell the hamburger with onions Willard had eaten for lunch, the synthetic mountain breeze of his aftershave.

"You know David Oliveira? Grew up with you down in Truro?" Willard asked.

Though Gus had played football with Dave at Nauset, he was in no mood for reminiscing.

"Yeah, well, Dave's got a cousin, Lunes," Willard continued, undeterred by Gus's silence. "He's from Brockton, but he lives in Orleans now. A lawyer. Supposed to be pretty good, too."

"I don't need a lawyer," Gus snapped. "All I need is a chance to clear this up."

Willard chuckled softly. "No disrespect, Father, but you're sittin' in the wrong end of a cruiser with cuffs on. A lady laying in a hospital bed made some pretty bad charges against you."

"I'm not worried about that." Gus stared straight ahead.

Willard glanced at him sharply. "Well, you better start worryin'. Or at least get out them rosary beads of yours. What the *hell* were you thinkin'?"

"Listen, the woman came to me for help in the first place, all right? I needed to make sure she was safe, and find out how he forced her to name me. Besides, I'm the hospital chaplain; it's my job to—" Gus began before Willard interrupted him with a bitter laugh.

"You also got yourself a past, Father Gus. And it's no further away than the archives over at the *Times*. How long you think before someone digs all that up? Then you'll see who's standing behind you. No one but your own."

When Gus didn't respond, they drove the rest of the way in silence.

No one but your own. Throughout his childhood and adolescence, he had never ceased to be surrounded by community—whether you wanted them there or not. Thus he was not particularly surprised when David Oliveira's cousin showed up an hour later.

*T*hough *Gus and Lunes were the* same age, their styles couldn't have been more different. In his well-cut suit, the attorney was clearly a man who was as comfortable and proud in his body as a panther. Obviously, he spent hours in the gym. Though his cousin had been light-skinned, Lunes looked more Cape Verdean. His eyes were as dark as coffee, his skin a smooth cinnamon. Gus admired the man's style in spite of himself.

After brushing off the seat in the cell and removing his jacket, Lunes sat down.

"So you're Codfish Silva," he said. Then he laughed. "Excuse me, it's *Father* Codfish now, isn't it?" He appraised Gus with a mixture of the reverence for all things connected with Church that families like theirs inculcated in their children—and the bafflement that his generation felt for a man who would choose such a vocation in this day and age. Not to mention *celibacy*.

"Codfish was my father," Gus said, bristling. "And much as I appreciate Willard calling you, I don't need a lawyer. This is nothing but a misunderstanding."

Lunes removed a notebook and a pen from his brown leather case. "All due respect, Little Cod, but that woman's injuries don't sound like a misunderstanding to me. Someone made their point loud and clear."

Little Cod. It was a name Gus hadn't heard in years. When he had walked the docks with his father, or watched the Captain's ropy muscles tense and relax as he hauled heavy nets of fish from the boat, he had been proud to be called Little Cod. How had this infuriating lawyer even heard it?

His jaw tightened. "As I told you before, I don't need an attorney."

"You telling me to leave, Little Cod? 'Cause if you are, there's no need to play games. I already know all about you."

"You read some old newspapers and your cousin played ball with me fifteen years ago. You don't know shit about me, Oliveira," Gus said. "And if you call me by that name one more time—"

"Whoa, Padre," the attorney said, holding up his hand. "A priest—cursing? I'm shocked."

Gus glared at him.

"Anyway, I didn't mean to interrupt," Lunes continued. "It almost sounded like you were about to threaten me."

Gus looked downward and emitted a long, slow exhale. "You deserved it," he said when he glanced up. "You're pretty good at getting under a guy's skin, aren't you?"

Lunes chuckled softly. "A necessary skill when dealing with a hostile witness—or trying to find out if a client is telling the truth."

"Well, since I'm neither, and this hasn't been the best day of my life, I'm going to ask you to leave."

"Your call." Lunes nodded and reached for his jacket.

"And one more thing?" Gus snapped. "She's not just some woman in a hospital. She's a mother desperately trying to protect her daughter. If you talked to her for five minutes, you'd understand . . . Ava Cilento is so terrified she could do or say anything right now."

Lunes cocked his head, appraising him openly. It was the same kind of frank assessment that Gus had made a moment earlier. "My cousin Dave says you were a helluva football player back in the day," he said, pivoting. "Not the biggest guy on the field, maybe not even the most talented, but the one who played with the most heart."

"Dave was no slouch himself."

Lunes nodded, watching Gus stealthily. "He also says there's no way you could have beat a woman like that. Just don't have it in you, Codfish's son or not. Guess that's the reason I'm here. I wanted to see for myself."

"So what do you think?" Gus asked.

"Haven't decided yet," Lunes said. "One thing I do know is you're gonna need me in court tomorrow morning. But if you're too foolish or stubborn to realize that, there's not much I can do. I expect bail's gonna be high—with you bustin' into the hospital the way you did. Hopefully, the parishioners have been tossing more than the traditional buck in the basket."

"I didn't *bust* into the hospital, Mr. Oliveira. I walked through the door like I always do," Gus said, rising to his feet. Though he was not particularly tall, he stood so straight that he sometimes appeared to be. "And I don't expect my parish to post bail, either."

Lunes Oliveira put on his jacket, preening in the small mirror over the small sink as he buttoned it. "You really have no idea how much trouble you're in, do you?" he said when he caught Gus's eye in the glass.

"Right now I'm worried about a woman's life—not legal red tape." Gus escorted him to the door of the cell like a host. "Sorry you wasted your time," he added before calling for the guard.

"Oh, it wasn't a waste of time. Truth is, I've always been fascinated by Codfish Silva. Sad story all the way around. A stand-up guy from the docks who turned into someone else when he was with his woman."

Lunes laughed shortly, then lowered his voice. "It's gonna come out, you know. There are just too many parallels."

He was hardly the first one to try to lure Gus into talking about his father, nor the first to fail.

"This case is completely different," Gus said.

"Maybe so. Or maybe you're more like Codfish than you want to admit. Maybe you're a different person when passion gets involved."

"I'm a priest, Mr. Oliveira. Passion had nothing to do with it."

Lunes opened his mouth to respond, but he was interrupted by a guffaw that promptly turned into Jack Rooney's familiar hack. The old priest looked like he had been called from the recesses of his usual afternoon nap.

"Don't add sanctimony to your crimes, Gus. You're in enough hot water already. We both know a priest without passion is a dead priest—or one who might as well be."

Then he turned his attention to Lunes Oliveira. "Are you Gus's attorney?"

"Actually, your friend here was just telling me he has no need of legal representation."

The guard opened the door, allowing Jack to enter the cell.

"Good job, Gus," Jack said. "You've done everything you can to make yourself look guilty. Why not fire your lawyer? Then you can go into court and tell the judge that you couldn't have done it because priests have no passion. Is that your defense?"

"I don't need a *defense*. All I need is a chance to talk to Ava Cilento—which is what I was trying to do when—"

"You show up outside a room under police guard, trying to visit a woman who's been seriously assaulted?"

"A woman who has accused him of the crime. Don't forget that detail," Lunes added.

"That's my point. There's no way she would have said that—not unless she'd been coerced," Gus said.

"Have you noticed where you're sitting?" Lunes asked.

Gus sank onto his cot and put his head in his hands. "All right, I give up," he said when he looked up. "Maybe I do need your help, Mr. Oliveira."

After he dismissed the guard, Lunes turned to Gus. "All right, then," he said. "But I won't have any friend of my cousin Dave's calling me 'Mr. Oliveira.'"

"How's this? You don't call me Codfish, Little Cod, or anything else that has gills, and I won't call you Mister."

"It looks like your curate and I have struck a deal," Lunes said, still smiling as he turned to Jack. "Now I hope you'll excuse us, Father, but the arraignment is tomorrow."

"Jack can stay," Gus interrupted. "In fact, I insist."

"Listen, Little—" Lunes began. "I mean *Father.* Let's get this straight. I need to know everything that went on between you and this woman. Every meeting. Every conversation. Every wet dream you ever had about her. And I can't have you censoring yourself because your pastor's tuning in."

Jack rose to go. "I'll be there tomorrow," he said.

Gus grasped his arm. "This is ridiculous. Ava Cilento came to the rectory because she was in trouble—just like a lot of people do. There's nothing more to it than that."

Lunes loosened his tie and began to strut around the cell as if it were a courtroom. "You're saying you had a purely pastoral relationship with this woman? Nothing unusual about it at all?"

"Can I be any more clear?"

"Then answer me this one," Lunes said in a voice that had

grown low. "What the hell are you doing here, smelling the last occupant's piss and answering my dumb questions?"

"*Merda*, Lunes," Gus shouted. "You think I haven't been asking myself the same question all day? None of this makes any sense."

At that, Lunes walked to the door and called for the guard. "Could you please show Father Rooney out?" he asked. He shook Jack's hand. "Thanks for coming, Father. I hope you meant what you said about being there tomorrow. Your curate's going to need you. Oh, and one more thing—don't forget the parish checkbook."

Before Gus could protest, Jack threw up a silencing hand and walked out. Gus noticed that his limp was more pronounced; he actually looked frail.

"Seems like a great guy," Lunes said.

"Never knew a better one."

The two men stared at each other as their smiles faded. Finally Gus said, "I told you before—she was forced to say what she did. She had to have been. Exactly how or why, I don't know, but it's obvious she's in danger, and—"

"Listen," Lunes interrupted. "Whatever her problem is, she's going to have to get herself another savior, 'cause there's nothing you can do to help her now. Nothing."

Silently, Gus thought about the last time someone had told him the same thing. It was the day he'd promised his mother he would be like a Jedi knight and swore not to interfere. "Are you saying you believe me?"

Lunes assessed him with a long stare. "I hope I'm not being fooled by my childhood indoctrination, but I'm actually starting to think you're telling the truth. Now, let's get to the more prosaic questions. What were you doing in the early hours of the morning? And, more importantly, who can vouch for your whereabouts?"

"I was in bed by midnight, and then—totally typical day. I got up at quarter of five, went to the beach to run and pray. Got back in time to say the seven-o'clock mass. After that, I went back to the rectory and had breakfast with our housekeeper."

"How far do you run?"

"A couple of miles. Sometimes three," Gus said.

"Two hours to run a couple of miles, maybe three? You going for the slow-man record?"

"I said I run *and pray*."

"And you can't do that simultaneously? Come on, Father. How long does it take to whip out a few Hail Marys?"

"That's not the kind of—listen, I'm not going to explain my prayer life to you or anyone else. You asked what I was doing and I told you. It's the same routine I follow every day."

Lunes rubbed at the lines that appeared on his forehead as if trying to erase a thought. "I don't suppose anyone else was on the beach at that ungodly hour."

Gus's mind leaped to the woman he had often seen on the jetty, her brown hair a forlorn flag in the wind, sitting knees to chest as if folded in to herself. How many times had he run past her, lost in contemplation, in the rhythm of his running? But Ava Cilento had not been on the beach since the night she came to the rectory.

"No one but me and my dogs," he replied.

"Pretty weak," Lunes said. "Not that I'm questioning your veracity. But obviously your chronology leaves you all the time in the world to run your three miles, go to the Cilentos' house, beat Ava within an inch of her life, and still have time to fit in a rosary on your way back to church."

"I can't imagine a more profane scenario."

"More 'profane scenarios,' as you call them, play themselves out every day," Lunes said forcefully. "Don't add naïveté to your handicaps, Padre."

"All right, say I *am* the kind of monster who can move from deadly violence to the consecration without missing a beat. Say I *am* that evil. That dead inside. It still doesn't work. You say this thing happened at her house with her husband present. You think the guy just opened the door to me?"

"Who said anything about Cilento being there?"

"He works till about ten at night. Eleven at the latest. He'd be home sleeping at that hour, in bed with his wife, wouldn't he? From everything I've heard, he rarely lets her out of his sight."

"You said you counseled the woman, Father. Surely, she mentioned that she and her husband were separated."

Gus was too stunned to respond, but Lunes read the answer in his confused eyes.

"Son of a bitch," Lunes said. "Looks like someone's been playin' you like a sax. And it's a sad tune, brother. A real sad tune." Seeing Gus's growing consternation, he picked up his notebook and returned to a more professional tone. "So if you weren't counseling her about her separation, then what exactly—"

"*Puta que pariu!* The woman came to me with a ring of bruises around her throat! They weren't painted on there. They were real. Now that he knows she's told someone, it's only going to escalate."

"Curse in English, will you?" Lunes said. "I don't speak old country."

"Sorry. I don't know what half the things I picked up on the wharf mean myself."

Again, Lunes chuckled. "I believe you, Father—not that it means shit, or *merda*, as they say on the wharf."

"So you *do* speak old country."

"A few words, but I speak common sense even better. Common sense and hard-headed facts. You ever heard of those languages, Padre?"

"Obviously, they're not my native tongue."

"Yeah, well, if you're gonna get out of this one, you better brush up. Where'd you go after mass?"

"I told you. Back to the rectory to check on my house-keeper. She just got out of the hospital and—"

"Then where?" the attorney pressed impatiently.

"It was my day off, so I decided to go to Provincetown. Visit my old house."

"Totally typical day, huh? You often make these little nostalgia trips to the place where your mom was killed?"

"This was the first time," Gus admitted quietly.

"And don't tell me. You were alone. No witnesses but those dogs of yours."

"Actually, there was someone else at the house," Gus said in a low voice. He put his head in his hands, and when he looked up, he said, "I'm so screwed, Lunes."

"You mean this story gets worse?"

"It was Hallie Costa. My old girlfriend from high school."

"The one you—"

Gus nodded.

"So now you got *two* women? Little Cod—I mean, Gus—*damn*."

"I know how it looks, but—"

"You know what? I'm not even going to ask you to explain what you were doing in that house with the Costa woman. Because if I know too much more, I might not be able to defend you." Lunes closed his notebook and left the cell.

After the door closed, Gus leaned his head against the bars as he listened to the confident click of Lunes's shoes as he walked away.

CHAPTER 18

The body of Christ," Gus said as he raised the flat, papery disc in the air. Lucia Spinelli opened her mouth like a bird, her veiny eyelids closed and trembling. At ninety-three, Lucia only occasionally remembered the names of her five children; she had totally lost the name of the village in Italy where she was born; and she still expected the husband who had died thirty-seven years earlier to walk through the door and take her out of the nursing home where she'd lived for eleven years. The raised Eucharist was the only stimulus she still responded to consistently.

Just as Lucia's mouth clamped shut on the host, a daughter Gus hadn't met before paused in the doorway, her movement impaired by two large canvas bags in her hands. "You're that Father Silva, aren't you?" she said. "The one I read about in the *Times*?" And then, while Gus blessed the old woman as he always did, she answered her own question. "Yes, that's *exactly* who you are."

Lucia's eyes snapped open in confusion, but Gus finished his prayer in silence before he acknowledged the daughter.

"Yes, that's who I am," he said calmly.

"Who asked you to come here?" the daughter snapped.

"Your mother did."

"My mother's incapable of asking an aide to take her to the bathroom, never mind calling a priest. If she had her wits about her, she wouldn't be within a hundred feet of you."

"When she identified her faith, she asked for me," Gus said, squeezing Lucia's hand. He nodded to the daughter, looking her directly in the eyes.

"You can take my mother off that list of yours, Father Silva," she called after him as he left the room. "She doesn't want you here."

"I'm sorry to hear that," Gus said, thinking of the comfort Mrs. Spinelli got from his visits. He kept walking.

In the hallway, a nurse named Nancy, who was passing out medications, stopped him. "Don't listen to that bitch," she muttered. "No one who knows you believes a word of that garbage in the paper."

"That's kind of you, Nancy, but I'm afraid a lot of people *do* believe it." Ever since Jack had posted bail, writing the check in his shaky hand, Gus had maneuvered between the hostility of people who had been quick to assume the worst about a priest, after all the scandals, and unwavering supporters like Nancy.

Seems like God's trying to teach you equanimity, Jack had said when he saw Gus tense up after a parishioner conspicuously avoided them in the drug store. *Well, I hope He knows I'm a slow learner,* Gus answered. *Oh, He knows all right,* Jack shot back, and Gus had felt his anger dissipate as the two shared a laugh.

Though the disdainful glances and quick judgments still bothered him, Gus had learned to react less as the days passed.

"See you tomorrow?" Nancy asked.

"Probably Thursday. I have some things to take care of tomorrow." Remembering his appointment with Lunes the following day, Gus frowned to himself. He still wasn't sure if the attorney believed in his innocence, and he also harbored a disquieting sense that to Lunes Oliveira, it didn't matter. He probably would have defended Codfish Silva with equal vigor.

"Are you back at the hospital?" Nancy asked.

"They've replaced me as chaplain," Gus said. "Temporarily. As you can see, some people feel uncomfortable having me around these days." Though Ava was reported to be recuperating with a private nurse and a guard at her side at home, Gus was still forbidden to go near the hospital.

Nancy pushed her meds cart toward the next room. "Sorry I brought it up."

"See you next week," Gus called after her, though he realized that nothing in his life was certain anymore. "And take good care of Lucia. She's always been one of my favorites."

"Will do. Bye, Father." To Gus, the pity in Nancy's voice was even more searing than the hostility he'd met in Lucia's daughter.

While Gus *made his rounds, the* dogs stayed in the day room, moving among residents who were in various states of consciousness and alertness, but who were always responsive to the silky feel of their fur, the simple wet love from their tongues. Now the animals were eager for movement, air, light. When Gus mentioned their favorite words—*the beach*—they wrestled and nipped at each other in excitement.

As the cold air entered his chest, Gus realized he had been suffocating in the nursing home; he hadn't taken a nourishing breath since he held up the host before Lucia Spinelli and pronounced the words of will and faith: *the body of Christ.*

But even the coastline had changed for Gus. The gray sky felt ominous. He jogged in the direction of the jetty, and walked along the mottled rocks, searching for some clue to the puzzle Ava had become.

He didn't realize he had cut himself on a jagged piece of

stone until he looked down and saw blood spreading across the stones. *Merda*, he said, looking down at the wound, which Jane, who had followed him out onto the jetty, began to lick. Maybe it was the cut or the taste of the curse in his mouth, but Gus suddenly felt overwhelmed with anger. Why hadn't Ava done more to protect herself? Why hadn't she come back and let him help her? And now she threatened to destroy everything he'd worked for with her false accusation.

Limping off the jetty, trailed by Jane, he spotted a couple holding hands. It had been years since the sight of two people clearly in love had brought such a sharp stab of loneliness. Leaning against the hood of his car while the dogs watched him with anticipation, he checked his messages for the first time in three days. In his former life, he had received a couple dozen messages every day. But now there were only two. The first was from Sandra, asking him to pick up a can of red beans on the way home.

The second message caused Gus to stand up straight. Ava had recorded two long minutes of frustrating silence just like the messages she'd tormented him with before the assault. After what she had done, the wordless messages felt like a game, almost a taunt. He was about to press delete when the sound of her ragged breath made him pause.

He listened again, remembering the night in the rectory when she'd bitten her lip, and how she'd been so distraught she hadn't even realized she'd drawn blood. Suddenly, he was back in the kitchen on Point of Pines Road, staring at his mother's swollen mouth. *Mama*, he'd begun, but before he could say more, her hand flew to her face, covering the injury. *I thought I told you to clean your room*, she said sternly. Again he was assailed by the helplessness he'd felt as he sat on his bed and looked around the impeccably neat room. When he went to the doorway, Maria had turned her back on him and switched on her tape player, filling the space between them with Amália Rodrigues's plaintive voice. He knew it was heretical, but sometimes his failure felt so heavy that even God couldn't release him from it.

He played the message a third time, wondering if the memories would have been different if Maria had someone she trusted enough to call. An adult who would have known how to help her. Before reason could set in, Gus hopped in the car and drove the dogs back to the rectory, where he stopped to look up Ava's address in the phone book. Jane and Stella watched vigilantly from the window as he fired up the car and roared toward Ocean Drive.

The stone house dominated the coastline, dwarfing those on either side of it. Gus thought he had never seen a more garish home. Even from a distance, it felt silent and closed.

Gus got out of the car and opened the iron gate before he pulled into the long driveway. He pounded on the door with the heavy knocker, but got no response. When he spotted a curtain flaring in a window on the second window, he trampled a flower bed and stood beneath it. "Ava!" he yelled. "Please, come down. It's me—Father Gus."

Finally, he heard the sound of halting footsteps. When they stopped before reaching the door, he felt chastened. He had called a badly injured woman out of bed. Still, he couldn't turn back.

"Please, I have to talk to you," he shouted insistently. "You owe me that much; don't you think?"

But when the door opened, Gus was confronted by a man

of about fifty-five. He was small in stature, but thick-bodied and muscular in a way that went beyond the physical.

"Tell me, Father Silva," he said, giving every word sharp corners. "Exactly what does my wife owe you?"

Gus stared into a pair of enervated eyes that were ringed from lack of sleep. "Where is she?" he asked.

Robert stepped outside and closed the door behind him. "It seems I've overestimated you. I never thought you'd have the audacity to show up at my house after what you've done to my family."

"*Your* house. *Your* family," Gus spat out, attempting to control his rising fury. "Tell me, Mr. Cilento, does anything belong to Ava?"

"Save your sermons. You're the one who's been charged with assault. *Aggravated* assault."

"Another way you've exerted your sick control. If she wasn't terrified, she—"

"What? She would have defended her priest lover? Did you really believe that? As I said, you are a greater fool than I thought." Robert emitted a short, caustic laugh as he reached into his pocket, pulled out a cell phone, and pressed three numbers.

If a call went through to 911, Gus knew he would be sent back to jail and Ava would be left alone in that house with her husband's wrath. In one deft motion, he ripped the phone from the older man's hand and threw it down. It shattered on the driveway. "Get out of the way," he yelled.

"Or what? I need to know exactly what you're threatening here."

In that moment, Robert Cilento disappeared. Instead, Gus saw his father standing before him. With a shove forceful enough to send Codfish away forever, he knocked Robert onto his manicured lawn, where he landed with a groan.

Gus didn't think he'd injured him—though clearly, in spite of all the hours of prayer, the life he'd dedicated to eradicating it, the violence was *still there*. Lunes Oliveira had known when he called him Little Cod. He pushed his way into a marbled entryway, calling Ava's name. Hoping to buy a few extra minutes, he locked the door behind him. He was aware that he was risking his freedom and the bail money Jack had posted, but he was sure she would recant if he could only speak with her alone.

He took the stairs two at a time. With every step into the cavernous house, Gus felt Robert's need—for stature, armature, protection. Such need, Gus knew from experience, was the most dangerous force in the world. "Ava! *Ava!*" he yelled into the silence.

Gus had almost convinced himself that something had happened to her when he heard a weak voice. "I'm here, Father," she called from the foot of the stairs.

He looked down and saw her standing in the overdone foyer. Her fragility, multiplied in the mirrors that lined it, stopped him for a second, before he raced back down.

Dressed in turquoise silk pajamas and a matching robe, Ava lowered her head, allowing a curtain of hair to obscure the right side of her face. "Like I told you the first night, you must be a mad man. Why would you come here, Father? Don't you know how dangerous it is?"

Then, clutching her robe at the center as if in pain, she went to the window and peered outside. "I don't see him. He's probably already called the police and is waiting for them outside the gate," she said.

"He tried, but I smashed his cell phone."

"Do you think that will stop him? There's a phone in the cabana. You have to—"

"Where's your daughter?" Gus interrupted. He wondered if a frightened child was hiding somewhere in the house, and if she'd heard the altercation outside.

"Mila's been with my friend Cynthia since the night I was—*hurt*," she said, choosing the word carefully. "At least for now, she is safe."

Gus nodded. "Good. Now is there a way we can get to my car without passing through the front door?" With only the sea behind them, the prospects seemed dim.

"Not to your car, but out. Yes, there is a way." Ava led him down a corridor into a room where a disheveled daybed and several magazines scattered across its covers indicated her presence. Unlike the rest of the house, the room was simple and unpretentious.

From inside a desk she produced a key and some cash, and then she pointed down the hallway. "Go into the library on the right and through the terrace doors. This is the key to the house next door. The people are in Spain. From there, you can call a taxi to the bus station in Hyannis."

"What do you mean—*I* can? Surely, you don't think I intend to leave you behind," Gus yelled, no longer able to control his anger. "I'm already looking at possible prison time, and I just made it a lot worse. Why did you do it, Ava?"

Ava glanced anxiously in the direction of the door. "Don't you understand? There's no time for this now."

"What I understand is that you've implicated me in a serious crime. I'm not going anywhere until I get some answers."

"Do you think I *wanted* to do it? The day when I woke

up in the hospital, I cursed the sun, I cursed the stubborn heart that goes on beating after everything I've done. When the doctors promised I would recover, I wanted to scream. But Robert was there beside me, holding my hand. The concerned husband. When we are alone, he promised me how different things would be—but first, I had to do one thing for him. One small thing."

"He threatened you. I knew it." Gus felt his chest constrict as the echoes thrummed in his skull. The words, the angry sounds of fists hitting walls, the weeping and begging—it had all come back.

"He doesn't have to *threaten*," Ava said. "I knew what would happen if I didn't . . ." She put her face in her hands and sobbed. "I tried to warn you outside the bar, but you wouldn't listen. Whatever goodness I once had, whatever love, I lost it years ago."

Gus paused and reached for his handkerchief, but he had forgotten it. "You want to know his worst crime? He told you those things for so long that you believe them; and then he created a world where it felt true. But still you had the courage to come to me. And enough hope to call when you were too afraid to say a word. Now you just have to take the next step."

Ava sunk into a chair. "Oh, Father, do you really believe there might be a chance for me? For my Mila? I used to dream; I even used to pray to find a way out. With no belief at all, I would say *Our Father* to the empty sky, *Hail Mary* to the sea. But no one ever answered. No one ever heard."

"That's where we disagree," Gus said. "Something led you to me, didn't it?"

"Even now, after everything I have done, you can say that? You still think there's hope for me?"

"I wouldn't be here if I didn't," he said. "But from now on, you have to be absolutely truthful with me. Why didn't you tell me that you and Robert were separated?"

"Because we're *not*. Robert made a show of that for a while. He told his friends; he even rented a small place near the restaurant. You see he suspected . . ." She shook her head, her words drifting off. "But he kept coming home, thinking he would catch me with someone else. I knew he never meant to leave."

"And then after he beat you, it became a convenient alibi . . ." Gus concluded. He attempted to tug her toward the door, but Ava remained rooted in the spot.

"Do you understand how dangerous this is—for both of us? Look at what he did to you already, just for meeting with me. He got you thrown in jail. If you still try to help me, he will destroy your priesthood. *Worse* . . . And if I tried to go . . ."

"The real danger in a situation like this, Ava, the *only* danger, is to do nothing. Do you understand that? You have to trust me."

Ava clutched her bathrobe and stared downward for a long moment. When she finally looked up, something in her face had changed

"My God, I must be mad, but yes, *I will*. Not this way, though. If I leave now, Robert will get to Mila first and take her away. We need to have a plan."

Gus glanced in the direction of the door, wondering how long they had before the police arrived. "I'm not leaving here unless you give me a time frame. When will you call me?"

"Soon. Within the week. Now go, before they arrest

you again and you're no help to anyone. Do you need more money?" She pulled out more bills from a messy pile in the drawer, treated as casually as grocery coupons.

"This time you have to promise you won't allow anything to change your mind."

"I said I would," she repeated, trembling as she took him by the hand and led him toward the library. "First go to the neighbor's house like I told you. After the taxi drops you at the station, buy your ticket and then wait at the coffee shop around the corner till you see your bus."

Gus was startled by her detailed plan of escape. He wondered if she had imagined it for herself but been too afraid to carry it out. His hand was on the door handle when he heard a forceful knock coming from the front of the house.

"Barnstable Police. Are you okay in there, Mrs. Cilento?"

Robert's voice followed. "Father Silva, do you hear that? Your only hope is to come out and turn yourself in."

"Why are you still here?" Ava asked.

"I'll give you one week," Gus repeated, squeezing her hand.

The pounding resumed, followed by louder demands for admittance. "We're coming in," someone finally yelled.

"I'll call. I promise," Ava said, pulling away.

Her arms wrapped protectively around herself, she started toward the front door, calling in a voice as strong as she could muster. "There's no need to break the door down, Officer. He's right in here."

Gus launched himself through the French doors that led outside and ran across the lawn, clutching the key and the crumpled cash that would hopefully keep him out of jail long enough to get Ava and her daughter to safety. Once she was free to tell the truth, he was sure the charges would be dropped.

His purposeful actions of the next half-hour provided their own momentum. He found himself adding to Ava's escape plan like a born criminal, anticipating questions he might be asked, choosing routes where he would be less likely to run into anyone he knew.

It wasn't until he found himself at the counter in the bus station, looking into the impatient eyes of a young clerk whose name tag identified her as Marnie, that he realized his aptitude for criminality was a joke. "Destination?" Marnie asked, as he stared at her blankly.

"Provincetown," he said without thinking. "One way." It may have been a foolish choice, but the only place he could think to go was home.

It had been just two days since he'd been to the house on Point of Pines Road, but so much had happened since, that he felt like he was returning again after a long absence. The door was still unlocked, and the beer cans he and Hallie had drunk from remained on the counter.

The scope of his crime spree seemed to be widening. Since his arraignment, he'd assaulted a man, accosted the woman he'd been accused of beating, and entered a house unlawfully. In forty-eight hours, he'd destroyed the life it had taken years to build, and proved everyone who ever doubted him right: he could wear whatever robe he liked, but beneath the skin he was still Little Cod. Gus picked up the empty cans and tossed one, then the other, into a trash can that reeked from the scraps of meals eaten weeks ago. "Two points," he said each time a can pinged his mark.

A groan emanated from the bedroom, followed by the creak of a mattress. The next thing Gus heard was his cousin's raspy voice: "Who the fuck is in my house?"

Gus realized he was committing the cardinal sin in a fishing family—waking a working man from sleep. But where else could he go? As he sat at the table, he imagined the police knocking at the door of the rectory and being greeted by the fractious Sandra, who would defend him fiercely. His tried not to think of how frail she had looked when he left the house. Gus got up and pushed open the door to the darkened bedroom.

Alvaro leaned on one elbow and used the other hand to make a visor as he tried to adjust to the light that rushed in and the figure who stood in the middle of it. "Jesus Christ," he grunted.

Gus went back to the refrigerator and removed two beers. He opened one, and shoved the other toward the empty spot at the table.

From inside the bedroom, he could hear Alvaro sputtering obscenities as he pulled on his pants.

Standing in the doorway, Alvaro rubbed his eyes. "Goddamn, if it ain't my long-lost cousin," he said. "Drinking my fuckin' beer, too."

"I thought we could have one together," Gus said.

"You haven't been around in what—thirteen years—except for a drive-by when Aunt Fatima died? Now you're in trouble, so you come running to your family? Well, I don't know you anymore, Little Cod. And besides that, I'm sleepin'."

"Yeah, I heard you," Gus downed his beer, staring doggedly at his cousin. "But in case you forgot, this was my house a long time before you ever parked your mattress on the bedroom floor."

Alvaro went to the sink, and poured a glass of water. He rinsed his mouth with it, and spat into the cluttered basin. Then he opened the beer Gus had left for him. "Anyone ever tell you you're a lot like your old man? Stubborn bastard just like Uncle Codfish."

"Lately, someone seems compelled to tell me that every day," Gus said.

Alvaro pulled up the chair opposite Gus, and rubbed the stubble on his chin. "So what the hell did you do now? When I think how proud Ma and Aunt Fatima were when you went into the seminary. I knew it was bullshit from the start. But the women, they went for it—hook, line, and sinker."

After spending the last twenty-four hours defending himself, Gus felt hollowed out. "Hey, thanks for the support, man. I mean, did it ever occur to you I might be innocent?"

"Chick turned you in herself, didn't she? Why would she lie? Not that I blame you. That celibacy shit's unnatural, you ask me. Man in the prime of his life doesn't get any for twelve years? Any guy's gonna get a little crazy."

"Twelve years and counting, if you want to know," Gus said. "And my mind's never been clearer."

"So if you weren't doin' her, why'd you go after her at the hospital?"

"*Filho da puta!*" Gus yelled in frustration. "I didn't *go after her*. I went to see how she was—and to find out why she lied about me."

"Smart move. I heard you ended up in jail."

"*Yeah, and it gets worse.* I went to her house this morning,

Varo. I won't go into the details, but her husband ended up calling the police."

Alvaro shook his head. "Man, you're either lying about this broad, or you're right: you're nothing like Uncle Codfish. In fact, you're way too stupid to call yourself a Silva at all."

"The woman came to me for help. What should I have done? Let her die like my mother?" Gus blurted out those last words before he could stop himself.

Instead of responding, Alvaro got up and walked to the sink with his beer. He took a long pull, then poured the rest down the drain. When he turned around, his eyes were glinting. *"Don't talk to me about your mother.* Who do you think's been takin' care of Aunt Maria's grave all these years? Hers and all the rest of the family's. There's more of us in that Cemetery on the hill than there are above ground. Doesn't that mean anything to you?"

"After Race Point, I did what I had to do, Varo. I couldn't live here anymore."

"Yeah, I know. You fucked things up with Hallie so you decided to go into the seminary and do penance for the rest of your life. On some crazy level, I could almost understand. But that doesn't mean you forget your family."

"I said I had to get away. I didn't say that was why I became a priest. Seems to me like you're doing your own form of penance. Look at this place. Look at how you're living. When my mother was alive, this was the nicest house in the neighborhood. Your mom's place, too—you could eat off the floor. No matter what else was going on, our family had pride."

"Pride? You grew up in that dump on Loop Street—or did you forget that, too?"

"I haven't forgotten anything. I tried, but this house, this town, our family—it doesn't let you go. My heart is a map of the place. And Aunt Fatima's house wasn't always that way, either. After Junior died, she put herself in a kind of cell. Just like you're doing now. You're thirty-eight years old. You should be raising kids, not sweeping graves and sleeping alone in that filthy room."

"So, what? Now you think you're a fucking shrink?"

"Are you kidding me? No shrink could have figured us Silvas out."

"They would have to rewrite the book, that's for sure," Alvaro chuckled as he tossed his empty can in the trash. "Listen, Gus, for the next fourteen hours or so I got a serious commitment to that mattress in there, and if I were you, I wouldn't stick around."

Gus rattled his own can and chucked it on top of his cousin's. "Looks like I'm done." He got up and peered outside, where it had started raining.

Alvaro didn't speak until Gus had reached the door.

"*Voodoo*," he said, imbuing the name with an ancient affection Gus hadn't heard since his Aunt Fatima died. "If it means anything, I'll be praying for you, man." He cocked his head in the direction of a small crucifix that had hung on the wall since Gus's childhood. "You're not the only man of faith in this family, you know."

"I never thought I was." Gus closed the door softly behind him. He was already on the street, the cold afternoon seeping through the lining of his thin jacket and into his chest when Alvaro called him again.

"Hey, one more thing. I don't know where you're going and I don't want to know. But don't make it the first place the cops are likely to look. I probably won't get two hours of sleep before they're hammerin' at my door."

Gus paused on the street, and put his hands in his pockets. "I'll see you, Alvaro," he said. "And next time, I won't let twelve years go by."

CHAPTER 19

Gus spent the afternoon walking on West End Beach—the place where he'd first met Neil, when he was five. Could he really remember his mother shyly talking to Donna Gallagher, pushing Gus forward and saying he would be entering kindergarten in the fall? *How old is your boy?* she'd asked. Or was the memory, like so many of his early images of himself—a story told by someone else and repeated so many times that it felt like his own? The years when he'd been part of a family, someone's beloved son, had been so short, and he remembered so little.

One thing he knew for sure was that he and Neil had instantly recognized something in each other. Whether it was a heightened sense of life, or just a greater propensity for joy, they had bonded that first day on the beach. Now, walking the beach that was so much smaller than he imagined it, he was assailed by a sense of loss. How had it all gone so terribly wrong?

Around six, besieged by hunger, he walked back into town with the intention of stopping in at Cap's for dinner, then changed his mind and chose a new seafood restaurant, where he was less likely to be recognized.

Ducking inside, he thought of Alvaro's warning: he was sure to be spotted and picked up by the police if he lingered in town. But he had no car—and, more significantly, he didn't want to leave the Cape until he heard from Ava.

He looked around furtively as he was shown to a seat in the corner, but there were no familiar faces among the staff;

the sparse group of diners were also strangers. He ordered a beer, and without looking at the menu said he would have fried scallops and a bottle of hot sauce. When they came, the scallops were astonishing—sweet and fat, but they tasted so strongly of the past that Gus only ate two of them before he pushed his plate aside.

"Is your dinner all right?" the waitress asked when she returned.

"Delicious," Gus said, shoving his plate in her direction without explanation. "I'll take another beer and the check."

He quickly downed the beer, paid his bill, and started out the door. On the street that was as much a part of him as the face he saw reflected in the store windows, he felt his sense of isolation burrowing deeper. Suddenly his destination was clear. He stopped to buy a flashlight before he headed for the highway. He would go to the shack in the dunes where Hallie was staying. Then he would wait for Ava's call.

The rain was heavy by the time he stuck out his thumb on Route 6. Drivers were more wary than they'd been when he and his friends used to hitchhike. By the time a trucker stopped, Gus was drenched, the road was lacquered with water, and it was dark. Even with the light in his pocket, it wouldn't be easy to locate Wolf's old place.

He was almost certain he had lost the way and would be forced to spend a cold, wet night on the beach when a light in the window of the shack came into view. He wondered what he was likely to find inside. But approaching the porch, he was reassured by Dr. Nick's familiar laugh, a resounding bark, mixing with Hallie's lilting voice. It hardly sounded like the death scene he'd been expecting.

Gus drew a deep breath and rapped firmly on the door.

Hallie's face, warmed by the kerosene lantern Gus had seen from a distance, greeted him. "Gus? What in the world—"

"I know you have enough to deal with right now, but I—" He hesitated, unable to think of an excuse for his intrusion. Fortunately, he didn't have to.

"My God, you're drenched." Hallie stepped aside. "Come in and get out of those clothes. Then you can tell me what insanity possessed you to venture out here on a night like this." Something in her voice, however, conveyed that she already knew.

While she ferreted through a drawer for some dry clothes, Gus found himself face-to-face with her father. Nick, propped up with pillows on a reclining chair, regarded him austerely. He was noticeably gaunt and gray, but otherwise largely unchanged. Suddenly, Gus's problems paled.

"Hello, Nick," he said, knowing that any apology would be useless and insufficient. The only thing in his favor was the doctor's well-known sense of mercy.

"Gus Silva." Nick's eyes glittered warily. It was clear that the new charges had brought back the feelings he'd experienced the night Hallie had been hurt. "I see you've gotten yourself into trouble again. "What's that cliché about the tiger and its spots?" He pounded at his chest, which caused a spate of coughing and drew Hallie protectively to his side.

"Tigers have stripes. You never did get your clichés right," she interjected gently. "And I already told you: Gus is innocent."

"You were there?" the doctor asked, his gaze still fastened on Gus.

"I didn't have to be there. Gus told me what happened."

"Thanks, Hallie," Gus said, touching her arm. "But your

father has every right to his skepticism, every right to hate me."

"*Hate?*" Nick's voice rose the way it did when a recalcitrant patient refused to stop eating french fries or to measure his days counting pills. "I've got weeks to live! You think I've got time for hate?"

"None of us do. The only difference is that you always knew it. I'm sorry, Nick."

"I know you are, *Gustavo*, I know you are," Nick said. Extending a bony arm, he squeezed Gus's hand with surprising strength. "Now you better listen to the doctor over there, and get out of those wet clothes." His pride in her was palpable.

Hallie held out a pair of blue hospital scrubs. "You can change over there," she said, indicating a portion of the room that was separated by a sheet—Nick's "bedroom." When her father stirred restlessly in his chair, she looked at her watch. "It's time, isn't it?"

After Gus had gotten into the dry clothes, he took a seat while Hallie prepared an injection.

"Tired?" she asked Nick, after she had given him the medication.

"You two aren't getting rid of me that easily."

"You've been going to bed every night around this time," Hallie said. And then, when Nick continued to stare at her, "Okay, Nick. Yes, I thought Gus and I could talk."

"Sorry, but I think I have a right to know what kind of trouble he's in." He turned toward Gus. "Did you break bail?"

In the flickering light, Gus's eyes roved from father to daughter. Then he nodded. "I went to her house."

Hallie leaped to her feet. "You *what*? Gus, are you suicidal?" She turned to her father. "Okay, so now you know. Now it's time to get some rest."

But Nick was more resolute than ever. "I'm not going to bed until I get an answer. "Why, Gus?"

"The woman's been abused for years, and it's getting worse every time. So when she called me today, what was I going to do? Go to the police?"

"That's what most reasonable people would do," Nick said.

"She's convinced her husband has someone on the inside. Whether it's true or not, the guy has almost completely broken her. That's why she lied—"

"To be honest, I don't give a damn why she lied," Hallie snapped. "She's implicated you in a serious crime. You could be sent to jail for a long time over this—especially with—" Abruptly, her voice broke off.

"Go ahead, say it. Especially with my past." Gus lifted his chin in Hallie's direction. "That's another reason I went there. I had to talk to her, Hallie—for purely selfish reasons. If she doesn't feel safe enough to tell the truth, the charges will go forward."

"Doesn't look like your plan turned out too well, does it?" Nick interjected.

"It will, though—as long as I can evade the cops for a few more days."

As usual, Nick got right to the point. "Tell the truth. Are you in love with her?"

"*Love her?* I hardly know the woman. She came to me for help. Maybe I'm a little bit like you in that way. I believe that when someone knocks on your door, you answer it."

"Obviously a dangerous practice." Nick glanced toward the window as if he expected the police to appear at any moment. Suddenly, he winced in pain.

"Your leg?" Hallie asked, moving to his side, and massaging his calf.

"Maybe I *should* lie down for a while," he said. He allowed his daughter to help him to bed. She was pulling back the sheet that separated his bed from the living area when Nick stopped her. "And, Gus? For what it's worth, I think you did the right thing," he said. "Not the safe thing, and certainly not the wise one, but since when have guys like you and me ever gone with safe and prudent?"

It was nearly thirty minutes before Hallie reappeared. There'd been no movement or voices for at least half that time. Gus imagined her watching Nick as he fell asleep, soaking in the lines and contours of her father's face.

"Hungry?" she asked. "I need to go for supplies tomorrow, but I've got hummus and pita, and a little bit of salad."

"Thanks, but I had dinner in town."

"In town? That doesn't sound too smart, either."

"Smart was your thing, Hallie. I was the guy who played football, remember? I run on instinct."

"Don't give me that," Hallie said. "If you weren't smart, you never would have been so engrossed by *David Copperfield* when you were nine. And you never would have fallen—" She broke off. "I'm sorry. This has been such an emotional month for me. I don't know what I'm saying half the time."

"No apology necessary."

Hallie got up and went to the stove. "Usually when Nick goes to bed I make tea and go outside to drink it on the stairs. It's my moment of sanity. Want some?"

"Tea or sanity?" Gus said.

"Tea," Hallie said, taking two mismatched mugs from the shelf. "When it comes to rationality, you're a lost cause."

Gus smiled in the flickering light. "Did you hear Nick? He said I did the right thing. That meant a lot."

"Mmm," Hallie said noncommittally. When she turned her back to the stove, the tiny crease between her brows became a deep shadow. "And when we were alone, he also said that he expected you'll pay a high price for it."

They sat down at a small table. Hallie had made a tablecloth out of what appeared to be a paisley shawl, and filled a vase with beach roses. The rain pelted the tin roof, and Gus noticed a small leak near the corner of the room. He emptied the pan Hallie had used to make tea and set it on the floor.

"I wish there was something I could do," he said, moving away.

Hallie wiped the tears from her face with the back of her hand. "I hear you priests are pretty good at miracles."

"Only those up for canonization. Guys with charges pending don't carry much weight."

"Then I guess there's nothing you can do except sit and be with me. Not unless you brought some tools to fix that leak." Hallie's smile was muted by her obvious sorrow. In the background, Nick had begun to snore.

"How's he been doing?" Gus asked.

"So far we've been able to keep the pain under control. The clots in his legs are what's bothered him most. Related, of course. But the actual cancer site's been quiet."

"And his state of mind?"

"You saw him. He's taken one piece of devastating news after another with the most amazing equanimity I've ever seen. And he's so open when he talks about it. Completely matter-of-fact."

"He's showing us the way, isn't he? Just like he always did," Gus said. "You know, when people ask who inspired me to become a priest, I tell them about cranky old Father D, and then I talk about Nick."

"Don't let him hear that," Hallie warned. "You know how he feels about the Church."

Gus laughed softly. "Yeah, I know. But that doesn't change what I saw growing up. Every day of his life, Nick preached a powerful sermon. No words needed."

Hallie got up and cleared their empty cups. "Honestly, Gus? I'm not sure I can handle this. I can't imagine coming home to Provincetown and him not being here."

Gus got up and hugged her, but this time she quickly pulled away.

"Damn you, Gus Silva." She walked to the window and looked out at the lashing rain. "Do you have any idea what a mess I am? If you touch me, I just might fall apart."

Gus turned toward the sink, where he began to wash the cups. A moment later, she was beside him, silently drying them and putting them away.

He looked toward his wet clothes. "I should go."

"That's crazy. Listen, Gus, I'm *glad* you're here; I mean that. And you can stay as long as you want. The only thing I ask in return is the truth."

"Like I told Nick, I didn't hurt that woman."

"That's not what I'm talking about."

Gus looked at her, feeling bewildered.

"You never really answered his other question," Hallie said. "Are you in love with her?"

"I'm a priest, Hallie."

"What does that mean? Nothing except that you're lonelier than the average guy? Come on, Gus. Falling in love is simply what people do—and it's a well-known fact that ordination doesn't preclude—"

"For me, it *does*." There was a flash of anger in Gus's voice. "And I'm *not* lonely—at least, not more than anyone else. My life isn't the sad compromise some of my friends think it is. I *chose* it, Hallie. I chose God."

"So you're no longer a sexual being? No longer capable of attraction? Infatuation? *Love?* Do you really expect me to believe that?"

"Attraction—yes. Outright lust? Nothing eradicates that. And love—most definitely. But *being* in love? No, Hallie. Not since you—"

They were silent for a few minutes. Then Hallie said, "You may believe that, but I don't. No vow could change a person that much."

"It wasn't the priesthood that changed me, Hallie. Being in love did that. Knowing what those kinds of feelings can do to me." He looked around the little shack, his gaze veering from the cot where Hallie apparently slept to a straw mat beside it. "Is that enough truth to earn me a spot on the floor for the night?"

In answer, Hallie searched a chest in the corner. "Sorry, but I don't even have a sheet to cover that mat," she said, tossing Gus a pillow and a light cotton blanket.

Once they were settled in, they lay there for several moments, each listening to the rhythm of the other's breathing. "Tell me about him," Gus finally said. His hands were behind his head and he was staring up at the ceiling.

Hallie hesitated. "He's . . . *strong*, and I don't just mean physically. He's the kind of person who's never paid a bill late once in his life, who thinks before he acts—sometimes to a fault. He hates Provincetown and fireworks, and he calls a day at the beach 'savage amusement.' Sounds like a bore, doesn't he?"

"Not necessarily," Gus said, but there was a hint of triumph in his voice.

"Well, the amazing thing is that he's not. He makes me laugh in a way I never thought I would again; and even though he hates beaches and fireworks, he goes anyway— just for me."

When Gus made no response, Hallie finally leaned over the edge of the cot, and said, "Hey you, down there. You're not jealous, are you?"

"Do you still intend to throw me out if I don't tell the truth?"

"In the rain. With cops crawling all over town looking for you."

Gus laughed softly. "Okay, then. Yeah, I *am* jealous. I've been jealous ever since I heard the words *Hallie's husband*. Are you happy now?"

"Yes," Hallie said, her smile visible through the dark. "I'm happy. It means you're human; and as much as I'm opposed to liars, I'm even more uncomfortable with saints."

"He still doesn't deserve you," Gus said after a moment of quiet.

"That's what I used to think about your God," Hallie said. "The ultimate heresy, right?"

Again Gus laughed before turning on his side. "We probably should get some sleep," he said, though he doubted they would.

Several times during the night, he woke to Nick's groans. They were promptly followed by Hallie's soothing voice; the beam of her flashlight slicing the darkness. The sight of her crossing the shadowy room in the thin drawstring pants and tank top she wore to bed affected him more than he wanted to admit. He rolled toward the wall, but he still felt her presence. What had she said? *If you touch me, I just might fall apart.* It was a broken, hallucinatory night of sleep. In the wind, the shack that stood on stilts shook like a houseboat tossed on mercurial seas.

It was close to dawn before Gus fell deeply asleep. A short three hours later, he woke to the smell of fresh coffee and the sound of a gull cracking clamshells on the roof and then skittering across the tin surface to claim his breakfast. Hallie was talking to Nick behind the sheet. Here, where the business of dying was being conducted, routine took over. Medications needed to be dispensed according to a precise timetable. Nutritious foods needed to be prepared, though neither father nor daughter had much appetite. The laborious business of living in a shack without electricity and only a small stove needed to be accomplished.

Gus slipped outside, and a few minutes later, Hallie followed him. He worked the rusty water pump, filling the basin for Nick's sponge bath, while Hallie lit a cigarette.

"I thought med school would've cured you of that nasty habit."

"I've been trying to quit, but now isn't the time."

He took one from her pack. "Believe it or not, this is the first one I've had in eleven years. It must be your corrupting influence."

"Excuse me? I think you were the one who introduced me to cigarettes and whiskey—all on the same day, too."

Gus chuckled, then turned serious. "How long are you planning to stay out here? This kind of life gets pretty hard when it gets cold."

Hallie exhaled a plume of smoke. "Nick wants to die as close to the ocean as possible—even if it shortens his life. He says it's a Portuguese thing." The rain had abated, but the grayness, and the wind remained. Hallie's hair was blown back. The face of the girl he remembered was marked by the weariness and determination of the woman she had become. "I have to go in to town. You need anything?"

Gus shook his head. "You're leaving me alone with Nick? What if he needs his pain medication?"

"Then you'll get it for him, and he'll tell you how to administer it." Hallie accepted the basin and carried it inside.

Gus sat on the steps, drinking his coffee, listening to the gulls. He took out his cell phone and frowned as he listened to the worried diatribes that Jack and Sandra had left overnight. He wondered briefly if the police could trace his location through his cell phone. He expected he wouldn't hear from Ava until the end of the week. Robert was likely to be extra vigilant after his visit, and it would take time for her to plan her escape.

He took a walk to the ocean with the intention of praying. There were so many desperate pleas he wanted to toss out to the God of sea and wind, but as always, his petitions were subsumed by the layered gray sky, the imposing darkness of the water, and the only prayer he could offer was one of wild gratitude. With her promise, Ava had taken the first step toward saving her life; and being here with Hallie and Nick was a gift Gus had never expected to receive again. He was climbing the big dune toward the shack when he saw

Hallie sitting on the steps with her bag. "I was afraid you'd gone," she said.

"Do you think I'd leave without saying goodbye?"

"Never know what a guy on the lam might do." Hallie walked down the steps and paused, her bag slung over her shoulder. "I won't be long."

Gus brushed away the sand that had begun to blow into his eyes. "Anything else I need to do while you're gone?"

"Just what you do in the hospital. Give him a little bit of your hope. Your strength. Whatever voodoo you've got."

He watched her tramp across the dunes toward the pitch pines. When he went back inside, Nick was asleep in his chair, his mouth agape, his formerly olive skin the color of oatmeal. Gus watched him for a few moments before he lay down on the cot and wrapped himself in the jasmine scent of Hallie's blanket.

He was startled by the ringing of his cell phone, and even more surprised that it was Ava.

"Robert knows," she blurted out, her voice thick with panic. "He came home early and sneaked into the house when I was talking to Cynthia. You have to come."

Gus kept his voice firm. "Did he hurt you?"

"I think he knew that wouldn't work this time. He can tell that I am—different. I have nothing more to lose, Father. It was a terrible scene, though. He cried like a child, cried and begged me not to leave. I almost felt sorry for him, but then I thought how little pity he has for me. And now he has involved you."

"So you told him what he wanted to hear?"

"Yes. I apologized; I swore he is my whole world and no one could ever love him the way I do—all the things he has said to me over the years. Then, later, when I was finally sure he was asleep, I left. But I don't have much time. When he wakes up and finds I'm gone, he will . . . well, I don't want to think about it. This isn't how I wanted to do it, Father, with no clear plan in place, but there is no turning back now."

"Where are you?"

"At the Pink Dolphin Motel on Beach Road. Room 4B."

"And your daughter?"

"Cynthia is driving her off Cape as we speak. Robert won't look for her or try to bring her home until he finishes with me."

Gus shuddered. "I'm more than an hour away. And I need to stay here until—"

"Did you hear what I just said? Robert is out looking for my car right now. I should have parked it somewhere else, but I'm still weak, and I'm afraid if he sees me walking . . ." Her voice trailed off. "You said you know people who can help me get away."

"I'll be there as soon as I can, but right now you have to call the police."

"No police," she said vehemently. "The moment a call comes in on the radio, Robert's friend would alert him . . . Please hurry, Father."

When Gus looked up, Nick was watching him. "It was her, wasn't it? That woman—"

"She's in trouble, Doc. Serious trouble. I promised Hallie I would stay till she got back, but something's happened. I have to go to her."

Nick attempted to speak, but pain stopped him. He grimaced as he rearranged his legs beneath the blanket.

"Can I get you something?" Gus asked.

Nick pointed at a bottle of tablets on the table. "One of those and water." He groaned again. "On second thought, make it two. And forget the water. I'll wash it down with a little glass of Madeira." He indicated a small chest in the corner of the room.

"I don't know if you should be combining the two. You better wait till Hallie gets back," Gus said, handing him the water.

"Who's the doctor here—me or you? Get me my Madeira. And then go. I'll be fine here."

Gus made sure there was enough wood in the stove, then obediently poured Nick his glass of wine. "I don't suppose you'd want me to bless you . . . ," he said.

"My daughter blesses me every time she walks in the room. That's all the blessing I need."

"Just thought I'd ask. Tell Hallie—tell her I'm sorry."

"No need to apologize," Nick said. "Not to either one of us." In the morning light, he was alarmingly small and weak.

Gus paused for a moment, and then reached out to touch a skeletal shoulder. "*Adeus*, Dr. Nick," he said, remembering the way his grandmother always said goodbye, literally meaning: *To God.*

Gus was walking through the door when Nick stopped him with his voice.

"You, too, sweetheart," he said, using the endearment he had uttered the day he found Gus in his mother's closet. *Adeus.*"

Gus closed the door softly and crossed himself.

CHAPTER 20

C*ould you drive a little faster?"* Gus asked, leaning forward in the cab.

"Faster, faster," the man mumbled with a Portuguese accent. Probably Brazilian, Gus thought. "Everybody wants faster. But nobody gonna pay my ticket when I get stopped."

"I've never known a cab driver to worry about speed. You're illegal, aren't you?"

The man regarded him broodingly in the rearview mirror. "You INS?"

"I'm just a guy who needed to be somewhere an hour ago. Please, I'm desperate, brother. I'll make it worth your while."

"*Filho da puta,*" the man muttered, clearly not expecting Gus to understand.

"That's me, the original *filho da puta,*" Gus shot back. Again, the driver shot him a suspicious look. Gus hoped he didn't recognize him from the Portuguese mass. The speedometer shot up to eighty.

At the Pink Dolphin, Gus reached into the pocket of his jeans and pulled out the handful of cash that Ava had pressed on him the night before. It was still sodden from his trek through the rain, but the driver stuffed the money quickly in his pocket.

"You have a nice day now, you hear," he said, smiling at the man he had just called a son of a whore. "You need a ride out of here, you call, okay? Ask for Marco."

"Thanks, but I can walk to the rectory from here," Gus said, made guileless by relief. *Ava's BMW was still there.* The only other vehicle in the sandy parking area was a pickup truck, parked askew in front of the office.

"The rectory?" Marco repeated, nodding, as if he understood the meaning of both the threat and the lavish tip. "Don't worry, Father. I keep your secret, you keep mine."

Gus smiled as the cab drove away. He knew how it must appear. He could already hear Marco telling his friends: *and the filho da puta was a priest.* Perhaps he would applaud his machismo. Even Hallie might take his absence as proof that he had lied about his feelings for Ava the night before. Not only had he fallen for her, but his obsession had trumped his promise to stay with Nick.

Though Gus sometimes passed the Pink Dolphin in his daily runs, he'd never really looked at it. A gaudy dolphin painted pink, its mouth open in a perverse smile, adorned the front. The building itself was salt-scarred, windswept, badly in need of paint—or demolition.

All the shades in room 4B were drawn. There didn't appear to be a 4A. Gus rapped firmly on the door but got no response. When he tried it, he was surprised to find it unlocked.

"Ava?" he called tentatively as he went inside. Again there was no answer, but he felt heartened by a strip of light under the bathroom door. The shower was running.

He knocked to let her know that he was there. "It's me—Gus," he said.

The only answer was the pounding of the water. It sounded like a cascade of small blows. Maybe she hadn't heard him. Gus turned on the light and took in the desolate room. Ava's keys were on the bureau beside a cold cup of coffee, the rainbowed cream on its surface indicating it had been there for hours. Seeing no sign of her purse or the phone she had used to call him earlier, he looked at his watch as he sat tentatively on the edge of the bed. Everything about the scene felt wrong, starting with the unlocked door.

A minute later, the shower was still running. His watch read eleven thirty-five. The exact moment when he began to suspect he had arrived too late: Ava Cilento was already dead.

"*Ava!*" he yelled, banging his fists against the locked door. "Are you in there?" But the room, the entire motel, indeed the whole curling peninsula resounded with emptiness. He kicked open the door, and encountered nothing but the vacancy he felt in his bones. No Ava, but no grisly scene, either. He almost laughed aloud at his garish, film-noir-inspired imaginings. Then he noticed a woman's top lying on the floor.

The garment was sheer and lacy, unlike the modest sweaters he'd seen her in before. But when he stooped to pick it up, the scent recalled her presence. He tossed the top in the corner and looked around. He picked up her keys from the bureau, willing the inanimate objects to speak.

Wanting to call her, he flipped open his cell phone before he remembered she had never given him her number. He threw it on the bed in frustration. Searching for something he couldn't name, Gus began to open and slam shut drawers and closets. All were empty. The noise of his footsteps stomping through the small space, the vigorous banging of doors and drawers, his curses felt like an assault on the deep silence he had struggled to create for himself. The hours of centering prayer and contemplation on the beach.

Through the back window of the motel room, he saw a cluster of cottages that would remain deserted until the season. Had she spotted Robert's car in the lot outside and escaped through the window? Could she be hiding in one of those empty cottages? But when he tried the window, he found it sealed with disuse.

Then something on the mirror above the bureau caught his eye. It was small, minuscule, like the drop of blood that beaded in the corner of her mouth when she bit her lip the first night he met her. This, too, appeared to be blood—a smear about the size of a fingernail. It could have been the result of a paper cut, it was so small. But the second Gus touched it, he suspected the worst.

His first thought was to go to the office and ask the manager if he had seen someone else enter the unit—or had some idea as to where Ava had gone. But the office was at the opposite end of the building, and its shades were closed as forbiddingly as those in 4B. It was unlikely the manager had witnessed anything; and if Gus introduced himself, *he* would be the one who was identified at the scene. Realizing how thoroughly he had painted the scene with evidence of his guilt, he decided against it. What he needed to do was go to the rectory and think things through. To replace the damning silence of the motel room with Jack's voice, and maybe even put in a call to Lunes Oliveira.

He imagined Lunes mocking him with his down-home common sense. *One drop of blood does not make a murder scene, Little Cod. Don't get carried away.*

And then he noticed a large rectangular square of carpet beside the bed that was stained darker than the rest. Four neat compressions in the rug indicated that the bed had been moved recently.

He had only pushed it about a foot to the side when he

saw another inky splotch. It was the sickening dark red he knew it would be, and it was still wet. Forcefully, he pulled the bed away from the wall, exposing the horrific design. Behind the place where the headboard had been, the wall was also splotched with blood.

As he stared at the soaked carpet and the bloody wall, he finally remembered what he had done after his mother died, and why he had blotted that hour so completely from memory. He knew because there, in room 4B, he lived those hours all over again. He recalled the utter darkness of the closet, the soft material of his mother's dresses that brushed against his face, assaulting him with her rosewater scent. Attempting to make himself disappear, he had curled his body into itself. But no matter how tightly he closed his eyes, he couldn't escape the narrow stripe of light under the door. The light that illuminated his mother's lifeless body. The dryness in his throat that he might have previously identified as thirst, it had demanded nothing of him beyond the shutting down of the senses, the heart's stubborn beating.

And he understood why he had sealed all these details from memory long ago: because instinctively, at nine, and more clearly at thirty-one, the hours now condensed into a few short minutes, he understood that the place he had gone that day was the darkest and most terrifying one imaginable.

When Gus shook off his stillness this second time, he was not a nine-year-old boy in his pajamas, but a grown man, and his mind was oddly clear. He considered straightening up the room and returning it to the state it had been in when he first entered it. Then he thought of all the fingerprints he had already left throughout the unit and decided it was hopeless. Besides, wouldn't cleaning up ultimately make him appear even more guilty? Instead of trying, he walked out, leaving the door open for the police.

It had begun to rain again, a downpour that prodded Gus up the hill and toward the rectory. Soon he was running— motivated not just by the lashing rain, but by something inside himself that had always found freedom in movement. By the time he reached the third mile, he felt that he could go on forever. He stopped briefly in town and called the police.

"Ava Cilento has been murdered in the Pink Dolphin Motel," he said, his voice flat with exhaustion. "You need to talk to her husband immediately." Then he directed them to the ostentatious house on the water.

He thought of the child he knew only from her photograph. *Mila.* For now, at least, she was safe with Ava's friend, but how long would her father allow her to remain there? Gus shuddered as he imagined her alone in the house with the man who had killed her mother.

At the sound of his entrance, the dogs tumbled down the stairs of the rectory and welcomed him with a cacophony of joyous yelps and barks. Gus was crouching to receive their exuberant licks and wriggling nudges when he heard Jack's desk chair being pushed back in the office. He stood up as the pastor walked into the foyer. Almost simultaneously, Sandra appeared in the doorway that led to the kitchen.

"Gus," Jack said, and nodded gravely. He appeared tired, and his old-fashioned white collar was slightly askew. Sandra stood in the doorway, forebodingly silent.

Then Julia came down the stairs. "Papa Gus! I'm so glad you're home. We were—" But she left her sentence incomplete as she raced past her mother and reached up to hug him.

"Thanks, Jules. I'm happy to be home, too."

"I'd suggest a shower, but I'm not sure you have time for that," Jack said, taking in his wet clothes. "The cops have already been here once."

In spite of the warning, Gus did shower, sloughing off the rain and sweat, hoping in the process to wash off the gloom of Nick's illness, and the grief that was already in Hallie's eyes, to pummel away the desolation of the motel, and the memory of the dark stain on the carpet he had found there. By the time he rejoined them in the living room, his essentially hopeful nature had already begun to war with the facts . . . *Maybe there was another explanation . . . Maybe Ava had come to the motel with a weapon . . . There was no proof, after all, that the blood was hers. Maybe she'd finally fought back . . .*

Jack, Sandra, and Julia were lined up stiffly on the couch. Gus smiled sadly. "I'm not sure what I'm going to do next," he announced, still standing in the center of the room. "But I wanted to make sure it was okay for the dogs to stay here if I go away for a while. Otherwise, I know a couple of people in the parish who might be willing to take them."

"You're worried about *dogs* at a time like this?" Jack interrupted. "And what exactly do you mean by 'go away'? You really intend to go on the lam? For God's sake, Gus, you've got to be the most inept criminal I've ever met."

"How many criminals do you know, Jack?" Gus sunk into a chair opposite the three of them. He sighed, feeling the despondency return. *What had he been thinking? Ava was too weak, both physically and psychologically, to fight back—or even to manage the artful cleanup he had witnessed.*

"Too many," Jack said, struggling to rise from the couch. "And, unfortunately, they all seem to live with me."

Sandra cleared her throat. "Excuse me, Monsignor! The law ain't messed with me in at least seven years."

"See what I mean!" The old pastor's eyebrows shot up. "Julia and I are the only ones who are clean around here." He went to his liquor cabinet and pulled out a bottle of Jameson, shaking his head as he filled a tumbler with strong drink. "Sixty-nine years old and I've never had a drink before four o'clock. Even at a wedding. The stuff took down too much of my family."

Gus got up and poured himself a shot. "If you can break your rule, I guess I can break mine." He hadn't tasted hard liquor since the night of his high school prom.

"Dammit, Gus," the old priest said gruffly. "You're the closest thing to a son this old goat is ever going to have."

"If you had been my father, Jack, my whole life would have been different."

Gus moved to embrace him, but, as always, the old priest roughly shook him off. "And for that reason alone, I'm glad I'm not. Codfish's boy turned out pretty damn good, if you ask me."

"Until now."

"This accusation doesn't mean anything, Gus," Jack scoffed. "It's how you handle it that's important."

"And we all know what a great job Gus has done with *that*," Sandra interjected. She got up and paced the room nervously. "I hate to interrupt this touching scene, but in case you guys haven't noticed, we got ourselves an issue here."

"Could you really be sent to jail, Father Gus?" Tears sprang into Julia's eyes.

Gus looked from one fear-stricken face to the other, then downed the rest of his shot.

"What on God's earth made you go to her house, Gus?" Jack asked.

Sandra continued to pace, her heels clicking rhythmically as she drew a narrow circle around him. "When you're talkin' philosophy, theology, contemplation, all that—you're a brilliant man, Gus. But when it comes to practical shit—I hate to say it—"

"Stop, Mami," Julia interrupted. "Let Gus talk—all of you."

"It's worse than you think," Gus admitted. "A whole lot worse than forcing my way into her house or breaking bail."

The clock on the mantle had never ticked so loudly as it did in the minute when they waited for him to continue speaking.

"Ava asked me to meet her at the Pink Dolphin this morning, but when I got there, she was gone. Then I started looking around and—" He was about to describe the dark-red blood he'd found beneath the bed and the chilling sight of the mattress when he looked into Julia's face and decided to exclude the details. "There was no body, but the amount of blood . . . It looks bad."

Jack's weathered face collapsed in compassion. "Oh, God—the poor woman. And there was a child, too, wasn't there?"

Gus nodded, thinking of the photograph of Mila Cilento in his pocket. He was haunted by her serious eyes, the way her head tilted slightly to one side as her hand gripped a pigtail.

But Sandra was sharply focussed on Gus. "And you're going to be the prime suspect. That's what you're telling us here, isn't it, Papa Gus?"

"If I'd signed my name with her blood, I couldn't have incriminated myself more."

"Gus, you didn't—" Jack's blue eyes were boyishly wide as he ran a hand through his brush of white hair.

"How could you even think that?" Sandra asked in an outraged voice. But then she spun toward Gus, her hands landing artfully on skinny hips. "Jesus Christ, Gus, answer the question. You didn't kill her, did you?"

"*Mami!*" Julia yelled.

"Sandra, there's no need to take the Lord's name in vain!" Jack bellowed at the same moment.

"I'm sorry, Father Jack, but if ever there was a time to get a little pissed with the man on the wall there, it's now," Sandra said, cocking her head toward the ever-present crucifix.

Gus pounded the coffee table to get their attention. "Excuse me, but does anyone want to hear my answer?"

"See! Papa Gus was about to tell us he didn't do it," Julia said. Then her voice grew small. *"Weren't you, Gus?"*

As Gus took a long, deep breath, the ticking of the clock again grew pronounced.

"The way things look, not many people are likely to believe me—even my friends in the parish," he said, looking up at them. "But it's important to me that you three do. No matter what you hear, remember what I'm telling you. I never had an affair with Ava Cilento. I never hit her, or hurt her in any way. And I didn't kill her, either. But someone did. The amount of blood in that motel room left no question."

While Julia glared in vindication at the two adults, Sandra sputtered, "Oh, for Christ's sake, Gus, I knew you didn't do it. I was only asking because Jack wanted to know."

"We've all got murder in us," Jack said. "It's just one of

the nasty skills we humans come equipped with. We can get angry or passionate or just blind enough to kill."

"And we can lie, too. So how do you know I'm not exercising *that* particular human skill?" Gus said.

"Because I've seen you do it before," Jack smiled. "I know how you act when you lie." He got up and refilled both his and Gus's glasses. "And because I know you."

"This is what I mean about common sense," Sandra interrupted. "Give either of you some two-line reading and you can pull more meaning out of it than I can find in the whole Bible, but when it comes to regular life . . . I mean, how's it gonna look when the cops show up to arrest you and you're dead drunk? You and your fine pastor both?"

"We're not drunk yet, Sandra, but we could probably use some snacks to absorb the alcohol," Jack said.

"You hear that? *Las mujeres* have just been sent to *la cocina*," Sandra said in the mixture of English and Spanish she used when she was angry. "Come on, Julia."

"Have we got an avocado?" Julia asked, following behind her mother as she headed toward the kitchen. "Whenever I'm stressed, I crave guacamole."

Gus and Jack sipped their whiskey in troubled silence while mother and daughter moved around the kitchen. They were both relieved when Julia appeared with a platter of fragrant nachos, followed by Sandra carrying a bowl of guacamole. Gus realized he hadn't eaten anything since the night before.

The mood remained subdued as the four of them pretended to focus on their food, each privately listening for the car in the driveway, the footsteps on the walkway, a knock at the door. Happiness, Gus thought, was never so sweet as when it was threatened.

"If you all don't mind, I think I'm going to lie down for a while," he said when he had finished his nachos. "I didn't get much sleep last night." He kissed each of them on the forehead before he left the room.

Though Jack usually complained loudly when Gus expressed his easy Portuguese affection, he said nothing this time.

Gus carried his plate to the kitchen and went upstairs, trailed by the dogs. The room was dark, like the motel room had been, but these shadows were familiar and hospitable. The dogs, grateful for Gus's return, settled into their familiar spots, Jane on her mat on the floor, and Stella curled against his body while he lay on his back and waited. The whole house was sealed in an unfamiliar silence, as if the other occupants had also withdrawn to their rooms to wait for the official voices, the rush of wind from the outside that would change everything.

As he lay on his bed, Jane snoring peacefully on the floor beside him, Gus thought back on the first night Ava had come to him and the terrible petal-like beauty of those purple thumbprints on her throat. Had it really been only hours since he'd spoken to her? Her voice had been so small, as if it was already vanishing. He had risked everything to save her, and he had lost. But worst of all, he had *failed*. As he waited in his room, "Gaivota," the half-forgotten fado song about a seagull, ran through his head. The knock at the door, when it came, was almost a relief.

PART FOUR

THORNE HOUSE

{ 2001–2009 }

The sign outside Thorne House announced the fate of Nick Costa's legendary medical practice, his wife's unfulfilled dreams, and Hallie's lost childhood: *SOLD BY RODERICK REALTY.* Hallie pulled the sign from the ground and leaned it against the fence, face in. Did they have to scream it in such bold colors? Felicia's brother, Hugo, had handwritten the second sign in purple Magic Marker the day before: *ESTATE SALE TOMORROW: Everything Must GO!!!* The exclamation points annoyed Hallie so much she was tempted to uproot that sign, too, but she resisted. She could dig out all the signs she wanted, but the truth would remain: the buyers were closing on the house in three days and she was contractually bound to deliver it clean and empty.

The day she'd signed on for the service Hugo called "cleaning and disposition of assets," he had handed her a business card that proclaimed him a "professional antiques dealer."

Hallie had confessed in Felicia's kitchen that there weren't many antiques in the house. But her old friend just licked the cream out of the middle of the Oreo like she used to as a child and laughed out loud. "You really think Hugo knows his ass from an antique? My brother's got a wallet full of those cards, and he's a serious drunk. It's not too late to change your mind—"

"I'm sure Hugo will do a fine job, and I'd rather give the business to someone local."

"Anyone ever tell you you're just like your father?" Felicia said with a familiar eye roll.

It was something Hallie had heard countless times in her life, but it felt different now.

Felicia stopped and hugged her. "I'm sorry . . . I've walked by that empty house so many times, I kind of got used to it, but this is the first time you've been home, right?"

"Since the funeral." Though he'd always claimed he wanted to be cremated, at the end, Nick had asked to be buried in St. Peter's—where Liz Cooper was interred with the Costas.

*H*allie *closed the gate behind her. Damn it, Sam should be with me*, she thought, but she hadn't pressed the issue at home. She knew how Sam felt about Provincetown. A single afternoon walking the streets and beaches she loved left him sullen, derailed by memories he refused to share with anyone, not even his wife.

She paused, threw back her shoulders, and loped up the brick walkway. It was something she'd done thousands of times, sometimes running, other times sauntering, distracted by an argument with Gus, barely thinking about the home she was entering. How she'd taken her life with Nick for granted.

She hesitated as she inserted the key in the lock, thinking of her husband's words. *It's just a house*, Sam had said gently when he urged her to sell it. *No matter how long you hang on to it, your father will never come home.* However, it wasn't until she stood at the front door that she felt that truth in her bones. The bitterness of *never*. Her father would never again stand at the stove, cooking macaroni and cheese with chorizo; she'd never find him sitting in his worn chair in the study, poring over a difficult case, or listening to Dizzy Gillespie, or reading an astronomy book.

When she pushed the door open, Hallie was assaulted by

the odor of rotting flowers. At first, she was spooked by the scent, recalling her father's wake. But then she saw the vase of dead blossoms on the kitchen table and smiled briefly. *Of course.* Cindy Roderick had bought them for the open house, hoping to cover the mildewy scent that had accumulated in every corner, and to remind prospective buyers of the former elegance of the old Victorian. The realtor wanted them to see it as Liz Cooper had envisioned, not what it had become under Nick's neglectful care.

Hallie grabbed the bouquet and looked for some place to throw it away. When she found the trash pail in the same closet where it had always been, she dropped the flowers and wept. Later, she would laugh to think that it was a trash pail that had finally broken her. She hadn't been able to cry since the day Nick died—not even at the wake, when she stood stiffly between her husband and Stuart. Aunt Del, Buddy, and the cousins who'd come home from around the country were lined up beside them. Hallie had shaken what felt like a thousand hands, accepted even more hugs, and listened to endless stories about Nick, all while numbly *absorbing* nothing. As for the corpse beside her, it clearly *wasn't* him. It was a pale old man with pursed lips, disdainful of the world in a way her father had never been.

Gus's trial had followed mercilessly soon after. She had faced it in the same spirit, strangely absent from her own body. At times, she wondered if she'd ever feel anything again. And then came the miracle that brought her back to life.

Hallie remained frozen before the closet, but in her heart she raced through the house and into the office, her tread light and free, the way it had been when she was a girl and she had news. *Nick! I got an A on my English paper . . . Nick, I've*

*been invited to a birthday party . . . I jumped the farthest in the broad
jump at school . . . I got a part in the play! Nick, oh God, Nick, I'm
in love with Gus Silva.* Though she never told him that last, he
had known almost from the first day.

However, now when she had her biggest announcement
of all, Nick was not there to hear it. *I'm pregnant, Nick! Pregnant, do you hear me? You're finally going to be a grandfather! And
it's a girl.* She didn't even say the part that would have brought
her father a bittersweet happiness. The baby girl would be
named for her mother: Elizabeth Cooper Costa Maddox.

She opened all the windows and admitted the unforgiving
east wind and the briny scent of the bay. Then she climbed
the two flights of stairs that led to the roof and took her
old perch on the chimney. *Nick, how could you leave me? And
where, where did you go?* she wept, looking out over the implacable waters. The only answer was the thrum of the tides.

She cried hard, but not long. That was one of Nick's rules.
You could weep—*of course you could.* In fact, Nick believed
that there were things so grievous in life that if you didn't
cry for them, it indicated a serious defect of character. But
though the world's sorrows were endless, tears had limits—at
least in this house. For Nick Costa, and for his daughter after
him, *to live* was an action verb. Hallie wasn't sure how long
she'd been sitting on the roof when she imagined her father's
voice: *Enough, Pie. Now get up and wash your face.*

And so she did. Not just because it was what her father
would have wanted her to do, but because Felicia was right:
she *was* like him. Like him in both the good and the most
maddening ways. She took comfort in the realization that
as long as she was alive, and her child after her, Nick would
never truly be gone.

There was soap in the dish, a hand towel on the rung—almost as if a family still lived there, though no one but realtors and prospective buyers had entered the house since Nick moved out to the dunes.

Looking in the bathroom mirror, she thought of the day when she had caught Gus studying his face at the house on Point of Pines. That was little more than a year earlier, but everything had changed for both of them. Though Hallie had girded herself for the jury's verdict, she still felt weak whenever she thought of the foreman's words: "Guilty on the charge of murder in the first degree."

She wanted to visit him, though she'd heard that, like his father before him, he had shut down in prison. Refused to see the many parishioners and hospital workers who had supported him throughout the trial. Even Sandra and Jack had been turned away, their letters and packages sent back unopened. In the end, it was only the miracle that had stopped her. Her own unexpected happiness. The child.

Two only children, Hallie and Sam had wanted babies right away. *Want* wasn't even the right word. It was more elemental than that. It was a hunger, a fever that never abated. On one of their earliest dates, Hallie was embarrassed when Sam caught her looking longingly at the beautiful children on the street, pointing at them, giving in to the inevitable clichés. *Did you see that one in the stroller? So cute. And that little girl in her bright leggings. Adorable.* But then she realized Sam was smiling, too, smiling and repeating after her. *Yes, cute. Incredibly sweet.*

Hallie, who had always believed she would conceive as easily as Liz Cooper had, was shocked when it didn't happen. After two years of trying, she and Sam had sought help. What followed was five years of studying calendars and taking temperatures, of futile fertility treatments and a persistent stalemate over adoption. ("I want our child," Sam insisted. "A little girl with your beauty and my, um, common sense." Invariably, Hallie countered, "It *will* be ours.")

But when she finally got pregnant, it felt like a vicious joke. Nick's death and the long trial had strained her marriage nearly to the breaking point.

Sam had accompanied her to the courthouse on the day she was to testify, but Hallie forgot his presence as Lunes Oliveira drew her back into the colorful streets of Provincetown where she had fallen in love with a boy with a troubled past and the kindest, saddest eyes she had ever seen. Before she had finished her testimony, Sam walked out. She never knew how much he saw or heard as she was forced to publicly relive her relationship with Gus and the accident that had altered their lives.

But it didn't matter. She carried the trial and all it had dredged up home with her. It was there in her quiet preoccupation, when she turned away from Sam in bed, and in the nights when she hardly seemed to come to bed at all. Like the sand of Provincetown, it had infiltrated the house, and no one could sweep it all away.

Sam responded by avoiding their condo that overlooked Boston Common. At first, he called to say he wasn't coming home for dinner, but eventually, it was just understood. She ate salads and baked potatoes, sardines on crackers—what her friend Abby called "spinster food." Usually, she was asleep by the time his key turned in the lock. Hallie knew she should worry, probably even "talk about it," but she was privately relieved by his absence. All she could think about was the trial, her own role in it, and Gus's face when they announced the sentence.

Alone in the condo, she folded her arms and paced, obsessed with guilt over her testimony and the question she could never ask out loud: *Had Gus done it? Had he killed the woman in the motel that day after he'd left her father's shack?* She would have given anything to be sure of him, but her doubts lingered. There was simply too much evidence that was impossible to explain away, not the least of which was memory itself. She recalled Neil Gallagher's body slamming against the Jeep and the moment when she realized Gus *couldn't stop*, that he just might kill Neil. And then she felt herself awakening from the coma in the hospital, her mouth unbearably dry, voice tiny—but already calling for Gus.

She'd always been so sure that he never intended to hurt her, but now? She was no longer certain of anything.

She used up almost an entire notebook of lined paper, attempting to write to him, but never got past his name. The typical questions felt like a mockery. *How are you? What's new?* Was there an etiquette for writing to prisoners that she hadn't yet learned? The only thing more cruel would be to tell him about her own life. The bright mornings she raced through, the satisfaction of using herself up as she tackled her patients' problems, and sometimes even solved them, the friendly greetings she got at the hospital. The *respect*. And all the while Gus was there. In a cell with an open toilet, and the person he'd loved and trusted above all others doubting his innocence.

She didn't even hear Sam the night he slipped into the kitchen and found her hunched over her notebook. He tore the letter from the table and read the name out loud, imbuing it with more disgust than the prosecutor had. "So this is how you spend your nights?" he asked. He ripped the unwritten letter to shreds with the same efficiency that he did everything.

"We should talk about this tomorrow," Hallie said. She attempted to angle past him and into the bedroom, surprised to catch a whiff of whiskey.

He stepped into her path, blocking her with his wide frame. "No, not tomorrow, Hallie. I want that murderer out of my house now. But most of all I want him out of my wife's heart." Up close in the still bright light of the kitchen, Hallie saw past the anger in Sam's eyes to the hurt. Abruptly, he kissed her. It was a harsh kiss that contained all the contaminated emotion between them. Hallie was amazed by how much she wanted it.

In the morning, Sam didn't wake her up to say goodbye before he left. The sex they'd had the night before couldn't erase the tension between them, but in the end, it accomplished something far more significant: it produced the miracle.

"I'm pregnant, Sam," Hallie had said into the phone when she knew for sure, her voice hushed and bewildered and shot through with questions.

First she imagined his silence as shock or disappointment, perhaps even dismay. A child—*now*? But then she realized that he was crying. "I love you, Hallie. If that means anything, maybe we can still make this work."

Hallie knew she should say that she loved him, too—and the truth was, she *did*. But she wasn't sure if he believed her anymore. Instead, she whispered, "We can, Sam. I know we can."

*N*ow, *two transformative months later, she* was alone in her father's house—and famished. She went instinctively to the refrigerator and was startled by its pristine emptiness. The cell phone rang just as the fridge door slammed shut.

"Look out the window," Sam said on the other end of the line. "A veggie pizza with extra artichokes and a carton of organic milk are being delivered to the house right this moment. It was no easy task to convince the driver to stop for that milk, so you better drink it."

"How much did you tip him?" Hallie laughed as she saw the lights of the delivery car blink out in front, followed by footsteps on the walkway. "And how on earth did you know they were arriving now?"

"I told them to call me just before they reached the house. That way we can eat together. I'm having the same thing."

Hallie heard the beep of the microwave, indicating that Sam's pizza had grown cold as he waited. It was quickly followed by the sound of a beer being popped.

She carried the phone to the door and tipped the delivery man even though she knew Sam had already done so. "*What,* no milk? I thought we were going through this pregnancy together."

"There's only so far a man can go," Sam said, exhaling with satisfaction after a long swig of beer.

Hallie could see his broad smile and his muscular chest, the way he tossed back his head when he drank. She carried the pizza and milk to the blue table where she had shared so many meals with Nick and their friends, and held Sam on the line until she had finished. They talked about his day at Wellesley, where his course in practical philosophy was easily the most popular course in the catalogue, and how he'd almost been clipped by a student on a bike when he was walking to his office. Finally, Sam asked about Felicia and the preparations for the estate sale. But there was an obligatory tone in his voice, a note he always assumed when he was forced to talk about her hometown.

"There's not much of an estate. Not much of value—"

She left the sentence unfinished. Not much of value—except Wolf's paintings, another forbidden topic between them. Other than that, there were the few pieces Liz Cooper had bought, and rooms full of her father's largely worthless treasures—also subjects Sam preferred to avoid.

He cleared his throat. "Well, that makes it easier, I suppose." Then, as always, he pivoted away from the subject and asked what time she'd be back on Thursday.

"The closing's scheduled for eleven. As soon as I sign the papers, I'll be on the road," Hallie said.

Only after she hung up the phone did Hallie think of all the things they hadn't discussed. How she felt when she opened the door of the house. The grief she'd finally released on the roof. What it was like to sit at the blue table without Nick. Provincetown was the part of Hallie that Sam could never have, and in many ways it was the deepest, truest part.

Like Hallie, Sam had strong visceral reactions to the crumbling Victorian on Commercial Street. Once in high school, he'd taken the bus to Provincetown from his home in Weston. He had walked past the place, and peered furtively up at the attic windows, but he had never knocked on the door. Nor had he ever been invited inside. If they had seen him on the sidewalk, Hallie and Nick would have thought of him as just another tourist, admiring the architecture and the view beyond it. No one would have guessed his real interest in the place.

Hallie put the uneaten portion of her pizza in the fridge for breakfast and walked upstairs to the rooms that she had once called the "ghost quarters."

Wolf's bold paintings still covered the walls. Since they'd been "discovered" by the art world, they had attracted increasing interest and higher offers. However, Nick had steadfastly refused to sell them.

Hallie studied her favorite painting of Race Point, the bolts of magenta Wolf had seen on the water. She could still remember her excitement as she had watched Wolf paint it, and how he'd become so lost in his work that he'd been startled to find her there. For a moment, he, too, felt present to her. In her grief over Nick, she had almost forgotten about the *other* grandfather her child would never meet.

Hey, Wolf, she said, talking to her ghosts for the second time that day. *Have you heard the news? Your son's going to be a father.*

CHAPTER 22

Hallie sat up with a start to the sound of hammering on the front door and raked her hand through her loose, wavy hair. It took her a moment to realize where she was: there in her high bed, peering out on her own glistening bay. *Home.* But before she could absorb the pleasure of that, the knocks resumed more insistently.

Hallie picked up the cell she'd tossed on her bedside table the night before: 7:25. She snuck out to the landing to catch a glimpse of the interloper. Then, realizing she was wearing only her bikini underpants and an old T-shirt that had grown tight across her chest in pregnancy, she quickly retreated.

Shit. Whoever the hell's banging at the door this early better be bringing coffee. She had thrown on her jeans and was searching for a bra when the pounding grew louder. Obviously, the bra would have to wait.

When she snapped open the door, she was almost struck by a man with his fist in the air. He was dressed in a sleek suit and smiling in a way that instantly annoyed Hallie.

"*Dr. Maddox.*" He looked her up and down. "I almost didn't recognize you. You look considerably less formal than the last time we met."

"*Lunes Oliveira?*" Hallie said, hardly able to believe Gus's attorney was standing in her doorway. She hadn't seen him since the trial. "What exactly—"

Undaunted, Lunes continued to grin. "So are you going to invite me in or not?" He consulted a black Rolex as he glided past her. "I've been up for an hour and five minutes and I still haven't had coffee yet. I thought you might—"

"This house has been vacant for a year," Hallie interrupted. "The only edible thing in the kitchen is last night's cold pizza. What's more, I don't seem to remember inviting you for breakfast."

"Cold pizza will be fine," Lunes said, pulling up a chair at the blue table. "By the way, I've gotta say I like that wild look. Maybe you should have worn your hair down in court. God knows it couldn't have gone worse."

Suddenly feeling self-conscious, Hallie hugged herself. She was about to toss her guest out of the house when a thought occurred to her. "Is there any new information about Gus's case?"

Lunes's smile faded, and she saw a hint of the man behind the fine clothes and the swagger. "I wish there was. It was probably my childhood brainwashing, but that was one client I actually believed."

"Too bad you weren't able to convince the jury."

"Ouch," Lunes said, rising from the chair. "My feelings might be hurt if I wasn't so confident in the work I did. If you recall, they had motive, a previous assault against the victim, and the testimony of the cab driver that put him at the scene. Not to mention all the physical evidence he left behind. But it was the abuse scandal that really killed us. The jury took one look at this young, good-looking priest and immediately decided he was guilty."

"Then why did you believe him?"

"Guess I couldn't imagine anyone would be that dumb. Sure, every criminal makes mistakes—even the smart ones—

but if Gus had written out a ten-point plan to implicate himself in the crime, he couldn't have done a better job."

"So you believed him because everything pointed to his guilt?" Hallie said, wishing Lunes could say something to erase the uncertainties that still haunted her. "That makes no sense."

Lunes shrugged. "We all have our weak spots, Doctor. The instances when logic fails, and emotion or a common history or . . ." He hesitated a minute before he continued. "Okay, all I had—all I *still* have is my gut—and the fact that a few good people who know him pretty well seemed to share my belief. Like Sandra. And what about her daughter? A National Merit Scholar who grew up in the projects. Can't usually put much over on that combination."

Hallie remembered the quiet, sloe-eyed girl and her sharply dressed mother who looked as if she belonged in a hospital bed, not a courtroom. "How are they?"

"Sandra passed away a few months ago, I'm sorry to say," Lunes said. "She was quite a woman."

"And her daughter?"

"There's a new housekeeper, and Julia's still living in the garage above the rectory. It's a rather unorthodox foster home, but the old priest has connections and he's made it work." While Hallie was considering that, he continued: "Then there was your actor friend, the guy Little Cod almost killed—what's his name?"

"Neil Gallagher."

"Poor bastard pretty much messed up his whole life trying to save his childhood buddy. Stopped showing up at his play rehearsals in the city, started drinking too much, blew his relationship with an up-and-coming actress, and ended up in Chicago, directing student theater."

Hallie knew about the job Neil had taken in Chicago, but the rest was news to her. "Shouldn't you be investigating Gus's case, instead of his friends?"

"That's where most investigations usually start, isn't it? With friends and family. Usually end there, too."

"So that's why you're here? You're researching me?"

"Nah. I already know all the salient facts about you, Dr. Maddox. Got yourself a thriving medical practice at the clinic in Mission Hill. Married—rather coincidentally, I might add—to the millionaire son of your former boarder. Someday you'll have to tell me how *that* happened."

"Yeah, someday we'll have a long chat about every personal detail of my life," Hallie said, feeling even more irritated.

Lunes seemed to enjoy the feistier Hallie. "Anyway, I figured you'd be in touch if you had any new information."

"So if you don't want to discuss Gus's case, why did you come?" Hallie asked.

"For the estate sale, of course. My ex-wife was something of an art collector and she taught me a lot. Aside from my kids and some pretty great sex, it was the best part of our marriage. Where are they?"

"Excuse me?" Hallie said.

"Your father-in-law's paintings. I hear his finest work is here, rotting along with a rather fantastic house. If I were still married, I'd consider buying it myself."

Though it was technically true, Hallie never thought of Wolf as her *father-in-law.* And as for his art, it was like the bay outside the window, or the slightly fishy scent on the air— simply part of the atmosphere she'd breathed as a child. It infuriated her that someone, especially the maddening Lunes Oliveira, saw it as a commodity.

"The paintings aren't for sale," she said curtly.

"Newspaper says otherwise." As if on cue, Lunes produced a clipping from the *Cape Cod Times* advertising the estate sale. He'd underlined the words *including artwork*.

"What?" Hallie tore the scrap of paper from his hands. "Well, it's a mistake. As I said, they're not for sale. They're . . . my daughter's legacy."

She'd blurted out that last before she could stop herself—and she wasn't even sure it was true. She and Sam had only talked about the fate of the paintings once, and his response had been blunt. "You want to know what I would do with them? Burn them. I don't care what they're worth—and frankly, neither did he." *He.* It was the only word Sam ever used to refer to his father.

Lunes cocked his head curiously, interrupting her reverie. "Daughter? I'm sorry; I didn't realize you had a child."

Instinctively, Hallie put her hand over her abdomen. "Um, I don't. I mean—not yet."

And there it was again, that voracious smile. "Well, I guess congratulations are in order. I'm happy for you, Hallie. Sincerely. And for Mr. Maddox as well."

Hallie nodded, appalled that she'd revealed her pregnancy to him. "I don't mean to be rude, Lunes, but I have a lot to do this morning; and the man who's handling the sale should be here any moment."

"I hope you don't mind if I take a quick look? I promise not to bother you." He drifted into the study, where he picked up Nick's telescope and began to examine it. "Pretty outdated, but still a fine piece of equipment. How much you want for it?"

Furious, Hallie bolted across the room and put her

body between the lawyer and his object of interest. "Don't touch it," she said before she could stop herself. Then, not sure whether she was flushing from embarrassment or just anger, she quickly added, "I'm sorry, but that's not for sale, either."

Lunes laughed. "Another of your daughter's legacies?"

"No, *mine*," Hallie said, recalling the clear nights when her father had packed a blanket and Thermos full of sweet coffee and headed toward Herring Cove, where he'd treated her to the wonders of the night sky.

"I see," Lunes said, walking through the room like a particularly agile predator, picking up and setting down various items.

Every time he touched an object, Hallie cringed and held her breath until he completed his careful examination and returned it to its place.

Finally, Lunes sauntered back into the kitchen and opened a cupboard. Hallie assumed the pushy intruder wanted to get himself a glass of water before he left. But instead, he pulled a cracked brown cup from the shelf and held it in the air. It happened to be the mug Nick has used to drink his coffee every morning. "How much for this?"

"Are you joking? You want to buy a coffee-stained mug?"

"Believe it or not, I've never been more serious in my life."

"It's an old diner cup. Obviously worthless. There's no way I would sell you such a thing."

"Then you're saying I can have it for nothing—a little gift to signify our growing friendship, perhaps?"

Hallie reached out to grab the cup, but the smiling Lunes lifted it higher.

"A thousand dollars, Dr. Maddox. I'll give you a thousand dollars for your *worthless* brown cup."

"It's from a place in Cambridge where my parents used to go," Hallie said in a low voice. "The coffee shop was torn down about twenty years ago and my father—"

"Ah, another family heirloom," Lunes said, holding up his free hand. "No need to say another word." He placed the cup on the shelf as if it were a delicate piece of crystal, then removed another mismatched cup—Wolf's favorite—and held it aloft. "How about this one? Will you accept my generous—no, let's be honest, *insane*—offer for this fine piece? One thousand dollars for a cup you couldn't get two cents for in a yard sale."

This time Hallie was successful when she reached out and grabbed it out of his hand. "Get out of my house, Mr. Oliveira," she said, shaking as she clung to the blue-rimmed mug.

Lunes laughed, again consulting his elegant watch. "I'd love to stay and see how the sale goes, but it turns out you're in luck. I'm due in court in less than an hour, and as you know, I still haven't had a cup of coffee. I'll leave you to your heirlooms."

Hallie closed her eyes in relief as he headed for the door.

But just before he reached it, Lunes made one of his dramatic pivots, which she remembered from the courtroom. "A little advice? I don't practice real estate law, Hallie; but if I were you, I'd get a hold of whoever's advising you on the sale right away. You've only got a couple days till the closing. And you better get that sign out of your front yard, too."

"What the—what are you talking about?" Hallie said, clasping the mug to her chest.

The lawyer smiled. "Look at you—you're not ready to part with a single cup. There's not a chance in hell you're going to give up your father's house. The sooner you break the news to the poor bastards who think they're buying it, the better."

CHAPTER 23

Hallie wrangled a bra on under her T-shirt, grabbed an old denim jacket from a hook, and ran a brush through her tangled hair. Then she walked into town and picked up a cup of coffee and a *malasada*, to go. She argued with Lunes Oliveira in her mind as she walked. *So she was having a little trouble parting with her father's things. That was to be expected, wasn't it? It didn't mean she wasn't ready to sell a house that had sat empty for over a year. Besides, she hadn't even come home very much when her father was alive. Why would she want to be here now?*

She could almost see him smirking as he made her face the question she'd been avoiding since her father's death: Why *hadn't* she come home more often? Why did she deny herself the pleasure of Nick's company when it was still available? Why did she deny *him*?

It seemed like they had so much time. All the time in the world, as Gus had once said about their love. Another lie, as it turned out. She would be there for the Portuguese Festival, she had promised her father . . . In late fall, when the tourists were gone . . . For Christmas, definitely.

When she noticed two men watching her suspiciously, she realized she was crying openly right there in the gallery district of Commercial Street. Fortunately, they were strangers. *What are you looking at?* she wanted to say. Or, more like, *What are you doing here in my town?* But of course, it wasn't her town anymore.

She swabbed at her face with the sleeve of her jean jacket and kept walking. She had a thousand excuses for failing to visit, but mostly she blamed her busy schedule and her husband's aversion to the place. *Can't you come here?* she ended up saying to Nick every holiday. And he had. Bearing *linguiça* and sweet bread, *trutas*, and the *vinho* no one but him found palatable, he would cheerfully trudge to Boston. He would sit at her mother-in-law's formal table in what looked like fishermens' clothes, watching with sly amusement as Sam's mother announced to every guest: Have you met Hallie's father? He's a *doctor*. As if she needed to bolster his image. Hallie finally saw him as he'd been back in his Harvard days, or when he'd gone to meet Liz Cooper's family, refusing to allow anyone to make him feel inferior.

Her friends had warned Hallie that the Provincetown where they'd grown up was gone. The fishing industry was waning, real estate prices were stratospheric, and most of the old families had moved to Truro or further up Cape. And yet every breath she took as she walked the streets told another story. From the salt-laced wind to the mixture of shells, sand, and multicolored pebbles that crunched beneath her feet to the sweet, greasy smell of the *malasada* in her white bag, Hallie was home.

The entrance to the alley beside her house was narrow, but it widened on the bay. It opened her lungs and split her heart every time she walked through it. She planned to watch the tide go out while she drank her coffee, but just before she turned in to it, she saw a cluster of unfamiliar cars parked outside her house; and even more alarming—a rabid-looking group of strangers inside the gate. Some of them had made themselves comfortable on the old wicker chairs while others were walking around the property, gaping in the windows. They exuded a strange tension, like competitors at the beginning of a race.

"Um . . . Excuse me?" Hallie said, a little too loudly, nearly spilling her coffee on the sidewalk.

The interlopers turned sharply in her direction. But instead of being embarrassed, they appeared put out. Those who were seated jumped to their feet and lunged toward the door, while one woman who was carrying a large, obviously empty shopping bag spoke up in a sharp voice. "Are you the seller?" she asked. And then before Hallie could answer, she added, "We've been here for almost a half hour!" The man beside her looked Hallie up and down, taking in the loose hair Lunes called *wild*, her old jeans with a hole at the knee, and a T-shirt bearing the logo of Doyle's Pub, one of her and Sam's favorite places to relax in South Boston. He nodded to himself, apparently deciding that she conformed to his stereotype of the typical Ptown resident.

Hallie glanced at her wrist, then realized she hadn't bothered to strap on her watch. "What time is it?"

"Eight-forty!" the man who'd nodded judgmentally at the sight of her yelled out. His tone made it sound like an indictment.

"Eight forty-*three*," a woman corrected from the porch. When Hallie looked in her direction, she realized it was none other than Mavis Black, her hair a brighter shade of neon orange than ever. Otherwise, she looked no different than she had when Hallie left Provincetown fourteen years earlier.

"*Mavis?*" Hallie mumbled, momentarily forgetting the mob in her yard.

"Very astute of you, Hallie," Mavis said, eyeing the pastry bag pointedly. "I've been waiting here for over a half-hour while you apparently wandered over to Ina's for a greasy Portuguese doughnut. We're here for the estate sale."

The idea of the nosy Mavis wandering through her house, touching Nick's things was even more repellent than Lunes's visit had been. Hallie quickly decided she didn't want *any* of these people stampeding through her rooms, gaping at Wolf's paintings, or running their hands over the spines of Nick's books.

"Well, the estate sale doesn't start till nine," she said. "I think that gives me seventeen minutes to drink my coffee in peace."

"But we're *early birds*," a woman who was guarding the door with the ferocity of a goalie shouted. "I'm sure you were told to expect early birds."

Safe behind the screen door, Hallie tried for the third time that day to be courteous in the face of extreme provocation. "If you could please give me a few minutes, there's something I've got to do."

"No more than five!" the woman by the door warned. "If you take any longer than that, the *regular* crowd will be here. It's not fair."

A surge of agreement bubbled up among the group.

True to her word, Hallie promptly reemerged from the house, carrying a large sheet of paper and a piece of tape. "The best I could do," she said as she covered the sign.

ESTATE SALE CANCELED
GOOD DAY TO ALL!

The people on the porch refused to forfeit their places until a loud murmur went up from those who were close enough to read the sign. "But it was in the *paper*," a man cried out, waving his cane in the air, and for a moment Hallie was afraid they might storm the place.

"I'm sorry, really I am," she said. "It's just that I—I can't do it." But since the bargain hunters were too busy venting to one another to listen, she slipped back inside and bolted the door behind her. Then she took her coffee and her *malasada* and went out onto the back stoop to be alone with her bay. She'd been avoiding fatty indulgences since she first learned she was pregnant, but this was an exception. The *malasada* might score poorly nutrition-wise, but it was desperately needed food for her soul. Just like the chilly breeze that rose from the water, and the sight of the boats spackled with salt and barnacles bobbing near the wharf.

A half-hour later she tentatively went inside and peered out the front window. The porch, the yard, and the street were empty, and for a minute Hallie missed the horde of intruders she had sent away. Without them, she was left alone with the decision that would enrage many people she hardly knew, and hugely disappoint the most important person in her life.

Sam had been calling all morning. But instead of answering her cell, she had switched it off. Before she could explain what she'd done, she needed to understand it herself.

When she got home from the lawyer's office, she paused briefly at the foot of the stairs, before marching up to the room she'd been avoiding since she first came home. Nick's bed was casually made and lumpy, as if some secret vestige of himself might still be hiding under the covers. Beside the bed a mountain of books teetered with a photo of Liz Cooper set on top. Nick's personal summit.

Lying down on the bed, Hallie spread her arms like wings and realized she had never felt more safe anywhere else. This was where she'd come when she'd woken from a nightmare; and there had never been a dark vision Nick couldn't quell. *It's not real*, he would say decisively. Then he'd let her lie in the crook of his arm. "*This*," he'd say. *This is real, Pie. Now tell me—is there anything to fear?* Hallie always believed that the fearlessness that was both her greatest strength and her most dangerous weakness had begun here. She turned on her side and found shelter in her father's room one more time. Within minutes, she was asleep.

Her rest was disrupted several times by pounding at the door, and by still louder voices at the open window. She didn't answer any of them. Not even when she heard Felicia's throaty voice: "Hallie, honey? Come on, I know you're in there."

Or when Aunt Del beat her cane distinctively on the window, and growled, "Hallie Costa! What've you gone and done now, girl?" But despite her words, there was no mistaking the triumph in her voice. Aunt Del had been trying to dissuade her from selling the house ever since she first heard that Cindy Roderick had put up a sign outside *her* office. Hallie knew she owed both Felicia and Aunt Del an explanation—not to mention her husband. But not sure what it was, she pressed her eyes closed and willed herself back to oblivion.

When she woke up, she was disappointed to find herself still trapped in the light of the same day. But even before she headed downstairs to choose between the uneaten half of her *malasada* and last night's cold pizza, she thought about her phone. Though she'd turned it off, she could practically feel it pulsing beside her. She wondered how many times Sam had called—and how long she could possibly avoid telling him about her impulsive decision.

A minute later the intense desire for an eggplant grinder with fresh mozzarella overcame nearly everything else. She waited till just before closing time when the streets were likely to be quiet before she slipped out. By then, she was sure the news had spread through town: Hallie Costa had canceled the sale of Thorne House.

She covered her hair with a hood and took a circuitous route to the market on Bradford Street. After she'd finished her perfect eggplant sandwich, she made her way up to the roof clutching her phone and what was left of her apple juice. By then it was nearly eleven and Sam was probably ready to call the Provincetown Police Department and request a safety check. She flipped the phone open, intending to call home, but instead found herself dialing Neil's cell. It was the same number he'd had for years, in spite of several moves.

He greeted her with the same upbeat, expectant hello he'd had as a teenager, but he couldn't maintain the optimistic tone for long. Hallie wasn't sure whether it was the trial or his stagnant acting career that had changed him, but something was clearly missing. She recalled the deterioration Lunes had described: failing to show up for rehearsals, losing parts, drinking excessively.

"You're in Provincetown?" he said after she had told him her location. "Hal, that roof was a hazard twenty years ago. Do you really think you should be up there?"

"It's safe," Hallie said, remembering the feeling she'd had in her father's room. *That*, not mugs or telescopes, or even this house, was her real legacy. Hers and Lizzie's.

Despite her ambivalence, there was so much she wanted

to tell Neil. About the grinder she'd had at Georgie's, and the golden light she woke up to that morning, and why she couldn't sell the house. She wanted to tell her story in narrowing loops, the way she and Gus and Neil had as teenagers until they eventually converged on the truth.

"It's not just the physical dangers I'm thinking about. That was your special place, yours and Gus's, wasn't it? You're probably up there reliving everything."

The whole town was our special place, but I have a new life now, Hallie wanted to say, but something in Neil's voice stopped her. There was a loneliness there, a *longing* that he only revealed when he'd had a drink or two. It filled her with sorrow and made her eager to get off the phone. She tried not to think about why none of his relationships ever worked out.

"Anyway, I shouldn't be bothering you. It's just being here . . . well, I guess I was feeling nostalgic," Hallie said. "I probably should let you go, and I need to call Sam."

"I get that feeling all the time, and I'm not even in Ptown," Neil said, ignoring the mention of Sam.

The wind had turned cold as Hallie stood there clutching her little phone, and she was shivering as she said goodbye. By the time she hung up, she regretted calling. Neil tried to keep in touch, but they'd only spoken once since the trial—when he called to say he was moving to Chicago. She was about to dial Sam when she heard the front door open and close.

She went to the hatchway and yelled in the direction of the stairs. "Hello?" There was no response. Clinging to both cell phone and flashlight, she descended the ladder to the attic cautiously—unsure if she should make the intruder aware of her presence or not.

But the tread hardly sounded like that of a burglar, or anyone who meant her harm. Instead, it recalled a tired man coming in from work. Hallie heard the refrigerator door opening and closing, followed by the sound of someone rattling through the junk drawer as if they were searching for something. The noises were so familiar that, for one crazy minute, she thought it might be Nick.

The footsteps echoed up the stairs toward the second floor.

"Hello?" Hallie repeated, resting her hand protectively against her abdomen. "Who the hell is in my house?"

CHAPTER 24

The only answer was a slow but determined creak of the stairs. Hallie was looking around the attic, searching for hiding places when she spotted the life-size painting propped in the corner. Wolf, who'd always considered it a failure, had faced it toward the wall. The intruder paused on the second-floor landing. Hallie held herself taut, thinking that he—and she was sure it was a *he* by the weight of his footsteps—must have been lured to the house by the paintings, which had been advertised in the paper.

She scanned the room, wishing her father or Wolf had kept a gun. She imagined herself bursting forth to defend Wolf's work, the impassioned swirls and furious dashes of color that would be all her daughter would ever know of her paternal grandfather. But there was no gun, and if there had been, Hallie wouldn't have known how to use it.

She was startled when the narrow door to the attic staircase opened and the visitor continued to climb to the top floor. The only exit was by the roof, and even the rusted iron ladder that Gus had ascended the first time they kissed was long gone. Heart banging against her ribs, she slipped behind the painting and made herself as still and small as possible.

The intruder strode to the middle of the room and then pulled a string, casting the chaotic space into sharp relief with a hundred-watt bulb. Hallie waited for his next move, but there was none. No movement. No words. Not even the clearing of a throat. The only sound Hallie heard was the low whisper of her unwanted visitor's breathing. What kind of burglar broke into a house and made his way up three flights of stairs, only to stop dead in the middle of the attic?

Hallie's first thought was that it might be the annoying Lunes Oliveira, come back to torment her one more time. Or maybe it was one of the thwarted early birds, returning to take revenge on a seller who had denied them the pleasure of sifting through her father's things. Both possibilities infuriated her so much that they banished her fear.

She poked her head cautiously out from behind the painting and found herself staring directly into a familiar pair of gray eyes darkened by indignation.

"*Sam?* What the hell?" she said, clutching her chest as she stepped forward. "You just about scared me to death. Why didn't you answer?" She attempted a relieved laugh but was cut short by her husband's implacable stillness.

"You *should* be scared," he said, indicating the door he had entered with the flat of his hand. "Jesus, Hallie. Anyone could have walked in and cornered you up here. I can't believe you didn't even lock the door."

"What are you doing on the Cape?" Hallie shot back guiltily. "Don't you have an eight-o'clock class in the morning?"

Sam continued to glare at her. "You know exactly what I'm doing here. I called you at least fifty times today—and that was before you turned off the phone."

"So you drove all the way . . . Oh, God, I'm sorry. I'm *so* sorry. There's no excuse, but coming home was a lot harder than I expected," Hallie said. "I just . . . I needed some time to process—"

"And you couldn't have picked up the phone? Am I such an insensitive prick that you couldn't talk to me about it?"

"Of course not, but—"

"But *shit*. If you didn't want to talk to me directly, you could have at least left a message. Let me know you were safe."

"I thought of that, but it felt like the coward's way out," Hallie said weakly.

"And not responding to my calls at all—that's your idea of courage?"

Hallie sunk down onto one of her mother's old boxes. "I was trying to figure out how I was going to explain what I'd done. I canceled the estate sale this morning, Sam."

"That's the least of what you did."

"You know about the house! But how—?"

"I called the attorney this afternoon."

"And he told you? Isn't there such a thing as client confidentiality anymore?"

"I'm your husband, Hallie. Or did you forget that once you crossed the town line? Williams assumed I knew."

"I know we agreed to sell the house, Sam. But when I saw that crowd swoop in to pick Nick's bones this morning, I just couldn't go through with it. I know it's crazy, but this place, his outdated medical books, the mug he drank his coffee from—they're all I have left of him."

Sam turned off the light, allowing the moon to outline them as he pulled up a box beside her. "Not true," he said more gently. He placed his broad flat palm over her chest and kept it there. "Not true."

Hallie covered his hand with her own. "I'm sorry," she repeated.

"I know you are." Sam smiled for the first time since he'd arrived. "And I'm sorry, too. I didn't realize how much I scared you when I came in till I saw your face. I was just so pissed, so goddamn frantic . . ."

Hallie nodded. "I love you." She leaned forward to hug him, and as she did, she saw a rectangle of dusky sky. Apparently she'd left the door leading to the roof unlatched and it had swung open.

"The wind must have blown that door open," she said. "Maybe before you leave, you can nail it shut."

H*allie met the only man who'd* interested her in years in the most unlikely of circumstances: at the reading of a will. Wolf's will, to be exact. It was two months after Nick had taken the grim hike out to the painter's shack and discovered his body that Nick and Hallie were summoned to the office of an attorney named Warren Kennett.

When she received the letter informing her that she had been named a beneficiary, Hallie was a first-year medical resident living in Boston's Mission Hill. She traced Wolf's real name with her fingers as she recited it out loud several times to her roommate, Abby.

"John Samson Maddox. I thought I knew him so well. I even used to tell people he was my uncle, and I never even knew his name," Hallie said, thinking of the hours she'd spent watching him work, thrilled as the vibrant splashes of color that at first seemed arbitrary and unrelated gradually recreated what she and Gus called the beach at the end of the world.

The attorney's office was a room of mahogany and glass, with Persian rugs and traditional paintings on the walls. Hallie's first thought was how much Wolf would have hated it.

Warren Kennett shook Nick's hand, and nodded toward

Hallie in a way she thought condescending. Though she only had two hours off from the hospital, she was wearing a short black skirt and an oversized sweater borrowed from the more fashionable Abby, with her own favorite plum-colored boots. She'd even taken the trouble to blow her hair straight. Now she wished she had shown up in her scrubs.

It was only then that she noticed the man who was already there. He rose politely.

"Sam Maddox," he said, extending his hand before Kennett had a chance to introduce him. "Your friend Wolf's son."

"*Wolf's son?*" Hallie and Nick blurted out simultaneously.

"But Wolf didn't . . . I mean he *couldn't* have—" Hallie stammered. "He didn't even believe in *involvements*." But as she spoke, she thought of the vague rumors she and Nick had never believed.

"*Hallie!*" her father muttered under his breath. She wasn't sure if he was correcting her for her bluntness or the inappropriate length of her stare.

Hallie blushed. "I'm sorry. I didn't mean . . . it's just—well, all these years—"

"No need to apologize," the son said graciously. "I'm well aware of my father's aversion to human relationships. I hadn't seen him since I was five."

If that troubled him, he gave no sign of it. Hallie immediately decided that the man couldn't possibly be related to Wolf. He was as self-contained and formal as Wolf was gruff and awkward. Even physically they were opposites. Wolf was tall and gaunt, while his son met her gaze levelly. Everything about him suggested solidity, from his body type to the equanimity of his expression.

Hallie couldn't help but notice, however, that he had his

father's eyes. The same shade of gray, the same laser-like focus. She wondered if he was trying to escape her stare when he positioned his seat slightly behind them—where he could observe their reactions, but they were not privy to his.

"I don't mean to rush things," he said. "But I have some business to take care of while I'm in the city. Do you think we could get started?"

Hallie cast a furtive glance backward, trying to figure out if his voice was calm or just cold.

The will was simple and straightforward. All of Wolf's financial assets, which included a boring complexity of accounts and stocks, annuities and trusts, went to his son.

"To my friend, Dr. Nicolao Costa of Provincetown, I bequeath the grandfathered lease to dune shack number 11 at Race Point, as well as all of my paintings and sketches, currently located in his home and at the shack.

Nick lowered his head, and Hallie could see that he was moved—not by the gift of the paintings, or even the coveted lease to the shack, but by the fact that Wolf referred to him as his friend. The doctor had only been hoping for access to the dune shack. But for years, he had been telling everyone in Provincetown that someday the paintings that hung throughout his house would be famous. Now he could help make that happen.

Hallie and Nick had almost forgotten the man sitting behind them when Sam cleared his throat and rose. He checked the time on his cell phone, apparently unimpressed by what was to Hallie a mind-boggling inheritance. "Excuse me, but if I'm done here, Warren, I'm going to take off."

"Dr. Costa. Hallie. Nice to meet Wolf's friends," Sam added. And then with a polite nod of his head, he was gone.

Nick was obviously ready to leave, too, but Kennett returned to his desk and to the will. "I know you need to get back to the office, Dr. Costa, but there's one more item to be discussed." He looked pointedly at Hallie for the first time. "John's bequest to you, Hallie."

"But my father got the paintings and the shack," she said. "What else did Wolf have?"

The lawyer chuckled softly to himself. "If you were listening a moment ago, you'd know that John Maddox had a great deal more than the lease on a barely livable shack and a few paintings of unknown value."

Hallie waited, expecting Kennett to say that Wolf had willed her his old paint brushes or the marble tablets that she'd watched with fascination as he mixed his colors. But instead, the lawyer returned to the formal language of the document. "To Hallett Costa of Provincetown, Massachusetts, I bequeath the painting entitled *Hallie at Race Point*, which is currently being stored in the back of Georgie's store."

For the third time in an hour, they were shocked into silence. It was Nick who spoke first. "That's not possible. Wolf never painted anything but seascapes," he said firmly. "And he certainly never painted my daughter."

"And why would he hide it in the back of Georgie's?" Hallie added. "Why not show it to us?"

Again, Kennett smiled. "It seems our friend Wolf kept secrets from all of us, doesn't it?"

While the attorney explained the legalities of transferring the lease, and taking formal ownership of the paintings, Hallie wandered toward the window. She was startled when she spotted Sam Maddox on the other side of the street. He stopped to buy a paper from a vendor and then slipped inside a little French café where Hallie herself sometimes picked up a coffee. *So much for his urgent appointment*, she thought, wondering if he was more like his father than she'd first imagined.

Hallie wished there was time for her and Nick to have lunch, but he had to leave immediately to make afternoon office hours. The only communication they'd had about their morning was through their eyes, and the *abraço* Nick gave her outside the law office. "You need to come home," he said before he disappeared. And then he looked back, reflecting the events of the day. "Soon."

The long ride back to Provincetown was probably just what he needed, Hallie thought—a chance to ponder it all, probably out loud, in the privacy of his truck. She would have liked to do the same, but she was due at the hospital in an hour. Fortunately, she only had to cross the park and trudge up Beacon Hill—an invigorating twenty-minute walk. She changed into the scrubs and clogs she'd brought with her in a restroom in the building, pulling her hair back in its usual ponytail and removing the slash of plum-colored lipstick that matched her boots. Looking in the bathroom mirror, she felt as if she'd reclaimed herself.

However, when she hit the street, she turned impulsively toward the café into which Wolf's son had disappeared with his newspaper. Hallie told herself she wanted to offer him the opportunity to see the paintings. But maybe she just wanted to catch him in his lie.

Sam Maddox was so engrossed in his newspaper that he didn't notice Hallie as she ordered her coffee and an almond croissant.

"The Arts section?" Hallie asked, turning her head sideways to see what he was reading. "I thought you were more of a business type, what with all your important appointments."

Wolf's son laughed softly, regarding her with the same deep attention he's shown in the lawyer's office. "Actually, I'm not particularly business or art oriented. I'm working on a doctorate in philosophy."

"It seems I guessed wrong."

Sam continued to smile. "Me, too. I thought you were the glamorous girl in black I just met across the street. That was quite a transformation."

"The glamour was borrowed from my roommate," she admitted. "This is the real me." When she dropped the heavy bag that contained what he called her transformation, her coffee sloshed over the top of her cup and splashed on his newspaper. She blotted it with napkins and apologized.

Sam gestured at the ornate iron chairs across from him. "Please. Join me," he said. Since she already had, it was hard to tell if he was being polite or sarcastic.

Sliding into the set, Hallie got right to the point. "I came here because your father left me a painting, and I really think that you should have it. I'm not sure what his early work was like, but the Race Point series is pretty remarkable."

"So you followed me?" Sam appeared amused. He folded his paper neatly before him, and studied her. "I guess I should be flattered."

"No. No, you shouldn't be," Hallie said, exasperated that her relentless honesty had trapped her again. "I just thought you should know I would be happy—"

"That's very generous of you, but I'm not interested."

"Well, if you ever come to the Cape and you decide you want to see the paintings, my father . . ."

But before Hallie could finish the sentence, his eyes stopped her. "Thanks again, but no," he said firmly. "As I said earlier, I hadn't seen my father since I was five, and I have no interest in his work."

Startled by his shift in tone, Hallie glanced at the clock. "I have one of those notoriously long resident's shifts coming up in about half an hour, so I should probably get going." She gathered her things. When she looked up, Sam was still watching her.

"Let me guess. You're going to be an internist like your father."

"My father is one of a kind, but yes, I'm studying internal medicine. How did you know?"

"I suppose I'm like Wolf in that way. An observer. The only difference is that he studied distant horizons. I'm more interested in what's up close."

"So what do you see?"

"I see someone who's going to be an amazing doctor someday. And also—" Abruptly, he stopped himself. "Well, it's obvious why my father liked you so much."

Hallie blinked, feeling as if he was looking into a part of her that had long been invisible.

"Thanks for following—I mean, for *joining* me," he said and smiled.

She was halfway to the door when he called after her. "Have you got a pen in that thing?" he asked, indicating her oversized bag. "Maybe you should give me your number—in case I change my mind about those paintings someday." He held out his newspaper so she could write on it.

Hallie studied him, wondering if it was a ploy. However, Sam's eyes were guileless. She went back and scrawled her number on the top of the Arts section he'd been reading when she came in. "I'm hardly ever home, but you can leave a message."

It was ten p.m. the next night, and Hallie was in her favorite pj's, hair braided, and about to curl up with her cat, when he called. "Sam?" she said, repeating the name into the phone. "Sam *Maddox*?"

"We only met yesterday. You mean you forgot already?"

"Don't tell me. You've decided you want to see the paintings."

"Actually, I was wondering if you wanted to have a beer. I'm going back to New Jersey tomorrow and—"

"Don't you think this is kind of an odd time to call someone you barely know? Especially when that someone is just coming off a twenty-four-hour shift?"

"Well, you said you were hard to reach. Besides, I thought you people from Provincetown were known for your spontaneity."

Now it was Hallie's turn to laugh out loud. "Maybe the artists, but not the doctor's daughter. Listen, Sam, thanks for asking, but I don't date." And then, realizing how odd that sounded, she quickly added. "Right now I'm totally focused on my residency."

"Who said anything about a date? I'm sitting in the Harvard Gardens all by myself. I thought you might hop in a cab and join me for a beer."

Hallie was about to tell him that she was planning to crawl into bed—*crawl* being the operative word. But then she thought of the way he had listened when she spoke, and his easy laughter. *Yes*, she thought, already pulling the braid out of her hair, and peering into her closet to look for her suede boots. "Just give me fifteen minutes."

They had ordered their second beer when Hallie looked at him frankly. "Can I ask you a personal question?"

"If it's about my father—then, no. I'd prefer you don't."

"I wasn't going to. I mean, not exactly," Hallie said quickly, feeling her color deepen. She wished she could explain that for a moment there his eyes had made her feel as if she knew him better than she did. As if she might have been able to speak to him as bluntly as she always had to Wolf.

It was only after the beer arrived that Sam spoke again. "I have exactly one memory of him."

"A good one, I hope," Hallie said tentatively.

"We were having dinner together as a family, Wolf, my mother, and me—apparently a rare event since it stands out in my mind so much—and they were arguing, which feels like something far less rare. In any case, it didn't take long before Wolf had enough. He threw down his napkin and walked out."

"And that was it?"

"No, that wasn't it. Not quite, anyway. Right before he left, he looked at me and said he was sorry—just like you did a moment ago, except that there were tears in his eyes. It may have been the most genuine moment that ever passed between us as father and son."

"And what did you do?"

Sam shrugged. "I accepted his apology. Maybe not then, when I was four or five. But over the years, I came to understand that Wolf simply wasn't equipped for family life. He never had been. I could either go on hating him for it—as I had as a kid. Or I could go back to that moment in the dining room and let him go."

"So all that stuff you inherited yesterday—where did it come from?" Hallie asked, emboldened by his honesty.

"All that stuff?" Sam laughed. "You mean *money*?"

"Yeah, that."

"Lots of places. My ancestors got in on the ground floor of this country. Railroads, real estate, and some less honorable things, too. After my father learned that the Maddox family had been involved in the slave trade in Rhode Island, he was pretty much done with it—and them, too."

"But he held on to the money," Hallie said, attempting to hide the shock she felt—and a flash of disillusionment with Wolf. "Even if he lived in a shack and wore the same two pairs of pants for ten years, he never let it go."

"I guess it was all he thought he could do for me. The only way he knew how to be a father. That was the real reason I wanted to get out of that office yesterday. For the second time in my life, Wolf nodded in my direction and said he was sorry."

*A*fter that, Sam had shown up in Boston every weekend. He even came when Hallie was on duty and their dates consisted of late-night dinners from the vending machine in the hospital cafeteria. And he called constantly, leaving long messages that made Hallie laugh, or think about something she'd never thought about before.

Four months later they were sitting on a hand-woven rug Abby had brought back from a trip to Honduras, enjoying a picnic-like feast of take-out Thai and a Singha beer and listening to her neighbor's salsa through the wall when Sam grew unexpectedly serious.

"I never thought I was anything like my father until you told me how he painted the same scene a thousand times, trying to get it right," Sam said.

"You plan to take up painting?" she asked, as casually as she could. Since the night at Harvard Gardens, Wolf had remained an implicitly forbidden subject between them.

"No, but I have that kind of determination," Sam said. "Except that you're my Race Point."

"What does that mean?"

"I'm transferring to BU. New Jersey is just too far away from the woman I love."

"But Rutgers has one of the best philosophy programs in the country, and you love it there. You said so yourself," Hallie argued before she allowed heself to absorb the most important part of his statement. *Had he really just told her he loved her?* Though they had been sleeping together for a couple of months, the relationship still felt comfortably undefined. "Oh, God, Sam—what did you say?"

"I think I have loved you ever since that day when you spilled your coffee all over my newspaper. Maybe even before that."

"Are you saying you fell in love with me because I'm a klutz?"

Sam laughed. "I fell in love with you because you were the most gorgeous woman I'd ever seen—even after you changed out of Abby's clothes. And because you were a struggling medical student who had just inherited a painting that might turn out to be very valuable, and you were already offering to give it away."

Hallie unfolded herself from her comfortable cross-legged position and got up to pace the room. She looked down and focused on her brightly colored striped socks. "Sam, I don't know. I'm not sure I even believe in—that kind of thing." Only when she heard the words out loud did she realize how much she sounded like Wolf.

"Well, let me be the first to tell you: *You do*," Sam said confidently, stopping her with both arms. "I've felt it, Hallie."

Hallie leaned her body against his and cried. Because she was afraid of loving him. And equally afraid of ending up like Wolf, all alone in a shack. Or like her father, shackled to his own loneliness by a distant past. She kissed Sam's neck, his cheek, his mouth. Then she unbuttoned his shirt and kissed the skin of his muscled shoulder.

"Is this your way of saying you love me, too?"

Hallie pulled him toward her room. She nodded slowly, more surprised by the word that rose up inside her than he was. *Yes!* Yes, she loved him. She loved him for all the ways he wasn't Gus. He was punctual, organized, driven. He rarely showed emotion, but when he did it was as solid as his body felt beneath her hands. In the end, however, she married him for the qualities that brought back her first love: his ability to make her laugh, his perceptiveness, and his simple, but oh so rare, *goodness*.

Now, *seven years later, Sam produced* a pint of milk for Hallie, then took Nick's seat at the table. He had the kind of presence the house demanded—one as stalwart as her father's. "So what's the plan? You want to keep the place and use it as a summer house? Is that it?"

"Could we?" Hallie couldn't believe he was even considering it. She breathed in sharply.

"Honestly? I don't know." Sam took a long drink from his beer. "It's not just Wolf's lingering presence. It's you, too. When I watched you on the stand at the priest's trial, I felt like I was seeing someone I'd never met."

Hallie was grateful for the dim bulb in the kitchen as she

felt her color deepening. *So he knew.* And then she realized that of course he knew. That was why she married him—because he understood her as no one else had. No one but her father and Gus.

"All that—what I testified about on the stand—it was so long ago," Hallie said, and for the first time, the words really felt true. "We can make this house—this town—*our* home. Ours and Lizzie's."

Sam filled a long moment with silence before he spoke. "Before today, I never really understood how much it meant to you."

"How could you? I refused to admit it to myself. But look at this place, Sam." She swept open the curtain like a game-show host to expose the moon-drenched water, the lights from town, the blinking eye of the lighthouse. "You've got to admit it's pretty incredible." She wasn't sure if she sounded more like a realtor or a travel guide.

"There are lots of incredible spots on this earth that aren't emotional land mines."

"But this is my father's house. My house. When I saw the estate-sale crowd in the yard this morning, I couldn't let it go. Not the house or anything in it."

Sam tossed his empty bottle in the trash. "It's hard for me to understand that, you know. I never felt that way about any place. Certainly not the house where I grew up with my mother and stepfather. And none of the places I lived after that. They were just rooms. Beautiful rooms. Utilitarian rooms, But in the end, just rooms. The only place I've ever missed is that funky little apartment you had in Mission Hill. The first place we had sex."

Hallie laughed. "With the Cure thumping in the background, and a couple fighting downstairs. I loved that place, too. Maybe we should move back."

"Or maybe we should just go upstairs and try out your old bed. If it's as good as it was in Mission Hill, we just may have found ourselves a new home."

CHAPTER 25

After they found an architect, Hallie and Sam spent most of their weekends in Provincetown, supervising the renovations. To them, however, it felt more like an exorcism. Doors and windows were knocked out, replaced and widened, walls were tumbled, and the ghosts who'd been there so long they'd even claimed their own bedrooms were finally banished.

Everything shined on the young, expectant couple in those weeks. People who didn't know them stopped to say hello, and longtime residents, curious about Wolf's son, warmed when they noticed the way Sam's hand drifted protectively to Hallie's growing abdomen in the middle of an ordinary conversation.

They were making coffee in Aunt Del's narrow kitchen the first time Hallie felt the baby flutter inside her. "Sam! Sam—" she cried. For the rest of her life, she would remember the slant of light across his face as his expression moved from concern to heightened attention to pure joy in the span of a second.

"Really?" he said. "She *moved*?"

All Hallie could do was beam and nod while the whole world shifted in a delicate dance beneath her hands.

That night, they lay in the dark under the same floral quilt Hallie remembered from her childhood. Their stomachs were full of Aunt Del's *sopas do Espirito Santo* and the crusty bread she had served with it. It was a labor-intensive stew that Aunt Del usually made for holidays, and they'd both had seconds.

"What did she call that soup again?" Sam said. "It was pretty awesome."

"*Sopas do Espirito Santo.* 'Holy Ghost Soup,' in English. And for a semi-vegetarian, you sure sucked it up. Did you know it contains beef *and* chicken?"

But Sam wasn't thinking about the excess meat. "*Holy Ghost soup?* You're kidding me, right?"

"Don't worry. I've been eating it all my life and I'm still a godless heathen."

"You are not," Sam said. Even though he never went to church, enough of his Episcopalian upbringing remained to make him uncomfortable when she voiced her strong feelings against faith.

"Aunt Del says you used to sleep in this room sometimes when you were a kid?"

"When Nick had a date." Hallie studied the familiar cracks in the low ceiling, a map of the sleepless nights she had sometimes spent, and her cruel prayers to no god in particular: *Please let it be a flop!*

"I didn't know Nick dated."

"He was a man, wasn't he?" Hallie said, repeating Aunt Del's explanation. The one she'd never liked. "Unfortunately, nothing ever worked out." Only as an adult, seeing her father's loneliness, had she realized just how *unfortunate* it was.

"I bet you chased them all away."

"I played my part. You have no idea how much I regret that now."

"Nick was his own man. If he'd wanted another woman in his life, he would have had one."

Hallie nestled against his shoulder. "How do you always manage to say exactly what I need to hear?"

"Seven years of training, baby. Imagine how good I'll be after fifty or sixty?"

Fifty or sixty years. It seemed unimaginable, but as Hallie fell asleep, she felt like she was drifting in a quiet boat on calm seas.

The next morning, Hallie and Sam stopped to listen to a street musician playing the accordion in Portuguese Square. They clapped enthusiastically before tossing a donation into her hat. Then Hallie showed Sam the War Memorial, delicately tracing her grandfather's and great-uncle's names on the stone. "Nick used to say we could never leave Provincetown, because he couldn't be too far from his dead," Hallie said, remembering the times when her father had lifted her up as a child and pointed out the same names.

"Do you think that was why he stayed?"

"Nah, he just liked it here." Hallie grinned, indicating an open bench. "You sit here and listen to the music while I go down the street and get us some breakfast."

The bakery had a line even in the off season, and there were several people lingering over coffee who were excited to see her. "The old house is looking great," she heard more than once. And most often it was followed by, "So when are you moving back? We need a good doctor in town."

"I'm just summer people now," Hallie said, silently grateful that she hadn't brought Sam with her.

"Summer people—*you*? Never," someone in the corner shouted out. Hallie recognized Sonny Rivers, one of Nick's former patients.

She had her order and was turning to go when she came face-to-face with Gus's cousin, Alvaro. He was standing too close to her in line, and though it was nine in the morning, she detected alcohol on his breath. Looking at his unshaven face, she suspected that he was just in from a fishing trip, and that maybe he'd stopped off for a traditional drink on the way home.

"Large coffee, Gracie. Black," he said to the girl behind the counter, ignoring Hallie.

But she refused to allow it.

She put her hand on his arm and lowered her voice. "What's going on, Alvaro? How's Gus doing?"

At first, he seemed determined not to respond as he shook off her arm, his eyes flashing. "*How's he doing?* Is that a serious question? How do you think he's doing?"

Hallie felt as if she'd received a physical blow. Inside her, Lizzie leaped in response. By then everyone in the bakery was watching them.

"You know I did everything I could to help him."

"Do me a favor, will you? Save it for the people who will always take your side just because you're Nick's daughter."

"Think whatever you want about me, Alvaro," she said when she could speak. "But there hasn't been one day in my whole life—not one day—when Gus and I weren't on the same side."

"You really believe that, don't you?" Alvaro snorted. "Man, you're even more deluded than I thought you were." He dumped his coffee into the trash, not even flinching when the hot black liquid splattered on his jeans. Then he slammed out the door.

Hallie was shaking as she made her way down the street to the bench where just a few minutes earlier, she'd been looking forward to enjoying some breakfast and street music with Sam. Still engrossed in his conversation with the accordion player, he didn't notice her at first. But as soon as he turned toward her, his eyes changed.

He touched her mouth with the tip of a finger. "Your lips are white, sweetie."

"Probably just a little morning sickness," Hallie said, pulling away so he wouldn't feel the tremor that had begun in the bakery.

"Morning sickness? You're long past that," Sam said. "Maybe we should drop off Aunt Del's croissant and head back to Boston early." He glanced briefly in the direction of the bakery, as if expecting to see someone—or something—that might explain what had happened.

Hallie quickly agreed, silently cursing her lifelong inability to tell a persuasive lie.

Though she couldn't know if it was true, Hallie would always feel as if the events that devastated her life and Gus's hard-won peace had occurred on the same day. At the same shattering hour. It didn't matter that her late-term miscarriage happened weeks before she got the call about Gus. In her mind—and, more importantly, in her heart—the two would always be linked.

She had just delivered good news to a patient who had been treated for leukemia three years earlier. Her blood counts were normal.

"Who ever thought *normal* could be such a beautiful word?" the patient said, hugging Hallie as if she herself had produced the result. Before she could speak, Hallie felt a sharp burst of the back pain she'd been experiencing, and trying to ignore, all morning.

In the bathroom, the whir and hum of everyday life in the clinic reverberated in her head. Laughter. Footsteps. Voices. She was about to see her last patient before lunch, and she could already smell the minestrone that someone was microwaving in the break room. When her nurse knocked on the door to say that the next patient was waiting, Hallie was startled by the calmness of her own voice. "Would you please call an ambulance, Lucy. I think I'm—something is wrong."

Lucy only hesitated a matter of seconds. "Right away.' You hang in there, okay, Hallie?"

She had never seen Sam cry before, but he wept that day in the hospital. Wept and stroked her hair, telling her repeatedly that he loved her. Hallie had accepted the embraces and the words; she'd even cleared his tears away with her fingertips, but inside, she felt hollow. No tears. No love to spare for anyone or anything. *No Lizzie.* She froze when he tried to say they would try again. "No, never." When it was clear he didn't hear her, she wondered if she'd even spoken the words out loud.

The physical recovery from the miscarriage, and the D and C that cleared every evidence of her daughter's life from her uterus, had been easy. *Too* easy, Hallie thought. Within a week, she was wearing her old clothes as if she'd never been pregnant. "One of the advantages of being fit and slender," her obstetrician had said. The words felt like a slap. *There were no advantages*, she wanted to shriek. For the first time, Hallie understood her father's grief over Liz Cooper, and Gus's months of silence after his mother's murder. She learned how grief could lock you into an isolation that no one could penetrate.

"It will be good for you to go back to work, Hallie," Sam urged her gently after several weeks had passed. "Get out of the condo. Out of your head."

"It *won't* be good for me," Hallie cried fiercely. "And it certainly won't get me out of my head. *You don't know*—"

"You're right, Hallie. I *don't* know. I don't know how to help you or what to say to you. All I know is that everything I do is wrong. Sometimes I think you're happier when I'm not around at all."

When she didn't contradict him, he got his jacket; and then, as he had after the trial, he left.

At first, Hallie was relieved, but when he stayed away for several days, she began a vigil that was reminiscent of the ones kept by fishermen's wives when they're husbands were too long at sea. On the rare occasions when the phone rang, she sprinted to life, but it was never him. It was Lucy from the office, calling to ask when she'd be back, the persistent Aunt Del, or her friend Abby, whose house bubbled with the sounds of her two young sons. A dozen times a day she picked up the phone to call him. But she never got past the first three digits of his number before she realized she had nothing to say. Nothing to give him but a hollow woman, a husk, a mother without tears.

Later, Hallie would learn that Sam had kept a similar vigil over his own phone, waiting to hear that she wanted him to come home, that she needed him. "One word of encouragement and I would have been there in an instant, even if I had to walk out in the middle of class," he would say.

But she got the other call first. When she saw Neil Gallagher's number on the caller ID, she suspected he'd heard about her loss and was calling to offer his belated condolences. She walked away from the phone and closed the door to her bedroom so she wouldn't have to hear his voice on the answering machine. She was already choking on sympathy. On flowers and cards and the tentativeness she heard in people's voices. As if she might implode if they said the wrong thing. The worst part was that it was true; she might. She *had*.

It took an hour for her to walk into the living room and confront the blinking phone. Her first instinct was to delete it without listening, but then, impulsively, she pressed the play button:

. . . *I thought you'd want to know. It's Gus. They* . . . . Hallie took a step away from the machine as if she were afraid she might ignite if she stood too close. The words blurred, even when she'd played them three times. *A pretty bad beating . . . He lost a lot of blood. Oh Christ, Hallie; I don't know.* And again the apologies. *I know this is a happy time for you, and I hate intruding on that, but I felt like you should hear it from me.* There was more, the social stuff oddly tagged onto the dire news. *My best to Sam. If you want to call me back . . .*

But Hallie didn't hear it. Her mind had caught on certain words and phrases . . . *Rush him . . . pretty bad . . . blood . . .* a lot of *blood . . . I don't know, Hallie.*

In her mind, Hallie saw Gus more clearly than she had in years. She saw him untainted by her old anger and guilt. Oddly, it wasn't the Gus she loved who appeared to her with heartbreaking clarity. It was the boy with his hair poking up in the back, who had accepted her gift of two minnows.

That vision was what finally released the tears she had been unable to cry for Lizzie. Every time someone, especially Sam, referred to her as "the miscarriage," Hallie felt like she was losing her all over again. Was she the only one who knew that the daughter who lived inside her for twenty weeks, who leaped and tumbled in her womb, was real? Hallie cried for that, too. For the crushing loneliness that had descended on her since she lost her baby.

She retrieved the phone, intending to call Neil, but then she replayed the end of his message in her mind. He said he hated to intrude on her happy time. So he didn't know. If she called, she would not only have to hear the terrifying details about what had happened to Gus; she would have to tell her own story, too.

It was dusk, but her hair was loose and uncombed, and she was still in her pajamas when she heard footsteps in the hallway. Footsteps and then the sound of a key in the lock.

She was so full of confusion that it took a minute for her to process her husband's presence in the doorway.

The first thing she was viscerally aware of was the armful of roses he carried—at least two dozen of them. Even across the room, Hallie felt accosted by their scent. They reminded her of the roses he'd brought to her on the day of the miscarriage. But most of all, they were too *red*. When she looked at them, she thought of the words she'd heard on the answering machine, and the blood she'd seen in the bathroom that day at the office.

The roses weren't the issue, though. After six days, her husband had come home. He was home, and it was clear from his expression that he still loved her. That she had never been nearly as alone in her loss as she thought she was. She was across the room before he had a chance to close the door.

He tossed the roses on the floor and reached for her.

"I thought you weren't coming back," she sobbed. "I thought you were never coming home."

"And I thought you didn't want me to. Do you know how crazy and miserable I've been? Why didn't you call?" Sam said. He smelled like the cold, crisp air of winter, and the piney aftershave she loved. But the embrace didn't last. Feeling the phone that she still held in her hand wedged into his back, he released her. "You were just about to, weren't you?" he said.

Of course, his conclusion made sense. There was no one else she would have called—at least, not until she'd heard Neil's message. If her face wouldn't give her away, Hallie would have lied. "I wanted to call you. Ever since the night you left, I wanted to call—"

Sam tilted his head slightly to the side in the sweet, bemused way she loved. "But you didn't," he said cautiously. "And you weren't going to call me now, either."

He squared his shoulders and walked toward the answering machine. Hallie cringed as he replayed the messages. In an instant, Neil's words filled the room, the house, their lives, with the latest episode in Gus's life.

Hallie sunk into the couch and put her face in her hands. "I didn't even answer the phone, Sam," she said. "I didn't call back, either." It was her last defense, and it was a weak one.

Sam looked down at her, his eyes drained of emotion. "And here I thought you were crying for our baby. But no, you had no tears for her. No tears for *us*. It was that sociopath priest you were crying for, wasn't it?"

"I desperately wanted you to come home, Sam," Hallie said. "I've tried so hard—"

Sam reached out and fingered the bright strands of her hair. "I know you've *tried*; that's what kills me. My wife gets an A for effort in her attempts to love me. She even tried to forget the guy who almost killed her, and who actually succeeded with his next victim. Poor tragic Gus Silva. Well, thanks, but no thanks."

He stood up abruptly and started for the door.

"You don't understand," she said, rushing to block his path. She wiped her face awkwardly on her sleeve, a childish gesture that seemed to soften him.

"I'm afraid that's the problem. I *do* understand, Hallie. When we first met, I knew there was a barrier there, some hurt that prevented you from getting close to anyone. But I loved you so much I believed I could make you forget. Even after you told me about the high school boyfriend who—"

"Gus is a *priest*. He's been out of my life for years and you know it."

Sam shook his head, and Hallie finally glimpsed the grief beneath his anger. "You know, I truly believed that for a long time—until the trial. That's when I first understood the hold he had on you. When you looked at him from the witness stand, it was as if everyone in that courtroom vanished. Including me. But then you got pregnant and for a while we were so happy I thought we were invincible. Even Gus Silva couldn't touch us. I sincerely thought I had won. *We* had won. And maybe if Lizzie had been born, we might have."

"We still have each other," Hallie pleaded.

Sam sighed. "If only that were true." Then he walked slowly and deliberately toward the answering machine and replayed the message. Hallie wanted to block her ears against Neil's voice, but she knew that would only fire her husband's anger. "Didn't you hear this, Hallie? Gus is in trouble again," he said, starting for the door. "He needs you."

CHAPTER 27

An accidental glance at the bathroom mirror caught Hallie off guard. Her eyes were red from weeping, skin pale from holing up inside, lips cracked from the dry heat in the condo. She probably had scurvy, too, she thought. In the two weeks since Sam had left for good, she'd lived on the kinds of foods she warned her elderly patients against: crackers, cereal from the box, the last olives in the jar.

She had avoided the mirror because it contained the truth: Sam was right. Though she'd tried to avoid thinking about Gus, she had called Neil right after Sam left.

"How is he?" Hallie had blurted out when he picked up.

"According to Alvaro, it was a pretty serious injury. There was some kind of knife involved; it came within an inch of his heart. But the last I heard he's probably going to make it: *this time*. That's an exact quote."

"I feel so helpless. What can we do, Neil?"

"Not a goddamn thing. Nothing but live our own lives as best we can."

"Something I'm not doing particularly well right now," Hallie said.

"Yeah, well, no one's screwed up more than I have. Seeing Gus sentenced to prison did something to me, you know? I'm not the same person, Hal," Neil said despondently. "I guess our holy friend would probably tell us to *pray*."

"A lot of good that's done him, huh?" Still unable to talk about her miscarriage, Hallie made an excuse to get off the phone. She hoped Neil hadn't noticed that as she said good-bye she was already crying.

Then she went to the kitchen window and opened it the way Nick always did when he lost a patient, a symbolic action of release. The cold felt sweeter than anything she'd experienced in weeks, and she took a huge drink of it. Somehow, though, she'd been expecting the ocean air. But once her lungs adapted, even the pungent smell of the city was salutary. She took another deep breath and then coughed.

She'd given up smoking when she began her fertility treatments, and had only relapsed once when Nick was ill. But now she was dying for the taste of her old vice. It was the first thing she'd truly desired since she lost Lizzie. In her jean jacket she found a crumpled pack of Marlboros containing one very stale cigarette. She lit it up right there in the house. Once she took that first drag, she wanted more. She wanted a spinach and mango salad from the café where she'd first had coffee with Sam, and a walk across the Commons. But as soon as she was outside, an even more undeniable want accosted her. Why hadn't she thought of it sooner? If just for a week or even an hour, she needed to go back to the place where she had always gone when she was in trouble or pain. As she turned in the direction of South Station, she walked faster, almost breaking into a run like she did when she was a child and she was racing home to Nick.

CHAPTER 28

Hallie was scraping paint from the office door with Hugo Bestler. Throughout an unusually harsh April, Hugo and Hallie had worked hard to get the office in shape. Hugo usually showed up an hour late, hungover and sucking hard on a cup of coffee, but he was a great listener. One who didn't judge. One who didn't even talk back, aside from the occasional grunt, usually when she said something that reminded him of his own divorce a decade earlier. Hallie had learned not to ask him a direct question before two p.m., a practice that seemed to work well for both of them. She could talk freely, not worrying how outrageous or silly she might sound, and he was left to his brooding silence. It was actually during one of these largely one-sided conversations that Hallie realized she was never going back to Boston. She was home to stay.

"I could have told you that the first day you showed up here." It was the first time Hugo had spoken that day.

Now she stepped off the ladder, rested her hands on her hips, and beheld their accomplishments. "Looks like we'll be ready to start painting tomorrow."

"You still planning to paint that door purple?"

"Absolutely. What have you got against purple?"

"It's supposed to be red," he muttered, not looking at her.

"I loved Nick's red door, too, but I'm not him, Hugo. People might as well get used to the idea."

Hugo peered down the street, apparently wondering if it was too early to stop at the Pilgrims Club for a drink, then began polishing his tools. Hallie admired his meticulousness.

"You're the boss. If you want to quit early, fine with me," he said, forgetting about the door.

Once she stopped working, Hallie felt the bite of the east wind. She was carrying logs inside to start the fire when she thought of Sam standing in the door at the condo.

"You know what really gets me?" she said to Hugo as he was preparing to leave. "He knew I would come back here and that I'd reopen Nick's practice. Damn, he probably even knew I'd paint the door purple."

Hugo laughed acidly before spitting on the sidewalk. "Kind of like my ex. In fact, right about now, Brenda's probably telling someone I'm about to head over to that bar. One of these days, though, she's gonna be wrong."

"You mean you're going to quit?"

"Nah. I'm just gonna start drinkin' in another town. I get sick of lookin' at the same old bastards every night."

Hallie laughed. "Sam was wrong about one thing though."

"What was that?"

"He said Gus needed me."

Hugo's head snapped sharply in her direction. "Man's a priest. He ain't supposed to need anyone. Don't tell me you're one of those jailhouse chicks. You know, the kind that get turned on by a man in an orange jumpsuit."

Hallie shook her head vehemently, clearly exasperated. "I haven't seen Gus since the trial."

She could hardly bear to remember the day when she had taken the stand in a defiantly red suit. She had been confident during Lunes's questioning, and fierce in her defense of Gus when the prosecutor challenged her.

No, Gus had not assaulted her on Race Point, she'd said in a clear, sure voice. It had been an accident.

But as the lawyer paced and raged and pummeled her with his questions, his voice started to feel like the relentless, staccato blows Gus had unleashed on Neil. The flashback didn't last long—maybe less than a minute—but during that time, she was there on the Point, a terrified eighteen-year-old in a torn blue dress, screaming the words that sometimes still resounded in her dreams. *Stop, Gus! Stop before you kill him!*

Hallie, who valued honesty above all other virtues, had lied about it in court, even as Gus and Neil looked on. Gus hadn't attacked Neil, she insisted. It had been a fight, a silly drunken fight, and Neil had been an equal participant in it. She couldn't even say for certain who had landed the first blow, or which one of the boys had knocked her onto the cement bumper.

From his seat, Neil watched her with an emotionless expression. And then he closed his eyes and nodded, giving his assent.

"Want my advice? Stay the hell away from him," Hugo said gruffly, tossing a hammer vehemently into his toolbox. "Shit Hallie, I liked Gus Silva as much as anyone else back in the day, but the man went into prison a convicted killer. You think a couple of years in Millette has brought out his better nature?"

"That's what bothers me, Hugo. *I don't know what it's done to him.* He's cut off everyone in his life. His friends, even his precious church. The only one who's seen him is his cousin."

"Like I say, Gus was a great football player in high school. But nothin' he's done since has made a helluva lot of sense to me—starting with the priest thing. Why would you want to—"

"Because he's a *friend*, Hugo, and he has been since we

were nine years old. Forget all the stuff that happened between us when we were teenagers."

Hugo snorted. "You really think you can forget that stuff,
Hallie? You think *he* forgot?"

"You're starting to sound more like my husband every
day."

Hugo flashed a broken-toothed grin. "I don't suppose that
means I get the privileges that go along with the job?"

"Not in this lifetime, buddy," Hallie grabbed the rag
he'd been using to wipe his tools and swatted him before
she started inside. "Now get out of here—and don't be late
tomorrow. We've got a lot of work to do if we're going to get
this office open by the first of March."

Inside, Hallie realized she hadn't eaten anything since breakfast. She surveyed the contents of her refrigerator. There were
almonds and apricots and a bit of sweet bread—enough to
pass for a meal. In the cabinet she found an old bottle of
Portuguese *vinho*. She was about to throw it out when she
reconsidered. How bad could it be?

The wine was surprisingly dry and good, and the view from
her back window always comforted her. The sun hadn't gone
down yet, and through its gray light, she could see the houses on
stilts, the wharf, and the boats, bobbing in unpredictable waters.
But her eyes were drawn to the narrowing arc of wild land that
culminated with the lighthouse. Impulsively, she leaped up, finished her wine as if it were a shot, and grabbed her jacket. There
was something she'd been avoiding, but with the office opening
so soon, she needed to take care of it now.

She hadn't seen Alvaro Silva since the encounter in the
bakery. His glare had chased her out of town that day, but

now that she no longer had a family to protect, she actually looked forward to running into Gus's cousin. This time, she wouldn't back down until she got answers to the questions that haunted her, no matter how furiously he reacted. *How was Gus? And why didn't he respond to his friends' letters? Why had he turned down their requests to visit?*

Halfway up Point of Pines Road, she could see that the old Silva place was dark. She opened the iron gate and walked up the narrow stone walkway to the house. When no one answered the door, she took in what was left of the garden Gus's mother had tended with such love: weeds, trash that had blown in from the street or been dropped there by Alvaro himself, an empty bottle of sambuca, and a large pile of cigarette butts. Hallie sat down on the stoop, inhaled the acrid smell of rotting garbage nearby, and lit a cigarette. She tried to imagine Gus, sitting on these steps as a small boy.

When she was finished with her smoke, she found a scrap of paper and a pencil in her bag and scrawled a terse message asking him to call her.

But she wasn't surprised when a week passed and she got no response. She and Hugo were hanging her new sign out front, HALLETT COSTA, M.D., INTERNAL MEDICINE, when she brought up the subject.

"I haven't seen Alvaro Silva around town much. Did he move away or something?" she said as casually as she could.

"Alvaro—*leave*? There's about ten people in this town who aren't goin' anywhere—even if a tsunami rolls down Commercial Street. One of 'em's Alvaro, and another one's me."

"And who are the other eight?"

"All those lonely nights you spend in that big-ass house, you should have plenty of time to figure that out." Hugo made a slight adjustment to the sign, and then stood back to study his handiwork.

"Excuse me, but I happen to *like* being alone."

"A Portagee who likes bein' alone? Hah! Creature doesn't exist. Never see one without seeing six cousins, and probably their grandmother, too."

"I'm only half Portuguese. Did you ever think I might take after my mother?"

"Nope, I never thought that—and neither did anyone else around here. Except for the blond hair, you're Nick's to the bone." After a moment's hesitation, Hugo cocked back his head. "What the hell you want with Alvaro Silva anyway?"

Hallie folded her arms across her chest. "I just want to talk to him, that's all," she said. Then, before she could stop herself, she added, "I went to his house, and it looked unoccupied. I even left a note, but—"

"Shit, Hallie," Hugo said. "That house has been a dead zone since they carried Maria out the front door in a bag. Why the hell would you want to go over there?"

"So you're saying Alvaro doesn't live there anymore?" Ignoring his question—and the image he'd conjured, Hallie's mind drifted to the trampled fall flowers. Blue mums. Fading hydrangeas.

"From what I hear, he's got a woman down in Harwich. But he still stops by the house. It's Silva property, and a damn valuable piece of real estate. I wouldn't expect him to answer no note, though."

"Well, if you see him, tell him I want to talk to him, okay?" she called out as she started into the house. Then she turned around in the walkway and spoke in a resolute voice. "And that I'm not going to give up until I do."

CHAPTER 29

By the end of April, Felicia was telling callers that Dr. Costa didn't have an opening for six weeks. Some of the reactions were so loud that Hallie could hear them from across the room. "But you're not even open yet! How can you be all booked up?" The most common complaint was that the caller had been one of Nick's very best patients. Didn't that count for something? If they were really angry, they might also point out that Felicia was a hairstylist, not a secretary. What was she doing working in Dr. Nick's office?

When that happened, Felicia quickly retorted that this was *not* Nick's office, and that she had made a career change—*if it's any of your business.* Unless they were particularly rude, or had done her or any of her family wrong in some way over the years, she waited till after she hung up to add that last bit.

Once the office opened, the days were long and full; and when word got out that Hallie never turned anyone away, regardless of their ability to pay, people started to come from as far away as Yarmouth.

Hallie was seeing her last patient of the day when the nurse she'd added to the practice knocked on the door of the examining room. Paolo was a recent transplant, who'd come to Provincetown for vacation and fallen in love with a man who owned a gallery down the street.

"Felicia says someone's here to see you. A personal matter."

"Well, tell her I'll be finished here in about fifteen minutes," Hallie said, galled by the interruption. The man in her exam room had come all the way from Orleans with a serious case of emphysema. Then, out of curiosity, she asked, "Is it a patient?"

"I don't think so. Some guy named Alvaro Silva. Says it's important."

Hallie felt a flutter of nervousness, wondering if he was finally ready to give her some news of Gus, but she hid it under her usual professional calm. "Tell him not to leave," she said.

However, by the time she had finished with the patient, there was no one in the office but Paolo and Felicia. Paolo looked oddly nervous, while Felicia covered her mouth and suppressed a grin.

"So where is he? Didn't want to wait?" Hallie said as she dropped her new patient's file on the desk. "I thought it was *important*."

"He was gone by the time I came out of the examining room," Paolo said.

"But he left you a little present," Felicia added. "Two of them, actually."

They both pointed in the direction of the front porch. Hallie cautiously opened the door. At first, she didn't notice anything unusual, but then she spotted them, tied to the gate: two of the most forlorn-looking animals she'd ever seen.

Puzzled, she turned back to her friends.

"Gus's dogs," they said simultaneously.

"What?" Hallie said, trying to avoid the dogs' plaintive eyes. "Well, they're going to the pound. I don't have time for a dog, let alone two." Then she eyed the larger one and something broke inside her. "You don't look very healthy either, do you, girl." She stepped forward to stroke her ears.

"I'll make an appointment with the vet," Felicia offered.

"Oh, and Hallie? One more thing. Apparently there's someone who has visitation rights to these mutts. Alvaro said to expect the girl every other Sunday, precisely at two."

Visitors were never a problem at Hallie's house because, like her father before her, she favored meal-in-a-pot type concoctions like chili or curries that would serve guests if someone stopped in, or keep for a day or two if they didn't. On the first Sunday that Julia Perez showed up, it was a particularly festive gathering. Stuart was there with a new friend bearing a chocolate raspberry torte for dessert, as well as Buddy, Felicia, and Felicia's mother, Luanne. Hallie's third cousin, Tony, who'd recently moved to town and was thinking of opening a café, was in charge of the CD player. He started with Chuck Berry, and moved on to Alicia Keys, but it was his Brazilian sambas that got everyone to their feet, hips swaying. Lunes Oliveira had stopped over just when the dancing began, and once he got a whiff of the fragrant smells coming from the kitchen, it hadn't taken much to convince him to stay.

"Obviously, your intention from the start," Buddy said, eyeing Lunes with inebriated pomposity. "What, may I ask, is your interest in my niece, anyway?"

Hallie wanted to remind him that he wasn't exactly her uncle—as Nick had once done—but it was too late for that. Instead, she just shrugged in Lunes's direction, as she poured him a glass of wine. "You better be careful. My uncle's watching you."

"And I'm watching you," Lunes said, as he pulled her to her feet for a samba. Since that first antagonistic visit, he dropped in whenever one of his two boys, age eight and ten,

had a game or a practice in town. Hallie saw a different side
of him when he was with them, and she had even attended
a couple of the boys' Little League games with him in the
spring. But when he hinted about going on a "grown-up
date—you know the kind that involves wine and dinner
and maybe even a kiss on the cheek at the end," she had
demurred.

"God, Lunes. The ink's hardly dry on my divorce papers."

"I wasn't expecting you to say yes, but at least be honest.
The ex has nothing to do with it." Lunes smiled in a way that
reminded her why she had initially found him so annoying.
"Anyway, I was just throwing it out there. If you ever get
over your pining, give me a call."

Hallie had slammed the door, and avoided him for weeks,
but to her surprise, she missed his friendship. She also missed
the boys, who tore through the house, trailing sand everywhere and lured her and Lunes outside to throw a football on
the beach.

Julia seemed uncomfortable from the moment she entered
the room. Within the first five minutes, she'd declined an offer to dance with Lunes's ten-year-old son, a plate of scallops
with bacon pressed on her by Felicia, and an illegal drink
from Uncle Buddy.

"I'm just here to see the dogs," she said, nervously studying the floor. Hallie wondered how such an introvert survived the raucous atmosphere of a dorm. She led the girl into
the bedroom where Jane, who had eaten little since she arrived, was sleeping heavily with Stella loyally at her side. Julia
instantly forgot Hallie as she sunk to the floor and stirred
them, prompting a joyful welcome.

Hallie sat on the bed and tried to strike up a conversation, asking about Jack, and her studies, but Julia answered tersely. Her straight, dark hair obscured her face as she focused on the animals, obviously waiting for Hallie to leave.

"A lot of the people I did my residency with went to Tufts, including my friend Abby. It's an excellent program. Any thoughts of going into medicine?"

"No," Julia answered, a little too quickly and much too sharply. It was the first time her voice had risen above a whisper since she entered the house.

Suspecting the girl had spent far too much time in hospitals already, Hallie instantly regretted her question. She had hoped she might ask the girl if she'd heard from Gus but decided that was probably a taboo subject, too.

Stepping out of the room, Hallie almost walked directly into Stuart, who was just outside the door. His eyes were closed and he was holding a hand over his heart like he was about to recite the Pledge of Allegiance.

"My God, you scared the shit out of me," Hallie said. Then, thinking of his cardiac condition, she took his arm. "You're not having pain, are you?"

Stuart put a finger to his lips, then led her away from the door. "My heart has never been stronger, but it broke just a little when I saw that girl come through the door. She reminded me of myself those first months after Paul died."

"You were *nothing* like that, Uncle Stuart. You went through the streets, wailing and telling your mournful story to anyone who would listen, even those who'd heard it a dozen times. And at night, you cried so loud that neither Nick nor I got any sleep for weeks."

"Excuse me, young lady. I might have cried, but I most certainly did not *wail*." Then, abruptly, Stuart's tone changed.

"That girl, on the other hand, looks like she needs to have herself a good keening. And she needs to tell her story as many times as it takes, to someone who understands—until she finally accepts it herself."

"And I suppose that understanding someone would be you," Hallie said. "Well, you can go in and talk to her if you want to, but don't be offended if she ignores you."

"Very little offends me these days. It's one of the only advantages of my advanced years." Stuart kissed her cheek before he started down the hall.

Hallie would never know what he had said in there, but when the two emerged he asked her to set another plate. "Julia has decided to stay, after all."

Julia's face was still closed, although she looked as if she had been crying. Hallie decided to sit her between Felicia and Luanne, partly as a buffer for their occasional mother-daughter sniping, and partly because Luanne talked so relentlessly, and with such animated outrage (usually about the latest "jerk" she was dating), that she hardly required a response.

Hallie walked Julia to the door when she was leaving. "I hope Luanne didn't wear you out, or ruin your opinion of the opposite sex."

"I liked her. She kind of reminded me of my mother." Then, looking as though she'd revealed too much, Julia quickly added. "So it would be okay if I come back in a couple of weeks? You don't have to give me dinner or anything. Just a quick visit with the dogs will be fine."

Hallie rubbed her forehead. "Maybe you should make it next week, honey. You probably noticed Jane isn't eating—and there are some other things going on with her, too. Bring

Jack along. Linda Soares, who used to be the librarian in town, is making her famous cod with tomatoes and beans."

"*Really?*" Julia said, her eyes filling. "You mean you . . . have you made an appointment?"

Hallie looked over at Jane, who was watching them from her bed in the corner as if she understood. "Not yet, but soon. We both know how much Gus loves those dogs, Julia. I've got to do right by her."

Julia nodded solemnly. "Next week, then. I'll ask my—" she began, and then corrected herself. "I'll ask Jack."

"Your dad." Hallie finished the sentence as Julia clearly intended.

Finally, Julia smiled. "Yes, my dad. One of them, anyway."

She was off the steps when she turned around and called back: "*Medical research!*"

"Excuse me?" Hallie said.

"That's what I want to do when I get out of school. Medical research."

CHAPTER 30

It was on a particularly busy Wednesday afternoon when Paolo knocked sharply at the door of the examining room and announced an emergency. A man had shown up complaining of chest pains.

Hallie excused herself and stepped into the hallway. "Someone we know?"

"Oh, you know him all right." Paolo hesitated. "It's the guy who left the dogs, Hallie." Since his partner was a native, Paolo knew the old stories as if he'd lived through them himself.

"Has Felicia called the ambulance?"

"As we speak."

In spite of herself, Hallie was taken aback when she opened the door to Room 1 and saw that Alvaro had removed his shirt. He was standing in the center of the room with the military straightness characteristic of the Silvas, his chest and arms as toned as Gus's had been in high school.

"Open your mouth," she ordered sternly. When he did, she popped in an uncoated aspirin she'd brought from the chest in the office. "Chew."

Alvaro grimaced. "A friggin' *aspirin*? That's all you've got? Pretty primitive medicine, Doc. Don't I even get a glass of water?"

"Chew," Hallie repeated, ignoring both his questions and his sarcasm. "It could save your life. And don't talk so much, either."

When she applied the cold stethoscope to his skin, Alvaro shivered. "Jesus Christ! If I wasn't already having a heart attack, that thing would give me one."

"You shouldn't have removed your shirt; it wasn't necessary." As Hallie tuned in to the even rhythm of his heart, she felt calmer. "Tell me about the pain. Where is it? What does it feel like?"

"It's right beneath your hand. And it hurts like hell. Shit, what's pain supposed to feel like?"

"Well, your heart sounds fine. I'd give you an EKG, but the ambulance will be here before I have time. They have everything they need to treat you till you get to Hyannis." It was the same reassuring spiel she gave to the emergency patients worried about the long drive to the nearest hospital.

"What the fuck, Hallie? You called an *ambulance*?"

"This is a medical office, Alvaro. When people come in presenting with symptoms of a heart attack, that's what we do," Hallie said brusquely. "And put on your shirt while you're at it."

"What's the matter? The sight of a man make you nervous? Or maybe I just remind you too much of someone—"

"Nothing you could do would make me nervous, Alvaro Silva—unless you tried to drop off another animal."

Alvaro grinned. "I knew you'd take them in. Neither you or Nick could ever say no to a stray."

"Well, it would have been nice if you had at least told me the old one had bladder cancer. The poor thing was nothing but a sack of bones, and she bled all over my good rug the first night."

"She's not just *the old one*, you know. The name was on her tag."

"Well, excuse me," Hallie said, galled that he refused to apologize for leaving a sick geriatric dog and an overactive Jack Russell at her door. "*Jane* bled all over my best rug."

"So how's she doing?"Alvaro asked in a low voice.

"About a week ago, we had to put her down. I was with her, stroking her ears as she went to sleep. Then we buried her in Maria's old garden."

The euthanasia at the vet's office had been peaceful. Beautiful even. But the burial was a dark comedy. Partly out of spite and partly just to get Alvaro's attention, she'd dragged a very inebriated Hugo out of the Pilgrims Club to help. Things had gone downhill from there. But if Gus's cousin had been home since the burial, he apparently hadn't noticed the grave.

"You buried her at my house? *What the*—?" He stopped mid-sentence, apparently having a change of heart. "I guess Gus would have liked that."

Before Hallie could respond, they heard the paramedics enter the building. There was a knock on the door to the examining room. "Provincetown Emergency."

Alvaro stepped aside and allowed the paramedic to enter. "How you doin', Eric?" He flashed a smile, as if he were encountering him on the street or in a bar.

A second man followed with a stretcher.

"Listen, I came in with a little indigestion—probably from the calzone I had over at Provincetown Pizza," He rubbed his stomach. "I thought the doctor here might hook me up with a script or something. But it looks like she overreacted."

Eric looked from Hallie to Alvaro. "It may well be heartburn, but we should probably bring you to the hospital anyway. Just to check it out; you know, bro?"

Hallie agreed emphatically, but she could already sense she would lose this fight.

"Any family history?" the second man asked, looking at Hallie. She had never seen him before.

"*Family history?*" Alvaro laughed bitterly. "Lots of it, right, Hallie? But none involving heart problems. Men in my family got hearts like lions. We're more likely to die by suicide or electric chair than a heart attack."

The new guy glanced at his coworker, obviously wondering if this was a joke, or if they were dealing with a psych case.

Hallie had folded her arms across her chest, and looked down. Though she was seething inwardly, she exuded calm. "The patient is right; I overreacted. Sorry I called you out, but don't worry. Mr. Silva will be happy to pay all the charges incurred. Won't you, Alvaro?"

"The hell I will. You're the one who called nine-one-one."

Eric looked from one to the other. "Listen, Alvaro, you get any other chest pains, indigestion, whatever, and Dr. Costa here's not available, don't hesitate to call. Heart attacks fool a lot of people."

Hallie nodded. "Thanks again for coming out, guys."

However, as soon as they'd left the room, she regarded Alvaro coldly. "Put your shirt on and get out."

"What? I thought you were giving me an EKG. You heard Eric. Better to be safe than—"

"Yeah, I heard him. And I think we'll both be a lot safer when you're out of my office. You've wasted enough of my time, Alvaro." She spoke firmly, refusing to show how shaken she was by his theatrics, and by the way his scent reminded her of Gus.

But as she was exiting the examining room, Alvaro reached out and seized her by the arm. "Meet me at Cantelli's at five—before the place fills up. There's something I need to say to you, and it's been a long time coming."

At first she thought Alvaro had stood her up, but then she saw him at a small table in the corner, his eyes flaming over the small votive candle. There were two martinis before him.

"What's this?" Hallie said, feeling annoyed as she slipped into a seat that faced the window. "You ordered for me?"

He lifted his glass in a mock elegance as if to toast her. "I figured this was something a lady like you would drink. You and Wolfman's son."

"Leave Sam out of it, okay? You know nothing about my ex-husband." She put up a finger and signaled the waitress. "What've you got on tap, Julie?"

Alvaro guzzled his martini as Hallie waited for her beer. He pushed the empty glass to the edge of the table before he reached for Hallie's.

"They're supposed to be sipped," she said. "And do you have to look at me like that? It's unnerving."

"*Unnerving*," Alvaro repeated. "Good word. I bet you and Wolfman's son used it a lot when you sat around drinking beer in your penthouse, pretending you were regular people. *Unnerving* that your old boyfriend was charged with murder. So *unnerving* that you had to go into that courtroom and talk about how he tried to kill you, too. *Unnerving* to watch the best guy you or I or anyone else ever met sit there and forgive you. Even as you were sending him to hell. And then when he was sentenced to life, my, my—I bet that was *unnerving* as hell. You and Junior probably had *two* martinis that night."

His voice rose a little higher every time he pronounced the word: *unnerving*. Hallie felt people watching them, though she refused to look back.

"You know what I don't understand? Why you hate me so much. We always got along when we were kids, didn't we?"

"I don't hate you, Hallie. I just love my cousin."

"And you think I don't?" Hallie whispered. It was the first time she'd admitted the truth out loud—or even in the privacy of her heart—in years. Maybe not since she ran away from Gus on the beach.

"If you loved him, you would have believed him."

"What are you talking about? You know I believed him. I got on the stand and—"

"You got on the stand and finished him, is what you did."

"That's ridiculous, Alvaro. I—" Hallie began, but the blaze of anger in Alvaro's eyes stopped her.

"They had a lot of evidence against him, but they had no body. He might have got off—until the tall, blond doctor walked to the stand in her red suit. So sincere. So reluctant. So fucking *sorry*. If you looked at the jury when you were testifying, you would have seen the turn. Something hardened in them then and there. There was no coming back from that, Hallie. Gus knew it; I knew it; and if you were honest with yourself, you'd know it, too."

"How can you say that? You were there. You know what I did. I practically perjured myself trying to help him."

The infamous Silva rage flared, and Alvaro slammed the table so hard that his martini glass toppled and shattered. When the waitress made a tentative step toward them, he stopped her with a look. "Shit, Hallie, it wasn't what you said. It was *you*. Anyone watching you on that stand could tell you didn't believe him. You loved him—I suppose even your idiot husband could see that—but you'd seen his other side; you knew what he was capable of."

"I didn't think he was guilty. Jesus, Alvaro, I *didn't*," Hallie said weakly. But then the image of Gus heaving Neil's body against the Jeep rose to her mind. The memory of Neil's blank eyes, his flaccid body. It was the same memory that had rattled her when she was on the stand. She covered her face with her hands and started to cry.

"I didn't want to believe it. God, I would have given anything to be sure he didn't do it. But I wasn't. I just wasn't," she said when she looked up. The restaurant was beginning to fill, and again she felt the other customers watching her. Hallie Costa, drinking with Gus's cousin and weeping openly. But she didn't care.

"No crying, okay," Alvaro said, softening. "You're making a fucking scene. And besides, I can't deal with a woman bawling."

"There was so much evidence, Alvaro. And I couldn't help but remember that night—how crazy he got. How could you be so sure?"

"Because I asked him, that's how. Gus may be a lot of things, but he's not a liar. And besides, he's blood. If he was bullshitting me, I would have known."

"If I could have talked to him like you did, if I saw him even once . . ." Hallie said. "I would have fought to get him a new trial. I would've hired private detectives. I would never have given up. You must know that, Alvaro. But I was afraid if we dug too deeply, we might find something—I don't know—even more incriminating."

"So what if you did? He's doing life, no parole, Hallie. Were you afraid they'd add another hundred years onto his sentence?"

"It couldn't get any worse for Gus, but there are so many

people who believe in him. People who love him, Alvaro. They would be shattered if it turned out he was guilty."

Again, Alvaro pounded the table. "For Christ sake, admit it, Hallie. *You're* the one who would have been shattered. The people who are sure of his innocence—people like me and Gallagher, Jack and that kid who seems to think she's his stepdaughter or something—we got nothing to fear. We been saying 'bring it on' since the trial. The only one who would be shattered is the one who wants to believe Gus is innocent, wants to with all her heart, but can't shake her doubts." Alvaro reached out and covered her hand with his own.

"*Come on, Hallie*," he said more gently. "What did I tell you about this crying shit?"

"The way he turned his back on everyone—I don't know, Alvaro, it felt almost like he was hiding something. You're right. I was afraid to know the truth. I was a coward."

Alvaro squeezed her hand and then released it. "Don't be so hard on yourself, okay? For one thing, Gus *was* hiding something. And after all these years, everyone stopped writing to him. I mean, you can only carry on a one-way conversation for so long. As far as that crap about you being a coward, everyone in this town knows—

But Hallie had stopped listening. "What do you mean he's hiding something? Something about the crime?"

"Yeah, something about the crime all right. But not the one Gus committed. The one that was committed against him the day they locked him up for something he didn't do. He didn't want you to see what living in that place did to him, Hallie. He couldn't stand for anyone else he loves to know who he had become."

Finally, the rage in Alvaro's eyes was quieted. "If we talked before, we might have cleared this up a long time ago . . . but like my girlfriend says, maybe things happen for a reason."

"Gus would call it *God's will*," Hallie said bitterly.

"And I'd call it timing. The last time I visited Gus, a little over a week ago, we were just sittin' there, not talking much—we don't usually—when all of a sudden, he looks over and asks about you."

"He did?" When Hallie looked down, her hands were shaking.

"He didn't say much. Just asked if I ever saw you, or how you were doing, something like that. But anyway, I've been thinkin' about it. I don't know if you'd even want to after all these years, but maybe you could write to him one more time."

"Did he say he wanted to hear from me?"

"Nope. Nothin' like that. But it was the first time since my dad died that he actually asked about someone from town. I don't want to get your hopes up, because he'll probably blow you off just like he does with everyone else. But then again, he might not."

When she rose to go, Alvaro stood and embraced her. "You don't have to run off, you know. You didn't even finish your beer."

"Some other time maybe?"

Alvaro smiled. "I'd like that. And next time I promise I won't break any glasses."

CHAPTER 31

Two Sundays later, Hallie walked up the familiar hill to St. Peter's and entered the church after the last mass. The hush, the shadows, the scent of burning candles all brought back the intrepid girl she had once been, the girl who had followed Gus here after hearing of his father's suicide. Almost expecting to see him hunched over a cigarette in the third row from the front, she slid into the empty pew.

When she heard footsteps, she closed her eyes and pretended she was praying, hoping to remain unnoticed. A young man with thinning hair, his skin dotted with pockmarks, glided past her toward the altar, where he appeared to tidy up. He wore no collar but he was dressed all in black down to his shoes. She was grateful that the few times she'd seen Gus after he entered the seminary, he had been wearing his usual jeans and sweatshirts—not this funereal outfit.

"Dr. Costa?" he said warily when their eyes met. "It's, um, good to see you here."

"*Hallie,*" she said, extending her hand. He wasn't a patient, and she didn't see him around town much, but she'd noticed him a couple of times at Lucy's Market. "And you must be the priest who replaced Father D'Souza."

"I wouldn't use the word *replaced*. From what I understand, Father D'Souza was one of a kind. I'm Matt," he said, extending his hand.

"No *Father* or anything? Just Matt?"

"Matt's fine. In any case, I'm sorry to interrupt your meditation."

"I wasn't—I mean, I *don't*—" Hallie began, and then when the priest grinned, she smiled back. "Thank you, Matt. You're very kind."

She left when he retreated to the sacristy. The wind was always particularly fierce in the cemetery, but she welcomed the cold. She sat down on the stone marked MARIA BOTELHO and folded her long legs to her chest. Then she pulled a spiral notebook from the messenger bag she used as Nick had once carried his backpack—a combination of old-fashioned doctor's bag and general catchall.

Since she'd met Alvaro at Cantelli's, she'd written at least a dozen letters to Gus. She told him about the people they knew, and her days in the office, about the changing color of the bay outside her window and how much she loved winter when the village belonged entirely to those who called themselves *town people*. But the letters always felt like a taunt—the brightness and productivity of her days, held up against his gray surroundings, his wasted years, an existence she could not even imagine. Particularly not for Gus. Other letters were extended apologies, crammed with guilt and regret—as if it were possible to put a stamp on it and be done. She never mailed any of them.

She wasn't sure why she'd brought her notebook to the cemetery. Her hands cramped in the wind, as brown leaves scuttled across the field of remembrance where Hallie found an odd peace and ease. She wrote about those leaves, and about the frozen weeds, trampled with unknown footsteps, about the yellow lichen on the ancient headstones, and how it often formed patterns like starbursts and daisies, about the flags and plastic flowers beside some of the newer ones. She described the grave that had been dug for the woman everyone called Jenny Z., who'd recently died at 102.

She admitted that she had become like the old *vovó* who used to take a folding chair and sit beside her husband's grave for hours. She planted flowers in the spring—delicate bluebells for his mother's grave, and bold red geraniums for Nick. On holidays, she said there were always flowers or wreaths left on the Silva graves; she suspected they were from Alvaro. There, in the cemetery, she smoked as she mused on the patients whose symptoms defied the usual explanations—often finding answers that eluded her in the office.

And then she told the truth that she'd been evading at home. Except in the strangely vivid dreams that still returned on occasion, she couldn't remember him anymore. Not in any real way. Though she searched for him near the tower where they used to smoke before school and on the corner where he'd first hugged her, on Loop Street, Point of Pines Road, and especially here, he was gone. As elusive as the mother she'd barely known. Sometimes she thought she was being punished for her lack of faith in him, or for her years of resentment after he entered the seminary.

When she was finished, she fished the envelope and stamp she always carried from her bag, and scrawled his address across it in bold letters. Fortunately, she'd memorized it. Then, before she could change her mind, before she could tell herself that the letter was too morbid or self-indulgent, she stuck the stamp on the envelope and dropped it in the mailbox on the way home.

She was disappointed, but not surprised, when there was no response. But then, nearly a month later, when she'd all but given up, she went to the mailbox and found a thin envelope addressed in Gus's handwriting. The letters, leaning forward optimistically, nearly caused her to break down right there on the street.

Inside, she set the letter on the table and made a cup of tea she was too shaky to drink. She stared at the envelope, as if it contained a bomb, or a message that would save her life—she wasn't sure which. She closed her eyes and was almost surprised when she opened them and saw that it was still there. The tea was cold before she reached for it.

Dear Hallie,

Do you have any idea how many times I've written those two words, thought them, dreamed them since I last saw you in the courtroom? When I gave up on everything else, they became my prayer, my mantra. Dear Hallie. Those two words, the beginning of the letter I was going to write someday, have gotten me through more than you'll ever know.

And then you wrote. For good or for bad, your voice has worked on me as nothing else has. You described the cemetery so well that I could feel that cold wind, and trace the deep cut letters of my mother's name in stone. I could see your face as it was the day my father died. You were too young and unscarred to take on my horrible story, but you let me give it to you anyway. I can still remember your innocence, your determination to grow up as fast as I needed you to.

Have I ever told you how grateful I am for that, or how lucky I've been to know you? Hallie, the child, the girl, the young woman? For a guy who swore himself to a life of celibacy at the age of eighteen, I have known as much of love as any man—and more than most.

Now I know why they call greed one of the seven deadly sins. Once I read your letter, I wanted more. If it wouldn't be too much trouble, I'd love to see a recent photo. Dr. Hallie Costa in her office maybe.

There are no class pictures here, but here is a snapshot: My hair has gone from black to gray with a tuft of pure white in the front. I have replaced running with weight lifting (one of the only acceptable releases here) and that's changed me too. In the mirror I see the face of a hard and bitter man, the man I never wanted—and still don't want—you to know. So as much as I would like to see you, I won't let you visit.

There are things about the human race that you learn in here that change you irrevocably. Once you see them you cross over to a barren place where there is no room for hope or faith or what I used to think of as redemption. I have no children, no church, no real family anymore. The only thing left to me is the wish that the few people I care about in this world will never cross that border.

But that isn't the only reason I'm writing, Hallie. The other day I received another letter that demanded opening—this one from Ava Cilento's daughter. The girl's name is Mila and she's sixteen now. She says she needs to talk to a priest, and she wants to visit me. At first, I thought it was a bad joke. Those were the same exact words her mother used when she pulled me into a storm that landed her in one hole and me in another. Obviously, the kid wants more from me than spiritual counsel. She's gone to the trouble of having a phony ID made, and claims that if I won't put her on the visitors' list she's going to come and stand outside the prison all day every Saturday.

I suppose I shouldn't care, but I do.

If you could possibly get in touch with this girl before the 21st, I'd appreciate it. Tell her that I'm not a priest anymore, I don't want to see her, and I have no answers to whatever questions she might have about her mother. Of course, you'll have to get past her bastard of a father first. But for a woman of your brilliance, that should be no problem.

Thanks, Hallie.

Gus

Hallie hadn't allowed herself to weep for Gus since she learned of his beating. Now as she set the letter aside, she cried a different kind of tears. They were voluminous, but silent. They rose up from the deepest part of herself, rinsing her clean. She cried for all the ways he had changed, but mostly for the constancy she felt when she read his words. No matter what prison had done to him, he was still Gus.

When the light changed, she got up and washed her face. Then she folded the letter and put it into her pocket, filled with resolve. The next day she would contact Ava Cilento's daughter and do what she could to change her mind. As for Gus's letter, she would carry it with her until she saw him again.

Within twenty-four hours, she wrote back.

Dear Gus,

I can't tell you how much it meant to hear from you. Like you, I've written that greeting so many times I feel my whole life is stained with it: Dear Gus. Do you remember what you said when we first got together? You said that we had time. I didn't know entirely what you meant then, but when I got your letter, those words came back to me, and I think I finally understand. I only hope that someday we will have time enough to say the things we've kept silent about for so long.

I'll write more later, but for now, I wanted to let you know how I made out with your request. I wish I could say I'd been more successful. Oh, I got past the father, all right, but the girl herself is another story. I tried my best to dissuade her, but I'm afraid my efforts only made her more determined to see you. All I can say is expect a visitor outside your window on Saturday.

Love,

Hallie

P.S. No pictures. If you really want to know how I look now, you'll have to see me.

PART FIVE

KAFKA'S CASTLE

{ 2009 }

The final mystery is oneself.

— OSCAR WILDE

Don't ask me how, but the third time I went to the prison, I knew that all the efforts I made to get there—the fake ID that says I'm eighteen, the lies to the Bug, the nasty bus ride—would be worthwhile. This time, I was sure he would put me on his list. If nothing else, I figured he had to be a little curious.

The guards already recognize me. "You back again, sugar?" one particular lowlife says. "Can't you see that man don't want to see you. Obviously, he's gettin' all he wants elsewhere. Guys change inside, you know. Me, on the other hand, I know how to appreciate someone with your loyalty, your devotion—not to mention that valentine-shaped ass."

There are other rude comments, too, but I just sit there on my little orange plastic chair and pretend I don't hear a thing.

"He's not my boyfriend, if it's any of your business," I finally snap when I can't take it anymore. One thing I've learned in life is to never let anyone know when you're scared.

And they all laugh. "Sassy little thing, ain't she?"

Anyway, I'm so involved in my dissing match with the apes I don't even notice that *my* prisoner had come down and taken his place opposite me, with only a wall of glass separating us.

Then he says my name. *Mila.* No hello or anything.

He looks absolutely nothing like I expected. At first, I even think it's a trick. That maybe he sent someone else in his place. I know it's sick, but I keep everything I can get my hands on about my mother's case in a hatbox under my bed, and let me tell you, this guy is *not* the guy in the newspaper. The guy in the paper had a runner's body and dark hair. I guess you could even say he was handsome in his own way. Someone I could easily imagine HER falling in love with. The man in front of me, on the other hand, has gray hair cut close to his scalp, a closed face, and the same hard-ass prison look everyone has here—even the guards. And though he's still lean, he's got the jacked arms and bulging veins in his biceps weight lifters get.

But what really shocks me is that there's absolutely nothing special about him—until he says my name. He doesn't just say it, he PRONOUNCES it, bringing me to life in some way I hadn't been before. If that makes any sense.

Then he gives me this incredibly intense look, as if he's seeing HER—just like my dad sometimes does. And though I'm hardly what you'd call shy, all of a sudden I'm feeling tongue-tied. It's like all the things I've been wanting to say to him have turned to marbles in my mouth.

He, on the other hand, is totally zen. "No wonder you've been having trouble with the guards. Your skirt is okay, but don't you own a more appropriate blouse?"

"No, I don't. And I didn't come here to get a lecture on my clothes." But in spite of myself, I pull my shawl a little more tightly around my shoulders. Ever since I went to Mexico with my dad and one of his old girlfriends a couple of years ago, I've been dressing like Frida Kahlo: long skirts, peasant blouses, clunky ethnic jewelry. I even dye my hair black so I look more like Frida and less like HER.

"So you're still living with him? I had hoped your mother's friend—Cynthia, I think her name was—would have gotten custody by now."

"Cynthia—against all my dad's money, his lawyers? Was that the plan? Anyway, I barely remember her. She stopped visiting when I turned eleven."

"I wish I had been able to help," the priest says with a sadness that confuses me.

He pauses for so long that I think he started to meditate or something. Then he launches into his spiel: "Listen, Mila. I understand why you might want to meet me. You must think I have some answers for you about your mother's death. Or maybe you just want me to listen to you tell me how difficult life has been without her, recite the victim impact statement you never got an opportunity to make. Well, if it's the latter, I'm here to listen. But if it's the former, I'm afraid I can't help you. I don't expect you to believe this, but I wasn't there when your mother died."

"*Former . . . latter.* What is this, English class?" I say, trying to pull myself together so that when I tell him what I really want, it will be comprehensible. "To use your terms, let's start with the *latter.* I don't think I have to tell you what it's like growing up as 'the kid whose mother was murdered.'"

For a minute, I get the feeling that if he could, he would reach out and grab my hand. I tuck both of them under my thighs.

"How did you know?" he asks.

"Um, I can read."

"Of course. The papers must have rehashed all that old stuff and you went back and looked it up. I did the same thing a few years after I lost my mother. Read those articles so many times, I practically memorized them, especially the quotes from neighbors and friends saying what a lovely person she was. It was almost like getting a little piece of her back."

"All I ever heard about my mother was that she was a whore."

For the first time, I get the reaction I want from Father Gustavo Silva. Until then, he thought *he* was the badass. Joe Lifer and all that. But inside me, there's a girl as hard as anyone in this godforsaken place. Sometimes she makes me strong. Other times, she scares the shit out of me.

He stares at me a minute, then gets to the point. "In your letters, you said I owed you something. So tell me—what exactly have you come to collect?"

Again, I start to feel a little uncomfortable. I automatically reach around in my little red purse for my cigarettes. But since I know you can't smoke in here, I end up stuffing a piece of gum in my mouth instead. The rhythm of my chewing calms me down. After all the effort I made to get here, I'm not sure I know the answer to his question.

"I want you to look at me," I finally say. "I want you to sit on a chair behind the wall where they keep people like you, and spend five minutes of your life looking at me. Me. Mila Cilento. Her daughter."

"I see you, Mila," he says. "I've always seen you. And I'm sorry for everything you've gone through. Is there anything else?"

For a minute, I wonder if that's some kind of a confession. Like maybe I should call someone and get them to write it down. But then I focus on that last question. "Yeah, actually there is something else."

He waits.

"I want to look at you, too. I want to see what a guy looks like who claims to be all about God and love and all that crap and then goes out and does what you did." I thought I was going to be so cool, but all of a sudden my voice goes wobbly.

"My dad did everything he could to protect me from knowing too much, but he couldn't stop me from growing up, going to the library, digging out the old newspapers just like you said. Now I can't even drive along the beach road because even if I don't look, I'm gonna see that dumpy motel. And you know what else? I'm gonna see the blood that was everywhere.

"I guess that's another reason I came here, Father Silva. I want to know if you see that when you're about to fall asleep."

He closes his eyes for the briefest second, and then he says, "Well, first of all, I'm not a priest anymore. I'm not even a believer. So whatever you think about me, the Church has nothing to do with it. If you want spiritual advice, you can go to St. Ben's and see a priest named Jack Rooney. And as far as the crime scene I was lured into that day—the *blood*—yes, I see it. There's not a day when it's not before my eyes. Does that make you feel better?"

The words sound sarcastic, but there's something else in his voice, and again, I'm confused. Before I can say anything, he seizes control. "Listen, I'm sorry for what happened to your mother, Mila. But like I said, I didn't kill her, and I don't have the answers you're looking for."

He gets up to walk away when I call after him. "Hey, one more question—"

Though he can't possibly hear me, he seems to sense that I'm calling him. He comes back and picks up the phone.

"Are you saying you don't believe in God either?" I don't know why that bothers me, but it does. Is *anything* about this guy real?

He rests his hands on his hips. "That's exactly what I'm saying, Mila. I don't believe in God or anything else—except a couple of friends and a cousin."

"You know what you are? You're a dead man," I yell at him. "And you're not even good-looking like the guy in the newspaper!"

By then the guard inside is telling him to come on, hurry up, but he just stands there, watching me. And it's like the moment when he first said my name. There is something so sad and deep about him, and it goes through me like a blade. I turn around and just about knock three people over, trying to get out of the place, tears wreaking serious havoc with my mascara, and people hollering at me to slow down, take it easy, until I finally reach the open air. By the time I make it to the street, the nasty bus looks like a limo with a driver; I'm that happy to get in it.

Last year, after I went through a weird Kafka phase, I renamed my dad after the Bug in *The Metamorphosis*, and started calling my house *The Castle*. Not only is it the biggest, gaudiest mansion in town, it's seriously goth. If my house was a person, it would be an emo girl with no friends who always wore black and cut herself in secret. Most people think I'm that girl. Especially my dad.

Why don't you bring friends home? the Bug says, his permanent scowl growing even deeper. *You're such a pretty girl, Mila. Why no dates? And why the fearsome eye makeup? Who are you trying to scare?* Stuff like that. But if I ever started acting like the so-called popular kids, dragging a bunch of people home to watch movies or sleep over and counting friends online, if I started shopping at Hollister's and spending my days texting, he could never handle it. And a date? *Please!* Bringing a boy to Kafka's Castle to meet the Bug would be like setting the kid up for a neo-pagan sacrifice. Besides, I *do* have a friend.

Just one, yes. But if you ask me, one true friend like Ethan Washburne is worth at least a dozen bitchy back-stabbers.

But back to my house. We know each other very well, the Castle and me. I swear I can tell something is wrong in the place even before I open the door. It actually *looks* different. It's made of stone (aren't all castles?) and when things are bad, the stones turn a darker, more mottled gray. I call that bad sign # 1.

When I get home from my field trip to the state prison, I open the garage door and see his Porsche parked inside which means he's home. Definitely bad sign # 2. Things are quiet, but it's a spooky kind of quiet. Right away, I know where my father is. I can either avoid it, or run and jump right into the heart of it. Since I tend to be a leaper, I go to the room we call the "guest room," though no guests have ever actually slept there. In fact, the last and only person to use the room was my mother. That was where she hung out when she wanted to get away from the Bug—which was probably a lot.

I open the door cautiously and find him sitting on her bed in his suit and tie, facing the bureau that still holds her things, her silky pajamas, the neat piles of tees and shorts she wore in the summer. There used to be a big envelope filled with letters written in her old language, and several photos of strangers who looked a lot like me in the bottom of her underwear drawer. But after the Bug caught me looking through it one day, the most interesting thing in the room mysteriously vanished. Her silver brush-and-comb set is still there, angled across her dresser just like it was when she was a little girl in Slovakia. Beside it is a bottle of perfume that condensed into pissy sweetness long ago.

I don't even dare to think about how often my father

comes in here or what he actually does in this room. Fingers her clothes? Sprays her dead perfume into the musty air? Runs her hairbrush through his own hair? (I confess: I've done all of the above myself, but not with the same sick reverence the Bug has.)

"Why aren't you at the restaurant?" I ask nervously, not mentioning how much he's creeping me out, sitting there in formal attire staring into a dead woman's mirror.

He doesn't answer. In fact, he's so deep in his own obsession that my words don't even penetrate. So I clear my throat and speak louder. "Sorry to er—*interrupt*, but I'm going to Ethan's. His mom invited me for dinner," I say (though Ethan's mom has been drunk for pretty much two years straight and she hasn't cooked dinner since she and his dad split up).

The Bug coughs, and readjusts his vision so that he can actually see something besides his memories of her. "I thought that's where you were all day." Then he gets up and ushers me out of the sanctuary. As soon as he comes into the hallway and looks at me, I realize he knows. Living alone in our haunted house, me and my dad have fine-tuned our communication over the years. Soon we should be able to eliminate talking altogether. I'll look at him, he'll look at me, and we'll be there.

"You're right. Maybe I'll just stay home." I start down the hall. "I've got a book report due next week, anyway." (We never do "book reports" in my school, but they were big in the Bug's generation, and he usually lets me go if I mention them.)

"Mila, stop right there," he says in the voice that used to scare the shit out of me when I was little. "I want to know where you went today, and I want to know now."

I spin toward him. "I told you—" Then, seeing that he's not buying, I change my tactic. "Let's go down to the kitchen and make tea, okay? Then I'll tell you whatever you need to know." One thing I learned from my mother is how *not* to react to the Bug's intimidation—like never, ever show him that you're afraid.

In the kitchen, Dad doesn't take his eyes off me. I concentrate on the act of making tea. I pretend I'm performing a Japanese tea ceremony and every gesture counts. I make green tea with extra honey for myself (so I can outlive all my enemies) and Lipton for the Bug, who hasn't tried anything new since 1981.

While the steam from our tea wreathes our faces, we study each other like cardplayers. *What have you got?*

Finally, the Bug antes up. "Jimmy, the new dishwasher, saw you down at the bus station this morning."

"Jimmy's only seen me once. How could he be sure it was me?"

"With that ink-black hair, and those long skirts you like, who else could it be?"

"Lots of people have—" I start to say, even though I know I'm just buying time. Useless time at that.

"I called your friend Ethan's mother. The woman sounded like she'd been drinking, but she was clear about one thing: you weren't there today."

"So how many issues do you want to deal with at once?" I'm still stalling so I can come up with some explanation for my presence at the bus station. A cigarette would really clear my head right about now, but lighting up in the kitchen would definitely be the final push. "Are we talking about my choice of hair color or Ethan's mother's drinking problem?"

"Right now, Mila, I just want to know what you were doing at the bus station."

Sometimes I just can't help pressing the Bug's nuclear button so I shrug and seal my fate. "Nothing much. Just looking for a little action."

In an instant, his hand is in the air, the flat of his palm taut with rage. The guy is just way too predictable. You put a quarter in the slot, you get the same gum ball every time. He hardly ever follows through and hits me, though. In fact, I think his raised hand scares him more than it scares me. And most of the time, that's all it is—a hand in the air. Sometimes I want to raise mine back. Like *Hi!* In my own sick way, I like it when he goes to the edge of losing it. It gives me the upper hand.

"Jesus Christ, I was kidding, Dad. You know, a J-O-K-E?" I pause and sip my tea.

"Don't curse like that," he says, his defeated hand falling to his side.

"Why not? You don't believe in God. Whose feelings am I hurting?"

"It just doesn't sound nice, that's all. Now, are you going to tell me what—"

"Okay, if you really want to know, there's this boy from school who works there, and I was spying on him."

"Spying? On a boy?" Now the poor Bug looks totally confused.

"That's what high school kids do, Dad. Get crushes. Stalk their victims. You're always saying how you want me to have a normal teenage life. Well, this is it."

Sometimes I'm so good at crushing the Bug I scare myself. And what's worse, I almost feel sorry for him. But then he goes into his self-pity routine. "It hasn't been easy for me raising a daughter alone, you know . . ." There's more, of course, but since I know this monologue by heart, I stop listening and focus on my cuticles, which are starting to look kind of ragged.

The Bug would like me to think our little family had this idyllic life before a sleazeball priest came along and mesmerized my mother. I don't remember a whole lot about those days, but I know better. I was six when she died so I should remember more. But most of my memories are nothing but a lot of random flashes. Like I'm walking into a dark room, but all I see is the little light that's plugged into an outlet in the corner. In the background, people are yelling and I'm cringing inside. So I just try to focus on that tiny light, to be absorbed by it. I fly into it like a moth.

Another memory: Again it's night, and I pull my blanket over my head. I can feel that blanket, its satiny edging which I hold between my fingers. And there is this muffled noise, the sound of something or (someone?) falling on the floor. *No*, a woman's voice cries in terror. *No. No.* In that memory there's no night light. No place to fly.

I suppose these fragments don't prove much, but they do suggest that life with Mom wasn't as perfect as the Bug would like me to think it was.

"I feel for you, Dad, I really do." I'm just daring him to raise his hand again. But he is too worn out for that. All he does is stare at me. Did I mention that my dad is old? Well, he is—not eighty or anything like that, but older than other kids' fathers. The circles under his eyes are so hollow they look like they were carved out with a blade. The same knife also cut deep lines between his nose and his mouth. His "love lines," I call them, because no one loves their own misery as much as the Bug does.

"I have to get back to the restaurant. We have eighty-four tonight," he sighs, measuring his life the only way he can—by the daily reservations at Cilento's. From what I've figured out, the guy has plenty of money, and none of it comes from his silly little restaurant. But if he gave up Cilento's, what would he do?

"Eileen left your dinner in the fridge," he adds. He kisses my cheek sorrowfully, and starts toward the garage. A few minutes later, I hear the Porsche starting up, and I am alone in Kafka's Castle with my home-cooked solitary dinner and a whole box of Klondike bars. But on this night the house is emptier than ever. On this night even God has vacated the premises. Thank you very much, Gustavo Silva.

I had almost stopped thinking about Gustavo Silva, his hot eyes and cold words, when I received the letter. And I'd forgotten about God, too. Ethan Washburne was already referring to that crazy time when I lingered in the theological section at the library and visited inmates at Millette State Prison as my "spiritual phase." We were both relieved when it was over.

E was raised a Methodist and used to go to church almost every week until his parents broke up. That's when his mother started inventing her own rules, including ones like "Thou Shalt not drink before 11 a.m.," and "Never sleep with a guy before he buys you dinner—unless it's Saturday night and you're really lonely." E says if I'd spent hours dying of boredom in Sunday school every week like he did, I would have given up on this stuff long ago.

I'm just getting home from school when a woman pulls up and parks her old Honda Civic in front of my house. Then she climbs out and leans against a fender.

"Mila Cilento?" she asks, looking me over.

Obviously, I ignore her. I continue fishing for my key in my purse, thinking I've got to seriously clean it out. I've collected so many lip glosses and receipts that I can't find a thing. Maybe I should just knock, I think, still ignoring the lady who is drilling holes in my back with her stare. But Eileen has gained so much weight lately that I discover my key before she manages to waddle to the door.

The woman, who's wearing jeans, a really cool pair of

boots, and a black sweater, isn't about to take a hint; she just says my name louder.

"Are you talking to me?" I glance over my shoulder as the key clicks in the lock.

"That's your name, isn't it?" she says. Then she tries to hand me this slightly grubby white envelope.

"Yeah, well, I don't know you, and whatever you're selling, I'm not interested," I say, even though her voice sounds strangely familiar. I push the door open.

"We've spoken before. I'm a *doctor*—and I've taken time away from my practice to bring this to you."

I look at her. "Seriously? What kind of doctor drives around in a shit-box Civic and passes out mystery envelopes to random people?"

"You're not random. This is a letter addressed to Mila Cilento, and it's from a mutual friend."

Okay, so my curiosity is piqued. I drop my bag and take a couple steps closer—close enough to get a look at my name etched on the grubby envelope. "I only have one friend, Dr. Whoever-you-are. And that's not his handwriting. Thanks, anyway."

"You remember Gus Silva?" she asks, just when I'm about to disappear into the Castle. "Maybe *friend* is the wrong word. I'm Hallie Costa."

"Hallie Costa? You mean, you're the rude person who called my house and tried to talk me out of visiting my mother's killer." I knew I recognized the voice.

"*I* was rude? As I recall, you told me to get lost and slammed the phone in my ear."

I shrug. "Not how it went. I told you to *please* get lost."

At that point, Eileen finally makes it to the door. "Can I help you?" she says warily to Dr. Costa.

"She's working her way through college selling magazine subscriptions," I tell Eileen. The fake doctor has some little wrinkles around her eyes, but she still looks pretty young. And since Eileen's half-blind without her glasses, she buys it.

I turn to the doctor and repeat, "Thanks, but we're not interested." Then at the last minute, I grab the envelope out of her hand. "I might as well take it," I say. "Even though I'll probably just throw it away."

I hate the smug expression on her face. *Mission accomplished.* So before she has a chance to say another word, I go inside and slam the door behind me. The first thing I do when I reach my room is toss the envelope in the trash just like I said I would. *Take that, Gustavo Silva!*

"Meee-la! Time for your snack," Eileen calls from the kitchen, in exactly the same intonation she has used every day since I was six. Eileen was thin when my dad first hired her, and she showed up every morning in jeans with creases ironed into them and shirts that matched her socks. Initially, the Bug thought she would be a mother figure for me. But calling me for my daily after-school snack is as motherly as Eileen gets.

"No thanks, Eileen." I was starving on the way home, but somehow that letter in the basket is messing with my appetite. Instead, I call E. Washburne, which is how he signs his name to the scathing letters to the editor he writes on a variety of subjects. E's letters appear so frequently in the *Cape Cod Times* that he's practically a columnist, but he's also had letters in the *Globe*, and one even made the *New York Times*. His favorite thing is to go online and leave a comment on a *Times* article. Most of the people who hang out there are old hippies and retired professors, but E's comments always get a lot of recommends.

Since he got home from school, E's probably been online reading the papers and eighteen blogs, and undoubtedly gotten himself worked up about something by now. But I'm not friends with E because I want to be better informed. No, behind all that angst about the world, the kid is seriously funny. It probably sounds ridiculous, but I don't remember laughing before I met E. *Ever.*

He also helps me knock out my homework every day on the phone. As for his own, he can't be bothered. And though they keep promising to pull his scholarship if he doesn't make more of a "traditional effort," the administration is afraid they'll end up looking like fools when E wins a Pulitzer or the Nobel or something.

I feel different about homework than E does. For me, getting it done keeps Eileen and the Bug off my back until I can escape with my trust fund which I'll get when I'm twenty-one. Of course I could run away. But let's face it: spoiled kids like me don't do well on the street. Even E finds the idea of "the ultimate freedom from parents" unappealing.

"What kind of rebellion would that be?" he says. "I'd end up living with a bunch of drunks just like my Mom. It would be home times twelve."

Anyway, by the time I reach E, it's too late. He's way too fired up about something he read to show even the slightest interest in my biology questions. So I pour a big glass of orange juice and go back upstairs. And there is the letter, absolutely *staring* at me from the waste basket where I left it.

I honestly don't think I would have read it if my name hadn't been underlined three times like it was urgent. Maybe I can read it to E later, I think, rescuing it from the trash. Then the two of us can laugh Gustavo Silva into oblivion.

I open it gingerly, like it might contain some kind of prison cooties.

Dear Mila,

   I don't know why you came to see me that day a couple of months ago. I don't truly believe you wanted to learn about God from the man convicted of killing your mother. A fallen priest. "A dead man," as you said when you left. But whatever the reason, your visit had a huge—and entirely unexpected—impact on me. Believe it or not, I didn't even know I was a dead man until a girl who looked disconcertingly like her mother told me I was.

   That night and for many nights that followed, I paced the way I used to when I was writing a homily or trying to figure out what to say to a twenty-four-year-old who was dying of leukemia. I also cried for the first time since I've been here. I've seen a man killed before my eyes, been through a few violent incidents myself, and have been locked in the hole for so long I would have given 20 years of my life just to hear a human voice. But nothing affected me the way your visit did.

   I doubt you took my advice and went to see my friend Jack Rooney. If you did, he would have taken you into the living room in the rectory and lit a fire in your heart.

   The night after you came, I was tortured with various visions (not the kind saints have, these mostly involved various execrable things I've seen and experienced here). What your visit did— what you did, Mila Cilento, was force me to say out loud what my life had become. A denial of all that is good and true.

   I will spare you the events that filled my "visions" and led me to my denial. In the end, they don't matter. What matters is that saying the words produced a sorrow in me that was greater than anything I've ever felt in my life.

Father Jack used to say that anyone who came to you, anyone who knocked on your door, as you did so persistently for those weeks prior to your visit, presented what he called "a sacred duty." To fail at a sacred duty, in Jack's book, was to diminish your soul. Mila, my soul is so diminished already that one more failure and it will shrivel up and blow away.

Please give me another chance. The woman who will be delivering this letter is a close friend. She has offered to drive you here so you can avoid the trauma of the "nasty bus."

Gus Silva

After I finish reading, I realize I can't share it with anyone—not even E. There are some things that are so private, you have to close the door—even on your best and only friend. When I get to the part about the doctor with the yellow ponytail driving me out to the state prison, I go to my window.

I expect to see nothing but an empty street. But she's still there, leaning against her car, smoking a cigarette. In one way, I'm glad she hasn't left, so I don't have to go to the trouble of tracking her down. But in another way, I'm seriously irritated. I mean, how did she know I would read the letter?

I'm thinking all this stuff as I'm walking down the stairs and out the front door, quietly enough not to alert Eileen. Outside, I break into a run down the walkway, waving the letter in the air.

"Thanks for the personal delivery, but you can tell our *mutual friend* the religious impulse has passed, and he can keep whatever hard-earned wisdom he got in 'the hole' to himself," I say when I reach her car.

"*The hole?*" the doctor repeats, and she looks so genuinely pained that for a minute I feel sorry for her. Then, all of a sudden, it comes to me who she is. *Dr. Maddox*, they called her in the newspaper reports, though she introduced herself as *Costa* when she first called me.

"You're the girlfriend, aren't you?" I ask. "The one who testified at his trial."

"I haven't been anyone's girlfriend for a long time." She squints at me, indicating end of subject. "So you want me to tell Gus you're no longer interested in visiting him?"

For some reason, I can't speak so just nod.

"Okay, then." She gets into her car. And that's it. No goodbye or anything.

"It was a phase," I yell after her, feeling a little offended that she doesn't even ask me why. "Call it my 'make friends with an inmate period.' Anyway, I'm over it."

She slams the door, and rolls down the window to dump the remains of some coffee on the ground. I try to say something else, but she puts up her hand to stop me. "No need to explain, Mila. To tell you the truth, I had no idea why Gus wanted to see you in the first place." And without looking back, she starts the car and disappears up the road.

By then I'm so pissed I go inside and rip his letter into little pieces. Then I do the same thing to the envelope with his handwriting and the underlinings that tricked me into opening it. I throw it all back into my metal waste basket, and before I get the urge to try to tape it together, I add a lit match. All it makes is a few scrappy flames, which I blow out when I hear Eileen calling me.

I don't answer right away, so she knocks at my door. Of course I'm not about to open it, because then she'll smell the fire. "Your friend Ethan is here," she says, when I still don't respond.

"Tell him I have PMS or something." It's the first time I can ever remember consciously lying to E.

For a long time, Eileen just stands there outside the door, breathing. Then she says, "Do you want some Tylenol?"

So I fling open the door. "I want to be left alone if that's all right with you."

Then, realizing that I sound exactly like the truculent little brat the good doctor obviously thinks I am, I'm even more annoyed. "Did you hear me? I said. *Leave me alone!*"

That brings E running up the stairs. He stands behind Eileen holding the newspaper that undoubtedly got him rattled up earlier. "You okay, Frida?" he asks, using the name he always calls me and proving that even geniuses ask dumb questions.

"Go fight the world somewhere else, E," I say. "I want to be left alone."

Then he tells me to get over myself, which is probably the best advice I've had all day. But all I can think is *How dare he?* So without thinking, I tell him to fuck off. And he does.

Afterwards, I'm engulfed in misery. When you've only got one friend, you really can't afford to tell him to go fuck himself. That night I skip dinner, which causes Eileen to panic and alert the Bug.

He comes home early from the restaurant, toting a carton of carrot ginger soup (my favorite). By then I'm absolutely starving, but I refuse it. I pretend I'm Gandhi on a hunger strike. The only problem is, I don't know what my demands are or who is supposed to meet them. Maybe I'm boycotting myself.

I don't tell the Bug any of this. If I did, he'd probably threaten to drag me to a psychiatrist. Then all I'd have to do was call his bluff and agree—which is the last thing he'd want. See, the Bug fears embarrassment more than death, and he's already lived with a wife who was murdered by her priest boyfriend. A daughter with mental-health issues would be the last straw. So I decide to spare us both the aggravation. I tell him to leave the soup; I'll eat it later.

"Are you sure you're all right?" he says, standing in the doorway with his usual funeral director's face (*This way to the coffin . . .*)

Just the sight of him makes me morph back into bitch girl. *Is it any wonder I'm screwed up, living with that face all these years?* I want to scream. But instead, I just say, "It's a headache, Dad. Not a brain tumor."

For once, he doesn't drag out the usual dusty lecture about "respect." He just shakes his head and shuffles away, leaving me to my own pathetic company.

That night, I don't sleep at all. I get up and walk circles in my room. I take off my pj's and open my window to let in the stars, the moon, the cold night air. Ben Franklin, or maybe it was George Washington, one of those founding father dudes, said that if you can't sleep, you should strip naked and stand before an open window. Then, when you get back into your warm bed, you go right to sleep. Doesn't work for me, though. Sorry, Ben.

For one thing, I'm too *hungry* to sleep. Even the cold soup congealing on my nightstand looks like a feast. But I refuse to eat until I figure out why I chase away everyone I care about. Will I end up in my own castle somewhere, walking around with a face like the Bug? Or will I turn out like my mother—another victim straight out of a made-for-TV movie? I'm not sure which possibility scares me more.

Around three I realize I'm probably going through the same thing Gustavo Silva did after my visit. The pacing. The horrifying look into my own black heart. Out of nowhere, I'm desperate to read his letter one more time. I go to the metal waste basket where I turned it to ash, looking for something—a scrap that survived my bonfire of fear and anger. I'm looking for the wisdom of "the hole" encapsulated in one secret message meant just for me. But the only piece I manage to dig out contains the words "offered to drive"—obviously referring to the doctor.

Okay, I admit it. I'm sleep deprived, hungry, and over-dosing on self-pity, but I take this as a sign. Something like a divine message. The words that survived my fire are clearly telling me that I have to go to the prison and see the priest one more time. After all, the good doctor did *offer to drive.*

Without further thought, I go downstairs and pull out the phone book. Hallett Costa, M.D., 535 ½ Commercial Street, Provincetown, is not hard to find. I pour myself a mixing bowl full of Cheerios and milk, gulp it down, and dial. I know 4 a.m. is not the best time for a phone call, but if I wait for the perfect time I'll change my mind.

The phone rings about ten times before the doctor picks up, sounding sleepy and disconcerted—and just a little scared—the way people always do when a ringing phone slices the night in two.

"Hello?" she says. "Hallie Costa here."

"It's me, Doc. Mila Cilento. Remember? You made a house call on me today?"

The line goes completely silent.

"Señora? You there?"

"It's four-oh-eight in the morning. Could you tell me the reason for this call? And, Mila? It better be good."

"From what I understand there's visiting hours this Saturday at the prison. I was thinking you could pick me up—say, around two-ish?"

"Oh, is *that* what you were thinking? Well, what I was thinking is something I wouldn't say to a child," she says before she slams the phone in my ear.

A *child*? Excuse me?

But even though she obviously isn't too impressed with my character, I'm very impressed with hers. In fact, I'm so impressed that I'm sure she'll show up at two o'clock sharp. I don't know her very well, but I can already tell that she's one of those people who always come through. I mean, she's still running errands for her old boyfriend.

After that, I have another big bowl of Cheerios. Then I go upstairs and sleep like a baby—as if I've got something resolved, though I'm not sure exactly what it is.

dear ava,

i seem to have lost my last friend in the world so once again i'm left with u, good old dead mom. that's right: e hasn't spoken to me in 4 whole days—not since i told him to go fuck himself. he walks right past me in school without even a glance in my direction, dragging his 50 pound pack of books on his back.

seriously, i wish u could have met e. not to brag, but all my life people have been telling me i'm pretty smart. my guidance counselor even said i'd probably make valedictorian if i weren't so antisocial. but next to e, i'm practically a moron. he's hot, too, tho he does have this acne problem, not to mention being totally skinny. ok, so probably, no one else in the entire world wd call him hot, but he's got great black hair & these incredible navy blue eyes. i even like the slouch he got from carrying around all those books.

don't get me wrong. it's not like i'm in love with e, but if i was ever in this lifetime going to fall in love, it would be w/ someone like him. someone w/ character and a brain in his head. not an old man who hasn't smiled since lincoln was president. no offense, but how could u? i suppose the answer is obvious. the bug's, well, a BUG w/ a nasty temper, but he was rich enough to build a castle around u.

after the letters i sent to u last yr, i made a vow i would never write to u again. for one thing, if anyone found out i was carrying on a correspondence w/ my departed mother, they'd probably lock me up. and besides, how long can u keep up a one-sided conversation w/ someone u don't even know?

*let's face it, ava: i slipped thru yr body to life & air, but since
then, u've never been much of a mother. that may sound harsh,
considering the circumstances, but i doubt we were ever very close.
all i know of u is the soft feeling of yr pajamas when i wear them
to bed & yr european featherbed. i know how the sun filters thru yr
gauzy curtains in the morning, gently waking me up. sometimes i
even picture u in that delicious bed feeling the same delicate sunlight on yr face & i wonder what u were thinking about the last
time u slept there. was it the priest w/ the gorgeous eyes?*

*i guess that's the real reason i'm writing to u. i wanted u to
know i'm going to see him again. don't worry, tho. our secrets are
safe—both the big one we share and the smaller one i told u about
the last time i wrote. i know it's pathetic, but if i shared them with
anyone—even e washburne—it would cut the last—the only—
thread that connects us as mother & daughter.*

mila

After I finish the letter, I tell Eileen I'm going shopping. In
Eileen's eyes, shopping is the safest, most normal thing I do. In
reality, nothing could be further from the truth. I'm such a
shopping addict that when I come home weighed down with
bags, I know exactly how a heroin addict feels when the nee-
dle first pops the skin. It's like totally letting go and exhaling
a huge satisfying *Yessss!* Tell me how healthy that is.

The good thing about being with E is that on some days he
makes me totally forget about the shopping rush. E hates "con-
sumerism" and video games, texting, and practically every other
thing that normal kids do. What he likes to do after school is to
take the B bus to Hyannis, pick up some coffee at Dunky's, and
hang out on the village green with the street people.

On this day, however, I seriously need to go to the mall. Eileen drops me off near the Macy's entrance. As I walk toward the heart of the complex, my sense of mission takes over. I need something totally provocative to wear to the prison on Saturday. My intention is to press every button on Dr. Costa's keyboard. It takes me an hour of intense hunting before I find exactly what I want: a skirt that is about a foot long, a pair of stilettos that make my calves muscle up, and one of those little shirts that rattled him the last time. The whole effect is very un-Frida, and I personally don't like it. But that's okay, cause it's not for me, anyway.

*W*hen *I clomp downstairs the next* day in my prison-visiting ensemble, a familiar little furrow appears between Eileen's brows. "New clothes?"

"Yeah, I'm meeting a couple of girls from school," I say, pulling out my high-powered ammo.

"Really?" The furrow irons itself out. "Well, I suppose that's how kids your age dress." Her voice is still doubtful, but I know she's not about to do anything to jeopardize my chance of making friends.

I'm almost out the door, my red purse in hand, when she is assailed with one final concern about her job security. "That skirt is *awfully* short, Mila. I don't know what your father—"

"Dad's already seen it," I say, then give her a fluttery little *see-ya!* wave, and slide out before she has the chance to call the Bug and check out the veracity of my statement.

The truth is the Bug would probably freak the way he does when he's forced to deal with any hint that I might be a sexual being. He acts like he doesn't even know I have my period yet. Once when I asked him to pick up some Tampax, he looked at me like I was speaking a foreign language, and ended up embarrassing us both.

Anyway, it isn't two yet when I set off down the street in my cute little skirt and my red bag to wait for the doctor's car. By two-fifteen, I'm starting to get pretty cold standing out in the wind in a skirt that barely covers my ass. It's April, but spring comes late on the Cape, if at all. Usually, the gray old winter drags into May, and then *bam!* It's straight into tourist season. So I'm practically *shaking* from the cold—and, okay, I admit it, I'm a little nervous, too. I mean, the doctor didn't actually say she was coming. In fact, she made it pretty clear she never wanted to see me again.

By the time her car rounds the corner, I'm glad to see her—though I do my best to look nonchalant—like I just got there, too. She pulls up and looks me up and down like she's deciding whether or not I'm good enough to get into her cheesy car.

"Nice outfit." She pops the lock so I can climb in. "For a hooker."

"Ba-da-boom," I say. Then I turn on the radio to let her know I have no intention of making conversation.

After a while, it's like she forgets I'm there. At first, I find her obliviousness a little insulting, but then I realize, she's thinking about *him*. She's got that fizzy, distracted look you get when you have a *boy* on your mind. It's so bad I consider asking her to pull over so I can give her the benefit of my not-quite-sixteen-year-old wisdom. I've already got my three-point lecture ready to go:

1. From what I've read in the paper, you were the lucky one. You got away. You ought to respect that.

2. If you want to meditate on something while you drive, think about the one who isn't here. She's everywhere, and nowhere. She sits between us in the car. She's in the fields we pass. You can ignore her if you want (believe me, I've tried) but she's always there.

And 3. Jeez! You're like thirty-five already! Aren't you a little *old* for this crap?

All of that is way too personal, though, so the two of us implicitly agree to ignore one another and occupy ourselves with whatever's rattling around in our own heads for the rest of the ride. But once we get there, she starts acting all motherly. She gets so pissed at the way some of the guards are looking at me that she gives them this hard, focused look. I really can't describe it, but somehow it works. Oh, they still look at me—her, too. Even if she's old and doesn't make much of an effort, she's still a stunner. But no one dares to come near us or say anything nasty like they did the first time I came. I'd never admit it, of course, but it feels kind of nice to be, well, *protected*.

We revert to ignoring each other again during the long wait. When they lead me into the visitor's room, I'm surprised when she gets up and follows. "I know this is your visit, but I just want to say hello," she says, trying to act like it's no big deal. As if I can't see her hands are shaking when she opens the door. She steps into the corner, and allows me to sit in the chair facing the glass.

When Gustavo Silva is finally brought into the visiting room, it's nothing like the last time. That day I had his full attention. Now all he sees is her. And though it's obvious that she's trying to keep it together, she can't. She doesn't gasp, or collapse, or even cry, but from ten feet away, I can feel her doing all those things inside. It reminds me of the first time I visited. All I had to go on was a photograph from the newspaper, but I was pretty shocked by how much he'd aged. And well, just *how* he'd aged.

Finally, he picks up his receiver. "Hello, Mila," he says. "Would you mind if I talked to Hallie for a minute?"

I quickly pass her the grimy phone and stand aside, feeling seriously pissed.

He does all the talking. Every time she tries to speak, he looks at her with so much love or forgiveness or *whatever* that it's just embarrassing. He covers his mouth so I can't see what he's saying into the phone, but it must be pretty intense because she can't keep it back anymore. She starts to cry. Or maybe he just has that effect on people. At one point, he reached out and touched the glass with his hand, which earned him a rebuke from the guard.

For a minute I almost feel something like *jealousy* on behalf of my mom. I mean, I still hate her, but my mother obviously loved this psychopath so much she put everything on the line for him—including me. And here is the guy looking at the doctor like she's the sun and the moon. I clear my throat to remind them that they're not exactly alone.

The priest says something else, and then the doctor asks if she could visit again some time. Alone. Apparently he agrees, because she mouths the words "thank you." Then she hands the phone to me.

By that time, I'm breathing fire. I mean, what is she thanking him for? For ruining her life? Or mine? Or probably every life he ever touched?

"I noticed a coffee shop a few miles back. I'm going to go

and grab a cup," she tells me in a shaky voice. "When you're ready, I'll be parked in the same area."

"Wait," Gus says. He's talking to me, but he is looking directly at her. And she at him. "Before she goes, there's something I need to give to her." He signals a guard, who promptly unlocks the door and without a word hands the doctor a brown paper bag.

So I admit it; I'm curious. What in the world could a guy doing life have to give to anyone? Some cute little keepsake he made in the prison shop, maybe? Whatever it is, it's so familiar to Hallie that she seems to recognize it by its weight. She shakes her head and insists she doesn't want it even before she reaches in and pulls out—drum roll here—some ancient *book*? I squint to read the title on the spine: *David Copperfield*. Are you kidding me?

"That book has been with me since I was nine," Gus says into the phone, and this time I'm not sure if he's talking to me or to her, or just to himself. "It was the only thing I took with me when I entered the seminary."

"Maybe you should tell *her* that." By then, I'm seriously confused at what all the intensity is about. I mean, it's just a book, right? It's not the Bible.

I'm about to hand her the phone when Gus speaks up emphatically. "No. *Please*. Just tell her."

The only reason I do it is because I'm starting to feel sorry for the poor doctor. The last thing I want is for her to start bawling again.

"With all the time I've had on my hands, I read it again," Gus says. "It was almost as good as the first time."

And then, before I can do my parrot routine, she speaks directly to him. "Gus, I *can't* take that back."

Though he doesn't respond, it's obvious that he's read her lips. "Well, I can't keep it here anymore. I don't want to keep it here."

I don't need to repeat that either, because whether Hallie deciphered the words or not, she understands something I don't. She stares at him for a long, probing moment.

Finally, she clutches the book to her chest. "Okay, then," she says. Just that—after all the drama. *Okay, then?* But somehow she manages to infuse those two words with more heartbreak than a whole book could hold. It's so bad that even *I* feel like crying. Then she turns toward the guard and walks out without looking back or even saying goodbye. I've got to admit, I kind of admire that.

After she's gone, I'm overcome with this crazy anxiety—like all of a sudden I don't really want to be alone with this guy, especially after the scene I just witnessed. It doesn't even matter that a guard is watching every move he makes. At first he keeps looking at the door, like he's expecting Sun and Moon to walk back in, or like he can't believe all that light shined on him, even for a minute.

Then he turns his full focus on me, and I wish she'd stayed—even if I *am* just a little bit jealous. It's as if my skin is transparent and he can look straight through my chest and see my ugly little heart pumping blood and ruin through my body.

"Didn't your mother ever teach you it was rude to stare?"

"My mother died before she had time to teach me much— just like yours did. I guess that makes us both rude orphans."

"Speak for yourself," I snap, feeling a weird twinge inside. Then, since neither of us can think of a follow-up, we just sit there. Two minutes seem like two days. I don't exactly back down, but he still wins. His eyes give off so much heat that I feel like I've been singed.

"In your letter, it sounded like you'd had some great spiritual experience after I visited you," I finally say.

"You could call it that. The night after I denied God, the glacier that had formed inside me over the last ten years turned to water. I don't think I've ever felt so sorry for anything in my life as I felt for saying those words."

"From what I hear, you Catholics are good at guilt—that is, when you're not diddling little kids and screwing around with people's moms."

Gus is unshaken. "I hate those things as much as you do, Mila. *More.* But if you think the Church—or any person, for that matter—is nothing more than their worst sins, you're blind."

He's staring at me, and I start to feel nervous again, so I pull out my pack of breath mints and pop a whole handful of them. "I don't care about your Church, Mr. Silva, or about your guilt for denying God. What I want to know is how you feel when you think about my mother."

"When I think of your mother, I feel tremendous sorrow— and yes, some guilt, too. If I had tried harder, maybe I could have prevented her death."

Then, before I have a chance to respond, he does something that completely freaks me out. He pulls out this picture of me when I was little. "She gave me this the first time she came to see me. I've been carrying it around ever since."

"Kind of like the book?"

"Yes, something like that. In fact, they're both tied to the same event for me."

I'm supposed to bite. You know, ask him *what* event. But I'm too sad to care. The guy who was convicted of killing my mom has been walking around for all these years with a picture of my little-girl self in his back pocket. I quickly turn my head, refusing to look into the scared eyes of the kid I used to be.

"You have no right to that picture. You never even knew that girl."

"Wrong on both counts. I have every right. Your mother gave me that picture on a night I have paid for dearly. And I *did* know that kid. The minute I saw her eyes, I knew her better than I've known members of my own family. Look at her, Mila. She's just a little girl, but she's already seen way too much."

I try not to look, but I do—and, God, I hate that kid. She's so vulnerable, a good wind would break her in two.

"Obviously, the picture didn't mean much to her," I say, fighting back tears.

"Wrong again. I really didn't know your mother very well, Mila. She didn't tell me a lot about herself, and I'm not sure if the things she did say were true. But I know she loved you very much. She had given up on herself, but she thought I could help you."

"What could you possibly do for me?"

He holds up the photograph of little-girl me again. "Maybe I could help you make peace with *her*."

"Don't play shrink with me, okay?" I say. "That's not why I came here."

"Then why? You wanted to look at me again?"

"Yeah, maybe I did."

"So what do you think?" he says, smiling again.

I appraise him openly the way the guards did to me in my skirt. I look from the top of his iron-gray head to the penetrating eyes, to the small white scar on his left cheek, and finally settle on the arms that are folded across his chest. There's a hokey valentine tattoo on his bicep that's partially obscured.

"To tell you the truth, I have no idea what she ever saw in you."

He laughs out loud. "Believe it or not, Mila, your mother and I were not lovers. In fact, I haven't been with a woman since high school. That sounds crazy to most people—impossible even. But it's true."

"Whose name is that inside your heart tattoo, then?" I ask.

He unfolds his arms, and lowers them so I can't see it anymore. Even though my intention was to *ping!* a few nerves, I wish I hadn't asked. Still, I can't help pressing a little further: "Is it my mother's? Or the doctor's?"

But instead of answering, he lifts a finger in the air again, signaling for the guard. For a minute, I think he's going to walk away on me like he did the last time, but this time he stops to say goodbye. "Thanks for coming, Mila," he says. "And if you ever need anything, don't hesitate to get in touch."

My first instinct is to say something bitchy like I always do—*As if I'd ever need anything from you.* But the plain kindness in his eyes stops me.

And then he's gone. Bang. I'm left sitting on my orange plastic chair, trying to blot the ridiculous tears on my face with a Kleenex. I mean, there's absolutely no way I'm walking out of this place bawling over the guy who ruined my life.

I'm not really sure how long I sit, going through my bag, and reapplying lip gloss. But when I finally get out of there, I'm confronted by the woman I almost forgot.

"You all right?" she says.

"Why wouldn't I be?" I snap. "You're the one who looked like you were going to have a meltdown in there—over a *book*, no less. And why are you still here? I thought you were going for coffee." I flip back my black hair and stand up as straight as I can, wishing I'd worn one of my long Frida skirts and the jewelry that goes with it, the costume that gives me strength. If I had, tears definitely wouldn't be streaming down my face the way they are.

I'm afraid the doctor's about to go soft on me and try to hug me or something, but all she says is: "You're crying."

"It's just that he's nothing like I ever expected him to be, okay? It shocked me when I first visited, but this time—"

"If Gus was angry with you, you have to understand. He's been through a lot."

"That's just it. He's *not* angry. He's—I don't know—*nice*— and I have no idea why. I don't deserve it."

"Apparently Gus thinks you do. So you like him."

"I didn't say that, did I?"

"But you did like him. You *do* like him. Most people react to Gus that way."

"You certainly do. I couldn't help noticing that the two of you were doing some serious *reacting* in there," I say. "God, you're still in love with the guy, aren't you? You've always been in love with him."

I only want to divert attention from myself and how I'm feeling—which is more confused than ever. But when I see the pain in her eyes, I'm actually sorry I mentioned it.

"Anyway, I'm not most people. The guy supposedly killed my mom. And my dad—my whole family—hates him more than anyone on earth. I shouldn't even be here."

But the doctor is focused on one word. "You said 'supposedly.' Does that mean you don't believe Gus killed your mother?"

By then we've reached the exit and I'm absolutely dying for a cigarette. I bolt out of the door, light up, and head for the car as fast as I can. But the doctor keeps pace with me.

"Is that the real reason you came here, Mila? Because you think Gus is innocent?"

I try not to look at her face. "Don't be ridiculous, Everyone says he did it. I mean, who else—"

Hallie knows she's hit a nerve, but she doesn't know why. Still, she can't let it go. "Do you know why your mother went to see Gus in the first place?"

The April wind is lashing my bare legs, and my hair keeps blowing in my eyes. I push back my hair. "She went to talk about God. Why else do you go to a priest?"

"You've read the newspaper accounts of the trial, Mila. The things that were said about your father."

"You know what? I'll take the bus." I start walking in the direction of the bus stop, even though my new shoes are absolutely killing me, I left my credit card at home, and I don't even have the twenty bucks for the fare.

Predictably, the doctor follows me—not because she gives a damn how I get home, but she thinks she has me on the ropes. I put my head down and talk into the wind. "Gus Silva was the one who said those things about my father. And for obvious reasons. No one else corroborated his lies, if you recall."

"Maybe because no one else knew what happened in that

house. No one but a dead woman and a small child who was too young to take the stand and tell what she'd seen."

"I saw nothing, señora. You got that? *Nada.* If I could have taken the stand, I would have said the same thing as every one else: my dad adored his wife. Forever and always. Just like you love your killer priest." We both know I'm lying, so I turn away quickly, and start fumbling through the cute little red bag that contains every necessity in life but cash.

"Look at me when you say that, Mila," she says.

So I spin around and face her. "My father didn't do it. That's one thing I'm sure of. Is that good enough for you?"

She lowers her head, then reaches out and touches my arm. "I'm sorry for badgering you. I mean it. I'm just so desperate to find something that will help Gus. If he knew I was treating you like this, he'd kill me."

"Not a very good choice of words, Doc." I'm hoping that if I piss her off enough she'll stop trying to be nice to me.

But she doesn't even seem to hear me. She slings her arm over my shoulder. "If you don't take the bus, I promise I won't say another word about Gus's case."

"One thing I can't stand is people pretending to care about me when they're just pursuing their own agenda." I shake her off, not about to admit how good her arm felt around me.

"You're right: I was pursuing my own agenda. The reason I used my only day off to drive you here was because I thought I might learn something about your mother through you. That wasn't fair."

"At least you're honest."

"Listen, Mila. Gus asked me to drive you here and back, and there's so little I can do for him. Please let me do this one thing."

"Throw in a chimichanga with extra hot sauce and you've got yourself a deal," I say as if I've got all the options in the world. "I'm starving."

We're pulling out of the taco shop when she asks me what all the *muchas gracias* and *señoras* are about. "Are you planning to study Spanish in college?"

"College is for middle-class kids hoping to pursue a career in business. In case you didn't know, I'm already *financially secure*, as my dad would say." Some sour cream squirts out of my chimichanga and I lick it off my hand.

"Maybe I read you wrong, but I thought you were the type who valued education for its own sake. Not to mention, you might learn a skill that could lead to a useful life."

"Why go to school and study Spanish when you can move to Mexico and actually live it?"

"So that's your plan—move to Mexico and sit by a pool, smoking pot for the rest of your life?"

"I didn't say anything about pot, did I? Though right about now it doesn't sound like a bad idea."

She tosses her yellow waves and laughs out loud in a way that reminds me of of the priest. On the way home, I sit back and study her, thinking how close they must have been. Close enough to *become* each other in some way. For just a moment, I wonder if by hanging around with E so much in these formative years, I might unconsciously assimilate part of who he is into my bloodstream. If it goes on much longer, twenty years from now, I'll probably end up carrying around a fifty-pound pack of books and railing about the Constitution to strangers in Dunky's. Thank God I told him to fuck off when I did!

But somehow I can't stop thinking about what I saw in

the prison. How they were with each other. The strange interaction over the book. "You two must have laughed a lot when you were together," I say, still watching her on the sly.

"Excuse me?" she says, obviously lost in her own thoughts.

"You and the Padre—you must have laughed a lot when you were my age," I repeat.

"All the time."

At this point, I'm in serious danger of starting to like Hallie. She's so young in a way. Not young as in immature; it's just that her heart doesn't seem to be scabbed over yet like most adults'.

"Do you have a boyfriend, Mila?" she asks. The dreaded question. Usually followed by the even more predictable comments on how pretty I am; surely a lot of boys would be interested, etc.

"Let's just say that with my mother's track record in love, I avoid it."

"I see," she says quietly. "How about a best friend? Someone you tell absolutely everything to?"

"I have myself."

"And that makes you happy?"

Now I'm getting annoyed. And as anyone who knows me well can tell you, when I get mad, I can't help it. My tongue automatically turns into a razor. "Obviously, not as happy as you were with your boyfriend. Until he tried to kill you, that is."

She doesn't say anything at first, but her lips tighten, and I can tell I've hit her in the solar plexus. Annoyingly, she turns up her dumb song again and tunes me out until it's over. Then she switches off the radio and we ride the rest of the way in silence.

When we reach the Castle, I don't even expect a goodbye. But to my surprise, she looks at me with this crazy sincerity and says, "Good luck, Mila."

Good luck? *Good fucking luck?* What's that supposed to mean?

I'm almost too flustered to thank her for an unpleasant ride to a place I wish I'd never been, but somehow I manage to get out an embarrassingly emotional *muchas gracias* before I escape.

The signs tonight at the Dismal Kingdom are not favorable: the stones are dark and forbidding, the Bug's Porsche is in the driveway, and when I look inside, I see Eileen standing in the window, watching as I get out of the doctor's shitbox car. Before she or the Bug can question me, I slip up to my room and lock the door, intending to plead a menstrual headache if anyone knocks. That should scare the Bug away!

But amazingly no one comes to the door. It's just me and my chrome-yellow walls and Frida staring down at me, her eyes as dark as Gus's were earlier.

My phone is blinking *número dos*—two messages—and for a minute my heart soars. I knew E would call! Take that, señora! I *do* have a friend after all, and one who's way too smart to do anything like join the priesthood or end up in jail. But when I play the messages back, the first is from my manicurist, reminding me of an appointment I made for the next day, and number two is from a girl in English class who was assigned to a project with me.

So after I change into my Frida clothes, I lay back on my bed and try not to hear Hallie's voice in my head, gently taunting me about my solitariness. *And that makes you happy?*

The answer makes me cry so hard that my bed shakes. Then I think about the other words she said and I breathe them into my room. *Good luck.* Does she really think that's possible for me? Maybe even something I deserve? The possibility would make the life I live in the Castle no longer feasible. I say the words louder. I say them over and over until I fall asleep and they become the very best dream I ever had. *Goodluckgoodluckgoodluck.*

dear mommy (did i ever call u that?),

i don't know how long i can go on keeping our secrets. when no one is home, i wander around kafka's castle looking for a way to escape. even my yellow walls don't make me happy anymore & Frida is no longer inscrutable when she looks down at me from the posters on the wall. she glares! that's right. my hero despises me, mommy. but not as much as i despise myself.

sometimes i still go into yr old room for comfort, and when i look in the mirror, i still see yr face, but that is where the similarity ends. i used to think i was like u (esp. since the alternative was taking after the bug) but now that i've met gus silva, i no longer believe that. admittedly, i don't have a lot of experience with good men, but even i know one when i see one. i hate to admit this, and believe me, i wouldn't tell anyone except u, but i'm starting to believe gus's only crime was his decency.

he still doesn't know how thoroughly u betrayed him, mommy, how thoroughly u betrayed all of us. but soon he will know. soon, mommy, everyone will know—even the bug, and i for one don't care anymore.

the only way u can stop me is to come back to "life" and do the dirty work yrself.

mila

As usual, after I write to dead mom, I feel kind of crazy. A couple of years ago I even went to see a therapist about it. It was after a particularly nasty little "episode" here. An episode so bad that Eileen turned against the man who signs her paycheck every week and agreed to drive me.

Eileen hates me. Sure, she feeds me and makes sure my clothes are clean, but I know. I even understand. Hating me is the only way Eileen can live with the secrets she's kept, the things she's seen since she came here. She survives by blaming everything on my mother, the faithless wife who drove my father to his current state of insanity. Ava's sins are etched on my face, as far as Eileen is concerned.

But this time was different. This time the Bug went a little too far. After it happened, Eileen came into my room, her face distorted with emotion. She even attempted an awkward hug. And since I was in a pretty vulnerable state, I let her do it.

"If there's anything I can do to help you, Mila . . ." The usual generic words. But I pounced on them.

"I really need to talk to someone, Eileen. You know, like a therapist or something . . ."

Of course she hesitated. "Are you planning to report—" she began, the little furrow opening up in her forehead.

But I quickly shook my head. "No, definitely not. Do you think I want to end up in some horrible foster home? I just want to talk to someone privately, someone who can never tell anyone what I say."

She'd made a call the next day.

By the time the appointment rolled around, however, Eileen was back to normal. She looked at me with mistrust as we pulled up in front of the office. "I could lose my job for this, Mila." She looked at me like I was Ava. "You better not say anything that could get your father in—well, in any kind of *difficulty*."

"Don't worry." I smiled politely, though I couldn't help thinking that Eileen was one of the most pathetic people I'd ever met in my life.

Truthfully, though, she had nothing to worry about. I barely mentioned the Bug. It was my own sanity that was on my mind. Sometimes I had hallucinations. A couple of times I even believed I'd seen the mother who died when I was six. I tried to giggle to make the therapist realize that deep down I knew none of this was *real*. But the truth was, I was no longer sure what was real and what wasn't. I mean, they never found Ava's body. But then, if she was actually alive and walking around town, other people would have seen her, too. *Wouldn't they?*

The therapist listened attentively. At first, I even thought she was taking my questions seriously, that there was a possibility my mother was not an apparition or a sign of psychosis. Maybe I really *had* seen her.

But then, Señora *psiquiatra* took off her glasses and made serious eye contact (which they must teach them to do in therapist school). "It can't have been easy losing your mother at such a young age, Mila, and, well, in such a traumatic way."

From then on the "session" went downhill—with her explaining that it was a common phenomenon for survivors to think they see the person they've lost. She described it this way: it's like when you have a new car, and all of a sudden you start noticing that car all over the highways. Usually, though, people just do a double take and then realize it's not their dead relative after all. But since I was so young when I lost my mother and probably couldn't remember her very accurately, she continued, I actually believed I saw her.

Even though I didn't much like the therapist, I wanted her to be right.

Obviously, Eileen was relieved when I said I wasn't going back. Instead, I began researching my mother's death, reading the newspaper accounts about the amount of blood loss, and the brutal nature of the crime. There seemed to be no doubts in the detectives' minds about my mother's fate. *She had to be dead.*

For almost a year my sanity seemed secure. No sightings. No obsessing. I didn't even think of my mother again until my not so sweet sixteenth birthday a couple of months ago when I got this card in the mail. My name and address were typed on the envelope, and the postmark was Weatherwood, California, a place I'd never heard of. It was one of those HAPPY BIRTHDAY TO MY DAUGHTER cards, and though it was unsigned, various words were underlined and starred like *love* and *special*. All the corny stuff. Some of the letters were kind of blurry, too, like maybe someone had bawled all over the stupid card before they sent it. Or maybe that was just my imagination, too. That's the thing about being crazy. The crazy person is always the last to know.

I put the card inside a pouch in my backpack (the only place safe from Eileen's fanatical cleaning and snooping) and tried not to pull it out and look at it every day. Some days I succeeded and other days I pulled the card out at least eighteen times to make sure it was still there, with the same words and phrases underlined. Every time I open it up, my heart beats faster till finally I have no choice. I write back to the address that's typed in the corner of the envelope:

General Delivery
Weatherwood, CA

Then I take a chance and scrawl the name that she would never dare to include on any mail the Bug or Eileen might see: AVA CILENTO. The next morning when it's time for school, I check my backpack one more time. Both the card and my letter are still there, tucked inside a book my Spanish teacher gave me: Pablo Neruda's *20 Poemas de Amor y una Canción Desperada*.

"You ready?" Eileen calls from the bottom of the stairs the next morning. "It's seven forty-three."

That's our Eileen, precise to the minute, but absolutely clueless about what actually makes a minute *matter*. "Be right down," I say. "Just got to finish blow-drying my hair."

Though Eileen hasn't said anything else, I can feel her presence at the bottom of the stairs, her stolid stare, dimply thighs jammed into those pressed jeans.

And when I finally emerge from my room, there she is, holding my smoothie in one hand, and jangling the car keys with the other. "We're going to be late, Mila," she warns just like she does every day, even though we never are.

Maybe it's just because I'm so giddy about my impending escape, but I get this weird urge to hug her. Fortunately, for both of us, it passes quickly.

As soon as Eileen's car pulls away from the academy, I turn around and head toward Route 28 before any nosy teacher sees me. It's a long walk, and by the time I reach Dunky's, my backpack feels heavier than E's and I'm exhausted.

I *clunk!* my backpack to the floor and order a vanilla chai, wondering how I can make it last till school gets out. I pretend to be fascinated by the books in my backpack. *World History, Biology, Latin*. The only one I don't bring out is the Neruda. Even though my trust fund is something like six figures, I don't even have change in my purse to buy a Bavarian cream.

At exactly 2:30, I head back to the school. By then, I'm sure the secretary has already alerted the Bug about my absence, so I lurk behind a tree where I'm likely to *see* before *being seen*. If my plan works out, I'll never have to enter that school again. Not that I dislike the place or anything—in fact, it's been my refuge these past eleven years. But there's no way I can go back to being the bitter misfit princess. Maybe I don't know where I'm sleeping tonight, but I do know what I have to do next.

Sometimes E's mother's rusted-out Escort is among the shiny Saabs and Mercedes that line the road, waiting to pick up students. But lately the spot where she usually parks has been empty. E says she's been working lunch at the restaurant, but I suspect she's just sleeping off whatever she did the night before.

When E emerges, he glances briefly at the empty parking place. Then he lowers his head and starts trudging toward home. Even though he refuses to take gym and lives on shit food, E stays healthy by carrying that heavy backpack miles every day.

I let him slip past before I pick up my own sack of rocks and begin my official stalking. Following about twenty paces behind, I feel the loneliness and anger and nobility that he has absorbed from all those books he reads. It rises off him like steam, and drifts toward me till I can't be silent any longer.

"E. Washburne!" I call after him, but he's far enough ahead, he doesn't hear me. "*E!* E. Washburne!"

Then, all of a sudden, I'm tired of calling him by his newspaper name. Tired of pretending my house is Kafka's Castle instead of just the miserable home it is, tired of the Bug and Frida and Mexico. All the lies E and I have created to pretend our lives are something other than what they are.

"*Ethan!*" I yell, louder this time. This time, the wind carries my voice, and he turns around.

At first, I'm not sure if he's still pissed at me for telling him to fuck off. He just stands there, his backpack on one shoulder as I walk toward him, throwing off my Frida jewelry as I go. I refuse to let him break eye contact. By the time I reach him, my neck is absolutely naked. He sets his backpack on the ground, and for a minute I think he's about to divest himself, too. But this is my nervous breakdown, not his, and he's actually just waiting for me to catch up.

"What the hell are you doing?" he asks. "And why'd you call me *Ethan*?"

"I'm throwing away my jewelry, that's what I'm doing," I say. "And I'm calling you Ethan because it's your name."

At that, E takes off his glasses, as if another (fuzzy) perspective might somehow clear things up. "You're acting really strange, you know that?"

"I've been acting strange all my life. So have you," I say, and the next thing you know we're both laughing. The dust from the road is in my nostrils and the road is littered with abandoned jewelry.

When our laughter trickles away, E puts on his glasses, hoists his backpack, and looks back on the trail I left behind.

"You probably should go back and get that stuff. You might want it later."

"Yeah, I might." But instead of looking back, I start walking toward E's house, and soon he falls into step with me. "Your mom home?" I ask.

"It's two-for-one happy hour at the bar. A good tip day." He tries to sound sardonic, but just ends up sounding tired. Like me.

"Then she probably won't be home for a few hours," I calculate out loud. "Good, because I want to talk to you. There's this, uh, well—there's a secret I need to tell you."

"Yeah? What kind of secret?" He sounds nervous—like he knows I could say anything in the state I'm in. And he's right, I could. But what scares him even more is that the famous E. Washburne, who has fiery retorts for pundits all over the country, will have no clue what to say to me. Me—a gringa with dyed black hair and a pale white neck, unprotected by its usual armor.

E's kitchen is a total disaster. Sink full of dishes, orange juice cartons and cereal boxes still on the counter from this morning. The living room is even worse. Every surface is littered with Lori Washburne's halfhearted interests, unfinished craft projects, books about medicinal herbs and reincarnation, every page scrawled with vigorous notations and underlinings, magazines piled up from the last ten years: *Vegetarian Times* (though Lori has never been a vegetarian, as far as I know), *Us, Family Circle, Yoga Journal.* The coffee table is marked with the deepening rings left by her wineglasses. An archaeologist finding this house a hundred years from now might consider the scarlet rings a telltale clue as to why nothing was ever finished or put away.

I plop down in the middle of the couch—right on a book that is wedged between the cushions. *Is Law School for You?* I read aloud, before I toss it on the coffee table, where it dislodges a pile of magazines. You can't brush against one item without subtly undermining the entire house.

"I think my mother has chai," E says, watching me from the doorway that leads into the kitchen. He still looks wary—like he wishes I'd start acting like the fucked-up girl he's always known.

"What I'd really like is a glass of wine."

"*Wine?*" E repeats. We're probably the only two high school kids alive who never drink—which is precisely why we don't. Anything *they* do, we're opposed to it. Being *anti-them* is our religion.

"You heard me. And please don't try to tell me you don't have any," I say, in what is probably my first reference to his mother's "problem." Though E and I are often brutal in our judgments about people at school, part of our code is that I pretend not to notice his mother's a drunk. In return, he never mentions that my dad's a total whack job.

"We have some, but it's tonight's supply," he admits, another sign that the code has crumbled. He stares at me a minute, obviously considering what to do, then goes into the kitchen. A few minutes later, he emerges with two juice glasses, and a bottle of white wine which he has already uncorked. "The wineglasses are dirty," he explains, making a space on the coffee table.

"I'm not fussy."

"This is her good stuff," E says, pouring shakily. "When Lori buys this, it usually means she's having a guy over. So hopefully, this secret talk involves something about running away to Mexico, 'cause my life isn't going to be worth shit after I drink this."

"We'll just have to finish the bottle. Then she'll think she forgot to put it in the fridge or something."

E hands me a glass, looking dubious, then moves a pile of unfolded laundry so he can sit on the chair opposite me. He removes his glasses again as if to protect himself from seeing me too clearly, and runs his hands nervously through his dense black hair. Then he gulps his chardonnay. "If we're going to finish the bottle, we've got no time to mess around." He takes another swig, not appearing to enjoy it much. "A secret, huh? Sounds pretty dramatic."

"It depends what you mean by drama," I say. I drink my wine, which tastes vinegary to my inexperienced palate. It's probably just psychological, but even that first sip makes me feel more relaxed. "The Bug's dating a woman named Cheryl," I blurt out.

E shrugs, obviously relieved. "That's what parents do when they're single, which most of them are. So?"

"Nothing—if you're talking about normal parents. But if you're talking about the Bug, well, it's cataclysmic."

E quaffs more wine. He looks so uncomfortable that for once in my life I actually wish I had a girlfriend. Or even that I was talking to Hallie Costa. At least, she would know enough to ask sympathetic questions, and she wouldn't sit there looking scared to death of the answers.

"Lori has lots of relationships, and she hardly fits the American Board of Psychiatry's definition of normal," he says. "I just try not to get personally involved. It's not like when I was a kid and some asshole would take me out in the backyard and play catch with me in the hopes of getting my mom in bed. Now I just exit stage left whenever I hear a voice in the house with a lower register than Lori's."

"There's two reasons my dad's never home. You want to know what they are?"

E stares straight at me, his hair so black and shiny in the dusty light that it's practically blue. "Shoot," he says, and he looks like he means it literally.

"The first reason is because he hates me."

"He can't hate you, you're his daughter." Like I say, the kid's a genius when it comes to geopolitical realities, but drag him into emotional terrain and he's lost.

"Don't you see? I'm the living embodiment of the woman who ruined his life. I've tried hard not to be her—with my hair color, my makeup, my whole Mexican thing. But I can't help it. I turn my head, or walk into a room, and I can see it in his eyes: *I'm her.*"

But E's not buying. "If he hated you, why didn't he send you to live with your aunts in New York? Or that woman Cynthia? With his money, he has a lot of options. He could have sent you to boarding school or—"

But I'm already shaking my head. "He wouldn't do any of those things. He couldn't. And that leads to the second reason he avoids me: because he loves me. He loves me more than anything on earth. For one thing, I'm *his*, and the Bug is a very possessive insect. And also because I'm all he has left of her. Don't you get it, E? I've become the receptacle for all his insane, obsessive feelings for my mother."

"In that case, I would think your dad's involvement with a third party would be beneficial to both of you. It would serve to mitigate—" he begins before the rage in my eyes stops him short.

"You want to see how fucking *beneficial* his last relationship was?" Then I stand up, turn around and remove the plate where my real front teeth used to be. I spin back and face E. No one on earth has ever seen me without my plate but Eileen and the Bug on the night it happened, and since then, only my dentist. I don't even look in the mirror without the false teeth to lie to me and tell me I'm someone other than who I am: an *abused child*, a pathetic label I would never for one minute allow myself to inhabit.

"Now you see who I really am," I say. "Not Frida, after all. Just Mila, daughter of the Bug. Ugly, ugly Mila."

E is naturally pale, so he has nowhere to go but to utter transparency. I can see a map of the veins beneath his skin as he stares at me. "He—*your dad*—did that to you?"

I turn around and reinsert my false smile, my Frida face. Then I sink back onto the couch. "That was the aftermath of Valerie, the final price of our happiness in Mexico." I say. "When he stopped seeing her, it was the worst time ever."

"Then one night he came home early and caught me smoking in the kitchen. I think he'd had a couple of drinks at work—or maybe he was just drunk on his own rage. He started off yelling about my smoking, what a dirty habit it was and everything. Then it got more personal: I was sneaky and lacked self-discipline. I could never be trusted. I was the curse she left behind. And finally, I disappeared altogether and he saw only her. *I was a whore*. Dirty. Destined to destroy whatever unlucky bastard I managed to ensnare. Imagine saying all this to a fourteen-year-old fucking *virgin*!

"Anyway, I was so freaked, I reached for the ashtray to put out my cigarette, but my eyes were on my dad, so I end up putting the unKool out right on his jade granite countertop.

I guess he thought it was deliberate, whatever, but he really lost it. It was like I'd put the butt out on his face. The next thing I knew I was on my ass, my mouth a pool of blood with a couple of little hard candies floating in it. Hard candies that just so happened to be my front teeth."

E's navy-blue eyes look almost black; his voice is a hoarse whisper. "Was that the only time?"

I want to answer, I really do, but I've used all my strength telling the truth I've never allowed myself to tell before. All I can do is shake my head. Then, I totally betray myself by starting to cry. And really, I don't know what I expect from E, but all he does is *sit there*, sinking lower and lower into the armchair, as if he wants to lose himself in the cushions with all the lint and coins.

"Maybe you should talk to a guidance counselor or something," he finally says. He pauses to gulp the rest of his wine. "That Miss Arnoff at school—"

At that moment I know just a little bit about how the Bug felt before he socked me in the mouth. "Fuck you, Ethan," I say. "Fuck you and your books and your head full of bullshit that's no use to anybody."

Then I march into the kitchen and pour the rest of my wine down the sink. I fling the door open noisily as I leave the house. Again, I don't know what I want E to do—maybe to follow me, or to try to stop me. He could at least reach out and touch my arm or something. But he just sits there holding his empty glass, looking so small and sad that I actually feel sorry for him.

I'm a mile down the road, half crying, half spewing rage, as I reclaim every piece of Mexican jewelry I dropped, when I see him running toward me. I've never seen E actually run, and it's so unnatural I almost stop right there in the middle of my nervous breakdown and laugh out loud.

"*Mila!* Mila, wait!" he yells, all out of breath and everything.

At first, I just turn back to my jewelry and ignore him, but then I realize that something monumental just happened: he didn't call me Frida. It's taken two whole years just to become Mila and Ethan to each other.

I don't actually turn around, but I do stop. And then E is behind me. *Right behind me.* I know because I can feel him breathing. And finally, I know because he's whispering to me.

"I'm sorry that happened to you, Mila. And I'm sorry I didn't know what to say about it. And especially because I have no clue what you should do now. All I know is that you can't stay there anymore."

Very slowly, I face him. He has removed his glasses and is staring at me with his unfocused navy-blue eyes. But even half blind, he's seeing me more clearly than anyone ever has before.

"And one more thing?" he says, letting his fingers run through my hair. "Mila is not ugly. Mila could never be ugly. In fact, Mila is the prettiest girl I've ever seen."

Then he kisses me; and even though neither of us have much experience, it's the kind of perfect, knock-your-bright-yellow-socks-off kiss that changes everything. And it happens right there in broad daylight.

Though I'm forced to go back home that night, there is this secret happiness inside me. I'm in darkness, but I can feel the sunny yellow of the walls all around me. By four in the morning, I can't wait any longer. I switch on the lights, and take all my books except the *Poemas* out of my backpack, and stuff as many essentials as I can fit in their place—makeup, hair products, a couple of outfits, and the expensive underwear I bought at the mall last week. When I'm finished packing I check to make sure my room is neat (a matter of pride, on my part). Then, just when I'm about to slip out the door, one final thing occurs to me. I take my credit card out of my wallet and toss it on the bed.

"Won't be needing that anymore, Mr. Bug," I say out loud. "No matter what I have to do to survive, I'll never have to ask you for anything again."

I'm walking down the hallway, about to make a clean escape, when her closed door stops me in my tracks. I've said goodbye to Frida, and in my own way to the Bug, but there still remains one final farewell I haven't said. In her room, I stare into the mirror where she saw her own treacherous face the last time she was in this house. But this time I realize Ethan is right: *I'm not her.* No matter how much I resemble her—and scrub-faced, without make up, standing among her abandoned things, I am an eerie likeness—I am not Ava Cilento. Nor do I bear any culpability for her deceptions.

As for my own, I take almost joyful responsibility for them as I remove the wallet she left behind, still containing a small amount of cash, from her drawer. Beside it, the keys to the Beemer are right where I left them the last time I "borrowed" the car.

The keys sit beneath the pile of scarves she wore to cover her woundedness.

"You owe me this much, Ava," I say, the keys safe in my pocket. Then I leave the castle, feeling like a princess freed from the darkest of fairy tales.

The car backs out rockily, completely demolishing a bed of flowers the landscapers planted a few days ago, and I have a minor crisis when I stall in the ruin. Since the last time I drove the car, I've been too busy for driver's ed, and my skills haven't improved much. But at four a.m., there are hardly any other cars on the road. Once I get to Route 6, all I have to do is draw a long, straight line till I reach the ocean.

The Bug has kept the car registered and occasionally even uses it, but I know he never listens to music while he drives. When I crank the radio I feel like I'm communing with the dead. I'm surprised to hear the last station my mother tuned into when she drove this car was classic rock. (Ava, I never would have guessed.) I don't possess anything remotely as melodious as Hallie Costa's voice, but when a song I like comes on (and even a few I don't like) I sing along anyway. I feel that good. After making it out of Qville, where I had torn up a few manicured lawns while taking the corners, driving on the empty highway is almost as easy as flying in a dream.

It's not yet morning, but there's a light on in the upstairs window, and when I gaze up, I see her bent over a desk like she's studying something—maybe a patient's file.

I knock boldly on the door, and a minute later, I hear her padding down the stairs.

"Just a minute, I'm coming," she says, her voice full of trust despite the hour. I wonder how I will ever explain my trembling, exhausted appearance at her purple door. But just as I knew I could navigate my mother's old car down the highway from Q-ville to Ptown, I know I will think of something. And I also know that no matter what happens, I'm never looking back.

PART SIX

THE PURPLE OYSTER

{ 2010 }

Feet, what do I need you for when I have wings to fly?

—FRIDA KAHLO

dear dad,

the other night i came into hyannis to see a movie with my boyfriend. (u remember ethan washburne?) after i dropped him off in q-ville, i drove by yr house. it's hard to believe it's been seven months since i last saw the place. i used to call it kafka's castle, but now i see it's just an ostentatious house that is too large for the lot it sits on, and much too small for the sorrow it contains.

sneaky as ever, i parked my car around the corner and waited. u rounded the corner in yr new red saab at the usual hour. watching from a "safe" distance, i actually cried—which is the last thing i expected to do. u hurt me a lot, dad, but i know u've saved yr deepest cuts for yrself & that knowing feels something like forgiveness.

i also know i have a lot of reasons to be grateful to u. above all, i'm thankful that u let me go. when i showed up at hallie's door, i wasn't planning to ask her to take me in. all i wanted was to talk to someone who was wise & kind. someone who would tell me what to do next. i didn't know hallie very well yet. in fact, i wasn't even sure i liked her, but i knew she was capable of the kind of love that simply didn't exist in our world.

i had given her no reason to help me, but it didn't matter. that morning, she made tea for me, and listened to everything i said, and heard everything i wasn't ready to say. then she hugged me & took me up to the guest room where she pulled down the covers. the sun was coming up & just before i fell asleep, i remember thinking i'm home, i'm finally home. i don't know how i knew. i just did.

i wonder if u would even recognize me now. i have cut my hair short & bleached it paler than pale blond with a streak of kelly green that really makes my eyes pop. ptown is the kind of place where u can dress however u want and be whoever you are so i feel right at home. i also got a job at a mexican restaurant as a bus girl 4 nites a wk, which gives me enuf cash to put gas in the beemer. thanks for letting me keep ava's car & for paying my tuition at the academy until i graduate. even tho the commute adds hours to my day, i would have really missed my teachers (& even a few of the kids, not to mention ethan!) there's also no way i would get such an advanced spanish class at ptown high. since spanish will probably be my major when i go to college, that's important to me.

education is practically the house religion here. hallie went to school for more than half her life. then there's julia, who stays with us in the summer. julia's mom died of aids when she was a kid, and the only "fathers" she ever had in her life were a couple of priests she met when she was about twelve. (yes, those priests.) she just started her medical residency.

thank u, too, for the checks u send hallie every month to cover my expenses—even tho she never cashes them. all she can see are the things u did to me—& of course hallie blames u for what happened to gus. but when i see yr ripped up checks in the trash, it makes me kind of sad. i know u are trying to be my dad the only way u can.

& finally thanks for the birthday card & flowers u sent & for the offer to come down & take me out to dinner. as much as i appreciate the invitation, i'm just not ready yet. maybe someday.

yr daughter,

mila

After I finish my letter, I jump on my bike and ride to the post office to mail it. I'm so happy I'm singing one of Hallie's favorite songs, "Friday I'm in Love," like I really think it's possible to put a stamp on the past and disown it. But when I peel out of the post office, my empty backpack is the heaviest item on earth. I feel like every inch of my skin is tattooed with the words of my letter. In particular, I can't stop thinking about one line:

of course Hallie blames u for what happened to gus . . .

But what about my part in it? How would she react if she knew my secret? Would she still stand at the sink beside me, singing Billie Holiday or old songs from the eighties while I wash and she dries? Would she bring me *malasadas* or pore over stacks of college catalogues, leaping up in excitement when she talked about visiting the campuses? Would she go down to the Tamale and yell at a thirty-year-old waiter for making a move on me till he blushed fifty-two shades of scarlet and swore I was like a little sister to him. (That just got Hallie more incensed. *Excuse me? Don't you mean a daughter?* she railed before she sputtered on. *You're lucky I don't . . . And if I ever hear . . .*) In the end, it wasn't embarrassment that made me run out of there, like Hallie and the waiter thought. It was just that no one ever stood up for me like that before, and if I didn't get out of there immediately, I was probably going to do something entirely stupid—like bust out crying. In the alleyway, I pulled myself together enough to tell Hallie that I appreciated her concern, but it wasn't like she was my mother or anything. I could take care of myself.

Deep down, I really wanted her to say that she was in every way that mattered, but she just looked kind of crestfallen. Like maybe I hadn't said what she wanted to hear, either.

Now, halfway home from the PO, the words from my letter still burning my skin, I think about the huge achy lump that formed in my throat that night and I can no longer keep it back. Not any of it. Abruptly, I skid to a stop and sob like a little kid. I left home to stop living a lie, and though I'm happier than I've ever been, I still have the word LIAR tattooed on my soul.

When one of Hallie's patients pulls over to ask what's wrong, it just makes me cry harder. I mean why do these people care about me? Don't they know who I am? Then I point to the perfectly intact skin of my knee and tell her I fell off my bike. She looks a little confused, but accepts it. If there's one thing I've learned from my parents, it's that if you speak convincingly, people will buy just about anything. "Don't worry, hon. Hallie will fix you up," she says and drives away.

If I wasn't determined to pull myself together, that one comment could have pushed me over the edge. Instead, it makes me realize that this time Hallie can't fix me up; this time only I can do that. So instead of going home, I turn around and pedal to the Hot Tamale, where I slip in the back door, scrub my face, and try to make myself semi-presentable. Then I pick up a couple of tostadas, one extra hot, the other with double sour cream. Somehow I manage to persuade my favorite bartender to slip dos Dos Equis and a bottle opener into my backpack when no one's looking.

"If I didn't know you better, I'd say you look kind of nervous," he teases. "Hot date?"

"Yeah, something like that."

There are still places on the beach where you can go to be alone no matter how many people fill up the town. Just you, the frigid purple ocean, and the dunes that can both shelter and trap you. Hallie finds a comfort I don't understand in the graveyard out by the highway, but the beach is where she goes to commune with the living and the dead. Though she doesn't say so, I know the "living" means Gus. As for the dead, I think Hallie mostly talks to her dad, who died in a shack overlooking the ocean, and some guy named Wolf.

A couple of years ago, the shack was burned down by an artist who was staying there. Once when I caught Hallie staring at the blackened spot where the shack had stood, I asked her if she missed the place much. But she just laughed. Only the beach mattered, she said. And besides, she claims she can still see her father sitting out on his steps, his wild hair loose in the wind, as he watched a sunset. Nothing can take that away from her.

On the way to Race Point, the sky turns this incredible cobalt blue, and on my bike I feel like I'm flying right into it, my pale hair sleek to my head, dinner bobbing on my back. Despite everything, the moment is so perfect that I want to frame it and keep it forever. I leave my bike in the parking area and trudge through the sand for what seems like miles with no sign of Hallie. I get so tired I almost sit down and drink both beers myself. Then I remind myself why I came out here, and I keep going.

It seems like every day, Hallie's walks take her farther out. The tostadas are cold by the time I spot her. When I come close, she looks annoyed. "Mila, what are you doing here? You know that this is my personal time."

"Is that any way to talk to someone who's just walked ten miles through the sand to bring you dinner?"

"*Dinner?* Well, in that case you can stay. Whatcha got?"

"Guess," I say, opening my backpack and pulling out my foil-wrapped packets.

"Some form of burrito, I'm sure. All I can say is you better not have forgotten the sour cream."

I make myself at home on the blanket Hallie carries in her car year round so she'll be ready when the urge to go to the beach hits. "Actually, I'm much less predictable than you think. It's happens to be a *tostada*."

"Bean, I hope," Hallie says. Then she spots the beer. "Where'd you get *that*?"

"You know that kid who tends bar on Wednesday nights? Seamus?"

"The one who stares at you like you're a supermodel and the Dalai Lama all rolled into one?"

"That's him." I pop the bottles.

She looks skeptical. "Number one," she says. "You really shouldn't be drinking that. And, number two, I hope you don't get in the habit of using your looks to get what you want."

I take a quick slug of beer since I'm not sure if she's about to take it away from me. "Pleeeze," I say, addressing number one, with appropriate exasperation. "Every Friday night kids come out to the Point and drink themselves into oblivion while I hang out with Ethan and a couple of homeless guys at Dunky's. You really think it's an issue if I sip half a warm beer with my guardian?" (As for number two, I don't respond, because it sounds kind of like she's warning me not to become my mother, a subject I avoid whenever possible.)

"I know you don't drink," she says. "That's why I'm not wrestling the bottle out of your hand right now."

She's right. I don't even like beer, and I was planning to drink only half of it. But I guzzle the whole bottle before I get the courage to say what I've come for. I promised myself that I'd keep my mom's secret for the rest of my days. But ever since I looked into Gus Silva's eyes, or saw his valentine-shaped tattoo, I knew I couldn't do it. Whenever I think of what I've been hiding, I imagine him cutting Hallie's name into his skin on some particularly desperate day.

"What if my mother turned out to be alive?" I blurt out in the middle of our silence. "Have you ever thought of that?"

"At the beginning, I thought of every possibility that might have exonerated Gus," Hallie admits after she wipes a dollop of sour cream from her lip. "But it's not possible. No one could have sustained that much blood loss and survived." She reaches out and seizes my hand. "I'm sorry, Mila. Have you hoped—"

I pull away, not about to be distracted by cheap comfort—not yet. Then I plant my empty beer bottle in the sand. "I've seen her, Hallie."

Hallie lets her hand drop and looks at me in an oddly unsurprised way, waiting for me to continue.

"She used to come back sometimes, and watch me outside my school."

"Did you ever speak to her?" Hallie says. She pauses to light a cigarette. Then she passes me one—something she *never* does.

I light one of her Marlboros, which I hate, and suck hard like it will save my life—or at least obscure the taste of my guilt.

"Speak to her? Well, no. I followed her once, though."

"And?"

"She got away."

"When was this? Recently?"

"The last time it happened, I was thirteen."

"So you saw a woman who reminded you of your mother a few times when you were younger, but she never spoke to you?"

"I know what you're thinking—that it was just the wishful thinking of a lonely kid. I used to think so, too. But if you could have seen the way she looked at me—" Then, I reach into my backpack, pull out the envelope postmarked from California, and remove the card inside. "Read it," I say. "Then tell me you still don't believe me."

Hallie studies the envelope in the weakening light, and turns the card over a couple of times, looking for something, anything to validate my claim. "You really think your mother sent this?"

"Well, did you read it?"

"Honey, it's a drugstore card with no signature. Anyone could have sent it to you. And, unfortunately, people can be very cruel. Especially kids."

"From *California*? I don't know a single person in the whole state."

"Maybe not, but I'm sure you know people who've traveled there. I'm sorry, Mila, but this looks like a particularly mean hoax to me." Apologetically, Hallie hands my card back to me.

"But I wrote back. Lots of times," I say, sounding pathetic in the face of all that blood. The blood that saturated the mattress, rug, floorboards. My mother's blood.

"Did you include a return address?" she whispers.

"Well, no. I mean, I *would* have, but if it came back and the Bug saw it—"

"You're a smart girl, Mila," Hallie interrupts gently. "You could have gotten yourself a post-office box in town. That is, if you really believed there was a possibility your mother would write back."

I put my cigarette out in the sand, and then wrap it in the deli paper from my dinner. Finally, I turn to look at Hallie. "I didn't have to prove it to myself, okay?"

"Why not?"

"Because I *knew* she was there. I feel her reading my letters. I feel her opening the envelope nervously. She's shaking so much she almost tears the letter inside. And she's crying, too. She soaks my letters with her tears. The ink blurs when I tell her how much I hate her for what she did."

But when I touch my face, I realize I'm the one who's crying. Big splashy tears for a mother who doesn't even know me. A mother no one believes in but me. And before I even know how it happened, Hallie is holding me. Holding me and rocking me and stroking my hair. *I'm sorry*, she whispers, as if it's her fault for destroying my fantasy. Or maybe just because she can't rewrite the story of my childhood. *I'm so, so sorry.*

It's dark by the time we get off the beach, so I put my bike on Hallie's rack and ride home with her. After my crying jag on the beach we didn't say much as we ambled down the coast. Somehow it felt all right to just walk and let the waves do the talking. But in the car, the silence loses its sweetness, and Hallie rushes to fill it.

"Julia and I are planning to drive up to Harry's in Hyannis tomorrow night. There's a blues band playing she wants to hear."

"A blues band? *Julia?*" (Julia rarely listens to anything but classical music, and she *never* goes to bars.)

"Yeah, she met the bass player somewhere last week. Guy named Spencer. She won't admit it, of course, but I think she's interested."

"Hmm . . . A musician might be just what Jules needs. A counterbalance to all the science in her life." It feels funny to be talking about ordinary things after my great confession. For years I imagined telling someone my secret. I thought it would be Armageddon. Even on this night, I went to the beach fortified with beer in preparation for a lot of angry drama. But now that I've finally done it, Hallie is smiling and talking about the prospect of Julia finding a boyfriend.

In a way, I wish she was right: that the whole thing was nothing more than the delusions of a lonely child. Then I wouldn't be partly responsible for every minute, and hour, and year that Gus Silva has spent in prison while I held dead mom's secret in my heart.

I don't care how badly my mother was hurt in that hotel room: *I know she survived.* And the reason I didn't get a post-office box wasn't because I thought she wouldn't write back. It was because I was afraid that she would.

But I now know that no one, not even Hallie, will believe me if I don't get more proof. So the next afternoon, after overhearing a particularly intense phone conversation between Hallie and Gus, I finally get the courage to call the post office in Weatherwood, California. When the clerk answers, I speak as calmly as I can, asking if anyone had come in to pick up the mail addressed to Ava Cilento. I know it's a long shot. That's why I'm so taken aback when the guy says, "Sure does. Miss Cilento's a regular here. Stops in every week to see if there's something for her." His voice has a raspy sound that makes me think he's really old, but he still perks up the way men do when they talk about a beautiful woman.

At that point, my hand actually goes limp, and the phone just slips out of it. From the floor, I hear the voice on the other end. "Hello? You still there?"

"Yes!" I practically scream as I retrieve the phone. Then I modify my voice. "Um, would you mind giving me your name? Just in case I need to ask you a couple of questions later."

"It's Wally," the guy says, sounding like he already regrets telling me that much. "And I won't be answering any more questions. Not now. Not later." The dial tone blares as sure and strong as I imagine my mother's heartbeat to be when she approaches the post office week after week, looking for my letters.

Wally. I write the name in all caps followed by exactly sixteen exclamation marks.

That night Julia makes a spinach frittata and a beet salad with goat cheese for dinner. It's one of my favorite meals, but I'm too distracted by those exclamation marks to feel hungry. I don't talk much, either. I can feel Hallie's worried eyes settling on me when she thinks I'm not looking, so I get up and scrape my plate into the sink, hoping no one will notice how little I ate.

"Julia and I were planning to go to Hyannis tonight, remember?" Hallie says as she helps me clear the table. "But if you want to talk, I can . . ."

"I'm fine," I answer, a beat too quickly. "*Really.* You guys go and have a good time. I have something to do, anyway."

She still looks dubious, so before she can ask me exactly *what* I need to do, I give her a huge hug. "You're sure?" she asks.

"Absolutely."

I clean the kitchen to perfection while they're getting ready, and when they leave, I go up to my room, sit up really straight in my chair, and write my very last letter ever to my mother.

dear ava,

do u want to know my dearest & most secret wish? the one thing i've never confided to anyone—not even ethan? i wish that hallie & gus were my real parents—mine & julia's, too. we would be the silva family, not the family of orphans we are now.

you will never know how happy hallie, julia, and i are when we're all together. if hallie's not working, the house is always filled with company, a mishmash of friends that includes matt, the priest from st. peter's, a sweet old drunk called hugo who does odd jobs for us, the gay couple next door, and some of hallie's doctor friends from boston. it sounds like an odd group, but everyone fits together. that's what being a family is, dead mom—something u wd never understand.

sometimes at night, i dream that hallie & gus are tangled together in sleep in the next room, "mom & dad." i dream so hard that when i wake up i almost believe it's true. reality has sharp edges after those dreams. then, slowly, i remember everything. the sounds i heard when u & the bug fought. yr empty room. yr face when i saw you outside my school.

and finally i see gus staring at me from behind glass. he's not my father, not hallie's husband, & what's worse, he's living a life that doesn't even belong to him anymore. there's no way to soften the edges of that dream, ava, but there is a way to end it.

the only thing i can do to restore this house and myself is to go to the police & tell them what i know. to choose my new family over u. it's a choice my heart finds surprisingly easy to make. consider

this your last chance to come back and do the right thing. and if
not, well . . .

goodbye, my mother.

mila

At the end of the letter, I break with tradition and add my
address and my telephone number. I look at the bold **2** on the
calendar at the post office when I mail it and mentally give
her two weeks. If she doesn't respond by August 16th, I'll go
to the lawyer who defended Gus and present my case. Lunes
Oliveira is so hot you could go blind looking at him, and
he's funny, too. Sometimes he shows up at the Tamale with
one of his glamorous girlfriends on Friday nights, or with his
kids on Saturdays after soccer, and he comes to Hallie's parties. The way he looks at her is almost embarrassing, but she
doesn't seem to notice.

Anyway, if he doesn't believe me, then I'll take my tattered birthday card, my collection of visions, suspicions, and
concrete details to someone who *will*. The Ptown Police
maybe. Or if I really want to get serious, I'll go to my father.
No doubt the Bug will have half a dozen of the country's
best private eyes on dead mom's ass before I finish my pre-
sentation.

The days drag at first, and then they speed up insanely.
Each hour, each moment, practically screaming in my ear: It's
not going to happen, you little fool. From the day I posted
the letter, I've dreamed that Ava is calling my name in a low
voice outside my window, and every night I've gotten up and
looked into the street. But each night it's more empty. More

desolate. More hopeless. Just like the streets where I have looked for her all my life.

In the final three days, my dreams abruptly change. Now I dream of blood soaking the sheets and carpets in my room and spilling down the stairs.

When I wake up on the morning of the sixeenth, I taste the question I don't want to ask. What have I got to counter all that blood? An unsigned birthday card? The words of some postal clerk in a town called Weatherwood? My irrational belief in Ava's toughness? Sometimes I mistrust myself so much I wonder if I invented Wally, imagined the words he said, just as I imagined the woman who watched me in the playground.

How can I go to Lunes? I already know he's never going to believe me. And neither are the hardheaded guys at the Provincetown Police Department. The only one who *might* take my story seriously is the Bug, and he's half-mad. In spite of my threats to Ava and the tough talk to my own mirror, I can't go to him. If Hallie's right, and I'm just a lost, delusional kid who misses her mom more than she's willing to admit, the Bug will never forgive me for raising his hopes. And if I'm right? If he actually finds her after all this time and grief? Well, let's just say I wouldn't want to witness the outcome.

*W*hen *the phone finally rings, I've* just about given up hope. Instead, I'm thinking about Ethan, who hasn't spoken to me for three days after one of our dumb arguments. As usual, it was my fault.

"E? I don't know why I was such a jerk, but really . . ." I begin, and then I go on some more before I realize that the person on the other end isn't saying anything.

Could be anyone, right? Wrong number. Bad connection on someone's cell phone. Telemarketer on another line. Even Ethan, too pissed to speak. But somehow I know it's not any of those things. The caller ID identifies it only as BLOCKED CALL.

"Ava?" I whisper to the ghost on the other end of the line. *"Is that you?"*

There are no words in response, but a sharp intake of breath answers my question.

"Listen, if you have something to say, *please . . .* say it."

A noise—some kind of fractured sob, maybe—interrupts me, shaking me more than I want to admit.

"Okay, that does it. I'm hanging up," I say, practically yelling into the phone.

But before I can, the strangled sound morphs into a word. A name. A fierce cry in a room that has been dark for over a decade. *Meeee-laa!*

Who ever knew those two short syllables could stretch to contain so much longing. Who ever knew that my name could snuff out years of dread, and a private wish, not to mention all the secret fears I've harbored about my own sanity.

Now it's my turn to fall silent.

"Mila? Are you still there?"she whispers.

"Who—who is this?" I say, as my voice shrinks and breaks.

"This is not how I dreamed this would happen. You don't know how many times I've wanted to speak to you. I've hungered—but always, it was too dangerous." There is little trace of the accent I remember somewhere deep inside.

Though I want to reply, I am so stunned that I can't speak a coherent word. Can't even make out the meaning of what she's saying. All I can hear is its texture: layers and layers of grief.

"I don't blame you for trying to help the priest," she says in the vacuum. "But before you do, you need to hear me out."

"Why?" I say, a surge of anger reactivating my vocal chords.

"I've always loved you, Mila. Never for one moment in all these years have I stopped loving you."

I snort into the phone, though there are tears flowing down my cheeks. "Even my father loves me better than you do," I say, bringing out the sharpest knife in my carving set.

There is a pause, and something enters her voice. Exasperation? Guilt? I'm not sure.

"I never wanted to leave you with him. Please, give me a chance to explain," she says. "I'm here on the Cape. Give me one hour; that's all I ask. I just want you to see me as I am. Your mother. Not a picture on the wall or a story you heard when you were little."

"That was your choice, not mine."

"One hour."

"The last person who trusted you ended up in prison for life."

"You're my daughter, Mila. Do you think I would do anything to hurt you?"

"Do you really want an honest answer to that question?"

"Please, Mila. I've risked everything—my freedom, my marriage, even my personal safety to see you. I'm asking for one hour in return."

"Your *marriage*?" I pick that one word from her entreaty like a shard of glass. All these years, I pictured her alone. A lonely phantom who hung around playgrounds and school buses, haunting her old life.

"I'm in Wellfleet," she says, ever the master of evasion. "Do you have transportation?"

"Answer the question."

She sighs into the phone. "Yes, Mila, I'm remarried. When I met your father, I was very young and new to this country. I made a mistake we all have paid for—you more than anyone—"

But I don't want to hear it. "So have you and *Señor* Right given me brothers and sisters?"

Again she hesitates.

"I asked you if I have any brothers and sisters."

Even before she answers, I hear the truth in her breath, her heavy sigh. "My son is nine. Maybe some time—"

"What's his name?"

"We can talk about all of that when I see you. If you don't have a car, you can call a taxi. I will pay."

"Tell me my brother's name. Or are you afraid I'll put the Cilento curse on him?"

"I named him for my grandfather in Slovakia. Alexander. Sasha, we call him."

I taste the name in my mouth. *Sasha.* It slips over my tongue like something exotic and bitter. Another child named for the family she left behind.

"If you come, I'll show you some pictures of him."

"Pictures of the child who was good enough to keep?" Immediately, I regret the whiney sound of the words. "Listen, there's a restaurant called the Purple Oyster on Main Street in Wellfleet. I'll meet you there in twenty minutes."

"That's too public. Come here and we can order in if

you're hungry. I'm staying at the Sandbar Motel on Route 6, right next to—"

"I'll be at the Purple Oyster in twenty minutes, and I'll wait ten more. If you don't come, this will be the last time we speak." Then I do it. I slam the phone down! After all these years sitting in her room, staring in her mirror, handling her things, and nurturing my own private dream that she might be alive, I have probably blown my only chance of actually seeing her. Shouldn't lightning strike right about now?

But no, I look around at the snapshots Hallie has hung on a wall in the kitchen, photos of her many friends in Provincetown, including a shot of herself with Gus on the beach, and I feel a surge of strength. By the time I climb into the old Beemer, I'm feeling relaxed. In charge. I will get there before the twenty-minute deadline, and when Ava arrives (as suddenly, I absolutely know she will) I will be sitting at a table facing the door. Will she recognize me with the blond hair that denies her plain brown genes?

CHAPTER 38

However, when I walk into the Oyster, Ava is the one who is sitting at the table opposite the door, watching for me. Her hair is shorn like mine, and the color has changed, too, as if we've been unconsciously imitating each other all along. It's the most dramatic shining platinum I have ever seen. She is wearing a jade necklace that emphasizes her eyes, and a deep plum-colored lipstick; and she is tanned from her life in California.

But no matter what color her hair was or how she was dressed, I would know her. Just as I knew her when I first saw her standing outside the fence at the playground. I don't recognize her from memory, or because she resembles the pictures I have seen. I know her because her face holds everything I have hungered for since the day my father came into my room and told me she was gone.

"Hello, Ava." I try my best to sound cold, but I can't quite pull it off. This is no delusion or hoax. *It's her.* I try to stop the tremor that is building like a volcano inside me, but when she gets up to hug me, I break.

"Mila, *Mee-la*," she says, like she did on the phone. Tears are streaming down her cheeks as she steps back to drink me in. Grudgingly, I admire the way she refuses to cover or even blot them. "You don't know how many times I've lived this moment in my mind—and now here you are. My beautiful daughter."

"Please, don't," I say, sliding into the seat opposite her. "It's way too late for that." But my voice, the tears that streak my own face, say otherwise.

At that point, the server approaches with menus in her hand, but stops several feet from the table. "You want to see these?" she says, nervously flapping them in our direction. "Or will it just be the coffee today?"

Ava asks for a refill, hardly looking up. I feel dizzy. Hoping a sugar rush will steady me, I order cranberry juice with lime.

"I told you on the phone I wanted to explain what I did," Ava says in a shaky voice. "But now I realize there's nothing I can say. No justification you can ever accept. All I can do is ask for your forgiveness, Mila. Beg for it, really. There have been days when I didn't think I could go on if I didn't get it."

She's so vulnerable, yet so luminous that I'm as mesmerized as the Bug must have been. I feel ashamed for doubting her. For that one moment, I feel rinsed with forgiveness. If I could, I would crawl into her lap like I did when I was a kid.

"Do you remember the first time you came to see me?" I whisper.

She closes her eyes. "You were nine, and someone—your father's housekeeper, perhaps—had braided your hair. That was the first thing I saw . . . that long plait hanging down your back. With everything in me, I wanted to run to you, sweep you up in my arms and never let you go."

"I was playing outside at recess, and I felt someone looking at me. It wasn't an ordinary kind of looking."

"It had been so long since I'd seen you, Mila. I didn't expect you to recognize me or even notice me. But then you came toward me."

"I thought I was dreaming you."

"Your face was so serious. No child should be as serious as you were."

"Then the recess monitor called me and I turned around. 'Do you know that woman, Mila?' she asked. And I remember thinking, *Oh my God, she's real! Other people can see her, too.* But when I turned back to look for you, you were gone. And again, I thought that there was something wrong with me, that I saw things, you know? But for years I clung to the monitor's words: *Do you know that woman, Mila?* I said them in my sleep, I prayed them over and over. I wasn't the only one who had seen you."

"I had come so far. I wanted so badly to speak to you, to touch you. But then I saw that woman questioning you."

"From that day on, I spent every recess waiting for you. I searched for your face wherever I went. But it was two years later before I saw you again. I had just gotten off the bus."

"You got out of the line of students and came running toward me. That's when I realized the kind of heart you had. It wasn't your father's heart, Mila. It was my heart." She almost upsets her coffee. "I'm so sorry I ran from you. But if I had stopped, I knew I would never be able to leave you again."

"You didn't come back again until I was almost fourteen."

"Do you know how dangerous that was for me? You were old enough to tell your father. And be believed. Not that I feared going to prison. I would have welcomed the opportunity to exchange my life for the priest's."

"Then why . . . *didn't* you?" I ask. "How could you let Gus—"

"By then there were other people to consider," she says, blanching at the mention of Gus's name. "Oh, Mila, you have to understand. When I got away, I promised myself I would never chance it again. But to never hear of you or contact you in any way? I couldn't bear that. On your birthday, I sent you that card, and then I started haunting the post office like a ghost, waiting for you to write to me."

"And when I did, you decided to come back and tell the truth so Gus can finally come home." I am so close to her, I almost slip and call her the M-word.

I feel so sure I hardly notice the long pause that follows. When I do, I rush to fill it.

"Gus has been in prison for ten years," I say. "You have to . . . I mean, you're *going to* go to the police, right?"

She lowers her head and stares into the blackness of her coffee as if the answer is there; and when she looks up, the very atoms of the room have shifted.

"Please, my darling," she pleads. "You are almost an adult now. A woman. Surely, you know that some things can't be so easily undone."

"*Easily?* Really? You dare to use that word with me? I mean, just how easy do you think Gus's life has been this last decade?"

"I know he's suffered, but why would the priest contact *you?* Did he have to turn my own daughter against me? Was that his revenge?"

"*The priest?* He has a name, you know."

"Mila, darling, you have to understand . . . I never thought he would go to prison."

"Say his name," I press. "Say the name of the man who's been sitting in jail, whether you intended it or not."

She is silent for so long that the waitress approaches with the check. Neither of us look up.

"He used to tell me to call him Gus," she finally says. "But I never did. I preferred Father. Not because I was a believer, but because I desperately needed him to be someone I could rely on. Someone I could trust. I no longer had any kind of father, Mila. For so long, there had been no one at all."

"And in return, you set him up—"

"Have you listened to anything I've said?" she says, her green eyes flashing. "I may have been weak and alone, but I'm not the monster he made you think I am. Your father was the only one I meant to deceive. I never thought it would go so far. But that doesn't give him the right to poison your mind against me."

"He has the right to do anything he needs to do to secure his freedom. In this case, though, I was the one who went to him."

"But why?"

I shrug. "Maybe I needed someone I could trust, too. Though I didn't know it at the time."

"But you haven't told him—not either of them?" Ava stares at me anxiously. "I don't believe you would—"

"I told Hallie. Unfortunately, she thought I was just a lonely child who had visions of her dead mother. That's when I realized I had to produce you if I wanted to convince anyone. Of course, I hoped that once you were here, you would do the right thing yourself."

"But you knew where I was. You could have sent—"

"Sent them where? I'm sure you never lived in Weatherwood. You wouldn't risk exposure."

"Until today," she says, but I can tell she still doesn't believe I would turn against her.

"Well, it just so happens I have a new family, too. And my loyalty is to them—not to you."

Her eyes are wet green stones in a river. They frighten me with the love they contain. But now that it is here before me, my heart is ice. After all the years of longing, I don't want to drink from this river after all.

"I could lose my son, Mila. It's true—everything you think of me—I abandoned you, and let you be raised by a cruel man. A sick man. And yes, a man ended up in prison because of my mistake. But never, not for one hour, or one heartbeat, have I been free of what I've done. Do you want to know how desperate I was?" She picks up a knife from an adjacent table, and puts it to her wrist, teasing the skin with the serrated blade. It leaves a visible scratch.

I seize her trembling hand. "Mommy—" And suddenly, the tough chica is gone and I am a little girl, running from the bus, my long braid flying behind me as I chased a mother I could never catch. *Mommy!*

I put my head in my hands, remembering the sound of her body hitting the floor, the darkness in my head the night the same thing happened to me.

"I had no choice," she repeats. "Do you see that now? If there had been another way, any other way—"

"But who hurt you in that motel room? The only finger-prints they found were yours and Gus's? They said you lost so much blood. How did you survive?"

"I told you I will answer all your questions," Ava says, looking around anxiously. "But not here in this restaurant. Not now."

"At least, tell me how you got away. You were badly hurt. You must have had help." But even before she answers, I know. She didn't meet her husband after she left. Her new life, the one that excluded me, began before she ever left the castle, long before she kissed me goodbye for the final time.

"My father was right. You *did* have a boyfriend."

She lowers her head, reaching for the long curtain of hair that used to hide her face, but there is nothing to shield her.

"I was already pregnant, Mila. Now do you understand why I had to go? My husband arranged everything. He'd already gotten me a new identity, a driver's license, everything I needed to become Cassandra Grayson."

"And then you found Gus. You knew how easy it would be for people to believe that it was just history repeating himself. He was just like his father."

"I knew *nothing* about that," she insists so forcefully that a couple across the room turns to stare. "The night I went to him I was telling the truth. What I wanted—the only thing I wanted—was someone to look out for you after I was gone. If you believe nothing else, you have to know that is true."

Strangely, in spite of everything, I do believe her. "So when did you find out? Before you accused him of assault? Or after."

She looks down defeatedly. "I didn't know when I told the police that terrible lie; I had no idea, but after the arrest, people began to talk about his past . . . I felt so terrible, but what could I do at that point? We had to go forward. Robert's suspicions—and his rage—they were growing every day. He hurt me so badly that last time, Mila . . . It was a miracle my baby survived, or that I did. If I had any hope of getting away, your father had to believe I was dead."

"Were you *in love*?" I ask, though it comes out more like an accusation than a question.

"It was the last thing I expected, the last thing I wanted, really, but when I met my husband, everything changed for me. For both of us. We were two people who shared so much. The same passions. The same disappointments. He had given up on the idea of ever being happy, too. I know it's hard for you to understand, Mila, but everyone has a right to love. Some people would even call it a duty."

"What about your duty to *me*?" I blurt out.

"I had a choice to make, a decision I wouldn't wish on anyone," she says, defiantly pushing her cell phone closer to me. "Now it's your turn, Mila. Call your Hallie. The police. Whatever will help to ease your bitterness."

The move throws me off balance. "What will they do to you?" I say, my voice embarrassingly small.

"Whatever it is, it's less than I deserve. We both know that."

I stare at the phone and freeze. Then I shove it in her direction, upsetting my cranberry juice as I get up and run. It seeps into the wood floor, just like I imagine my mother's blood spreading across the motel room all those years ago.

CHAPTER 39

*D*riving *toward Ptown, I've never felt* more lost. How can I even think about going back to Hallie's house after what I just did? *I let her go.* I could have reached for the cell phone and made the call that would free Gus, and I didn't. Instead, I gave Dead Mom a chance to go back to the Sandbar, pack up as quickly as she came, and get away.

When I reach the stretch they used to call Helltown Road, I'm not crying; I'm wailing. Not the kind of wordless howl my father set loose when he first heard she was dead, the fearsome keening I still hear in my dreams. No, my wail takes the form of a word. One word echoing in the confines of the car where for years I swore I could still smell her perfume: Mommy! *Mawwwmeeee!*

But the Mommy I've been holding on to is deader than everyone who knew her as Ava Cilento thought she was. Though I was just a little kid, I knew how much she'd been hurt; I experienced her fear right down to my spindly little skeleton. But somehow I always believed her love was stronger than anything the Bug could do to her. The way a mother's love is supposed to be. Knowing that hers just wasn't is like losing her all over again.

When all I've got left are those little hiccuppy whimpers, I park the car and walk to the beach. The beach that Gus loved more than any place else on earth. The beach he's unlikely to ever see again. And though I know it won't help, I whisper, *I'm sorry.* At first, I'm talking to Gus. Then, before I know it, I'm breathing apologies to everything in sight. I'm sorry to the dunes and to the gulls; I'm sorry to the dark-blue waters, to the wind, and to the shiny stones beneath my feet.

I even say I'm sorry to the broken green beer bottle that the waves will pound into sea glass. Looking at the shards, I realize why I'm apologizing to the whole world: because they will be transformed into something beautiful, but right now it looks as if nothing can ever change or forgive the crime my mother committed against Gus. The crime that became my own when I couldn't pick up the phone.

How long did I spend at the beach? Honestly, it was one of those pieces of time that is impossible to measure. It might have been an hour, but it felt like my whole life fit neatly inside it.

Even before I get to the Sandbar, I know it's too late. There are two cars in the parking lot. One SUV outside the office that I assume belongs to the manager, and another car with North Carolina plates. But what hits me is not the emptiness of the parking lot, which is pretty predictable at this time of year, but the utter desolation of the place. It reminds me of the squat, forlorn building with the grinning dolphin out front. The place where the former Ava Cilento staged her death. I wonder she would choose to stay in such a dump.

"I'm looking for a woman by the name of Cassandra Grayson," I say when I approach the desk.

There's a TV and an Xbox behind it, and the so-called clerk is seriously lost in some mindless mayhem.

"Grayson?" he says, not even looking up. "I don't think so."

"Yeah, I don't think so either," I say, more to myself than to him. Did I really think she would register under her own name? For that matter, do I believe she's told me her true name even now? "But I need you to check."

This time, he pauses the game and looks me up and down, taking my whole ruined life in with one quick glance: the mascara streaking my face, my punk haircut restyled by the wind, the crazy grief that's got to be etched all over me. "Are you okay?" he says.

"Listen, this is a police matter. I need you to check your computer and see if you have a Ms. Grayson registered here."

"You expect me to believe you're some kind of cop?" He gives up a stifled guffaw. For the first time, he seems to have forgotten his game.

"Did I say I was a cop? What I said was that this was a police matter. And a serious one. So if you wouldn't mind checking your computer—"

Once again, the guy seriously annoys me by breaking into a laugh. "Listen, hon, this is a family-run operation. We don't even have a computer. I've got an old-fashioned log book; and I can tell you right now, there's no one by the name of Grayson staying here."

"Anyone from California?" I ask, though I can tell he already hears the hopelessness in my voice. If Ava, or Cassandra, or whoever she is now, had been here, I'm sure she was driving a rented car with no out-of-state plates to call attention to her.

"Nope." At that point, the guy is clearly losing interest and eager to get back to his game. "You want a little advice? If this is really a police matter, maybe you should let them handle it."

"Thanks. Now you want to get that log book of yours out? I need to see it."

He reddens, and I'm starting to think that maybe I've aggravated him even more than he did me. "Listen, there's such a thing as privacy laws and—" he begins. But then he notices how desperate I am.

So I play it. "She's my mom," I say, tears springing into my eyes on cue. "She and my dad had this huge fight a couple of days ago, and I think she's been staying here. I'm really worried about her."

It would have been easy just to describe her. A stunning woman with a platinum cap of hair and an indescribable air of fragile elegance would be instantly remembered, but I need to see that book. Need to see the name she used, and what she gave as an address. Or maybe I just need to see her signature, the familiar handwriting that is both delicate and aggressive.

As soon as I open the book, it jumps out at me. But what really sends me reeling is not this visible proof that she was here, not even the evidence that she checked out two hours earlier— just as I'd known she would. She may have pushed the phone at me and urged me to call the police in a dramatic moment, but once she had time to think, self-preservation would rule just like it always has. What gets to me is the name she registered under: *Mila Cilento*. Against my will, the shaking starts again.

"I'm not surprised she was hiding from someone," the clerk says, apparently knowing who I was looking for all along. "We usually like to get a credit card number in case the room is trashed, but she had nothing but cash. And when I asked for a license, she said she'd left it in her other purse and would bring it in later, but—"

"She never did." I finish his sentence. "So why'd you let her stay here?"

"Hey, business has been off. We need to fill rooms, and besides, there was something—I don't know—*lost*—about her. I felt bad for the lady."

"Do you have any idea how dangerous it can be to pity someone like that?" Then while the clerk stands there, looking mystified, I turn around and walk out. From the car, I watch him through the window. He shakes his head, as if to expel both my mother and me from his mind, and returns to his video game.

My *predicament hasn't changed. In fact,* it's gotten worse. Dead Mom has escaped—this time probably for good; and the only home I have is with a friend I've just betrayed in the worst possible way.

I start down Route 6, and when I pull off the highway, I head to the little cottage by the beach as if I had known where I was going all along. And maybe I did. Maybe I've known ever since that day in the prison when I told Gus I'd come to learn about God. I didn't mean it. At least I didn't *think* I did, but his answer stayed with me just the same.

"If you're serious, there's this old priest named Jack Rooney. Wisest man I've ever known."

Gus's wise man is hardly a stranger. Jack has been a fixture in my life ever since I moved in with Hallie. He's had two knee replacements, but he still visits the prison regularly with Hallie. And whenever Julia's home, you can count on him showing up for dinner, a six-pack of beer and a crappy store-bought cake in his arms, beaming like a proud dad.

The shades are up, and I can see the old man inside, the TV screen flashing behind him.

And, yeah, I'm hesitating. Hesitating and wondering what the hell I'm doing here. For one thing, Gus's sainted wise man doesn't seem to like me much. Oh, he's been kind and everything—but what choice does he have? It's his *job* to be kind. But every now and then I look at him, and I know he doesn't quite trust me. His eyes say he hopes I don't hurt Hallie the way she hurt Gus. His eyes say, *I'm watching you.*

As I watch him limping around his kitchen, I know life is probably tough enough for him as it is. He deserves a little peace, and I'm honestly sorry I can't give him that.

When he answers the door, he doesn't look much like the respectable old grandpa type who shows up for dinner at our house. He's wearing a stained Red Sox T-shirt and his hair looks like it hasn't been combed in three days, like one of those old men the world has forgotten. But the moment he speaks, the pitiful old man disappears and someone else— Gus's wise man, maybe—takes his place.

"Mila! Come in, dear," he says, more welcoming than I deserve, as he pulls the door open.

There's nothing bleaker than the dinner he's prepared. A frozen Salisbury steak in a little tin plate that smells like the worst cafeteria food, and a bottle of lite beer. In the background, two sports announcers are ranting about something so heatedly that you'd think the fate of the world hinged on it.

"Got one of those for me?" I point at the beer—just to break the ice.

"Why, sure." Then he opens the fridge and pulls out a can of Coke, which he plunks down in front of me like a big exclamation point. "That's the only brand of beer you're going to get around here, young lady." He lowers the volume of the TV, but doesn't turn it off.

I was hoping he'd make this easy for me, maybe ask what I've come for, serve up a little small talk, but he doesn't. He just waits.

"Are you still licensed to hear confessions?" I say at last.

First he laughs out loud. Then he stands up and pulls his wallet out of his pocket, his eyes as mischievous as a little boy's, and makes a big show of rifling through his tattered cards. "Yep, seems like my papers are still in order."

But when he sits back down, he is serious again. He even closes his eyes and starts some kind of blessing over me. And when I try to tell him as politely as I can that I don't particularly believe in that kind of—um, *hocus pocus*, he continues anyway.

Then, abruptly, he opens his eyes and the smiling old man who tells corny jokes at Hallie's dinner table returns. "So what's on your mind?" he asks, rubbing his white stubble.

"Gus sent me," I explain when he continues to stare in a somewhat disconcerting way. "He said if I ever needed to talk, you wouldn't turn me away."

At the mention of Gus's name, he gives me the same baleful smile Hallie wears when she talks about him.

"Actually, I was about to turn you out, but since Gus sent you, I'll reconsider . . ."

It's a joke, but all of a sudden, I start to cry—for about the third time that day. A personal record.

Jack passes me a clean white handkerchief that looks like it's been ironed, which I immediately drench with messy tears. Meanwhile, he pats me on the shoulder in a rhythmic way, saying something like "There, there, dear." Normally, I would find the antiquated phrase laughable, or even infuriating, but now the words feel oddly comforting.

I finally look up and sniffle. "Father Jack, you just may be looking at the worst person on earth."

He takes the handkerchief from my hand, and wipes the last tears from my face with amazing gentleness. "That's quite an accomplishment. You want to tell me what you've done to earn such an impressive title?"

And so I do. Beginning with the first time I saw Dead Mom near the schoolyard, and ending with our final encounter in the Oyster, I omit *nada*. I even pull my own cell phone from my pocketbook to reenact the moment when I let her get away. The moment when I didn't have the strength to make the call that could have saved Gus.

At first the priest's face is neutral, and I'm not sure if he believes me. But then, as I pile detail upon detail, I see a fire building in his eyes. It's an angry fire, but it's also a triumphant one.

"So what should we do? Go to the police?" I whisper. "Or maybe we should call Gus's friend Neil. Hallie says he knows a really good PI."

"We'll do both of those things, but by now, your mother's probably on a plane to California, so it's not urgent. First, I need to give you your penance."

"Penance? Like I said, I don't exactly believe in that."

"Yes, but you see, *I* do," he replies. "And you're in my house now."

So, okay I'm listening. And suddenly, his messy three-room cottage, with the nauseating TV dinner on the table, feels like the house of worship I was always hoping to find.

"First, I'd like you to say three Hail Marys. Good ones. If you don't know it, I can give you a prayer book."

"I know it," I say, surprised that I still remember the words the Bug taught me. When I finish, I get up to make the call I should have made a few hours ago.

However, when I reach for the phone, Jack stops me. "Not yet. We go to the police tomorrow, but there's one thing you have to do first."

I'm mystified, but then slowly I begin to understand. "Father Jack, I can't—"

"You *can*," he interrupts firmly. "And what's more, if you don't, you'll never be forgiven."

Now this seriously pisses me off. "I thought you preached a merciful God. My father was right. You're all—"

But Jack is having none of it. "I'm not talking about God, Mila. I'm talking about *you*. If you don't go to that prison and tell Gus exactly what you know and how long you've known it, you'll never forgive *yourself*."

CHAPTER 41

Later, after Jack has called Millette and persuaded the chaplain to arrange for an emergency visit tomorrow, he offers to make up the couch for me, to cook me one of his frozen dinners, even to ride up to the prison with me tomorrow. He also wants to know if I want to talk about *her.* My mom.

Not able to lie to his face, I hug him when I say I have plans. Apparently, I can't keep my soul clean for even an hour.

Jack doesn't question me, though. Like Gus said, this is a man of *faith.* The religious thing is only part of it. He follows me to the door. "Drive careful, now."

"Don't worry, I'll keep it under ninety." Then I back out of the driveway and head to the place I've been avoiding all my life, the Pink Dolphin. I park right in front and stare down the door marked 2B. Here my mother carried out the lie that would send Gus to prison and leave me alone with a very toxic Bug. Up close, it's not the nightmarish portal I imagined for so long. It's just a door.

Still focusing on 2B, I take out my phone and call E. Then, for the second time, I tell him the ugly truth about who I am and the secrets I've kept for so long.

"Where are you now?" he asks. "Because wherever it is, you have to leave."

"*Why?*" I whisper, afraid that he's about to tell me that there's no room on the planet for people like me.

"Because you need to get over here, that's why. And tomorrow? I'm going with you."

"You don't have to do that," I mutter, as tears blur my view of the ugly motel.

"Actually, I *do*. Not because I'm a nice guy, or the world is counting on me to save it or anything like that. We're talking pure selfishness here, Mila. I need to be there with you." He sounds as surprised by the revelation as I am; and when I'm too dumbfounded to reply, he continues. "Besides, you can't drive. Not this time."

Though E is probably the worst driver in the state of Massachusetts, it feels like the best offer I've ever had. "Would you? Would you really drive me?"

"Are you on your way over yet?" he says in reply. " 'Cause I'm already out on my front steps in a T-shirt and bare feet, watching for you, and I'm freezing my ass off."

After I call Hallie and leave a vague message about staying with a friend so she won't worry, I turn my phone off. *Incommunicado* until I talk to Gus.

The next morning I get up early and dress in the long skirt and the warrior jewelry that I put in my backpack before I went to see Jack.

"Does this mean you're Frida again?" E asks as I get in his mother's old Escort. Fortunately, Lori sleeps in, because E hasn't exactly asked if he could use the car. It's obvious that we're both kind of nervous—him, because he's only driven about twice, and me because even my Frida disguise can't protect me from what I'm about to do.

"I just don't want those guys at the prison harassing me," I say, trying to sound nonchalant. "I figured if I went in there covered head to toe like the last American virgin, they might leave me alone."

"Yeah, well, it's not working," E says, tightening the ribbon on my Mexican shirt. "You're still way too sexy."

Once we cross the bridge, I watch Ethan obliquely from under my mascaraed lashes while he concentrates on the road. He actually looks really good these days. He's kind of filled out and must be using a new acne medication because there's not a single live pimple on his face. Fortunately, most of the ride is on the highway, and after surging onto it with little regard for the yield sign, Ethan hugs the right line, clutching the wheel like he's piloting a plane.

I stare out the window, trying not to think about how badly E is driving, or what I'm about to do. I was so certain after I left Jack's cottage, but now I'm arguing with the old priest in my head. *What's the point of this penance stuff? Isn't there enough suffering in life without manufacturing it?* And . . . *Wouldn't it be better to wait till we've found Dead Mom to tell Gus?* And . . . *What if I can't do it? What if I explode inside before I get the words out?*

Ethan drops me off outside the gate. I wave breezily, but as soon as the car turns the corner, I feel like I'm about five years old and lost in a train station. I actually consider chasing after the car, and telling E that I've changed my mind. But then I remember Father Jack's creased face telling me that I would do this, that I *had to*, and, what's more, I *could*. I force my feet to move toward the door.

By the time I reach the building, I'm deep in the middle of a fantasy. I imagine Gus is in there wearing his priest outfit—not the plain pants and shirt priests wear now, but the long black dress thing they wear in old movies where the priests are known to burst into song at odd moments. And when I tell him what I did, he asks me to kneel. Then he prays over me and takes it all away. All the cowardice and confusion and selfishness that I call my life.

The worst thing about visiting a prison is the constant reminder that its sole function is to grind time into fine sand. Here time clouds the windows and clogs your lungs. You take a deep breath before you enter and when you leave, knowing that inside these walls, you can choke on time, be poisoned by it, even die of it. When I'm finally ushered into the visitor's room, I wonder if my hair hasn't gone white like Ava's while I waited.

Gus takes his seat and picks up the phone. "Mila, what's going on? The chaplain came in this morning and said you needed to see me right away. Is Hallie—"

"Hallie's fine. She doesn't even know I'm here."

Gus's relief is so palpable that I can't help myself. I tell him what I've been thinking ever since the first time I saw them together. "I've never seen two people more in love than you and Hallie—even after all these years. Do you think that someday, I mean, if you could—"

This time it's Gus's turn to interrupt me. "I love Hallie more than I've ever loved anyone. But being in love? That's for people like you, Mila. Not people like me."

"I shouldn't have asked. That was way too personal. And, like I said, this isn't about Hallie. Maybe you could start. After all, you're the adult."

Gus laughs. "I'd be happy to, but unfortunately I don't know the topic we're here to discuss."

I hesitate long enough for us both to feel the noise of the prison filling in the space around us. The sound of time being obliterated. "It's secrets. That's our topic."

Gus folds his hands in front of him. "Sorry, Mila, but I'm an inmate. Watched day and night. No secrets allowed."

"Tell me about your tattoo."

He glances at his forearm, as if he's forgotten it was there, though something tells me that he never forgets it, not for a minute. Then he shrugs. "It's a heart. Universal symbol of love and affection. I'm sure you've seen one before."

"It doesn't look like it was done at a tattoo parlor," I say, knowing I've touched a nerve. "Well, it was. Millette State Prison. Most thriving tattoo parlor around." He turns his head, searching for the guard. "Listen, Mila, it was great to see you, but I think this visit's over."

"No, wait. It's important."

"It was important for you to ask me where I got my tattoo?"

"Not where—*how*?"

Gus sits back in his chair, and there is nowhere to hide. "That comes under the category of things you really don't want to know."

"You're right, I don't want to know, Gus, but I *need* to." I don't know why, but it suddenly feels like the truest thing I've ever said. *I need to know.*

"Well, for me it comes under the category of things I want to forget."

The guard appears before I can answer, and Gus rises from his seat, obviously eager to escape my question.

I mouth the words *Pick up your phone. Please. Just for one minute.*

He's still standing, but he complies.

"Remember when you showed me that picture of myself when I was a little girl?" I ask. "You said you knew that little girl. You knew her better than she knew herself."

Gus doesn't respond, but the softening I see in his eyes

is a kind of answer. We both know that the little girl in the picture is not just me; it's him, too.

"You know what that little girl's first memory was? It was hearing my mother being punched so hard her body hit the floor, and knowing she didn't even cry out because she was trying to protect me. But I knew, just like you did, Gus. I always knew. I sat in my bed in the dark on the hottest night of the year, shivering against that sound."

"Is that what you came here to talk about, Mila? What happened to your mother?"

I shake my head like a horse. "My point is that I have a category of things I'd like to forget, too. But when all the other memories of my first six years got painted over, those things still came through. I can handle it, Gus."

Gus studies me for a minute, then says something to the guard that I can't hear. Whatever it is, it pisses off the man in uniform. He's still shaking his head as he walks away. Gus returns to the orange plastic chair, which he turns around, and straddles. Then he extends the forearm he has done his best to hide on every previous visit, and allows me to see the crudely fashioned black heart. In its center is the letter X. "What do you want to know?"

And all of a sudden I feel like that small child shivering in my room, listening to something I'm far from ready to hear. "What's the X inside the heart stand for?" I ask, my voice a hard shield around that little girl.

Gus looks down at the tattoo himself, almost like he forgets. But then I realize he's remembering; and it's a *hard* remembering. He's remembering not only with his mind, but with his gut, his nerves, with the blood that flows from his heart to his arm and back again.

"The X is for Xavier. It's what we call a brand."

"A *brand*?" I whisper. "You mean, like they put on cattle?"

"Exactly. It's a sign of one man becoming the possession of another." For the first time since I've known him, his eyes avoid mine.

"You mean this Xavier—"

He nods, and when he looks into my eyes again, he shows me a part of himself that I don't believe anyone else has seen—not even Hallie. "When I came in here, I was a prime target until I got enough muscle—physically and in a lot of other ways—to say no to Xavier in a way he understood."

I don't know how I must look right then, but it's obviously pretty bad. "Mila?" Gus says. "I didn't want to tell you. Are you okay?"

What I really want to do is to get up and run out of the prison as fast as I can, to leave Gus Silva and his awful reality in the dust. Forever. But I remember how I felt after I told Ethan what my father did to me. Then I think of how Ethan followed me and told me I was beautiful, and how he made me believe it. Made me *know* it. The least I can do for the universe is to return the favor.

"Of course I'm okay," I say, willing my eyes to meet his. Willing myself to act like I hear stuff like this every day. I pop a piece of gum in my mouth and shrug. "I figured it was something like that."

Then I reach into my purse and pull out the most tattered, cried-upon, folded, thrown-away, and pulled-out-of-the-trash birthday card in existence.

Gus studies it for a long moment. "Was this the last card your mother sent you?"

"You could say that. I got it on my sixteenth birthday, Gus."

"But that's not possible."

Then before he can point out that the card's not even signed, I tell him the truth. "I saw her Gus. I talked to her."

"Mila, your—"

I raise my voice above his and continue. "Yesterday in Wellfleet. She called me and—"

"Your mother's dead, Mila. I was the first one at the crime scene, remember?"

"Let me finish, because if I don't get this out now, I might never have the courage to say it again. Ava's alive. She faked her death so she could get away from the Bug; then she let you take the blame. She's gone on with her life all these years while you sat in jail. That's who she is. And I'm her daughter."

By then my eyes are so full of watery grief and guilt and misery that I can't see Gus at all. Since he isn't saying anything, I don't know what he thinks—or even if he believes me. He can't touch me, but he reaches out and puts his palm against the glass the way he did when he saw Hallie for the first time.

"It's not your fault, Mila. Whatever she did, whatever your father did, none of it was your fault. And I wasn't to blame for what happened to my mother, either. We were kids. Little kids who should have been dreaming of furry blue monsters, not dealing with real ones." And somehow, in forgiving me, I think Gus finally forgives himself.

I wipe my eyes with the back of my free hand. Gus still looks doubtful, so I plow on. "I tried to tell Hallie, but she didn't believe me. Not that I blame her. I wasn't completely convinced myself—until I saw her in person. She was as close to me as you are now, Gus. She told me she always called you Father even though she wasn't a believer."

It's the smallest little detail, but it hits him. "I asked her to call me Gus, but she never would," he recalls. "She insisted on *Father*. Father Gus. How could you know that, Mila? How could you possibly know that?"

"She told me, Gus. She sat at a table, drinking coffee at the Purple Oyster, alive as you and me, and she told me."

For the longest moment in history Gus just stares at me. Then he runs his hands through his hair, which has gotten kind of long since I saw him last. "Holy shit," he mutters. Then he stands up and yells it out loud. He doesn't care that the guards are obviously on alert. "*Holy shit!* What are you telling me here, Mila?"

"The truth. The horrible, disgusting, amazing, *holy shit* truth."

He walks a small circle as the two men in uniform walk toward him. "Time's up, Silva," one guard says, roughly seizing his elbow. "This visit's over."

Gus and I just stare at each other because goodbye is way too inadequate. I make no effort to move as Gus walks away. Just before he disappears, he frees himself from the guard's hold and turns around. I read his lips: *What does this mean, Mila?*

"Not as much as it should. Not yet, anyway," I say, though he can't hear me. Then, finally knowing what I have to do, I get up and run out of the suffocating room, tripping on my long skirt like a clumsy colt. I keep running until one of the guards feels sorry for me and walks me out.

"Sometimes I wonder why kids like you come here," he

says. "You probably love your dad and all, but people like that—well, put it this way, he's here for a reason."

That stops me, and I turn around. I don't even bother explaining that he's not my dad. "Actually, he's *not* here for a reason. He went through all of this for no reason at all."

The guard chuckles. "Just like everyone else here. Not a guilty man in the whole place, to hear them tell it—"

But before he can complete his spiel, I reach the door where I reclaim the change and jewelry I shed so I could pass through the metal detector. With any luck, it's a ritual I will never have to repeat.

I expect to wait a while for Ethan to show up, but he's already there, parked across the street from the spot where he let me off. Hunkered down over a book, he really does look like a car thief. When I get closer I can see that he's eating a Boston creme doughnut.

I fling the door open. "Let's get out of here." It sounds like I'm talking to some kind of getaway driver or something. Then I land in the car, my skirt flouncing, my shawl on crooked, mascara smeared on my cheeks. I drop the jewelry and change I'm clutching on the floor. All Ethan does is look at me, book in one hand, doughnut in the other, glasses stuck on the ridge of his nose.

"What are you waiting for?" I snap. "Drive!"

Have I mentioned that one thing I really love about Ethan Washburne is that he never says or does the obvious thing. For instance, he doesn't ask, "What's the matter?" or "What the hell happened in there?" or any of the other questions that nearly any other human being would raise in this situation. Instead, he passes me the squishy doughnut, then points at a line in the book before handing that over, too.

"I was right there," he says. "The writer had just brought up a really salient point. You'll have to read the rest of the chapter out loud. Where we headed, anyway—home?"

"The police station in Ptown. Right away!"

So, sitting there in Ethan's careening car, a vision of a crudely cut black heart with the letter X in the center before my eyes, I read at least seven pages without ever knowing what the book was about. When I came to the end of the chapter, Ethan pulls over in a rest area and gently takes the book from my hand, tosses the doughnut in the backseat with the rest of the detritus from Lori Washburne's life, and cleans up the crumbs it left behind. Then he takes off his glasses and allows me to look straight into his naked eyes. They are the color of the ocean at dusk.

"Two things," he says. "Since this is starting to feel something like a chase scene in a movie, and I'm not sure what or who we're trying to outrun, maybe you should drive."

I change seats with him, and am just about to pull out when I stop. "You said you wanted to tell me two things; that was only one."

"It wasn't important," Ethan responds. It's not till we're on the highway that he speaks again, obviously making his best effort to sound casual. "I was just going to tell you I love you, that's all."

So there I am, flying down the highway toward the most dramatic moment in my life, when I will turn Ava in to the police—the lying, treacherous, negligent woman who is still my mother—and *dammit*, Ethan picks this time to say he loves me?

All I can think of is the words Gus said in the prison: *Holy shit!*

CHAPTER 42

While I was in the prison with Gus, Jack said he would meet Hallie. I picture them sitting in a formica booth in Quissett Pizza and Mexican, drinking a beer. I see Hallie turning pale as she hears the truth about how I kept my suspicions to myself while Gus sat in prison. I'm sure she argues with Jack at first, refusing to believe that the girl she treated like a daughter is the ultimate traitor. The enemy who weaseled her way in for breakfast and never left. I cringe when I think of him relaying the part no one can deny: my meeting with Ava at the Purple Oyster. I cry out like I stepped on something sharp when I ponder the moment when he tells her how I let Ava go. And with her, Gus's chance for a new trial.

The priest has promised to do his best to help Hallie understand. But even Jack, with his halo of white hair, his pure blue eyes and his book of spells, can't perform miracles.

They're already at the police station when Ethan and I get there. But in spite of everything, I finally feel like the absolutely fearless girl I once pretended to be. I hold Ethan's hand and stand really straight like Gus always does as I walk into the station on Shankpainter Road and tell the whole crazy, mangled truth as straightforwardly as I possibly can. When I'm finished I feel like the last girl standing in the national spelling bee.

I don't break until Jack steps forward to hug me. That's when I notice that while I was nailing the spelling bee, Hallie has slipped out the door.

"Give her a little time," Jack says, following my eyes.

"When she gets over the shock, she's going to be so proud of what you did today."

After leaving the station, I hike out to the spot where old Dr. Nick's shack used to stand. It's just past five and the coffee I picked up at the bakery is cold by the time I reach the place. I had hoped to find Hallie in her usual spot, but there's no sign of her.

I sit at the ghost shack, drinking my cold coffee, long enough to see the moon rise. Just when I'm about to give up, I see her lonely determined figure heading down the beach.

"Hallie! Over here!" I call. In the diminishing light, her face looks older, prouder, marked by a life I don't totally understand, and never will.

"Mila. What are you doing here?" After she lets Stella loose to run, she sits down beside me and lights a cigarette. These days, this is the only place she allows herself to smoke.

"Looking for you. What else? I need to talk to you about what happened with my mother. What I did."

"You mean what you *didn't* do." Hallie looks out at the ocean and exhales.

"Listen, Hallie, I know I should have called the police at the Oyster, but I was in shock—"

She puts up her hand, like she doesn't want to hear it—or just can't bear to hear it. Then, abruptly, she gets up, calls the dog, and starts down the beach, hugging her parka around her as if it's the only thing that's holding her bones together. "There's nothing to talk about, Mila," she says when I follow her. "Not till we find her. *If* we find her."

Then she makes a sharp turnaround. "Damn it, Mila. I took you into my *home*. I treated you like a daughter. How could you let her go?"

I'm about to cry, but then I think of what happened this morning in the prison. I think of Gus. For the rest of my life, the truths we both faced down today will be with me, my totem, my secret strength.

"I know she's done horrible things, unforgivable things, Hallie, but she's still *my mother*! Don't you understand? I still remember her holding me, singing to me. To this day. Ever since I was a little girl, I've been clinging to her memory. I thought that the worst thing that could happen would be to forget. Then I'd be totally alone."

I'm glad I'm on the beach because I'm practically shrieking these words into the wind. "But it wasn't easy turning on my mother. I'm sorry if you think it should have been, but it wasn't."

She studies me as if she's trying to figure out who I am and why the hell she ever took me in. Without a word, she starts heading toward the road again. At first, she's marching, moving fast, her arms swinging back and forth, anger shooting from her fingertips with every step. Then she breaks into a run. Poor old Stella is trotting behind to keep up.

I'm not sure if she's running toward the car—or just away from me.

The hour I spend on the beach after Hallie leaves me has to be the most miserable sixty minutes of my life, and what's worse, the wind is merciless. Sure, I've been through some bad shit before, but this time the bogeyman isn't the Bug, or Ava, or anyone else. It's *me*. I cry when I think about the Victorian with the purple door and the broad front porch. The house I foolishly began to call home.

Maybe I can sleep all night on the beach. Then, in the morning, in the face of a bright sunrise, I will think of what to do. I find shelter behind a dune, drink the last of my coffee and make a pillow of my two hands. I am curled up like that when I open my eyes and see Hallie standing over me, her hands resting on her hips.

"What do you think you're doing?" She squints at her watch through the darkness. "I've been waiting in the car for an hour."

"You were *waiting*? But I thought—I thought you *hated* me. I thought you never wanted to see me again."

Hallie sighs, then reaches down and pulls me up. "Just because I got mad at you doesn't mean I'd let you ride that bike home in the dark. Or stop caring about you. It doesn't even mean I don't understand *why* you did it. God, Mila, you really have no idea what it means to be family, do you?"

My face streaked with tears, I shake my head. "Are we really—" I say, and then add the last word, the sacred word, in a teeny tiny voice, "family?"

She gives me a huge hug, what she calls an *abraço*.

"One thing I want to make clear," Hallie begins, before stopping abruptly and taking my shoulders. "None of this was your fault. You were as much a victim as Gus was. And what you did—walking into that prison and telling Gus the truth, then reporting your mother to the police—that was incredibly brave. In fact, I think you're the second-bravest girl I've ever met—even if I did get mad. *Especially* because I did."

It is the closest thing to absolution in a dark confessional that I'm likely to get, and I have to fight back tears. "The *second*-bravest?"

"Next to me when I was your age," Hallie says.

"Oh yeah? What was so brave about you?"

Hallie looks out at the ocean that glints under a brazen

stripe of moonlight. "I used to test my strength by swimming out a little bit farther than I thought I could every day. I liked the feeling I got when my body was telling me I couldn't go any farther and I had to make it back on sheer willpower."

"That sounds more *stupid* than brave to me."

"It was. I used to call it refusing to fear death, but it was really more like communing with my inner idiot."

"That doesn't count."

"Okay, how about this one?" she says, still looking out over the water. "I was brave enough to love a boy who was damaged almost beyond repair from the age of nine. To love him so irrationally and completely that I've never been cured of it. And I probably never will be."

She starts to walk again and I follow slightly behind her, keenly aware that I don't know Hallie Costa nearly as well as I thought I did. And painfully certain that she is crying.

CHAPTER 43

The Dismal Kingdom, with its spectacular view of the beach, never looked more desolate than it does the next day when I pay an impulse visit to the Bug. It is nearly nine a.m., but there is no response to my knock at the door or to Stella's jittery bark. The dog looks up at me, her head cocked to the side, wondering where we are and why. Fortunately, I still have my key to the Castle on my ring.

I figure my father is probably asleep, so I go into the kitchen to make tea. But there, sitting at the island where I stared into the bottom of so many cups of chai, is the Bugman himself. His hair is a mess and he is wearing this velour bathrobe that's probably as old as his obsession with Ava. Normal people probably wouldn't believe this, but I've never seen my so-called "Dad" just hanging out in a robe, stubble on his face, no expensive cologne covering up the animal scent that I should know by heart but don't.

As soon as the Bug catches sight of me, he climbs off his stool, looking like a stranger. I almost think I've wandered into the wrong Castle. I don't know what I was expecting, but what I get is an angry-looking Bug, who is apparently put out in a major way by my unannounced appearance. "Mila. You should have called."

I feel this weird lump in my throat. "Good to see you, too, Dad." Sensing the ancient sorrows that fill the room like a gas, Stella begins to bark: *Let me out of here!*

"Don't worry, I'm not staying," I add as I rest my backpack on the floor. He eyes it with suspicion, like it might contain a bomb.

I start feeling some of the old anxiety of life in the Castle coming back, so, resorting to a familiar defense, I put on the kettle. It's almost sad to see that my old Japanese pot is right where I left it. My father returns to his stool as if he, too, has been calmed by my ritual. Once she realizes we're not going anywhere, Stella curls up on the familiar island of my backpack.

Through a wreath of steam, I look furtively at the hunched-up Bug in his ratty robe. After years of hating him for beating my mother and punishing me for my resemblance to her, I now feel nothing but pity. Not that he isn't responsible for his actions, but it's simply the nature of some bugs to be red-fanged and full of venom. You can't spend your life resenting them for it, can you?

He pours himself some tea from my pot and pronounces it *first rate*. "I could make you some French toast if you'd like," he offers. "Or an omelette."

"No thanks," I say, startled by this sudden eruption of hospitality. "The tea's fine."

But for some reason the Bug suddenly wants to keep me here. Is it possible he's *lonely*? "Ava loved omelettes. She used to say I made the fluffiest ones she ever had."

I shudder visibly and clutch my cup for warmth. Honest to God, I've never heard the Bug speak my mother's actual name to me. Never heard him indulge in an ordinary recollection about their lives together. *She liked omelettes.* Does that mean they were happy—at least for a little while? I don't know whether the thought comforts or incenses me.

When he reaches for the omelette pan, I stop him. "Let's not do this, okay?"

"What?"

"Pretend we're something we're not."

Gently, he sets the pan on the counter, as if he's afraid it might break. Or maybe he's just afraid he might slam it down if he doesn't maintain every ounce of self-restraint. "What do you want, Mila? Why did you come here?"

"I suppose you've read today's paper." I look down, concentrating on my tea.

"I read the paper every day," the Bug responds nonchalantly. But when he lifts his teacup, his hands are unsteady.

It isn't till we're seated at the table that he acknowledges what I told the police. "So you have some idea that your mother's alive."

"It's not *some idea*. I met her in Wellfleet less than a week ago, Dad. She was as close to me as you are right now." I remember the green river of her eyes.

"It's been a long time since you've seen her, Mila. You were only six when—"

"Jesus, she's my *mother*," I snap. "If I hadn't seen her for a hundred years, I'd know her. I can't believe you didn't call me when you read about it."

The Bug's eyes are morose and dark behind his glasses. "Ten years ago—even five—the possibility that she was alive would have driven me to God knows what. But now, ever since that day when I—" He stops and sips his tea, apparently about to let that sentence dangle into eternity.

Stella whimpers in her sleep, disrupting the silence.

Though I know he is alluding to the day he punched me in the face, I ask, "What day, Dad?" I'm hoping that just maybe we can talk about it. Exorcise it.

But when my father removes his glasses and stares at me through those hooded eyes, I know it's not going to happen.

"I'm glad she got away from me," he says, his voice drained of passion. "I only wish she took you with her."

"That wouldn't have fit in with her plan. Besides, you would have never let us go."

"Children weren't part of *my* plan. Ava knew that, but she wouldn't give up the idea. It was the only thing she—" He lets his sentence drift until it collapses: "I'm sorry, Mila."

I'm sorry. Two words that are supposed to compensate for the morose years I spent in the Castle, for the flash of light that sent me spinning across the room and left me without my front teeth, for the memories of my mother being beaten in the next room. Suddenly, the life I lived and finally escaped is in my throat like dust and I'm choking.

I jump up abruptly. "I've got to go. Thanks for the tea."

The Bug makes no move to stop me. He just sits there, nodding at his cup, at a particularly fascinating piece of lint on his bathrobe, at the cold stone floor. But when I reach the door, I hear him calling after me. "Mila!"

I stop, but don't turn to face him.

"You know the worst part? I was raised in the Church, too, and in some way it never leaves you. But I was so convinced it was that priest; I blamed God—and then I started to hate Him."

"No, Dad, that's not the worst thing." As I turn around, I'm enraged that he seems to be making this about *him*. "The worst thing is that a man's been sitting in prison for over ten years now. Not just an innocent man, but an incredibly *good* one."

"It's still hard to believe," he continues, as if I hadn't spoken at all. "Not just because he was seen outside a bar with her or even that he was there that day in the motel. I suspected him long before that. There were dozens of calls to his number on her phone bill."

"All part of the setup. She never even spoke during those calls. Just created a record," I say, figuring it out as I go. "And as far as the motel goes, think about it, Dad. If the local priest was having an affair with a parishioner's wife, do you really think he'd take her to a place a couple of miles from the rectory?"

"That was a reckless move, but they only went there once when—when she tried to break up with him. He was desperate." It's a story he's told himself for so long, he obviously can't let it go.

"So where do you think they went before that? There was nowhere in town where Gus wouldn't be recognized."

"That's why he took her to a quieter town where he'd be less likely to be seen, where no one knew her. Not his hometown, but somewhere close to that."

He doesn't sound like he's speculating. "What are you saying?"

"Ava had a credit card and a post-office box. She thought I didn't know about it. But of course I did. She could hide nothing from me. Almost all the charges were made in the same town."

If I were a dog, my head would be cocked to the side the way Stella's is when she's confused. I'm so shocked I can't even utter the word that is screaming in my head: *Where?*

"Wellfleet. That summer, while I was at work, she slipped off to meet him there three or four times a week."

I shudder, thinking of how she'd also stayed there in her recent visit. Even when she met me, she was probably mooning over her putrid love affair.

"But what about me? Where was I when this was happening?" I wonder out loud, feeling abandoned all over again.

"There was a full-time nanny in the house, of course. Your mother paid her not to tell me when she went out."

"But you knew anyway?"

"Unfortunately, Crystal's loyalty belonged to the highest bidder. Your mother gave away her trust foolishly—first to Crystal, and then to that priest."

Crystal. The name brings back the memory of plump, freckled fingers tugging my hair into a braid. Just that and nothing more, but it's enough to trigger an ancient revulsion. She may have duped both my parents, but, obviously, six-year-old me knew what she was about.

"And the post-office box—Crystal told you about that, too?"

The Bug nods. "I got the bill before she did. There were charges from a package store on Route 6, numerous visits to a tawdry motel like the one she died in, and meals for two—all take-out from a place in Provincetown. I figured someone Gus knew delivered it. How else would they convince the driver to come that far?" He looks at me as if I could provide an answer—both to that mundane question, and to the deeper one: *How could it be anyone but Gus?*

And though the Cape was undoubtedly swarming with tourists at that time of year, I don't have an answer, either.

"You wouldn't happen to have those old bills?" I ask, already knowing what the response will be. When it came to Ava, the Bug saved everything—even, or maybe *especially*, the items that caused him the most misery. I wonder how many times he pulled out this tangible record of her duplicity and festered in his rage. And I wonder how many times he took it out on me.

Without a word, the Bugman disappears up the wide marble staircase. He's gone so long I sit down on the cold floor, leaning against the door. Stella falls asleep in my lap. We're in the same position when he finally returns, holding an envelope. His face is dark with the moth-eaten shame of her betrayal. A shame that predictably morphs into anger.

"Why would you want to look at this?" It sounds like an accusation.

And the sorry truth is that at that moment, *I don't.* The details of the affair that ended with my abandonment in the Dismal Kingdom, and Gus's heart-shaped tattoo, already feel like pinpricks on my skin. But Hallie's voice is so deep in my head—or in my heart—that there's no escaping it: *When there's a choice, always do the brave thing.*

"You should have turned this over to the police during the investigation," I tell him as I reach for it.

"The police already had plenty of evidence. They didn't need further proof of my humiliation." The Bug's fury is so concrete it feels like a buzzing in my head, and the word— *humiliation*—raises the noise several decibels.

I pull out the thin piece of paper and wince when I see that the "tawdry" motel the Bug referred to was the Sandbar. Why am I not surprised? Obviously, my mother has been tempting fate for a decade. Why not return and revel in the scene of her crime?

But then something else jumps out at me so powerfully that my eyes blur: I count seven charges to the Wellfleet Theater. Always one ticket.

"You didn't say anything about theater tickets?" I say as calmly as I can.

The Bug's face is an interesting shade of purple. "It's obviously where they met." He leans down to grab the bill from my hand, his eyes bulging as if he's reliving the discovery. Then he shakes the deadly piece of paper so close to my face I feel a harsh wind. "The very first charge was to the theater!"

Instantly awake, Stella whines to get out of the Castle and I'm desperate to be gone, too. Away from the oppressive air, and the Bug's escalating rage. My head hurts from thinking, but I can't leave. Not yet.

"But why did she only buy one ticket?" I wonder aloud, talking more to myself or the all-consuming emptiness of the Castle than to the Bug.

"What?" the Bug blinks as if he's just awakened from a decade of sleep. And maybe he has.

"It looks like she bought wine and dinner for two, but every time she went to the theater, she went alone. It doesn't make sense. Unless—"

The Bug is so mystified that for a minute he forgets to be angry. "Unless what? Maybe the cheapskate bought his own ticket, but not hers." It might even have been a "moment" for us, a chance for father and daughter to go over the facts that devastated our family. Maybe even to heal. But all I can think of is Hallie. And *Gus*.

When it hits me, I leap up so quickly I stun the Bug. "Or maybe he didn't need to buy a ticket. Did you ever think of that?" The phrase that Gus yelled in the prison is coming in increasingly handy, though this time it definitely needs an embellishment. "Holy fucking shit, Dad!"

The Bug, who clearly has no idea what I'm thinking, mumbles something about not cursing. Not in *his house*.

Meanwhile, Stella has caught my excitement and is doing her trademark triple spin and barking joyously.

Is it really possible? I think, beginning to doubt myself. I want to snag the bill from my dad's greedy hands, but he is clutching it so hard his knuckles blanch, and he's looking even more Bug-eyed as he pores over the items to see what he missed. And what I saw. What I'm seeing.

Unfortunately, what I'm seeing is not on the bill. Not in the Castle at all. It's one of the photographs Hallie has tacked on the bulletin board in the kitchen. In it, she and her ex-husband loop arms with a third man in front of a small, unimpressive-looking building near the harbor. THE WELLFLEET THEATER.

The third man is Neil Gallagher. When I asked about the photo, Hallie told me he had acted in a long-running play that summer. I'm trying to piece together other things I've heard, and I'm almost sure he left the East Coast right after the trial— just months after my mother disappeared. Of course, my rational side and the Bug's dubious expression are already making me doubt myself. What does any of that actually prove? Couldn't Neil's move be a coincidence, and Ava's presence at the play-house only further incriminate Gus? As Neil's friend, he almost surely attended the play that summer. But seven times?

The chaplain's log, which Jack had held on to all these years, listed all the evenings when Gus had been called to the hospital for an emergency. "There's no way Gus could have had an affair—especially that summer, when it supposedly started," he'd said whenever the subject came up. "The assistant chaplain had heart surgery in June and Gus was on call almost all the time for emergencies. As someone who had their sleep disrupted almost every night, *I* remember."

But it's something else that finally convinces me. Something only I know. Something that, for me, obliterates all doubts. It's the way Neil looked at me when he visited Hallie last summer. There was something about his expression that felt queasily familiar. Not because I'd met Neil before, but because I'd seen that expression on other faces. It was the same wary, surreptitious glance I got from the Bug's sporadic girlfriends. The twisted-up smile of someone sizing up an adversary. The barely concealed glare of someone who knew I had a claim on a heart they wanted to own.

"God, Mila, what's wrong with you?" the Bug mutters, looking more confused—and *older*—in his ratty bathrobe. I almost wish I had time to explain, even to stay for breakfast like he wanted me to do. But I have to get home and talk to Hallie. *Now!* I'm so delirious and scared that I actually kiss my dad on the cheek, which freaks us both out. Then, before he can stop me, I grab his precious relic, stuff it in my pocket, and dash out the door with the frenzied Stella leaping at my heels.

When I look back, I see the Bug standing in shadows behind the glass door, his hand clapped onto the cheek where I kissed him. As if it were a wound.

But I've already left him behind. I'm on that highway, racing toward Provincetown. I'm bursting into the house with the purple door that's already filling up with the inevitable visitors who usually wander in on Saturday. And even though I know it would be better to wait till the guests leave to tell Hallie, I'm pulling her outside onto the back deck. And there, with her beautiful bay shining in the background, I'm shaking and crying as I tell her the truth that just might free Gus Silva.

CHAPTER 44

As exasperating as he can be at times, there are three things I love about Lunes Oliveira:

1. He knows how hot he is, but somehow it hasn't ruined him.
2. No matter when you call him, he'll tell you how crazy busy he is. What, did you expect him to just drop everything and be there? Then he will.
3. He's got a laugh that can make the house shake, and I doubt he's ever had a day so bleak that he hasn't used it at least once.

He was in Truro with his boys when Hallie called and told him we had something. *Something important*, she'd added, trying to keep the elation out of her voice and failing. Immediately, he launched into his spiel: this was his home she'd reached, not his office, in case she didn't know, so if she wasn't calling to ask for a date . . .

Then, abruptly, he stopped. "Something important? Really?"

Though he ended by telling her to come by the office on Monday, Hallie starts grinding his favorite coffee beans as soon as they hung up. By the time the coffee had brewed, Lunes walked through the door, in a pair of jeans and a cream-colored parka that emphasized the rich color of his skin.

"Coffee? You've got to be kidding, right? You think I gave up time with my kids to sit around and drink coffee?" But even as he's objecting, he's pulling a mug from the cupboard and pouring himself a cup. "All I can say is this better be good."

He kisses me on the cheek like a favorite niece. "If you could give us a little time, sweetie, your stepmom and I have some business here."

Like I said, I have a minor crush on Lunes, and I love it when he calls Hallie my stepmom, as if a court or somebody official said that we belonged to each other legally and forever. But there's no way I am going to disappear. Hallie and I speak at once—reminding him that their so-called *business* concerned my mother. My past. My life.

Lunes puts up his hands in surrender. "This is starting to remind me of my mom's kitchen. Can't walk in the door without three women talkin' at me all at the same time. If it's not my mother and my sisters, it's a couple of aunts and my bossy cousin Nicole."

"This could be it, Lunes," Hallie says.

"It?" Lunes raises his eyebrows, as if he didn't know what she meant.

I see her fingering something in her pocket, and I know what it is. The Visa bill. The evidence. Our flimsy piece of hope.

"Okay, you've got my attention." Lunes sits across from her at the table in what used to be Nick's seat.

I'm between them as Hallie starts to speak. For the next ten minutes, Lunes's eyes flicker from her to me as we tell the story together, her picking up a thread, and then passing it to me until we've sewn up the taut, implausible theory that we're convinced will free Gus. By the time we're finished Hallie's sprawling house is too small for Lunes. He is up and pacing from room to room. And every now and then we hear him emit a loud "God*damn!*" or a quieter "But what about . . ."

A few minutes later, he leans against the doorway. "You know what's really insane? I almost bought your story—and probably for the same reason you knuckleheads believed it. *Because I want to.* But there's one little detail that keeps getting in the way."

Hallie and I wait for him to continue.

"Ava Cilento is dead." He looks in my direction as if he just gave me the bad news. "I don't know who came and met you at the Oyster, Mila, but it wasn't your mother. Maybe the Ptown police and some reporter from the *Cape Cod Times* bought your story, but they weren't in the courtroom. They didn't see the crime-scene photos. An estimated four quarts of blood were spilled in that motel. *Her DNA.* I'm sorry, Mila, but no one walks away from something like that."

"Not unless someone with a rudimentary knowledge of phlebotomy and a proper place to store the blood had been systematically drawing her blood weeks in advance," Hallie says. "It just so happens Neil's brother Liam was working the night shift in the ER—"

"Whoa. *Whoa,*" Lunes interrupts. "Do you have any idea how crazy you sound? In fact, I'm glad you told this little story of yours to *me.* Anyone else would have the two of you in straitjackets by now." But in spite of his words, a match is struck behind his eyes, and in a minute he's pacing again.

"Liam Gallagher is a doctor. Why would he risk—" he begins.

"He believed he was saving a woman's life, Lunes," Hallie answers. "And maybe his brother's life, too. Obviously, everything was falling apart for Neil in New York. He was almost as desperate for a new start as Ava was."

"But Ava was in California, right? I mean she had to be. She couldn't have been flying across the country to pick up her mail. And you talked to Neil in Chicago on a regular basis, right? You had an address for him?"

Lunes sinks into a chair, rubs his eyes, and answers his own question before Hallie has a chance to speak. "Don't tell me. All you had was a post-office box, and every time you talked to him, it was on a cell phone. The man could have been anywhere."

Then he gets up and stands in front of me. "Are you sure it was your mother?"

"Absolutely one hundred percent."

"*Of course she's sure*," Hallie says, stepping between us as if she can protect me from the pain of that truth, or from what all this means for Ava. "A person doesn't forget her own mother, Lunes!"

"It's insane," Lunes says when he resumes his pacing. "Completely insane. In fact—"

He leaves those two words dangling and an index finger in the air, as we take a huge simultaneous inhale. I'm so scared he's going to say that *in fact*, he's not buying it, and that if he leaves now, he's still got time to get to the rink before the open skate is over. I don't even dare to exhale.

But then he finishes his sentence. "In fact, it's so insane there's no way you could make it up. Damn, Hallie, let me see that bill again."

CHAPTER 45

It's only two days later when Lunes's secretary calls and asks Hallie and me to come to his office. *Immediately.* The first irrational thing I do is look at the clock. It's after five. Isn't Lunes's office supposed to be closed? And of course, I know.

"Oh my God, did they—" Hallie looks like she's about to do one of those swoon things you read about in Victorian novels so I grab the phone from her hand, and finish the question.

"Did they . . . find them?" After Hallie's exuberance, my voice is a scared, cheepy little bird.

"Lunes will explain everything when you get here," Sue says, but her voice is screaming: *Yes! Now get over here already, will you?* Then she hangs up.

The reception area in Lunes's office is in darkness, and we're almost surprised when the door opens. Then we see the narrow rim of light coming from Lunes's closed door.

"Hallie? Mila? That you?" he asks in a voice that's pure silk. "Come on in."

When we go in, he's behind his desk as if he's working, except that he's pulled off his tie and is drinking from a snifter. A matching glass filled with golden-brown liquid is set in front of the chair that's clearly meant for Hallie, and there's a glass of ice and a soda for me.

Hallie hardly seems to notice. "Come on, Lunes. Tell me! Is it really—" she says. Or screams. Or maybe I just hear it that way.

Before she gets the words out, a slow smile consumes him. It starts in his eyes before it lifts his cheeks and exposes his teeth. Finally it pulls him to his feet and opens his arms. "Yes, it's really truly over. All but the annoying details."

Then he abandons all pretense of professional detachment as he comes out from behind the desk and hugs Hallie so hard he lifts her off her feet. "We got 'em, Hallie. The PI I hired found out Neil's never worked in Chicago. Never lived anywhere near the place, though he apparently stopped there long enough to pick up a cell phone with a local area code.

"So he's been—" Hallie says, and then shakes her head, unable to finish the sentence.

"That's right. With the information Mila provided, we were able to track him to a little town less than a hundred miles from the post office where Ava posted her birthday card. Even acting occasionally in small productions, and teaching classes."

It's only a second before Hallie tugs me into their circle and strokes my cheek as if she understands that for me, happiness will come later. Right now I feel like I just stepped on a grenade.

"You need to sit, Mila—right here beside your stepmom," Lunes pulls out my seat. Then he pours my soda and pushes the snifter in Hallie's direction.

Hallie waves it away as she collapses into her chair. "Thanks, but I never drink that stuff," she says. Then, before he can take it away, she abruptly seizes the glass and for a minute, she peers into the dark gold liquid as if she's mesmerized by it.

"What is that—Jack Daniels?"

"Something like that," Lunes laughs. "Why?"

But whatever she sees in the drink, Hallie isn't about to share it with us. Instead, she throws it back like she does that kind of thing all the time.

"That was almost as sweet as the last time I had it," she says mysteriously. Then she turns to me, and adds, "I hope you know you're driving home."

"In that case, how about one more?" Lunes asks, producing a bottle of Irish whiskey.

"No, thanks, that was perfect. The last thing I want to do is dull this moment. I want to feel this, Lunes. I want to feel every bit of it. Have you called Alvaro and Jack yet?"

"Nope," Lunes says. "I called the next of kin first."

Hallie just smiles—and then she starts crying. "What about Gus? Does he even know?"

"I thought you might want to take care of that. I talked to the warden a little while ago and he's going to permit Gus a call tonight around nine."

Hallie closes her eyes, shutting out everything but the idea of the call she will make. Tonight. Nine p.m. Until now, until they were found, no one has wanted to break the news of Neil's involvement, or to let Gus know how close his release might be. It still felt too fragile to all of us. But now she will have to find a way to explain that it wasn't only a desperate woman who conspired to send him to prison and keep him there. His childhood friend was part of it, too, probably even the mastermind.

When she opens her eyes, she takes my hand, as if she felt the wobbling inside me. "You okay?"

I want to say that I'm doing great. That this is the best day of my life. But instead, I hear myself saying, "What do you think they'll do to her?"

"Whatever it is, it won't be enough," Hallie says. Then she puts her arm around me. "I know she's your mother, Mila, but it's hard—maybe even impossible—for me not to hate her."

"It's hard for me, too. But it's also hard for me not to love her."

"Of course it is. You wouldn't be Mila if it wasn't."

And then, I ask Lunes if he'd mind if I used his bathroom. Hallie's chair scrapes against the wood floor as she rises to follow me, but Lunes stops her. "Let her have her time, Hallie."

When I flick on the fluorescent lights, I come face-to-face with what feels like the biggest mirror in the world. I've always hated my reflection. It reminds me of the face I saw at the bus stop when I was a little girl. The face of a mother who hasn't seen her child in two years. The hungry face. I also see the girl in the photograph Gus carried with him for all those years. The child who'd seen too much. The pathetic daughter Ava abandoned and betrayed, not once but with every breath she has taken for the last ten years. It's an image that makes me want to run away.

But someone else is there, too. It's the girl my surrogate mom showed me I could be. The girl who was stronger than anyone ever knew—even without her warrior jewelry. It's the girl Ethan loves, the girl I dream into existence every night I fall asleep in Thorne House: Hallie's daughter.

I come out of the bathroom, stand in the hallway, and listen to Lunes. "What I don't understand is why Neil felt compelled to stay in touch with you. It's almost as if he wanted to get caught."

Hallie is quiet for a minute. "No, that's not it," she says

with a certainty that floors me. "He called and visited and wrote because he had some kind of perverse need to control Gus and me. He couldn't let it go. And also because he believed he was so smart, so completely in charge, that we would never figure him out."

Lunes sips his drink. "Maniacal arrogance. It's a common trait in cold-blooded killers—not that our friend Neil actually murdered anyone."

"What he did was worse than murder," I say, surprising them with my presence as much as my words. "He sentenced his enemy to a slow death, and then he sat back and watched."

"*His enemy.* How could anyone in the world see Gus—" Hallie leaves her question unfinished—maybe because she's afraid to contemplate the answer.

That night, just before nine, she places the portable phone on the table between us. "I've been thinking about it for three hours, but I still have no idea how I'm going to tell him about Neil."

Unconsciously, my eyes drift to the photograph on the wall in the kitchen that she hasn't yet taken down. The picture of Hallie, Neil, and Gus on the beach.

"Just say it. However it comes out, it will be okay. Gus will be okay." I think of how black his eyes had been when he told me about Xavier. Obviously, the dark potential of the human soul was not news to him. If he needed a reminder, he only had to look down at his own forearm where it was carved in the form of a ragged heart. It's one secret that even Hallie will never know.

At 8:55, when I get up to go upstairs, she seems surprised—maybe even a little alarmed. "No, Mila. I want you to be here when I tell him. You were the one who made this happen. Without you, we never would have found them."

But much as I'd like to take credit, I shake my head. "Maybe I helped, but you were always the driving force. And this right now? This is between you and Gus."

Then I go up to my room and bolt the door, as if it's possible to lock out twenty years of Hallie's pent-up emotion.

CHAPTER 46

Around three, when I get up to go to the bathroom, I see the door to the attic is open and I know that Hallie is on the roof. It's usually my cue that she wants to be left alone, so I almost go back to my room. But I know there's a very particular loneliness waiting for me there and I'd do just about anything to avoid it.

Peering up the dark stairs, I truly understand why Hallie started making dangerous pilgrimages to the top of the house when she was a little girl. It was because she knew the ache I feel. *Saudade*, she calls it. Despite my bare feet, I walk through an attic littered with sharp objects and climb the rickety ladder to Hallie's cathedral.

She is leaning against the chimney, looking out over the water, and at first I don't think she even notices me. If there was any chance I could sneak downstairs without speaking, I would. But then Hallie looks up. The moon has illuminated a shadowy path of tears on her cheeks.

"Do you want to be alone?" I stammer.

But Hallie scoots over. "Sit with me, Mila."

When I do, she wraps her arm around me, seeming to invite me to take in the wild beauty of the night that surrounds us.

I speak first. "I know why you're crying. You're thinking of what it will be like when Gus comes home."

"I wish I could say those were happy tears, Mila," she says, wiping her eyes. "But actually, they were the selfish variety. And this is the last—the absolute *last*—time I'm ever going to cry them."

At that moment, I'm wishing Hallie had someone else to talk to. Someone wiser—and, okay, *older.* Like Abby, Jack, or maybe Stuart, who's lived next door since she was a kid. Even shy Julia would know what to say. But I'm the only one here. "Selfish tears? I don't understand."

"As long as Gus was in prison, he needed me. He waited for me. He belonged to me like he did in high school."

"But now that he's coming home again, won't you two—"

Before I get the words out, Hallie is shaking her head—not only in answer to my unfinished question, but to the tears that fill her eyes, despite her resolution to keep them back.

"I don't think Gus has decided what he'll do when he comes home. He hasn't had time yet. But I know. Jack says I've always known—even when I wouldn't allow myself to face it."

"You mean he'll go back to the *Church*? No chance! Gus has told me a million times he's not a priest anymore. And it's not like the institution gave him much support over the last ten years."

"His friends in the Church—and there were a lot of them—never stopped believing in him. And, besides, it wasn't about the institution for him. It was about something he found in a lonely pew in St. Peter's all those years ago. Something he saw in people like Jack and Sandra, and in the experiences he shared with the sick and dying at the hospital. Prison almost took it away from him before you came along and reminded him."

"But I've seen you two together. It's so obvious you belong—"

Again, Hallie shakes her head. "There was a reason he decided not to be with me all those years ago, Mila," she says. "In every way that counts, nothing has changed."

"But he told me that you two—that he—I mean," I stammer. "He said he loved you, Hallie. More than anyone else on earth."

"You want to know what really breaks my heart? He *does* love me more than anyone else. But my competition was never another person, Mila."

It's then that I finally remember—and even begin to understand—the rest of what Gus said that day: *He loved Hallie, but being in love was for people like me, not for people like him.* I don't want to cry in front of Hallie, but I can't help myself.

"Don't, Mila." Hallie says with mother-style firmness. "This is a happy day. This is the day we waited for. It really is. Now, if you don't mind, I think I'm going to go inside and try to get some sleep."

CHAPTER 47

Hallie and I don't talk much on the way to the jail where Ava's being held. It's the sunniest day ever, but for us it's the midnight hour. Within twenty-four hours, Neil and Ava will stand before a judge and hear their crimes pronounced out loud. Undoubtedly, the Bug will carry his sorry bag of flesh into the courtroom to stare down the woman he could never release, and Alvaro has made sure that the courtroom will be packed with Gus's friends. People who used to brag about the almost famous actor they went to school with, who had faithfully come home to see Neil's plays in Wellfleet during the summer and paid more than they could afford for good seats at his shows in New York. People like Hallie, who thought they knew him.

But the ones who love Gus best, Jack and Julia, and of course Hallie, will not be there. You see, they—or I should say we, because they've invited me to come along—will be at Millette State Prison. Or, rather, we'll be standing outside that ugly fortress, watching a certain door. Yes, it's true. In exactly twenty-one hours and thirty-seven minutes, Gus Silva is scheduled to be released.

"Are you *sure* you want to go in?" Hallie asks when we arrive at the jail where my mother is being held. Not imprisoned exactly. Just held. We're standing outside, smoking a cigarette in the parking lot, her on one side of the car, me on the other. "You know how I feel."

"Yeah, I do. And you're aware of my opinion, too." I mash out my cigarette with the heel of my new lace-up boots.

"There are some things I need to say to this woman—your mother—and, well, it just might be better if you didn't hear them."

"I know," I repeat, but I'm already heading toward the entrance.

"Did anyone ever tell you that you're the most stubborn girl on the Cape?"

"Just the Cape? Jeez, give a kid some respect."

It's a standing joke between us, but this time neither of us is laughing.

Even in her orange jumpsuit, Ava is stunning. Her pallor, the dark half-moons beneath her green eyes only add to her enigmatic appeal. She looks as vulnerable and alone as she must have been that first night she appeared at the rectory, asking for "Father Gus." It's hard not to notice her grace as she slips into her chair, the artful way she uses a tilt of her head, her hands. The hair that was platinum when I saw her last has been restored to a lustrous chestnut brown. Determined not to fall for it, I give her my coldest glare.

But a moment later, she greets me as *my little Milena*, the name I haven't used for more than a decade, and something collapses inside me. No matter how hard I try, the abandoned six-year-old always betrays me. With more fortitude than I feel—and my best imitation of Hallie's *cortesia*, I thank Ava for allowing us to visit.

"I don't have much to say, but Hallie wanted to come," I add, since Ava is obviously ignoring her.

Ava's eyes openly settle on the woman beside me. She nods her head warily, not even pretending this is a friendly visit. "But why? Did you come to prove that my daughter is more loyal to you than—"

"Mila is loyal to the truth, and she's been incredibly brave. If you were any kind of mother, you'd be proud of her," Hallie snaps.

Ava's eyelashes flutter the way they did the last time I saw her. "So you're here to judge me? Well, fine. But leave Mila out of it. You know nothing about my feelings for my child."

"I'm here because I need answers, and Neil refused to see me. Why did *you* agree to the visit?"

Ava adjusts the rolled cuffs of her jumpsuit, but I can see that she is shaking. It frightens me that I can't stop feeling her emotions. Will I ever? I have an irresistible urge to rise up and stand between them—though I'm no longer sure who I want to protect. Is my loyalty with Hallie—as Ava thinks—or not?

"Do you think I would miss a chance to meet the woman who has tormented my husband for so long? The rival I could never really fight? He tried to hide it at first, but a wife knows these things, Doctor."

"*Tormented? Rival?* I don't know what you're talking about," Hallie fires back. "Neil and I were friends—from the time we were nine years old. At least, I believed we were. Now I wonder how I was ever so deceived."

"Neil also thought he had been deceived, and in the cruelest possible way. He told me all about it. You knew how strong his feelings were for you; you encouraged it. Then you used him to get close to Gus."

"If he said those things, he's delusional. I never used anyone—"

Ava raises her voice and continues as if she didn't hear her. "And finally you both betrayed him. Do you have any idea what that did to my husband, Dr. Costa? He never had a good relationship with his family, but it almost didn't matter. He had a friend who was closer than any brother—and he had you, the girl he'd loved as far back as he could remember. The orphans of Race Point, right?"

"What a twisted interpretation of something that was meant to be innocent and good. You have no right to even talk about it."

"I have every right. Neil is *my husband*," Ava yells, briefly attracting the attention of the guard. "I've lived with the consequences of your blindness for the last ten years."

"If I was blind, or if Gus was, it was only because Neil was so good at hiding his dark side. You, on the other hand, were obviously aware of it from the start. Why don't we talk about what he did out of love for you?"

At that, Ava emits a caustic sound from her throat. It takes me a minute to realize that it's a kind of choked laughter. Now that the focus had turned to her marriage, the present, she seems distinctly uncomfortable. "Neil has obsessions, not loves. And, yes, for a while I was one of them. But as I said, I never had the power over him that you did. Or the good Father. Him above all."

Ava gets up and shivers like she is cold. She begins to pace in circles around the little room, which arouses the guard's attention. But she doesn't seem to notice or care.

"Did you ever wonder how we met—your Neil and me?" she asks stopping abruptly. "I mean—think of the unlikelihood of it. A scared, reclusive wife, living in a coastal town, and a gregarious actor from New York. *Fun-loving*. Wasn't that the adjective most used to describe him? What on God's earth would such a man want with someone like me?"

"You went to see one of his plays in Wellfleet. Maybe

you ran into him somewhere afterwards. Obviously, you're an attractive woman."

"The playhouse was an hour away, and you have no idea how constricted my life was. *You* remember, Milena," she says to me, though her eyes remain on Hallie. "I could scarcely take my child to the beach without arousing Robert's suspicion, much less wander off to the *bohemian end* of the Cape, as he called it. But that summer something happened inside me. That summer I was free in spite of him. Love did that for me—but not the love you think. Before I met Neil, there was someone else."

Hallie refuses to ask the question my mother is leading her toward. When she fingers her keys, I think we might escape relatively unscathed. But never one to back down, she clatters the keys on the table like a challenge. "Go ahead."

"I met Gus first. It was such a desperate time for me. The only hope I had was a vial of sleeping tablets I'd hidden in my closet. I counted them every morning, waiting for nothing, hoping for nothing but the day when I would have the courage to use them."

"You didn't even know Gus; he told us that himself," I interrupt, trying to forget the day I found that vial of sleeping pills. I was nine—surely old enough to know better, but I was hungry for anything that was hers. I can still remember the bitter taste of the pill I tested on my tongue.

But Ava is so focused on Hallie she doesn't hear me. "Robert and I had fought—*argued*, as he called it—the morning I first walked into Gus's church. I don't know what started it—I almost never did—but it was bad. When it was over, my eye was swollen shut; and my side hurt so much I could hardly breathe."

"A fractured rib," Hallie muttered.

Without answering, Ava continues. "When he began to dress for work, I ran to the bathroom and turned on the light. I had a secret fascination with my injuries. My scars. They were how I measured my life's progress. Worse than last time. Much worse. *Almost there*, I thought. You don't know how much I wanted to die.

"But this time, Robert followed me. He was so furious when he saw my face in the mirror; I thought he would hit me again—especially when he shut the door. 'You always have to push me, don't you, Ava? There's no way you can go to Mila's school play looking like that, and what about the wine tasting on Friday? I'll have to come up with some excuse for you—again.' I can still see his eyes, the way he shook his head in disgust."

"Then you apologized," I whisper. "He hurt you so bad, he could have killed you, and you *apologized*. Why would you do that?"

"You heard that, Mila? My God, *you knew*?"

"Of course, I knew. I followed you. I cried when you couldn't. I was standing in the hallway when he yelled at you for what he'd done. Your voice was so small, but it felt like a jackhammer to my heart. Why would you say you were sorry?" Ava lowers her head, revealing the vulnerable whiteness of her neck. "I pray to God that you will never understand the answer to that question. I apologized because this man—your father—had convinced me that I was wrong. It wasn't just what I did that was wrong. Or what I said. *I* was wrong, Mila. Every breath I took."

She almost looks afraid, as if she's still trapped in that bathroom, in her terror. "Do you remember his radio?" she asks.

I'm ashamed that this woman still has the power to draw tears from me. "He turned it on whenever you fought—always to a news station. He was so afraid that someone might hear the truth of who he was. What went on in that house. Even now, I still can't listen to radio news."

"Neither can I," my mother admits.

Then she turns back to Hallie. "That morning, the announcer was talking about a storm—a n'oreaster he called it, high winds, heavy rain. People were advised to stay off the beaches. I can't tell you the joy I felt. Not just relief, Doctor, but real *joy*. Fortunately, Robert always left for work at dawn, and even earlier when I *provoked* him.

" 'You won't want to go outside looking like that,' he said before he left. And, yes, I think I said I was sorry again. Sorry for my bruised face, for the pain in my side that is with me to this day in certain weather. Sorry that I was an affront to all the good people who shouldn't have to look at lives like mine. Who didn't want to see it. As it turned out, when Robert left the house, it was the last time he would ever have power over me.

"It was still dark and so wild when I reached the beach, but I didn't care. I got out and walked against the wind toward the water. My plan—if you could call it that—was to dive into the ocean and swim until I couldn't go any further. But as soon as I felt the undertow at my ankles, I knew I couldn't do it."

"If only you had," Hallie can't keep from saying, making me understand why she didn't want me to be there.

"Not until I found someone to look after Mila," Ava continues, ignoring Hallie's words. "Someone who would make sure my daughter would not become my replacement."

"But you didn't go to the rectory and ask for Gus's help until a year later. Are you really trying to tell me you met him before that night? Because that's impossible."

"Yes, that's exactly what I'm saying. That was not the first time." Ava's eyes remain closed, as if to lock Hallie and me out of the private story that is unfolding in her head. "I had no faith left, none; in fact, I hated the Church. But the morning of the storm I was so desperate. I could think of nowhere else to go. I don't know why—perhaps, I thought I would find something I had lost when I was a little girl. A remnant of innocence. Some sense of goodness and light.

"It was so early, I never expected anyone would be there. I thought the door would be locked, the church empty."

"But it wasn't." The resignation in Hallie's voice breaks my heart.

"Do you want to know the strangest thing? Just the way the light came through the windows, that certain hush, I felt like I was at home in my little chapel in Bratislava. I felt like a child again."

"And Gus—"

"The Father was on the altar, saying mass. Saying it for no one but himself and his God. Honestly, my first thought was: What's wrong with him? He was so handsome, so young. I couldn't fathom why he would choose such a life. But he performed his ritual with such reverence, such—there's no other word for it, *love*—it became obvious. Just the sight of him filled me with shame. To this day, I can't explain it. I wanted to run away from it, but I couldn't. I was transfixed."

"Did you speak to him?"

Ava shakes her head. "When he went into the sanctuary, I left. Then I went out into my car and cried."

"You say you had no faith. Why would you be so moved?"

"I wept because I had betrayed everything that was good. Because I was so filled with darkness. I cried because I loved nothing and no one but my daughter. And what good did my love do her? I was too weak to protect anyone—even myself."

"So you went back to look for him," Hallie says, and it is not a question.

"Every day at the same time. At first I hid in the candle room like I had the first day, and watched him say his private mass. But one day I dropped my bag, and he stopped. He looked back to see if anyone was there. After that, I waited outside on the street. The man's habits were so predictable. He said his mass, and then he went to the beach to run with his dogs, and, finally, winter or summer, he pulled off his shirt and swam in the ocean."

"You stalked him. If you can't tell the truth to me, at least stop lying to yourself."

Ava shrugs. "Call it what you wish. I stalked. I spied. I followed. To me, it was something else: *I loved*. For the first time since I came to America, I loved."

Every word my mother speaks seems to make Hallie more incensed. "You never even spoke to him. How could you say you loved him?"

"That's right. I never spoke. I never wanted anything from him like you did, or like Neil did. Nothing but a chance to see him with his dogs, to hear the words he said in the church. To be reminded that there are such people in this foul world."

"That explains one thing. Gus always said that from the first time you came to the rectory, he felt as if he knew you.

He even checked the records at the hospital to see if you'd been a patient. Did you go to Sunday mass, too?"

"Only once with Mila and her father. It was torture. Robert played at piety, but he sat there like a blind man in his polished shoes. He saw nothing. He heard nothing. Little did he know how that day would change all our lives. When we passed the priest, I heard him tell someone he was going to a play in Wellfleet that afternoon. His friend was in it," he said. He even bragged about his name, as if he was famous. *Neil Gallagher.*"

Hallie looks at her skeptically. "But you said you weren't allowed to go anywhere on your own. How did you get away?"

"I just went—like free people do, like women who are not married to madmen do. I didn't care anymore. I took the credit card I had applied for but never used, then I got in my car and drove down Route 6 and bought a ticket. The only thing that mattered to me was seeing the Father, watching him in his ordinary clothes, blending in with the crowd. I even had a glass of wine during the intermission. Beginning that afternoon, I no longer belonged to Robert. I belonged to myself. I knew I would pay with my life for it, but I didn't care."

"So Gus recognized you during the intermission and introduced you to Neil," Hallie guesses.

"No. The priest, your Gus, he was focused on other things. Other people. Sure, he saw me that day. He even smiled at me—but he didn't remember how he knew me. And before he had time to think about it, Neil came out. Within minutes, they were in the center of a circle. They were laughing, and talking—especially Neil. In all the years we were together, I don't think I ever saw my husband as happy as he was that day. Even when our son was born."

"And Gus?"

"I could see that something was wrong. In the Father's world—at the beach or the hospital or in his church, he was always at ease, but not there. Not among his old friends. He watched the exit like I did when I was forced to attend an event with Robert."

She pauses a moment before she continues. "After the play, I looked for him, but I knew he was gone. It was as if the light, the sound had been drained from the building. I was so disappointed I didn't even notice that someone had followed me out to my car."

"Neil."

Ava nods. " 'Excuse me, but I saw you watching my friend in there,' he said. I'm not a woman who blushes—not at all, but that day I did. 'You are mistaken,' I said, climbing into my car and locking the door. But it was useless. It was a hot afternoon and the windows were open. He put his long arms on the roof, leaned into the window, and laughed. 'When it comes to women checking out my holy friend, I'm never mistaken. Anyway, there's nothing to be embarrassed about. It's been happening since he was about ten. There's some-thing just so—I don't know—*tragic*—about the guy, don't you think? So young. So good-looking. So fucking unavailable.' "

"He said that?"

"There were no masks between my husband and me. Not even then. From the start, we recognized something in each other. I suppose that was why I said yes."

"Yes?"

"When he asked me to go for a drink. Oh, I protested

a little at first. 'I'm a married woman,' I said. 'I have to get home and make dinner.' As soon as I'd said the words, I felt how provincial they probably sounded to a man like Neil. After all, he'd only asked me to share a drink. But instead of laughing at me, he said, 'I know. You're a married woman, and obviously an unhappy one, but you haven't "made dinner" in years—if ever.'" He took in things that other people didn't see. The quality of my haircut. My jewelry.

"'There's a little place about a mile from here where we could grab a beer,' he said. 'Or if you'd feel more comfortable, we could go to my cottage . . .' Imagine the audacity. I suppose that was why I agreed—because he was the first man I'd met who was more audacious than Robert."

"So you went?" Hallie asks incredulously. "To a stranger's cottage? You must have been mad."

"I *was* mad; that's what I've been trying to tell you, Doctor. Mad with fear. Mad with loneliness. Mad with self-hatred. But, no, I didn't go to the cottage—not that day.

"I didn't know his reasons for asking me to the bar, but I had my own. I hoped he might tell me something about the Father. That he would explain why the man who was more at home in the world than anyone I'd ever known, had looked so uncomfortable. Why he had left the theater early."

"Did he tell you?"

Ava shakes her head again. "All we spoke about was my unhappiness. Or rather *he* spoke. Even though there were no visible bruises on me that day, he saw everything I took such pains to hide. When I asked him how he knew so much about me, he called for the check. He got so quiet I was afraid I'd angered him in some way. But instead of taking me back to my car, he drove down Route 6 in the opposite direction."

"And you let him?"

"I was frightened at that point—frightened of Robert, yes, but probably even more scared of this stranger. 'I really need to go home. My husband—' I said."

" 'Don't worry, I'll get you home in time to put your apron on and make dinner,' he teased. We were probably doing eighty, but I grabbed the door handle, and insisted he let me out. Immediately, he pulled into a patch of sand and sea grass."

She pauses for a moment, as if considering what would have happened if she had taken the opportunity to get away. "He covered my hand with his and said, 'I'm sorry. I realize you don't know me, Ava, but I swear—you can trust me.' If there was an instant when my life changed, that was it. I hadn't felt any genuine affection from a man in such a long time. And there was something so intense about him I believed him."

Hallie looks away. "My God, I think I know where he took you."

"Yes, it was to the cemetery in Provincetown. The same place where you fell in love with Gus."

Though the visiting room is overheated, I feel Hallie shiver.

"At first, I had no idea why he brought me there," Ava continues. "And then I saw the dates beneath Maria Botelho's name. She was thirty-one when she died—two years younger than I was.

" '*That's* how I knew,' Neil said when he saw the flash of light in my eyes. 'The last time I saw such a quietly desperate woman I was nine years old.' He took my hand again, this time with a kind of certainty. 'Let me take care of you, Ava.'

You have no idea how hungry I was to hear those words—and to believe them. Little did I know that he was playing the role of a lifetime."

Hallie looks confused. "But it was Gus who had promised himself and his mother that he would never allow another woman to be hurt the way she was—not if he could do anything to prevent it. And right there in that spot. Nothing meant more to him. Not even his vows to the Church."

"Now you're beginning to understand. At that moment, my husband *was* Gus—though it took me years to see it. Believe it or not, we didn't talk about the Father again for nearly a year. By then, Robert began to suspect there was someone else—and I hadn't had my period in two months. Then it was three. We had to act.

"Neil had thought of everything. People he knew in New York helped me to get a new identity. and once the time came, he had a nurse at the hospital draw my blood and store it. We needed enough to convince the police—and especially Robert—that there was no chance I could have survived my injuries."

"A nurse? Are you sure it wasn't Liam?"

Ava shakes her head. "He would never have agreed. They weren't close, though Neil did his best to pretend they were. He showed up at the hospital cafeteria almost every day for lunch, making friends with Liam's colleagues, until he found the right person."

"The *nurse*," Hallie says. "But I still don't understand why anyone would—"

"She was a married woman with three children, and, as you know, Neil can be very charming. There was never even an affair, just a few steamy e-mails and some voice messages. But it was enough."

"You mean he threatened her?"

"He would have ruined her life without blinking an eye. You must know that by now."

Hallie gets up and begins to pace, nodding as she absorbs the story. "So after Neil blackmailed her, he sent you to the rectory, where he knew you would find the perfect fall guy. Were you even hurt or was that a lie, too? A little theatrical makeup maybe?"

"Robert put his hands around my throat and tried to kill me the night before, Doctor. Do you know what that's like? Can you begin to understand?"

"But you'd seen Gus on the beach and followed him to the church. You knew the kind of man he was. How could you do that to him?"

Ava's eyes well up. "I never wanted to hurt the Father . . . and I had no reason to think Neil would, either. I wanted him to look after Mila when I was gone."

"And when you called him, leaving your number on his cell phone over and over again? When you asked him to meet you at the Pink Dolphin . . . *Jesus*, when you accused him of assault? How can you possibly say you weren't trying to implicate him?"

"We had to throw Robert off the track . . . But without a body, Neil promised me no one would ever be charged for the crime."

"And when someone was? When someone was not only charged, but sentenced to life—"

"Neil said there would be an appeal. He claimed he was talking to a new attorney and raising money, that the conviction would never stand."

"And how did your husband reassure you when Gus was

sent to prison? When he was attacked by some animal and nearly killed? When the weeks and months turned into years? How did you ease your conscience then?"

"Do you think it hasn't haunted me? I even told him we had to go back; we had to tell the truth," Ava cries. "But Neil said . . ."

"Go ahead," Hallie prods. "What did he say?"

"He said Gus didn't care when he ruined your life—or his. And if he wanted to waste his life converting sinners, what better place to do it? That was when I truly understood how much he'd come to despise the Father."

"If it bothered you so much, why didn't you go back yourself?"

"Don't you understand? I couldn't. Neil and I were bound together—not just by our son, but by this terrible thing we had done. I was afraid."

"Fear," Hallie replies disdainfully. "That seems to be your excuse for everything. In another situation, it might almost make me sympathetic to you. But other people were involved."

"What do you know about marriage, Doctor?"

Hallie's eyes burn. "I'm in no mood for riddles."

"But sometimes life *is* a riddle, don't you think? Sometimes you believe you have escaped a man, only to find you have married him all over again, that cruelty is something you attract. No more than that. *Worse* than that—it's something you need."

"Are you trying to say Neil beat you? Because as callous as he is, as much *evil* as he's done, I don't believe—"

"No, Neil never hit me. But, like Robert, he drew a line between us." Ava holds up an elegant hand. "*This* close you may come, and no closer. *This* much you may know, and no more. This you may ask, say, do, *think*—but not that. *Never that.*

"Neil worked so hard; the only time he was truly happy was when he had become someone else. Underneath it all, though, there was a terrible torment. And rage. That was the line I couldn't cross."

"Rage at *whom*? The man he sacrificed so the two of you could have your life?"

"Yes, that man. Sometimes when he'd had too much to drink, it would come out. I remember one night, after I'd gone to bed. He was alone downstairs, yelling, caught up in a ferocious argument. Sasha was so scared he crawled into bed with me."

"So who was he fighting with?"

"His orphan brother, of course. The one who had everything Neil wanted, but threw it away. Neil could copy it; he could bring an audience to tears with his brilliant imitation; all those years when they'd been friends, he had basked in Gus's light. But he himself could never possess it."

"What are you talking about?" Hallie asked.

"His *voodoo*, Neil called it. The power he had over other people. I experienced it, too. Don't pretend you don't know what I'm talking about."

Though I've been still and silent as a shadow while Ava and Hallie talked, all of a sudden I see Gus's eyes as they were the day he told me about Xavier and his tattoo. "It's not voodoo," I say, startling them both. "It's just *love*. Pure and simple."

Ava casts her eyes downward, but Hallie squeezes my hand. "Yes," she whispers.

Then she takes a long, deep breath before she speaks, obviously measuring every word. "Do you want to know what I think of you—you and your sad, tormented husband?" she says. "You are the worst kind of cowards. The most despicable of liars. The lowest of thieves. You stole a man's life and felt sorry for *yourselves* as you did it. You don't just prove the banality of evil. You *are* that banality."

When she turns to me, I see the immensity of sorrow behind her anger. "I'm sorry you had to hear that, Mila. With all my heart, I'm sorry." But when she says "my heart," she puts the palm of her hand on my chest, not her own.

PART SEVEN

MILLETTE STATE PRISON

{ OCTOBER 23, 2010 }

The next morning, Hallie woke so early that the sky was still lit with sharp stars. While Mila and Julia slept, she showered and dressed and made coffee, enjoying the quiet hour as she always did. She was sipping her coffee at the table when she noticed that her father's old diner mug, which she had grabbed at random from the cupboard, was cracked, and it occurred to her that it was time to get rid of all the old things. The objects that seemed to hold the past, but did not. Could not.

She took her coffee up to the attic and opened the box where she'd put the book Gus had given her the first time she visited him in prison. Inside the cover, her father had written his name in the looping open scrawl that was never afraid of taking up too much space. Hallie touched the faded ink, smiling faintly. The light was like weak tea. If she hadn't memorized the first line of the story long ago, she probably couldn't have read the tiny print:

Whether I shall turn out to be the hero of my own life, or whether that station will be held by anybody else, these pages must show.

She switched on the overhead light and continued, her voice as bright as it had been that day when she first knocked on the Barrettos' door, naïvely, optimistically, bravely believing that she, one small girl, could cure a tragedy like the one that had visited Gus—with a book and two fish. How foolish she had been. When she reached the second paragraph, she was stopped by a line she had deliberately skipped the first time. It had seemed too cruel to read then, but now she repeated the wise old crones' predictions for David Copperfield slowly:

> In consideration of the day and hour of my birth, it was declared . . . first, that I was destined to be unlucky in life; and secondly, that I was privileged to see ghosts and spirits . . .

As she closed the book, she remembered Gus's long silence after she told him about Neil's betrayal, and the calmness of his voice when he finally spoke; and she knew, with absolute certainty, that whatever curses Gus had endured, his gift was far greater. She shut her eyes and imagined him as he'd been when he was a child, sitting on the couch in his aunt's living room, his huge eyes full of heartbreak and his own luminous kindness, and she realized it had always been apparent. That was his voodoo.

It was nearly seven when she heard the sound of Julia padding to the bathroom on the second floor. Hallie slipped back downstairs, the book in hand. She had planned to return it to Gus when he was released, but staring at her father's cracked cup, she realized that he, too, had been carrying the past for too long. He needed no reminders. The cup shattered when she tossed it into the trash, but she resisted the impulse to hurl the book on top of it.

Instead, she replaced *David Copperfield* in her father's library, as if it were possible to reach back through thirty years and return the house to what it had been before she walked across town to visit a boy mute with shock and pain. She was just a child. She could never have imagined how his grief would infiltrate her life. But even if she had known, she would not have turned back.

Julia, the steadiest among them, drove them to Millette in her boyfriend's van. Hallie sat up front, while Gus's dog, Stella, who had just turned fourteen, rode in the back with Mila and Jack. Though Jack had been diagnosed with lung cancer only three weeks earlier, and had just begun chemo, he was determined to be there. Usually, Julia and Mila would be absorbed in their phones or arguing about what to play on the radio. But on that day there was so much emotion, so much inner noise and excitement in the car, they all seemed to understand that just one note, just one word might cause the van to suddenly combust. No one noticed the silence until they arrived, and then everyone seemed to be speaking at once.

It was one of those frigid days that fall occasionally spits out in warning. *This is the last time,* Mila said, speaking for all of them, as they each recalled their dreary visits to the prison. *The last time,* they echoed in unison.

When they reached the desolate parking lot, Alvaro's truck was already there, and he was standing outside it, leaning against the fender, just as he'd been the day when Nick had gone to the house on Loop Street and tried to coax Gus into speaking. He beckoned to Hallie.

"I'll be right back." She got out of the van and walked toward Alvaro, who pulled her into a strong *abraço*.

They waited until exactly eleven, when Gus was scheduled to be released, and then they all got out and stood outside and watched the door, inured to the cold. Hallie had tried to persuade Jack to stay in the van, but he had quickly rebuffed her—"I didn't come all this way to sit in the car"— and no one tried to argue with him.

It was only a few minutes before Gus Silva emerged, holding a small gym bag stuffed with eleven years' of his life. He started toward them slowly, almost as if he were reluctant to leave the place that had been home for so long. But as he got farther from the building, something propelled him forward into the bracing light. The walk was only about ten yards, but it felt like miles to Hallie as she watched him. Before he reached them, Gus stopped right there in the middle of the parking lot and let the gym bag fall as he opened his arms.

Stella, the still energetic Jack Russell, was the first to run to him, with a wild canine joy that remembered everything. Julia let out a small cry before she and Mila rushed after her, while Jack limped behind them on his cane, alternately sobbing and coughing as he cursed his former curate for "reducing me to this."

Alvaro followed. "Hey, cuz. Helluva nice day out here, wouldn't you say?" he said, grinning broadly at the white sky.

Meanwhile, Hallie stood back, almost shyly, until Gus's eyes found hers, and years of despair, mountains of loss, were swept away in one blinding smile. The first time he spoke, he just mouthed the word, the name he had carved on a tree in Beech Forest when he was a child. Then he whispered it, and, finally, he shouted it: Hallie. *Hallie!*

Bring all of yourself to his door:
bring only a part
and you've brought nothing at all.

— HAKIM SANAI

Nantasket Beach
June 23, 2011, 5 a.m.

Dear Hallie,

In just a few hours, this beach will be covered with a patchwork of colorful towels, sand chairs, and umbrellas. Music will blare; children will shriek; adolescents will strut their bright new bodies down the coast the way we once did. In the background, the ocean will hum and roar. But right now it is the solitary and silent domain of one monk. I come here most mornings before Lauds and run the way I used to when I was a parish priest. Maybe Nick was right when he said it's in the blood because a key criterion in my search for a monastery was that I had to be able to smell the sea.

It was good to see you last week—even if it was for a funeral. I laughed when you said that Jack Rooney was such a great guy, that he almost made you feel like joining the church. Then before I could haul out my conversion speech, you arched your eyebrows and emphasized "almost!" Well, no need to worry. You are already one of the holiest women I've ever met. No conversion necessary. (Holy? I can see you cringing now.)

I've been feeling the resonance of Jack's life particularly keenly in recent days. I usually go to bed too exhausted for insomnia, but one night last week was an exception. Sometime in the middle of the night I sat up in bed laughing out loud as I recalled the day I told Jack I'd decided to enter a monastery. That white hair of his stood straight on end.

"So you're going to sit around and pray all day? Might as well have stayed in jail."

"What—you have something against prayer?" I asked him. He had to think about that a minute. "It's all right—in its place," he finally admitted. "But don't you think you could pray and do something at the same time?" Jack was such a man of action. I think he saw the monastic life as an excuse for laziness, but I've never worked harder. We raise chickens, keep bees, and bake bread to support ourselves. Then there's the work of taking care of this place and each other. But the real labor is the prayer itself. The most intense work. The greatest joy.

The last time I visited Jack in the hospital, he brought it up again. "With all that praying, you and the Almighty must be on a first-name basis by now," he said, showing me his famous scowl. I laughed, but the truth is, the more hours I spend in contemplation, the less I know about God—and the more I realize how arrogant it is for us poor humans to squeeze the Infinite into our limited definitions.

Enough of this God talk, you're probably saying, so I will stop. I hear that Neil and Ava divorced shortly after they were released. It's a sad case all the way around, especially for their boy. Kids take the worst of it in these situations, as we all know.

You may have heard I visited Neil in prison—probably because I refused to see my father before he died and I've always regretted it. When my aunt and uncle tried to drag me there, I sat in the parking lot, stubbornly smoking cigarettes. It's an hour that still haunts me. In Neil's case, though, it would have been better if I'd stayed away. It brought me back to our fight on Race Point, though this time the blows were verbal instead of physical. Strong as the desire for answers might be, I can only hope you will never try to contact him again. I don't know what happened to the friend I knew in childhood, or when, but the man I saw that afternoon, like the one he briefly revealed all those years ago, is as troubled and dangerous as anyone I ever met in prison or elsewhere.

After the visit, I went out to my car and wrote the very last entry in the journal I started when I was first sent to prison. When I finished, I looked up at my old cell block. Then I went home to my room at the monastery and tossed it into the box full of notebooks I'd filled when I was in jail, knowing I didn't need them anymore. In many ways, those journals had been the only thing that kept me sane through all those years. And though they were often full of nothing but bitterness and rage, I believe that I was also unconsciously seeking Grace when I felt most abandoned. That night I took the box down to the fireplace in the monastery and burned them all.

What you probably don't know is that I also saw Ava. I know you still have a lot of bitterness toward her, but I can never forget how wounded she was the night she first came to me. Despite all the lies she told, that was something she couldn't fake. We only spent an hour together, but I hope it was the start of some healing—for both of us. Yes, she caused immense pain, but she endured just as much. Does that exonerate her? I suppose not; but when I visited her, I was strengthened by the message from a sign in your father's office: IF YOU JUDGE PEOPLE, YOU DON'T HAVE TIME TO LOVE THEM. *I'm sure you remember, and I'm sure you also know it wasn't the words that fortified me. It was my memories of the man who lived them.*

Mila still writes me fat, rambling letters, though never with-

out grumbling about my refusal to use a computer "like normal people." Her letters are a great source of delight in my life, especially when she tells me stories about you, or about her growing connection with her brother. It's limited to e-mail exchanges now, but I know that will change—and probably soon. For an honorary member of our orphan tribe, Mila is amazingly rich in family. I give you credit for that.

They will soon be ringing the bells for Lauds, so my hour at the beach is just about over. But before I sign off, there's one more thing I need to say. Last week at the funeral, I caught you studying me in secret. When I looked back, you turned away. But in that instant, I saw something like sorrow in your eyes. Something like regret. I may be misinterpreting here, but I suspect it was sadness for the years I lost in prison. If there's any truth to that, please let me clarify: I will soon put this pen in my pocket and walk down the beach with my arms wide open to a life more beautiful than I have the right to inhabit. Nothing of value has ever been taken from me. Nor can it be.

Love always,

Gus

ACKNOWLEDGMENTS

This novel and its characters are entirely fictional. Only the spirit that inspired it is real. I am grateful to my husband's dear friend, Yvette Roderick Freller, and to Debbie Roderick Maseda, who generously shared their memories of growing up in a tight-knit community that shares its fate with the sea. Though both women passed away far too early and the town they remembered continues to evolve, the spirit remains. I have done my best to honor it.

Alice Tasman provided advice, enthusiasm, friendship, and, above all, an unshakable faith in these characters and this story over the course of many years. My debt to her is beyond words.

It has been a great privilege to work with Claire Wachtel, whose thoughtful questions and suggestions improved the novel immeasurably.

Rona Laban, my lifelong friend and partner in adventures of all kinds, also accompanied me on this one, reading through many drafts, and offering a perfect balance of criticism and love.

Thanks are owed to Jonathan Burnham for suggesting the prologue, to Amy Baker at Harper Perennial for her early support, to Hannah Wood, and to my copy editor, Edward. R. Cohen, for his keen eye and for teaching me, among other things, that only a dolt heats pizza in the microwave.

I am forever grateful to Anjali Singh for believing in this novel and for helping to shape what it became.

Alison Larkin Koushki, Sarah Nalle, Jessica Keener, and

Tish Cohen provided valuable feedback at various stages in the journey, as did Laura Biagi and Jennifer Weltz at JVNLA.

Many thanks to Helena Ferreira for suggesting the song that Gus's mother teaches him as a child.

To the Heneys and the Lukacs for years of support and encouragement, and to Mary Larkin for wise counsel in all matters.

And finally, to my husband, Ted, and our family, Gabe and Nicola, Josh and Stacey, Nellie, Jake, Lexi, Emma, Hank, Will, Jude and Sebastian, much love and gratitude.

ABOUT THE AUTHOR

Patry Francis *is the author of The Liar's Diary* and the blog *100 Days of Discipline for Writers.* Her poetry and short stories have appeared in the *Tampa Review, Antioch Review, Colorado Review, Ontario Review,* and *American Poetry Review,* among other publications. She is a three-time nominee for the Pushcart Prize and has twice been the recipient of the Massachusetts Cultural Council Grant. She lives in Massachusetts.